# Russian Puppeteer

By:

## Jeffrey H. Fischer
## Colonel (R)

Website: www.jeffreyhfischer.com
Facebook: www.facebook.com/ColonelFisch
LinkedIn: www.linkedin.com/in/jeffreyfisch/
Twitter: @jefffisch

ISBN: 979-8-9857053-5-5

*As the war in Ukraine rages, Russian agents launch a series of devastating covert missions, including the assassination of U.S. Vice President Banks.  As Moscow planned, Washington D.C. devolves into chaos.  Unbeknownst to Russia, however, Admiral Hershey & Dr. Curt Nover have plans of their own. The bell rings, setting the stage for an epic political, diplomatic and military battle on the world stage. The outcome?  It is far from certain.*

*"The views expressed in this publication are those of the author and do not necessarily reflect the official policy or position of the Department of Defense or the U.S. government."*

*Full notification letter at end of the novel.*

# DEDICATION

For
BB, Tobi, & Zoe
My Everything

# ACKNOWLEDGMENTS

Many thanks to Abigail Dold for her exceptional work on the cover (and patience in dealing with me). You can find more of her work on Instagram at @absart11.

# NOTICE TO THE READER

This book is the fourth in a series by the author. Some of the plot and character development will make more sense if the reader were to consider reading *LIVE RANGE, BALKAN REPRISAL* and *AFGHAN GHOSTS* prior to this book. Just scan the QR code with your camera to find them on Amazon.

# Chapters

# *FOREWORD* by
# General (Retired) Philip Breedlove

As the Supreme Allied Commander of NATO from 2013 to 2016, I was challenged firsthand by the political, diplomatic, and military aspects of Russia's illegal invasions into Ukraine. Prior to the invasion I had engaged with the Russian Chief of Defense, General Valerie Gerasimov, as well as a handful of senior Russian diplomats and politicians. What we saw in the first two invasions of Ukraine in Crimea and the Donbass was stunning. Russia's true colors had emerged once again. I've just finished reading *Russian Puppeteer*... there are few books, non-fiction or other, that better capture the essence and underlying dynamics of Russia and the Ukraine War.

For background, I stumbled upon *Afghan Ghosts* when learning General (Ret.) 'Cobra' Harrigian, a friend and colleague, crafted the foreword. Little did I know, the book's author was a former subordinate of mine from days in the Pentagon, Colonel (Ret.) Jeffrey 'Fisch' Fischer. Soon thereafter, I was in contact with Fisch, who was finishing his fourth book in the Dr. Curt Nover series. His offer to pen that foreword touched me. I relayed my intent to read the book, and if moved, I would agree.

*Russian Puppeteer* transported me back to my time as the Commander of the European Theater. Russia's broken promises, the urge to support Ukraine, emerging and disrupting technologies in the battlespace, the heightened threat to the Eurasian theater; all resonate clearly in Fisch's novel. To a degree, I found his strained political-military relationships uncomfortably realistic. In 2014 during the Crimea invasion, both Fisch and I took part in a handful of White House video teleconferences, him in Austria advising the OSCE Ambassador and me at my command. His memory and grasp of the complexities is phenomenal.

## Russian Puppeteer

Today, in the fall of 2023, I reflect on the current Ukraine War. Ukraine has a right to its sovereignty, in the Budapest Memorandum, we in the U.S. were one of three nations that assured them we would protect it. Ergo, whether they are able to regain and hold their sovereign territory depends completely on U.S. leadership and western policy makers. The outcome of this war will turn on how the west supports or fails to support Ukraine. Political dynamics are a Pandora's box and Fisch presents a vivid 'behind the scenes' look into some of the more distasteful aspects of conflict at the highest levels.

I hope you enjoy this book as much as I. Of note, I've already ordered Fisch's first two books in the Dr. Nover Series. Fisch has captured my curiosity and I'm eager to learn how a former U.S. Navy SEAL who ended up as a medical doctor somehow continually finds himself saving the world while trying to save himself from the scars of war.

*U.S. Air Force General (Ret.) Breedlove was raised in Forest Park, Ga., and commissioned in 1977 as a distinguished graduate of Georgia Tech's ROTC program. He has been assigned to numerous operational, command and staff positions, and has completed nine overseas tours, including two remote tours. He has commanded a fighter squadron, an operations group, three fighter wings, and a numbered air force. Additionally, he has served as Vice Chief of Staff of the U.S. Air Force, Washington, D.C. Operations Officer in the Pacific Command Division on the Joint Staff; Executive Officer to the Commander of Headquarters Air Combat Command; the Senior Military Assistant to the Secretary of the Air Force; and Vice Director for Strategic Plans and Policy on the Joint Staff. His final assignment was Commander, Supreme Allied Command, Europe, SHAPE, & U.S. European Command. He is a command pilot with 3,500 flying hours, primarily in the F-16.*

*Chapter One*

# Welcome to the World

The Buffalo Wild Wings restaurant in Pentagon City boomed with exactly the atmosphere Curt and Allison sought. Their first born, baby Bo, was only three months old, and this would be one of the first meals he'd have out on the town with his faux uncle's Smitty and Buck. Noorullah, Curt, and Allison's adopted son from Afghanistan, was at his language training class. While he had only been in the U.S. for months, Noorullah's English was gradually improving. At the age of sixteen, learning a new language was challenging, but his life was far better in the U.S. Noorullah's time in language classes also afforded the couple some quality time with baby Bo.

College basketball games dominated the restaurant's television screens. Other less popular sporting events were barely broadcast. The Sunday lunch crowd filled 75% of the restaurant. They were louder than Allison was hoping for, but she'd roll with the flow. 'Such was the life of parenting,' she thought.

A half pitcher of Yuengling sat on the table. As usual, Buck was running late, and neither Curt nor Smitty had a gumption of guilt not waiting for Buck before imbibing. Buck, a former Special Forces pilot, had grown to be habitually late for any informal event now that he'd departed the Air Force. As for Curt and Smitty, the two were former Navy SEALS and nearly inseparable as friends. Too many life events, both in and out of the military, bound them for life. Allison would drink unsweet tea; she was the designated driver, and breast-feeding baby Bo. Finally, Buck strolled in without a care in the world. "Yo! Hey guys!" He quickly noticed them already drinking. "You couldn't wait fifteen minutes?"

"Buck," Smitty said as he stood to give Buck a bear hug, "Awaiting your arrival shares the risk of dehydration."

"Smitty, God Bless you, ya jackwad." 'Jackwad' had become Buck's 'go-to' derogatory name since he began practicing to refrain from cussing in front of baby Bo.

3

Curt also stood to greet Buck and said, "He may be a Jackwad, but he's right. Buck, how on earth did you fly for the Air Force and make your target times? Jesus, you are always late!"

Buck hugged Curt as well. "Easy buddy. Initially, we had navigators. Now we have GPS. I can do magic in the air. This ground navigation shit confounds me. Streetlights, traffic jams and construction. No such issues in combat aviation." Buck bellowed out his signature laugh.

"And how about you, beautiful?" Buck queried Allison. "How are you and my favorite nephew doing?" Buck leaned down to kiss her head in the booth.

"We are good, Buck. Thanks. Bo just got a perfect bill of health last week from the doc, and not the one I'm married to." Allison smiled as both Buck and Smitty laughed. Curt shared his 'not amused' face but chuckled inside. As Allison spoke, Smitty poured Buck a beer.

Changing the subject, Curt asked. "So, Buck, how's the new job?"

"It's good! I miss Europe, but the time has come for me to be in the States. I love the company and meeting cool folks. Just flew Madonna this past week. Crazy." After departing his work for NATO, Buck landed a job flying charter service for the world's wealthy, but not wealthy enough to afford their own aircraft.

A waitress picked up the empty beer pitcher while looking at Smitty quizzically. American sports bars were perhaps the world's best at nonverbal communication when it came to slinging rounds. With barely a nod from Curt's noggin, she was off to the bar, fetching another. Allison was impressed. "Madonna? Wow! Just don't tell me what she was like. You'll ruin it. She was one of my favorites growing up."

"You're probably right. I'll keep my mouth shut. She wasn't the most cordial customer I've had," Buck smiled as he drank his beer. "What about you, Smitty? How's the job? Kill anyone in D.C. lately?" Once more, Buck's hearty laugh bellowed across the restaurant.

"No, Buck. Not yet. Still hoping," Smitty replied. His job as part of a personal security detail for the Chairman of the Joint

Chiefs, Admiral 'Squirts' Hershey, provided just enough excitement to keep him happy. "Actually, I do have some interesting news. As you may know, Squirts is retiring next week. He seems to be working on some big plans post-retirement. I don't know what it is, but I overheard a bit of a conversation. He told me to keep it quiet."

Curt's eyes rose. The Admiral's retirement wasn't expected for a few more months. "Interesting. I'm curious. What drove his retirement? We all know he and the President share little love loss. Did Squirts get the dreaded White House message? 'Your service to the nation is no longer required.'"

"Dunno," Smitty replied. "Just know he's posturing for some post-retirement start up project."

"What?" Allison replied. "Why would he want to take the risk of a new start? As the former Chairman, he can walk into any Fortune 500 defense company and make mid six figures."

"You're right, but as we drive him around in the motorcade, it's clear he has little appetite to follow that established path. He doesn't appear to be a big fan of corporate America, at least the one that currently exists." Smitty raised his beer and took another pull. "What about you, Dr. Nover? How's your gig going?"

"Actually, it couldn't be better," he said as he looked at Allison and squeezed her hand under the table. His words were convincing; only because he'd practiced the phrase over and over until he believed it himself. Curt had now been serving in a senior Veteran's Affairs administration position for a while. It was an extremely important job, but afforded him little opportunity to engage with patients, a key reason he had transitioned into the medical field. The money, however, was good, and with Allison caring for baby Bo, a stable and significant income was a luxury in a struggling economy.

Curt changed the subject quickly. "Hey Smitty, have you heard anything scuttlebutt from our SOF brothers who are training Ukrainians in Poland?" While Russia's invasion into Crimea dominated nearly every conversation across the U.S. years ago, it was unfathomable Russia would launch a full out offensive, but it was now 2022, and a very different world than one could have imagined a handful of years earlier.

"Yeah," Smitty replied. "A buddy sent me a quick note. He says the Ukrainians are receptive and quick learners. It's perhaps not surprising the incentive a shooting war can have on a combatant's desire to quickly learn the tradecraft. That said, most of our guys are salivating to get into the fight. But just like in nearly every other similar conflict, U.S. forces are limited to a training and assisting mission."

Buck set his beer down after gulping a drink. "Yeah, too bad that 'train and assist' definition isn't like it was in Vietnam, when things were far more relaxed." Buck was right. Years of increased Congressional oversight placed substantial burdens on such missions, and as the keeper of the purse, Congress and was certain to get its way.

The young, energetic waitress had been standing near the table for the last ten seconds and interrupted, "Are you ready to order?" As she did, she slid the new pitcher of beer onto the table.

"Yes! I'm starved!" Buck said, ignorant of the fact that it was his own tardiness causing his hunger. As Buck prepared to speak, one by one, the Buffalo Wild Wings television screens switched from their current sporting event to breaking news. Eventually, the TV which was playing audio also switched. The establishment hushed.

"We apologize for interrupting the current programming, but we've just learned Vice President Steven Banks has been rushed to Walter Reed Medical Hospital with an apparent illness. At present, the White House is not reporting the severity, but sources have confirmed his condition is grave and he has been admitted into an intensive care unit. When we learn more, we will report it, but again, the Vice President of the United States has been rushed to the hospital and is in intensive care with a serious ailment. We now return you to your regular programming."

Smitty looked down at his work phone, curious if there was chatter among the other security detail teams. There was none. Curt, surprised by the news, couldn't help but wish he was still a floor Emergency Room doctor and providing hands-on care.

"Jesus," Buck said. "Ukraine, Inflation, a crap economy, lingering Covid and now this? I thought bad news only happened in threes?"

The table grew quiet, as did the entire restaurant. It was the National Capital Region after all and nearly everyone was somehow tied to the Government. All were looking at their mobile devices, sending texts, making calls, or receiving instructions. Protocols for such events were long established across every department.

## *Chapter Two*

# Toxic Shock

*(The night prior)*

The ballroom at the Omni Shoreham Hotel was lively, serving as the prefect fund raising venue for Vice President Steve Banks. He'd invited a good number of political high rollers, as well as some special guests to bolster his stump speech messaging. The Omni sat high on a hill overlooking Rock Creek Park in the foreground, as D.C.'s city lights flickered off in the distance. The hotel was also only half a mile from Washington D.C.'s Naval Observatory, the official residence of the Vice President. Conveniently, Vice President Banks could quickly return home post event; after all, it was a Saturday, and in Steve's book, that was time best spent with family.

The ballroom was arranged in a spacious fashion, with ten circular tables, each seating ten guests, then a rectangular head table. Seated there was the Vice President, his wife, Senator Jackson from his home state, and his guest of honor, Ukrainian Ambassador to the United States, Ambassador Andriy Ubyivovk. Off in the wings and along the walls were a handful of journalists, waiting to report on the upcoming Vice President's speech. Additionally, dozens of staffers and fortified plain clothed security details were strategically dispersed throughout the room. Back in Ukraine, a war raged, but Ukrainian officials around the globe were targets for Russian assassins. Ukraine was gracious for the West's continued assistance while Russian leaders seethed at the amount of support Ukraine received.

As the restaurant staff bustled and the chatter of background noise filled the room, Vice President Banks rose, preparing to tap his water glass with a fork to garner the crowd's attention. It wouldn't be needed. A 'shhh' fell across the crowd before he could make one clank. Steve was unique in the sphere of U.S. Politics. He was a likable fellow with few opponents. He had friends on both sides of the aisle and always sought political positions which resonated with the populous, often upsetting his own party's fringe elements. Tonight, all in attendance were enamored with Vice President Banks. He was a man of great integrity, seeming to always be above the fray and noise of modern-day U.S. politics. Even those in disagreement with his policies were at least welcoming of his gentlemanly political approach.

Steve addressed a now silent ballroom. "Guests and friends. It is my honor to welcome you here tonight... along with your checkbooks." The crowd let out a good chuckle.

The remaining speech was as expected. A scathing rebuke of Russia and her reprehensible actions, a firm demand for their withdrawal from Ukraine, recognition of, and a toast to, Ambassador Andriy Ubyivovk, then gently raising a handful of soft hitting policy positions, all intended to appease the donors in the crowd.

The speech would resonate. No matter which side of the aisle one sat upon, the 'rational middle' found the Ukraine War a popular subject. For decades, Americans were conditioned to view Russia as the adversary. Bashing Russia in the U.S. was akin to beating a horse incapable of dying.

At the end of the speech, the crowd afforded a standing ovation. The serving staff scurried under the thunderous applause. In a controlled hurricane of activity, dinner was served. To ensure no potential donor had to wait on their food, the Vice President's staff and political party paid for over staffing. Tonight was not the night to frustrate, but rather cajole a generous opening of wallets. The food was spectacular, and the drinks flowed.

Vice President Banks, after taking only a few bites, stood and began walking around the tables to press some flesh. As every D.C. politician knew, speeches were important, but it was one-on-one engagements that truly secured the larger political donations.

Vice President Banks' ability to work a room was like a well-rehearsed ballet. His aides had arranged guest tables by issue. One on the environment, one for big business, one for defense industry, etc. He'd memorized the layout and what to say at each table. More importantly, he'd speak at a volume that would ensure only those at that table were within earshot. For each group, he'd offer a few bits of policy gold and a sincere 'thank you' for their gracious donations, all the while ensuring his comments were at least close enough to existing presidential policy that he didn't get sideways with his boss.

The dinner was much like other festive political events. Guests at each table congratulated him, thanked him and a few even offered their five second elevator speech in an effort to influence him. Paralleling all the communication were numerous offers to refresh Vice President Banks' wine glass and dozens of toasts. It was the life of a politician: never refuse food or drink offered by a hand that also holds money. Steve was a pro, however. He'd only accept a small refill, and barely sip any wine during each table's toast. If he didn't pace himself, inebriation would be on this doorstep in minutes.

The evening was a hit. Reporters now congregated outside the ballroom, feverishly typing into their hand-held devices, rushing to push their story into the media cycle. For most, it would garner less than a minute in the headlines, but it would make the news. As the evening drew to a close, Vice President Banks offered his farewell, blaming his lovely wife for their early exit. The two held hands as they departed the ballroom and with a team of professional secret service they walked to their awaiting motorcade. They would be home in three minutes.

*********************

Across town, Russian Ambassador Anton Tarlov just finished his evening meal at Washington D.C.'s famed Russia House restaurant. The scene could not have been in greater contrast. He ate alone, no fanfare, no press, and no friends. In western nations, it was a similar situation for most Russian ambassadors around the globe. There was no mistaking the diplomatic fallout Russia was suffering from their war in Ukraine. Tarlov paid his bill, buttoned his trench coat, and walked out of the restaurant towards his waiting chauffeured limo. A few Washington, D.C. Metro police officers stood outside the restaurant as part of an increased protection detail. Russian ambassadors were high interest security.  The United States and many other nations were unwilling to put themselves in a position that could be leveraged by Russia, no matter how much they disapproved of Russia's policies.  An attack on Tarlov would be a lottery ticket for the Kremlin, enabling Russia to redirect global focus away from the conflict in Ukraine.

As the ambassador walked down Russia House's famed, red-carpeted steps, a stranger in a black trench coat approached. "Ambassador!  Ambassador!"  He shouted and sped up towards Tarlov.  Alerted, D.C. Metro police grew suspicious.

"Yes?" the ambassador replied.

"I am with Russia!  I am with you!  Victory will be Russia's!" He announced.  "May I have a photo with you?"

Tarlov's chest bowed out.  He was flattered.  "Of course," Anton replied.  The man handed his phone to Tarlov's driver. The two embraced and shook hands with big smiles.  Once the photo was secured, the exuberant man retrieved his phone and graciously thanked both the driver and ambassador.  Somewhat expediently, he disappeared into the night, much in the way he arrived.

Washington D.C. Metro police relaxed, as did undisclosed U.S. special agents serving incognito following the ambassador. While casual pedestrians wouldn't know who the agents were, there were plenty.

The ambassador's driver opened the rear door of the limo and Tarlov poured himself into the vehicle, clearly having perhaps a bit too much vodka.  For him, it was a simple mistake given The Russia House maintains nearly one hundred different types of vodka available at their bar.

Once inside the car, he opened his hand and looked down. A small piece of paper was in it, passed secretly to him by the exuberant stranger.

In Russian, it simply said, 'Mission Complete.'

Tarlov smiled.  Things were turning around for him... and for Russia.  Still angered over losing the political power associated with the video associated with the President's scandalous affair, he, and more importantly, Russia, were making a comeback.

Tarlov enjoyed the ride back to his residence. *'What a wonderful feeling,'* he thought to himself. Being a diplomatically protected senior representative in an adversary's land was truly enjoyable for him. He chuckled as he believed himself to be imperviously dancing in his enemy's impotent claws.

********************

After kissing his wife for bed, Steve Banks began to feel ill. He was certain it was the food. At such events, the food is often bad. He just needed some Tums and sleep.

Through the night, his condition worsened. Within hours he'd be rushed to Walter Reed with an unknown ailment.

## *Chapter Three*
# Failed Attempts

The White House Medical Unit (WHMU) and Walter Reed medical staff worked feverishly to cure and comfort the Vice President. While an emergency medical and trauma facility was available on the Naval Observatory, specifically designated for the Vice President, his condition had deteriorated so fast, the head medical officer at the WHMU directed an immediate movement to Walter Reed.

Test after test was performed, trying to discover what was causing his rapid demise. Within a few hours, the medical staff had their answer... Polonium-210.

The head doctor called Steve Lewis, the White House Chief of Staff. "Sir, it appears the Vice President was poisoned. We've identified the toxin as polonium-210. It's the same poison that killed Alexander Litvinenko in 2006. Now that we know the cause, our team is pushing in as much antidote as we can, known as Prussian Blue, but the prognosis isn't good."

Steve took notes, right up to the last line. Given all the political turmoil the President had undergone, Vice President Banks was the White House's 'safe harbor' on their political ticket. He was also a great man. "Thanks, Doctor. Can you give me even a percentage as a chance of survival?"

"Sir, based on the amount we found and the severity, the answer is zero. Litvinenko lived for a few weeks and his dose was 200 times the lethal amount. Based on our screening of the Vice President, he likely has up to five times that amount, but we won't know until the autopsy."

'*Autopsy?*' Steve thought. Any optimism abandoned him. His heart sank. "I'll notify the President."

"OK, but please, encourage him not to come here. Polonium-210 is radioactive. We are taking every precaution with our medical staff, which is already demanding. A visit by the President would only compound the problem."

"I will inform him. Thanks." Steve hung up the phone and walked over to the President. It was Sunday evening, and the

13

President was enjoying a lovely dinner with his wife at the Camp David dining room.

"Mr. President, I am sorry to disturb you, but I have some urgent information."

Steve shared what he'd learned with both the President and First Lady. Their meal was ruined. The President would fly back to the White House in a few hours. The First Lady was already on the phone, trying to comfort the Second Lady, who herself was suffering some effects of the drug, just from mere contact with her husband.

*******************

That evening, news channels would somberly report the Vice President's passing. Curt and Allison, just like millions of other Americans, were watching Sunday evening television, relaxing in their D.C. row home living room. Noorullah sat at the dining room table, completing his homework. Bo was asleep upstairs in the baby room. Others around America that had tucked in early would awake on Monday to the news of Vice President Banks's passing.

News outlets cited 'unnamed sources' claiming Steve's death resulted from poisoning. While news anchors across the U.S. maturated over that narrative, things were different in the beltway. Both governmental employees and journalist networks knew exactly what drug had delivered the fatal blow, and they'd also grew convinced the poisoning took place at the prior evening's fund-raising event. Every eye was on Russia.

## *Chapter Four*
# Services Re-required

Admiral Hershey kissed Kathy goodbye, leaving her with the movers and the calamity of boxing up their belongings for the pending departure from the Chairman's residence. His motorcade waited out front and departed once he was inside. The lights turned on and the motorcade rolled, just as it usually did, headed to the Pentagon. As they approached, Admiral Hershey could see the Pentagon flags were already positioned at half-staff. He expected a deep intelligence assessment regarding the Vice President's death on his desk first thing.

The Chairman walked into the building then down the halls. staffers eerily gazed as they passed him by. He had seen such emotion before, but not since serving in the Pentagon on September 12th, 2001. There was a sense of uneasiness and uncertainty. A look of desperation matched with a plea for strong leadership. Anything that would assure them the future would be OK.

As he passed each one, he nodded with a slight, reassuring smile. It was the best he could offer.

Once in his office, the Admiral would review the intelligence briefing. It was just as he expected. Russia was the likely culprit, but who was the assassin? Every guest at the event was vetted by both the Vice President's staff and the Secret Service. All of them checked out, to include the hotel staff. U.S. Military Presidential aides were hand-picked, the best of the best. It couldn't have been one of them, but NCIS would take no chances. Each military member present that night was undergoing thorough questioning. Whoever it was, the FBI was already at work trying to solve the mystery and they'd need time.

A brief knock at the door disturbed his reading. "Admiral, good morning," the youthful female lieutenant colonel said. It was Lieutenant Colonel Andrade, one of his front office staff.

"Yes, Colonel Andrade, good morning. What is it?"

"Sir, the White House Chief of Staff called. The President

would like to see you this morning. We've arranged your transportation."

"I presumed that was the case. What time are the Defense Secretary and I going?"

LtCol Andrade did a short double take. "Sir? It's just you this morning. I was informed the Secretary would travel later for the National Security Council meeting."

The Admiral nodded and thanked his trusty staff member. Perhaps his last office call with the President. '*Finally*,' he thought.

*********************

Steve Lewis escorted the Admiral into the Oval Office and then remained in the room, prepared to take notes. The President stood gazing out the window overlooking the rose garden.

"Good morning, Mr. President. How are you holding up, Sir?" The Admiral offered.

"Good morning, Admiral. I'm good, thanks. And thanks for coming on such short notice." The President turned and walked towards the two facing sofas in the middle of the room. "Please, have a seat."

The Admiral stood at the sofa, prepared to sit, but would only do so after the President sat first. Even as the highest-ranking military officer in the United States, he would still maintain military bearing and only sit once his superior had done so. Steve had sat earlier in a chair adjacent to the two sofas.

The President would not talk about the Vice President situation. He'd save that for later in the National Security Council. "Admiral, you've served our nation exceptionally, and I can't imagine anyone performing better under all the circumstances."

The Admiral knew this was most likely political fluff but appreciated the sentiment. "Thank you, Mr. President."

"Later this week, I had planned to meet with you as a final

office call. However, given the horrible passing of Vice President Banks, I would like to ask you to cancel your retirement and remain for another year, or at least until things calm down. Right now, the U.S. appears vulnerable to our adversaries, and it's not the time to shake up staffing. I hope you understand."

Admiral Hershey was stunned. "Mr. President. I... Um... I don't know what to say. Frankly, I was certain this visit was my last official office call."

The President shifted the conversation to a more personal and desperate nature. "Eugene, I need you. Your nation needs you. Look, I know we've had our differences. Hell, D.C. is full of bloody elbows, but our differences were never insurmountable." It was the first time the Admiral could remember the President using his first name.

Hershey bit his tongue. He was not a politician, and clearly did not see things the same way. "Mr. President, I appreciate the offer, but I tendered my retirement papers long ago. My replacement, General Gott, has already passed Senate confirmation. He's an outstanding officer and will perform exceptionally."

The response was not one the President had expected. A four-star Flag Officer *wanting* to walk away from the most powerful military position in the world? "Admiral?" He said, "You don't wish to remain the Chairman?"

"Mr. President. Our nation suffered a significant attack last night. And I agree, our adversaries may perceive us as weak. But I disagree with your assertion that keeping me on will make our nation seem less vulnerable. In fact, I'd argue the opposite. I believe following the long-standing customs and protocols of our nation, such as uninterrupted senior staff rotations, makes the United States an image of strength and resolve. So, yes, Mr. President, I am saying I believe it best for our nation that I no longer serve as the Chairman, Sir."

The President wouldn't relent. "But again. I cannot stress enough. At this very time, your nation needs you."

Admiral Hershey took a long, deep breath. He stood up. "Mr. President, I couldn't agree more. And that is why I must resign. Sir, if there is nothing else."

The President slowly rose with a puzzled look on his face. *'What was Hershey up to?'* he thought. Was he entering politics? A Congressional Representative? A Senator? Whatever it was, the President would accept the continued course of retirement. Perhaps the Admiral was correct. Maybe the planned transition would serve his administration well. At least better than forcing Admiral Hershey to remain against his will. "OK, Admiral. We will play it your way. But do you mind if I inquire as to your future plans?"

"No, Mr. President. I don't mind at all. I presumed you'd ask. But at this point, I am not at liberty to share. I can say with near certainty, however, that we will again soon be working together."

"Fair enough." The President reached out his hand, and the Admiral shook it. They offered polite farewells, and Steve walked the Admiral out. As the two walked down the hall, the Admiral informed Steve that finalized retirement paperwork would be submitted to the Defense Secretary within the week.

********************

The mainstream media was in hyper mode. Coverage of the Vice President's presumed assassination dominated most of the channels. Just a day prior, the news cycle was governed by the war in Ukraine. In both cases, the focus was on Russia, but the Vice President's death hit far closer to home. Pundits had a field day, speculating as to the U.S. response. Would the U.S. see this as a red line crossed by Russia? Would the U.S. drastically increase aid to Ukraine? Would they send forces? Would they attack Russia directly?

The Executive Branch had another agenda. During every interview, Senior White House did everything to tamp down news analysts' speculation with phrases like *'It's an ongoing investigation... we don't know with certainty... we'd like to focus on the Vice President and his legacy... this is the time for the family to grieve.'* In fact, all of these statements were true, but much of America had long ago transitioned to a nation of 'guilty until proven innocent' and one that sought rapid response, if not retribution.

Americans wanted blood, Russian blood, and had little patience to wait for the investigation to run its course. Deep down, so did the President, but extracting blood from a fellow nuclear power already heavily engaged in a conventional war proved to be a complex proposition. A proposition far more challenging than most armchair politicians or pundits realized.

The National Security Council would convene in a few minutes. Prior to the President's entry, acting Secretary of Defense Stacy Crawford and Admiral Hershey held a brief sidebar discussion, much in the way many other Secretaries and other NSC members did around the table.

"Admiral, how was your meeting with the President this morning?"

"Well, Madam Secretary, different from what I anticipated."

She was surprised. "How so?"

"The President asked me to stay on with the administration for another year. I had presumed it was a final office call."

Stacy's eyes widened. She, too, was surprised. "Interesting. Was it because of the Vice President?"

"Yes ma'am. I graciously declined and said my retirement is a done deal. He relented."

Just as Stacy was about to respond, the President's arrival was announced. "Take your seats," he said.

The council members sat. A briefing as to the Vice President situation was provided. All indications pointed to Russia.

"Thank you," the President stated to the briefing officer from the Department of National Intelligence. "OK." He redirected his attention to the staff. "We don't have a smoking gun, but I think we are all fairly certain who pulled the trigger. I need response options now."

Secretary of State Marleen Baker would be the first to speak. She had risen through the ranks of the State Department and was now the head of that organization. Although a political hire, Marleen pulled few punches, often advocating positions best for the nation yet a death sentence to any future political career she may entertain. Such was the life of a good White House Cabinet secretary. Marleen spoke, "Mr. President. We are currently exacting the toughest sanctions against Russia in history. Our allies are boycotting Russian oil and seeking alternative sources. We've provided billions of war aid to Ukraine. From a soft power perspective, I am not sure there is much more we can do other than summon the Russian Ambassador and or expel a few more Russian diplomats."

While the President was not pleased with Marleen's answer, he knew she was right. There was only so much soft power arm twisting in the playbook. He turned towards the Secretary of Defense, hoping for something far more substantive. Stacy felt the glare and responded. "Mr. President. As Marleen mentioned, we are pushing weapons and supplies into Ukraine. There are only a handful we have not sent due to your specific direction based on political or policy sensitivities. To this point, we've not considered sending U.S. forces. Is that something you'd like to entertain? If you wish to revisit that decision, we can."

As Stacy stated the last part, tension within the room increased and everyone looked at the President. Could the U.S. truly stumble into a conventional war with another nuclear superpower? The thought was frightening. Alternatively, doing nothing in response to the assassination of the Vice President was not an option.

"Thanks Stacy. Let's shelve that for now, but keep it on the table. Anyone else?" The President knew the answer. There were few, if any, instruments of international diplomacy available among the other attendees. Surely, the CIA would work feverishly to find the assassin. The Treasury and Energy Secretaries both were already implementing State Department directives—the lead agency for international issues. They had nothing more to offer without State Department consent.

The room was quiet for too long. "OK, Marleen, I want Russian Ambassador Tarlov in my office no later than close of business today. I also want a list of twenty Russian diplomats to expel."

"Twenty?" Secretary Baker inquired.

"Yes. Twenty."

"Yes, Mr. President. But I must inform you, if we kick out twenty, they will kick out twenty, and we only have twenty-eight U.S. diplomats remaining in Russia."

The President didn't flinch. "I didn't stutter. Twenty." He stood up, as did the rest of the room. He departed without saying another word.

Secretary Baker's staff was already working to contact Ambassador Tarlov. Telephonically, it would be impossible. As with most Russian embassies, they rarely answered phones. A messenger would be dispatched immediately to knock on the Embassy gates, requesting a hand message be delivered to the Ambassador. That message demanded an immediate call to the Secretary of State.

As the State Department messenger arrived, he observed white smoke billowing out of the rarely used chimney within the Embassy. *'Geesh. They're already burning classified,'* he thought to himself. It was a troubling sign. The message was delivered. As requested (and expected) Russian Ambassador Tarlov called Secretary Baker. They would arrange a meeting in the White House at 1600Hrs.

## *Chapter Five*
# Slights of Hand

LtCol 'Alfi' Andrade, the long-time executive officer of Admiral Hershey, stuck her head beyond her office door frame into the main Pentagon 'E' Ring hallway. "Mr. Smith, the Chairman would like to see you," she said.

Mark 'Smitty' Smith spun towards her, disrupted from admiring some of the artwork hung on the wall. "Got it, Alfi," he said and scurried into the Admiral's office. "Sir, what's up? You OK?"

"Yes, fine Smitty. Thanks. Hey, my retirement ceremony is in a few days. When General Gott assumes command, I will ensure you maintain your job on the future Chairman's detail. Should you wish?"

"Thanks, Admiral. I appreciate that. Frankly, I can't see myself doing anything else. I'm not a desk jockey." They both grinned and knew an office job was a death sentence for Smitty.

"Smitty, one more thing. The retirement ceremony will be at Fort Myer. After that, The Commandant of the Marines will host a private event at his installation on 8th and I Street. I want you, Dr. & Ms. Nover, and that 'Pooh-bear Buck' Thiessen guy to be my personal guests."

"Sure thing, boss. I'll pass the word."

"Thanks, Smitty, but I want this to be official. Get Alfi everyone's contact info and she'll pass it to the Commandant's protocol officer. I think his name is Flanagan, or something like that." Admiral Hershey paused, clearly thinking about something else, then continued. "I have some important news for you, and it's somewhat killing me to not share yet."

Smitty was puzzled. "Boss, if it can't wait, why not tell me now?"

"In due time. In due time," the Chairman responded. "Let LtCol Andrade know I'd like my motorcade in five minutes. I want to head home early today and see how Kathy is doing with the pack out. She's probably killed the movers, or killed her third margarita, or both." The two smiled.

Smitty did as requested and helped to arrange the motorcade, after all, it was partly his responsibility being Admiral Hershey's lead personal security detail (PSD). He was loyal to a fault. There was nothing he wouldn't do for Admiral 'Squirts' Hershey.

\*\*\*\*\*\*\*\*\*\*\*\*\*\*\*\*\*\*\*\*

The President stewed in the Oval Office, pacing aimlessly. He looked down into his hand at a note from his secretary. In some excellent penmanship, the text said the First Lady had called and desired a return call. He crumpled up the note and threw it on his desk. *'There was no time for such things,'* he thought. *'Where was Tarlov?'*

1600Hrs had come and gone, the scheduled meeting time with the Russian Ambassador. Now 1615Hrs, Secretary of State Marleen Baker was politely barking orders to her staff within earshot of the Oval Office. She and her staff were frantically placing calls, attempting to track down the whereabouts of Ambassador Anton Tarlov. At 1620Hrs, White House Security notified the President's secretary a Russian motorcade was arriving. Marleen was furious. *'Protocols be damned,'* she thought. There would be no formal greeting at the front door. Under escort of the President's military aide staff, Tarlov would be escorted to the Oval Office. It was exactly the message she wanted Tarlov to receive.

Tarlov stood outside the Oval Office with a military entourage. Casually, he looked around, as if this meeting was just yet another of many he'd had with the President, clearly acting ignorant to the Vice President's assassination. Eventually, the large Oval Office doors swung open. Steve Lewis stood there looking out at the ambassador and curtly requested he enter.

Secretary Baker, also loitering outside the Oval Office, hung up her phone and walked towards the Oval Office, looking at her watch and then Tarlov, sending yet another nonverbal message.

23

Steve was placed in the uncomfortable position of informing her she'd not be welcome in this meeting. In fact, Steve was also not welcome. It would just be a meeting between the President and Tarlov. In the President's eyes, Anton Tarlov was a loose cannon. He'd already blackmailed the President once. The potential he'd attempt such a scandalous maneuver again could not be ruled out. The President wanted no part of exposing any of his indiscretions to Steve or Marleen. He'd clearly done enough of that in front of the planted Russian camera in the White House master bedroom.

Tarlov sauntered into the Oval Office as if he owned the place and had not a care in the world. It felt wonderful. He would regain his status. "Good afternoon, Mr. President. I do wish we could meet under more pleasant conditions given the untimely death of Vice President Banks. He seemed like a good man. My deepest condolences to you, Mrs. Banks, and the people of the U.S. This aside, it is good to see you. It's been too long. What may I do for you?"

The President and Tarlov sat on facing sofas. They did not shake hands. The President just looked at him for a moment, then responded. "Mr. Ambassador, I believe we both know why you are here. Why don't you start by telling me what you know about my Vice President's death?"

Tarlov shrugged his shoulders. "I don't know anything about this. I am somewhat confused. Do you think I would? Mr. President, I need you to be clear. Are you accusing Russia of this act?"

The President deflected the question. "Well, Anton, I don't have any proof it was Russia, but I do know this. The poison that killed him is extremely rare, and therefore it's highly likely the assassination was a state sponsored act. Further, given recent history, only one nation has used such a poison for a heinous act."

Tarlov, knowing far more than he was letting on regarding Vice President Banks' death, knew exactly to whom the President was referring. Nonetheless, Tarlov smiled and replied as if he were disappointed the U.S. could even consider accusing Russia of such an act. "Mr. President, if you are referring to the untimely death of Mr. Litvinenko in London, that case has never gone to trial. To this day, it is not known who committed such acts. Perhaps he committed suicide in an effort to tarnish the excellent reputation of my country."

The President smiled. "So, you want to play it this way? OK. But we both know the European Court of Human Rights and an independent British investigation identified the Russian assassins. They also have strong evidence orders for the murder originated at the highest levels of the Russian government. And let's not forget, the polonium 210 was traced to a Russian nuclear reactor."

"Mr. President. I'd suggest you be careful. Russia has never had the opportunity to confront these unfounded allegations in a court of law. Isn't it your nation that preaches 'innocent until proven guilty?' Until the international community can identify a fair trial opportunity and not yet another kangaroo court, Russia will not subject itself or its citizens to any unfair criminal proceeding." Tarlov paused, somewhat proud of himself for so eloquently delivering Moscow's long standing talking point regarding the assassination of former KGB and FSB intelligence agent Alexander Litvinenko. Oddly, Moscow wanted the world to unofficially believe Alexander was killed by Russia for being a turncoat spy. But in official or legal realms, they'd deny it to the end.

Tarlov continued, "Sir, nothing from the tragic death of Mr. Litvinenko ties to or implies Russia is at fault for the unfortunate death of Vice President Banks. If, as you say, the poison was polonium-210, there are many nuclear capable nations that could have manufactured it. Have you demanded to meet with the ambassadors from each of those nations as well, or is this yet again another tiresome, unwarranted, and unfounded attempt to badger my nation?"

The President grew angry, exactly what the ambassador wanted. "Anton, stow the fucking act. You and I both know those other nations are not to blame. I'm staring at my lead suspect, and he's given me nothing to help pronounce his innocence but rather deflected blame... exactly what I expect the guilty to do."

"Oh, but Mr. President. I am innocent. I was at dinner last night, nowhere near your Vice President," Tarlov shot back.

"Right. And can you provide just as concrete alibis for all your operatives in Washington?"

Tarlov smiled, then slowly leaned forward from his sofa towards the President. "Mr. President, here is what is going to happen. Your government will investigate this tragic event and determine it was the work of Chechen rebels who wished to frame Russia." He grinned. Chechnya had long served as a thorn in Russia's side. A global misstep by their rebels would be just the excuse Russia needed to do some heavy 'cleaning' in the region. "I am certain this is where your investigation will lead you. Should you be willing to do this, I am sure future doors between our countries will open. Should you choose not to, I am fearful the video of your granddaughter skating will…"

Before Tarlov could finish, the President had heard enough, cutting him off. "Enough about your fucking video. I buried that blackmail effort long ago. My discredited former Defense Secretary fell on that sword. The world thinks it's bullshit. And I'm fed up with your threats. One more and I'll have you ordered out of D.C. Do I make myself clear?" Just as the President expected, Anton again raised an effort of blackmail. He was right to keep Steve and Secretary Baker out of the room.

Tarlov softly chuckled out loud. In fact, he laughed so long it grew awkward. Eventually, he stood up. "Mr. President, did you really bury it? And forgive me for saying, but it is not 'my' fucking video, but rather 'yours.' Unless you have anything else, good day, Mr. President." It would be all he said… all he needed to say. Seeds were planted. Russians were exceptional at such games.

The President did not stand but rather reached into his suit coat pocket. In a single move, he tossed a piece of paper at Tarlov. "Here. These diplomats. Twenty of them. They are out. Persona non grata (PNG). 48 hours. Further details will be made available to your staff from Secretary Baker." The paper hit Tarlov on the shoulder and fell to the floor.

Tarlov didn't flinch. He casually bent over and picked it up. "As you wish, Mr. President. I will inform Moscow and make preparations for their departure. You can expect a similar list from me within 24 hours. I'll take the liberty of pre-notifying Secretary Baker so that your twenty diplomats in Moscow have just a few more hours before their lives are too disrupted by silly diplomatic games. I truly do hope they have ample time to pack up. Unfortunately, Russian moving companies are not as responsive as those in the U.S. Good day, Sir."

Tarlov casually held the paper and walked out. As the door opened, he saw both Steve and Marleen stand up. "Marleen. I have your PNG list. We both know Moscow will respond in kind. Please be prepared for a similar one by tomorrow. Again, my condolences to you and the American people. Vice President Banks was a great man and would have made a fine President. Perhaps even better than the current one."

Tarlov didn't wait for a response. He just walked to his motorcade and departed the White House grounds. Everything was going as planned. Looking down at his phone, a text message in Russian stated, 'Vehicles 5 minutes away.' He smiled as they drove away.

\*\*\*\*\*\*\*\*\*\*\*\*\*\*\*\*\*\*\*\*

In the sleepy little town of Mount Vernon, Virginia, two large black SUVs with U.S. Government license plates drove into a small subdivision. Such vehicles were not uncommon in the area, given Mount Vernon was also the home of the first President, George Washington. His residence, a long-standing national landmark, was visited by thousands every year, to include many senior U.S. Government officials and politicians.

In broad daylight, the two SUVs crawled to a stop in front of a small ranch style home. The doors swung open, and four heavily armed gunmen emerged, all with fully automatic long guns. Indiscriminately, they opened fire at the house without warning. The shooting lasted for thirty seconds, each shooter unloading a full cartridge of ammo. Each gunman then tossed their gun back into the vehicle, only to grab another and repeat the unadulterated firing onto this small, undefended residence. They were exceptionally quick and the use of multiple weapons eliminating reload times. After a second round of firing, the gunmen jumped back into the vehicles. In their haste, however, one weapon fell from the vehicle as they drove away. It lay in the street in front of the house. There was no time to go retrieve it.

As they drove away, a woman in her mid-thirties emerged from the house screaming in fear. Neighbors rushed to her comfort. Her house was destroyed. Police arrived on the scene. A few neighbors with personal security systems feverishly worked to capture their video and provide it to the police. Things like this did not happen in Mount Vernon, and everyone was working to ensure those who committed this crime were punished.

After the police arrived, it would be mere minutes until the media descended upon the crime scene. Gun violence was fairly common in downtown D.C. but not in the suburbs. For the next six hours, the news would continually broadcast this 'breaking news.' Slowly, facts mixed with speculation would surface. According to unnamed sources, black U.S. Government tagged SUVs shot up the home of Rachel Benson, a thirty-five-year-old single mother who worked at a U.S. Government cafeteria in Washington, D.C. Neither she nor her seven-year-old daughter were injured. A single weapon was recovered by the police and was being investigated. Inquiries from the media to the FBI, Secret Service and other governmental departments that have armed personnel all were answered with, *'No Comment.'* While this was yet another significant news event, it paled compared to the Vice President's passing, and eventually, the news stations migrated back to that story. For now, however, Rachel

Benson would have her few hours of fame, regardless of how horrific and life-changing that it was.

\* \* \* \* \* \* \* \* \* \* \* \* \* \* \* \* \* \* \* \*

In the White House private residence, the President and First Lady were lying in bed, watching the news. They both wanted to ensure the coverage about Vice President Banks was fair and glowing. As the breaking news cut in regarding the Mount Vernon shooting, the First Lady said, "Honey, look at the TV. There, isn't that Rachel Benson your nutrition chef?"

The President looked up and within seconds, knew his lovely wife was correct. "Well, I'll be damned," he said. He grabbed his phone.

"Steve, hey...."

Before the President could finish. "Sir, I'm watching it too. I'm already reaching out to the FBI and others. This is bullshit. I have no clue how this happened. Last thing we need right now is another Waco, Texas."

"Good. I want to know first thing in the morning. And if it wasn't us, tell the God Damn Directors to change their 'No Comment' to 'It was not our agency.' Thanks, Steve, Goodnight."

## Chapter Six
# Replacing Legends

The next morning, the Vice President's desk sat empty. A small flower bouquet sat in the middle of it as an unneeded reminder of the painful loss. The key staff and personnel did their best to manage the office, but it wasn't easy.

Along with all the wild speculation as to how the Vice President died, the media also enjoyably matured over who would replace him. Adding to the drama, news anchors hypothesized as to what if the President were to pass away? Per the Constitution, the Speaker of the House would assume the Presidency. While unlikely, such discussions make for good news media, beating the drum of fear and concern.

Inside the White House, cooler heads were prevailing. The President had asked Steve for a list of potential replacements to fill the Vice President position. Unsurprisingly, within hours of the death, Steve had received texts, emails, bar napkins and phone call nominations from everyone who could get to him. While Vice President Banks's death was tragic, there was opportunity, and no matter how poor the optics, few in D.C. would allow a crisis to go to waste.

Before the morning meetings, Steve walked into the Oval Office with the list of his top candidates. The President stopped him. "Steve, is that your suggested list of Vice President candidates?"

"Yes, Sir. It is. I also had our party chairman's input." Steve was confident regarding his homework.

"Good. Good. I'm gonna make you a bet. I can guess the top name on your list."

"Mr. President, you're on. For five bucks?"

The President didn't pause. He blurted out. "Stacy Crawford."

Steve's face drooped. "How did you know? Did you talk to the party chair as well?"

"No, Steve. I've been at this game for a long time. The Midterms have just passed, and the next presidential election campaigning will start soon. We need a strong and clean candidate. She's perfect. A female from California, married to a retired Marine Officer, years of public service, and a newcomer to the political scene and therefore very little political baggage. And she's done a great job as Defense Secretary, even if for just a short while."

Steve agreed with everything, but there was one problem. "Sir, your points are spot on; however, there is one downside to Secretary Crawford. You're replacing the Joint Chief this week. Replacing that position and the acting Defense Secretary at the same time could cause some unnecessary churn in the Pentagon."

"True, Steve. But under the circumstances, our options are limited. Should anything happen to me right now, the Speaker of the House would catapult to President and that would infuriate many in our party. We can't let that happen." The President paused to let Steve digest what he'd said, then began again. "Let me see the rest of the list you and the party chair put together. I'd like to see the other options." The President's mind wasn't fully made up, but it was close. "Tell the party chair which way I am leaning. Also, tell Secretary Crawford I'd like to have lunch with her today. It's not optional."

"Will do, Sir." Steve departed the room as the President began reading through the day's schedule.

\*\*\*\*\*\*\*\*\*\*\*\*\*\*\*\*\*\*\*

The Pentagon's third floor E ring hosted a rare event on Tuesday. Admiral Hershey's farewell lunch was in full swing, with countless Flag Officers and senior OSD civilians passing on their best wishes. Tables of food and drink lined the walls, anchoring the festively palpable atmosphere, a thanks for decades of service to a grateful nation. For the Admiral and Kathy, it was the culmination of a decades-long career.

Just fifty yards away, however, in a vaulted and secure room, things were undertaking quite a different tone. United States

Air Force General David Gott was receiving numerous in-
briefings. From nuclear missile programs to pre-positioned war
reserves around the globe. The briefings seemed endless, but
General Gott kept drinking coffee and demanded it continue.
On day one of the job, he wanted to be up to speed.

General Gott was a stocky man, standing just shy of six feet.
He was born and raised in Iowa, a lifelong Iowa State Cyclones
fan. He loved his state and loved his nation. The General was a
moderately religious man, but far from a zealot. As for his work
ethic, it was extraordinary, as he rarely needed sleep… the man
was a machine. He'd started his career as a pilot, flying F-16s.
Although a strong aviator, he was unfortunately forced to eject
during a training mission when his aircraft caught fire. He
suffered significant burns to his legs and a 1.5-inch spinal
compression fracture. Flight Surgeons recommended he be
medically discharged from the service. To then Captain Gott, a
medical discharge was not an option. After months of physical
therapy, he was walking, then running, demanding not only to
remain in the Air Force but also retain his flight status. After a
long review, a medical board approved his retention in the Air
Force but limited his flight duty to non-ejection seat aircraft,
arguing another ejection would likely kill him. Begrudgingly,
Captain Gott relented and accepted his fate, continuing his flying
career in X-135 type airframes such as the KC-135 Stratotanker
and the RC-135 Rivet Joint. Flying these airframes would teach
him about the worlds of strategic airlift and national intelligence
gathering. Such career breadth made him an exceptionally well-
rounded officer, having firsthand experience in both fighter and
heavy aircraft. More importantly, he had an infectious positive
attitude. It was impossible to be uninspired by his comeback
story, and even harder to ignore, he never sought favor or
excuse for it. Annually, he'd proudly complete his physical
fitness run, no matter how awkward his gate appeared. His
optimism was infectious, encouraging others to do better, to be
better. It was this attribute, nurtured over a decades-long

career, that would secure his position as the future Chairman of the Joint Chiefs.

*********************

Across the Potomac River, roughly at the same time, a small dining table was set in the Oval Office for two. The President's personal chef stood over the table. She was meticulous, inspecting it for exactness. Steve Lewis approached and nodded, a quick approval regarding the setup. He was pleased as she and her staff had prepared the table perfectly.

Steve spoke, "Rachel, this is perfect. Thanks."

"Thanks, Sir. I will personally serve the food today, given it is just a meal for two," she responded.

Steve transitioned the discussion away from work to a more personal nature. "Hey. I saw the news last night. Are you OK?" He was referring to yesterday's attack on her home.

"Yes. Thanks for asking. I'm OK. But very shaken up," she replied nervously.

"Well, I am confident everything will be OK," he replied.

Rachel's composure slipped. "Mr. Lewis, do you have any information as to why my house was shot up by what appeared to be U.S. Marshals, or FBI, or somebody? I want to talk to the President. Now."

"Rachel, I understand your anger. The President and I have already reached out across the government. It was not U.S. Marshals, or FBI, or CIA. We don't believe it was anyone in the government but are still running that to ground. Our best guess is the attack was carried out by individuals attempting to appear as U.S. Government officials. The president has directed that someone from each agency makes a statement today clarifying their earlier comments and ensuring this was not a governmental act." Steve moved closer to Rachel. "Seriously, are you OK? Is your family OK? You can take the day off. We can cover this."

"Yes. We are fine. Just shaken. Mr. Lewis, I truly need to

talk to the President."

"I understand," Steve replied. "Let me try to find some time on his schedule later today." Rachel nodded and scurried into the kitchen to place the final touches on the meal.

The President stood at the front door of the White House. He greeted Stacy Crawford as her car approached. It was extremely rare, a breach of traditional protocol, and she was unsure what it meant. Her car door was opened by a Marine security guard, and she stepped out. "Stacy!" The President said with a bit more enthusiasm than he'd normally share. "Thanks so much for accepting my invite."

She shook his extended hand and responded, "Well, Sir, based on Steve's call, I wasn't sure I had a choice," somewhat joking. "You seem to be in a good mood. Can I presume the meeting with Russian Ambassador Tarlov went well yesterday afternoon?"

"No. It was horrible. But thanks for asking. Stacy, that question right there is why I wanted to meet you. Please. Let's go in and eat." The two casually walked to the Oval Office. Stacy was carrying her trademark worn leather satchel. She'd had it ever since starting her career in civil service and believed it was good luck. Stacy's look was exquisite. She had stylish shoes, expensive clothes, and perfectly done hair and makeup. The old leather satchel stuck out like a sore thumb, but inside were talking points and papers for what she deemed to be the likely top ten issues the President wanted to discuss. While she didn't know which topic it would be, she'd be prepared. It was her modus operandi. Stacy was a demanding boss, but always placed credit where it was due... on her staff.

The two sat down and lunch was served.

"Stacy, do you have any ideas as to the reason I asked you here?"

"Well, I have about a dozen guesses. My best one is you'd like to discuss how I see General Gott's transition into the Pentagon. Or perhaps, escalatory military options to assist Ukraine in their war against Russia. Or a recent assessment of our European allies with respect to Ukraine... or."

The President stopped her there and chuckled. "Stacy, OK.

Enough. I'd love to discuss all those, but not at this time." He paused. "Can I ask you? How is Ryan doing?"

Ryan was Stacy's husband. A retired Marine Officer. "He's great. Thanks for asking. He also wanted me to pass along his thanks for letting us sit up on your balcony and watch Marine One practice their approaches and departures to the White House. He always loved his assignment with that unit years ago. It really was a nostalgic treat for him."

"Ha. Yes, I confess, it was a strange request, but he was such a fine gentleman, and our grand kids loved having him explain everything on the helicopters." Rachel approached, quietly placed two bowls of soup on the table and poured water into their glasses. The President nodded with approval. She smiled and then vanished to prepare the rest of the meal.

While Stacy appreciated the small talk, she was growing uncomfortable. "Sir, why am I here?" She stared at the President and picked up her soup spoon, preparing to eat.

"Very direct, Ms. Crawford. You've never been one to beat around the bush. We may have to work on that if you're to assume the position as Vice President."

Stacy's spoon dropped into her soup. "Excuse me, Mr. President?"

"You heard me. I want you to be my Vice President, taking Steve's place. If things go well, we can discuss your running with me in the next election. Your name was surfaced by many in the party as a great option, and the national party chairman endorsed you. All I need now is a yes."

Stacy was overwhelmed. "Mr. President. I am honored and humbled. But I'm a little speechless." Stacy paused. "Sir, what role would I have as a Vice President? Historically, in many administrations, there's little actual work, or impact. Plus, I'm not really a politician. I've dedicated myself to civil service. And.."

The President cut in, "Stacy, I'd ask you to pick up where Steve left off. And we both know he had a significant portfolio of work in my team. I want you to be my Vice President because of your ability. I'd be a fool to let that go to waste."

Stacy was eased by the answer but was savvy enough to

know there were political overtones in his comment. "Sir, I appreciate your offer, but it's all a bit much. I can't make this decision at a table over lunch. Please, I need to talk to Ryan, and we both need to truly weigh this out."

"Yes. Of course," the President responded. "I completely understand."

"Sir, can I have an answer to you by tomorrow morning? I will tell you in person at Admiral Hershey's retirement."

"Sure. Frankly, I planned to give you a few days. But tomorrow is great," replied the President. "Now, let's eat. And why don't you brief me on the issues you raised earlier? No point letting our meeting go to waste."

Stacy smiled and pulled a folder out of her brown leather satchel. "I thought you'd never ask." She began covering everything in perfect detail. As the President listened, he hoped more and more that she'd take the offer. She'd be an exceptional Vice President.

*******************

Later that day, Stacy Crawford and her husband, Ryan Murphy, would take a motorcade from their residence to the Army Navy Country Club. It was a beautiful country club and the one most centrally located in the National Capital Region. The club's history held a long-standing list of famed members such as President Clinton and Eisenhower. Should Ryan and Stacy agree, another famed name might adorn the walls. Stacy and Ryan had long been members of the club. It was a favorite of theirs. The half mile drive from the entrance, through the golf course, to the main club building was almost magical. Somehow, it absorbed the stress of D.C. and could reduce a member's blood pressure by twenty points. It was an oasis of normalcy in the cesspool of the Capital.

Once inside, they sat in overstuffed leather chairs next to a gently burning fireplace in the Eisenhower bar. There, they would share a first drink to remove the day's edge. The two made small talk. Work discussions would normally be delayed until later at their private table; too many wondering ears filled the bar. The club, while beautiful, was also a haven for the defense industry, lobbyist and other government big shots, who'd love nothing more than to overhear some inside baseball directly from the Defense Secretary's mouth.

Stacy could wait no longer. "So, I'm not sure I told you, but I had a no notice lunch with the President today."

Ryan was mildly surprised. "Really? Hey, did you tell him I said thanks..."

Stacy was about to burst and cut him off. "For watching the helicopters, yes, Ryan, I told him. He wants me to be his Vice President."

Ryan's mild surprise escalated quickly as he nearly spilled his drink. "You're kidding, right?"

"No. Not one bit." She shared the details of her lunch with the President.

"What did you tell him?" Ryan asked, with an ever so slight smirk on his face. He'd been married to Stacy far too long and knew she wanted the job.

"I told him I wanted to discuss it with you first."

Ryan grew a bit more serious. "Well, I thank you for that. But as you know, this will really disrupt the plans we laid out and I'll be the one who must sacrifice again in our relationship."

Stacy's eyes widened, although she tried to hide it. His response was unexpected. She loved Ryan with all her heart. If Ryan was opposed, she'd turn it down, no matter how much she wanted the job. The wheels in her head churned rapidly, seeking reasons the job would benefit them both. "You're right, but I think in this position, both of us..." She stopped talking as Ryan stood up out of his leather chair.

Ryan walked over to kiss her on the cheek. Before he did, he said, "Congratulations, Madam Vice President." He kissed her and pulled his head back roughly a foot and stared into her eyes, smiling at his funny, albeit inappropriate, practical joke.

"Why did I fall in love with an asshole?" Stacy rhetorically asked herself. Then reached out and pulled him in tight for a hug. "Thank you, Ry. I love you."

Ryan returned to his chair and his drink. They'd continue with their drinks and dinner; the only two in the world who knew she would be the next Vice President of the United States of America.

*********************

It was near the end of the workday in the White House. Steve escorted Rachel into the Oval Office. The two approached the President, stopping short of his desk. Steve provided a detailed briefing regarding the events of the previous day, as well as what the executive branch attempted to learn about the attack.

"Rachel, is this true?" The President said.

She began to sob. "Yes. My house! It's destroyed!"

The President reached over his desk and passed her a Kleenex. "Steve, why don't you leave us? I got this."

Steve did as directed, walking out of the office.

As he closed the doors, Rachel lunged into the President's awaiting arms. He held her. In a comforting manner. Slowly, however, the hug clearly transitioned to one of passion. Before it went too far, Rachel partially pulled away and said, "I don't know who did this! Can you please find out and fire them?"

"Rachel," he replied. "Of course. I'm sorry this happened, and I am sorry I haven't been more attentive to you. I'll have the FBI put their best team on this. I promise you, sweetheart."

The two kissed. Passionately. His hands raising and lowering up the small of Rachel's back. They took a breath. "Thank you. Thank you!" She kissed him again... and again, kissing ever more passionately. In a rushed fashion, the two disrobed. The President, now standing naked with his pants around his ankles, was quietly penetrating Rachel from behind as her naked chest pressed down onto the Oval Office desk. Although they made little noise, the event was a ruckus, bordering on violent. It was how the President liked it. Her hips and thighs pounded against the edge of the desk. Towards the climax, the President grabbed her hair and pulled her head back, placing both hands around her neck. Tightening his grip, he began to choke her. To Rachel, it wasn't pleasant. In fact, she disliked it, but she dared not complain. She was with the most powerful man in the world and, for whatever reason, was attracted to his power. Rachel didn't try to remove his hands. She would fake an orgasm while deprived of oxygen, hoping he'd let her start breathing again. As much as she disliked it, her partner conversely loved it. The President found the event empowering and dominating. He, too, would orgasm for real shortly after her faux effort.

Exhausted, the two quickly cleaned up and re-robed. There was no time for cuddling. The President led her to the door; they kissed one last time. He opened the door. "Steve," he called. "Let's reach out to the FBI and find out who the officer is that is investigating the shooting. I'd like regular updates on the case, and please let the investigator know I take a special interest in any case involving my personal staff." He looked at Rachel, who blushed.

"Will do, Sir." Steve had written everything down. Later that night, he'd reach out to his FBI contact and have a full report the next day.

## *Chapter Seven*
# Transfers of Command

The morning sun glowed over the Pentagon as Stacy met Admiral Hershey and General Gott just outside the north entrance, used by senior staff and executives. Now, the 28th of February and the last day of the month, it would be Admiral Hershey's administrative last day of employment. Officially, he'd still have over two months of leave time to burn before he was truly 'Mr. Hershey.' "Gentlemen! Good morning!" Stacy cheerfully offered as a greeting.

The two, almost in unison, replied, "Good Morning, Madam Secretary."

They all shook hands. "Big day today for us. How about before the ceremony we park at Arlington Cemetery on the way and take a short walk? I'd like that and believe the day's events perhaps warrant such."

The two officers agreed, and each hopped into their respective motorcades. Security protocols demanded they ride separately in the event of an attack. Within minutes, the SUVs were at a quiet section of Arlington Cemetery and slowed to a stop. The three exited their respective cars, and they began strolling along the paved road. Stacy was flanked by the two most powerful military officers in the world and surrounded by thousands of heroes resting under white headstones. It was exactly the backdrop she wanted.

"I love this place," Stacy said. "It's where I found my calling to be the best Defense Department employee I could be. My idealistic dream was to be so good, not one more service member would be laid to rest under my watch."

The two officers looked at each other. She gently shot back. "Hey, I said it was idealistic, and I was 23. Give a girl a break." The two flag officers snickered. Stacy paused as she kept walking and then became serious. "I have something to tell you both. Yesterday, the President asked me to assume the role of the Vice President. I have not accepted it yet but have discussed it with Ryan. We are both inclined to take on the opportunity, but before I do, I want both of your thoughts."

Admiral Hershey was initially stunned, but as he thought through it, her selection made sense. "Madam Secretary, I don't have much of a dog in this fight. I'm on my way out the door. I believe you'd make a great Vice President, but as for the impact on the Pentagon, I think Dave has far more skin in this than I."

General Gott didn't need to think long. He'd been in the Pentagon years earlier and knew the game. He also realized that once a new Defense Secretary was appointed, he'd have an additional advocate, for lack of a better word, in the National Security Council, in the seat of the Vice President. "Madam Secre.." He stopped and corrected himself. "Madam Future Vice President, I could think of nothing better. I've always admired leaders who advance their best people and hated those who stifled a subordinate's advancement for their own selfish needs. I can see why the President wants you. Your vacancy in the Pentagon will hurt, no doubt. But the country will be better. And I pray you help us find your replacement that's at least half as good as you."

They'd stopped walking and no one really noticed except for the inner and outer cordons of Secret Service. "Eugene, Dave, I have one last request, if you don't mind, and I realize it's far from the most professional thing I've ever asked."

"Shoot, boss." Admiral Hershey said.

More formally, Dave responded, "What is it, ma'am?"

"Can I hug you both?"

They all smiled agreeably. Stacy reached up her arms towards Admiral Hershey. "Squirts. Thanks for everything. I could never have done it without you."

"My pleasure," he replied as he gave her a good Navy bear hug.

She turned to General Gott. "And Dave. I want you to know. You were my top pick. You have all the traits of a history-making Chairman. I believe in you."

The two hugged. It was a bit more formal; understandably, as these two had not yet served together in the trenches. "Ma'am, I promise. Everyday, I will do my best."

The three walked back to their vehicles and then proceeded

to Fort Myer.  Their brief detour would remain a secret to only them.  As Secretary Crawford entered her vehicle, she shot a text to the President and Steve.

> 'Mr. President,
> Ryan and I are in.  Honored to join the team.'

The flood of vehicles had overwhelmed the Fort Myer gate guards.  Every International Senior Defense Attaché assigned to D.C. would be escorting their chief of defense along with their ambassadors from around the globe.  Generals from around the globe descended on Admiral Hershey's retirement ceremony.

Cannons lined the hilltop of Fort Myer, pointing out over Arlington Cemetery and towards the Potomac River.  Dozens of American flags gently billowed in the soft air, all of them anchored at half-staff, by order of the President for thirty days, paying respects to former Vice President Banks.  Both the U.S. Navy band and the President's Marine band played traditional military music as guests arrived.  It was a spectacle worth seeing.

Briefly, the music stopped.  A staff officer asked for everyone to stand.  Ruffles and Flourishes played loudly.  Secretary of Defense Stacy Crawford, followed by both Admiral Hershey and General Gott, took the stage.  The Secretary opened the comments, both thanking Admiral Hershey for his service and welcoming General Gott, clearly stating he was up to the challenge.

Eventually, the ceremonial change of command took place as Admiral Hershey relinquished command and its token guidon, which was then passed onto General Gott.

The change of command ceremony then transitioned to Admiral Hershey's retirement.  He spoke, thanking his lovely wife, then family and friends.  His speech was brief.  What more could he say?  He had served at the highest level in the U.S. military.

To the crowd, the content of his speech mattered little.  He would get a standing ovation, not for his words, but rather his service career and the caliber of man he was.

Before the ceremony ended, two large flat panel screens on

either side of the stage burst to life. The protocol officer announced. "Ladies and gentlemen, the President of the United States."

In an instant, the President appeared, sitting behind his Oval Office desk and prepared to offer a statement.

"Madam Secretary, Admiral Hershey and General Gott. What a wonderful day for your change of command. First, I want to thank Admiral Hershey and his wife Kathy. Your joint service to our nation has been extraordinary. I could not be prouder to have had you on my staff as a critical part of my innermost sanctum on security issues. General Gott, I have no doubt in my mind you'll pick up the torch and continue right where Admiral Hershey left off. I look forward to our time together."

The President paused and directed his next comments to the audience. "To the visitors here today, and perhaps more broadly to the world, make no mistake, the United States military, and her might across all instruments of power remain steadfast, even as we mourn the loss of our dear Vice President Banks who lies in state at the Congressional Rotunda. To nations that should wish harm upon our great nation, I caution them. Never misconstrue our reserved nature for weakness."

As he spoke, a rustling in the crowd grew. People began to turn around in their seats as a handful of police motorcycles led a massive motorcade. Few were still listening to the President's speech as he was wrapping up.

Again, the protocol officer took the microphone, "Ladies and Gentlemen, the actual President of the United States." Quickly, the President's Marine band began playing hail to the chief and everyone jumped out of their seats.

Up between the seats in a wide aisle, the President and his wife approached. The first lady took a seat in the front row as the President helped her sit down. Once seated, the President continued to the stage. Stacy smirked. She knew the President couldn't pass up an opportunity like this.

As he jumped up onto the stage, he shook hands with Stacy, then the two flag officers. He then took the podium with authority.

"Hey everyone! Surprise!"

Laugher and applause broke out from the crowd.

"I didn't have much time, but wanted to say a personal hello. Kathy," he looked down at Kathy Hershey. "How did you put up with this guy for so many years?"

Again, the crowd laughed as they saw Kathy shrug her shoulders.

"I wanted to come and present this personally," he said as he turned his head back to the seats on the stage. "Admiral Hershey, will you come join me up here? Also, can my military aide come on up?"

Admiral Hershey rose from his chair and walked up next to the President. Meanwhile, a perfectly dressed Army lieutenant colonel wearing a Presidential aiguillette approached holding a folded U.S. flag, and on top of it, an adorned folder and box. He handed the flag and the box to the President, then opened the folder. In a voice made for radio, he read the citation of the Presidential Medal of Freedom. As he began, the crowd stood. Admiral Hershey's chest bowed out. The President pinned the medal onto his chest, shook his hand and whispered in his ear, "Thanks for everything, Squirts. You deserve this, and I look forward to seeing how you plan to serve our nation further. Any hints?"

Admiral Hershey smiled and gripped the President's hand, a bit firmer, and leaned in, "Thanks, Mr. President. As for my plans, still no hints… but I respect your tenacity."

To the crowd, it looked as if the two shared a funny joke between good friends. It was exactly the image the President desired, and it could not have been further from the truth. Such were the ways in D.C.

The observers applauded, and at the end of the ceremony, the President and his wife slowly moved to the Presidential motorcade, with Stacy and Ryan by their side. As the four walked, the flock of reporters scurried along, barking out questions. Eventually the President stopped.

The loudest reporter yelled, "Mr. President! Do you have any more information about Vice President Banks's assassination?"

"At this time, they are still running tests, but it's clear there was foul play. To speculate further would be unwarranted. Next question."

"Mr. President, what agency was involved in the massive shooting in Mount Vernon? Neither the FBI, U.S. Marshals are commenting." While the incident wasn't as big as a Vice President assassination, the media was already drawing parallels to the unfortunate event in Waco, Texas. It was not a linkage the administration desired.

"That's a good question," the President responded. "I understand there is a report on my desk from the lead investigator and I'll read it when I get back to the Oval Office. After that, I'll be able to answer. Next question, how about one for Ms. Crawford?"

"Madam Secretary," another reporter was able to quickly belch. "What is your response to allegations the U.S. is employing Special Forces against Russian forces units in Ukraine?"

Before Stacy could respond, the President jumped in, "Hey. Now is that any kind of question for my future Vice President? No more questions, good day." Stacy's eyes lit up, and Ryan did a double take. Neither were informed nor prepared for such an announcement. The scenario played out just as the President desired. Off the cuff, he'd announced his next Vice President.

The press pool exploded, growing louder and more active. Camera flashes were so rapid, it felt like a rave. With the feverous snapping of photos, one would have presumed there were no existing public photos of Stacy Crawford. The rear door of The Beast, the Presidential Limo, opened, and the four entered. Secret Service pushed back the press pool, and the motorcade began to pull away.

Within minutes, media outlets, internet pages, and social media were splashed with the headline. *'Stacy Crawford to be next Vice President.'*

\*\*\*\*\*\*\*\*\*\*\*\*\*\*\*\*\*\*\*\*

Rachel stood in her front yard, meeting with insurance estimators and a local building contractor who had already boarded up the outside and was working to make the house habitable again. As the group began to disperse, a black limo pulled up, and the window rolled down. "Ms. Benson," a voice called out to her.

She excused herself from the two and looked back into the vehicle. "Excuse me, may I help you?" She replied. She walked towards the car, stopping just feet away.

"Ma'am, I don't believe you can. But I can help you. I must warn you. You're in grave danger. Both you and your daughter."

Rachel's fears had been assuaged by the President, but she could not say such. "Thanks, but I think there are some pretty powerful folks working to figure this thing out."

The voice from inside the limo was unconvinced. "Rachel, you look like a bright lady. Who do you think could have pulled this off? And before you answer, we know about your affair with the President."

Rachel froze. No one was to know. How did he know? And who was his *'we'*? How many were in his *'we'*? She blurted out the question, "What affair? Who are you?"

"Ms. Benson, I am not the U.S. government. You would be wise to consider me a good Samaritan. You have placed your trust in the wrong hands. Your confidence in the President could be your demise. I have little time. When you need help, and you will, here is my number." He handed over a business card that merely had a phone number on it. As she took it, the car rolled away.

"Wait!  What's your name?"  It was no use; the car was gone.

## *Chapter Eight*
# The Pitch

The Private NCO club at the Marine Corps Barracks was packed. Drinks were flowing, and both the Commandant and Admiral Hershey stood at the prime location in the bar. Both had already imbibed quite a bit, and they had unbuttoned the top portions of their uniforms, a no-no in public for a military officer. They didn't care. No cameras were allowed in the bar, and no one there was foolish enough to consider breaking that rule in a location full of Marines.

Buck parked his car in Curt and Allison's driveway on 7th Street. From their row home, it was a five-minute walk to the Barracks. Together, Buck, Allison and Curt walked up to the Marine guard, and after a quick check of names, they were escorted into the Commandant's house, one of the few governmental structures to survive the razing of Washington D.C. during the War of 1812. It is also the only four-star Flag Officer billeting quarters visible to the public. Of course, the house was constantly guarded by armed Marines, a select few that were authorized to carry firearms other than police in the nation's capital. As the story goes, when the D.C. mayor ordered the city to be gun free, a press reporter asked the Commandant, "What do you say to the mayor who is demanding to disarm your Marines at this location?"

The Commandant smiled and said, "I wish him luck."

The Commandant's house was beautiful and looked out over the parade grounds of the barracks. A sharply dressed Marine offered his arm to Allison and led the three through the house, out into the back garden, over the parade grounds, and then to the NCO Club where the party was in full swing. Once inside, the young Marine gentlemanly returned Allison's arm and departed to escort other guests. He'd not be able to partake in the festivities.

Smitty, now off the clock, saw his friends enter and pushed three beers their way. "Hey buddies! Glad you finally made it!

What a party, eh?" Smitty was clearly into his fourth or fiftieth drink.

"Smitty," Allison said sternly. "Do you ever learn? I'm still breastfeeding and cannot drink alcohol." As frustrated as she was, Allison knew she would still be reminding all of them well into the next few months.

Buck was in luck and the beneficiary of a second beer. Eventually, a Red Bull would make it across the crowded room to Allison.

Smitty was clearly well imbibed. Thankfully, he was no longer carrying his sidearm. In true Smitty fashion, however, he did have his security earpiece and wire still on. Not for the show, but because he always wanted to know what was going on.

"Yeah. This place is hoppin," Buck replied. "Hell, I didn't even know this place existed."

"It's a private club, Buck," Allison said. "In the summer during the Friday Evening Parades, some are lucky enough to get invited into the bar. It's always an interesting crowd. Flag officers, politicians, dignitaries, diplomats, and billionaires. Additionally, the young Marines assigned to the barracks invite quite attractive counterparts whom they'd like to get to know a little better. Luckily, this event appears to be a bit light on the latter crowd."

Curt looked at Allison quizzically. "How did you know that?"

"Curt, sweetheart. You aren't my first rodeo. There isn't a girl on this earth not giddy over a well-dressed Marine."

"What? You've been here before?" Curt asked.

She kissed him on the cheek. "You're cute," she replied.

Smitty and Buck laughed. Curt turned a slight shade of pink from jealousy. It passed quickly. Allison was his until death do they part, and a little humble pie was always good for the relationship.

"Dr. Nover!" Curt heard from across the bar. "Dr. Nover!" As he looked up, he saw it was Admiral Hershey calling and motioning his hand to come over. Interestingly, just two seats down from the Admiral was Don Denney, the wealthy political donor and D.C. player. Don did not see Curt, as he was clearly locked in a serious discussion with another man in civilian attire. The four moved towards the Admiral, as he requested.

"Dr. Nover. I'm truly happy you could come. This is General Tyce Havens, Commandant of the Marines. Tyce, this is Dr. Curt Nover, the guy I was telling you about. Here is his wife Allison, and their friend Pooh Bear, er, uh, Buck." The Admiral still smiled when he said that name.

Buck tried hard to hide his anger at the nickname. He hated it, but if he let on that he hated it, there was a good chance he'd be 'Pooh bear Buck' for the rest of his life. Smiling, he extended his hand, "Commandant, it is nice to meet you." He then turned to the Admiral, offering his hand. "Squirts, good to see ya again. Did you get that constipation situation all cleaned up?"

In unison, everyone within earshot opened their mouths wide. Smitty jumped in and said, "Easy, Buck. Easy."

The Admiral looked at Smitty. "No, Buck's right. I need to be able to give as good as I get. Hell, since I've been Chairman, that's the first ribbing I've gotten in two years. Thanks Buck! But you'll always be Pooh Bear to me. And one last thing, how's that dick drip situation you caught from the Russian honeypot?"

Buck hung his head as the bar rolled in laughter. Someday Buck would learn not to fuck with the biggest bull in the room. Today was not that day. As they laughed, someone rang the bar bell. Normally, that meant a free round, but tonight, all the rounds were free.

"Hey, Curt. What do you say you and the guys come with me outside for a second? I want to talk to ya."

"Sure thing, Sir," Curt replied. He quickly glanced at Allison to ensure she'd be OK.

Allison smiled. "Curt, don't be too long. Who knows how fast a girl can fall in love surrounded by Marines?"

The four smiled, then walked out of the NCO Club and stood in the corner of the parade grounds. It was a grand lawn, surrounded by towering solid brick structures, as if it were a fortress' inner courtyard. At the other end of the parade grounds, chandeliers inside the Commandant's house shone softly out onto the surrounding shrubbery.

"What a day," the Admiral started. He pulled out four Cuban Cohiba cigars, offering the other three to partake. No one refused.

"Thanks, Admiral," they all said at different intervals. The cigars were lit. Out in front of them was another Marine guard position which looked out onto 8th Street. The Marines on duty at the position were clearly grateful the weather was unseasonably warm for February. They noticed the Commandant approaching and straightened up quickly. The two were dressed flawlessly in their uniforms, and would intentionally fail to notice, or mention the Admiral's uniform was now half unbuttoned and clearly out of regulations. It was a wise decision.

The Commandant spoke, "Gentlemen, again, I want to thank you for coming to my retirement party. It means a great deal to me." They all nodded, respectfully, also commenting the honor was theirs. The Admiral continued. "Look, I have decided. I don't want to follow the standard route into the defense industry or be a lobbyist. I want more, and frankly, I am hoping you all do as well." The Admiral paused to watch their faces. "I have secured financing and am starting my own company. If you are interested, I'd like to hire all of you."

Buck and Smitty were intrigued, and nearly ready to sign up. Curt, however, needed more. "Sir," Curt asked, "What is the business?"

"I'm glad you asked Curt. My company, working closely with the U.S. Government, is going to right some of the wrongs that currently plague the world."

Curt's eyes opened. "You mean yet another mercenary firm acting as private security or some other cover?" Curt was nearly disgusted just by the mere notion.

"Call it what you will, but yes. Curt, I know your past and I know how you felt about NISSASSA. To be fair, I wasn't fond of them either. It was run the wrong way."

"You knew about NISSASSA?" Curt quickly responded.

"Curt. I was the Chairman of the Joint Chiefs. I knew everything. Like I said, though. I didn't agree with their business model. They lost their way, ethically. I want to start a company that, at the core, is ethically bound to what we all know to be the laws of armed conflict, minus the definition of a combatant, of course."

"I'm out," Curt said quickly as he began walking back towards the bar.

"Curt, you are not even a quarter of the way through your cigar. Can you at least hear me out?" The Admiral said. Curt nodded. "Good. Curt, you need to understand, I too am not enamored by the notion of private mercenary organizations. When I first learned of the ones that stood up in Russia, I was angered. I grew even more frustrated when I learned from our State Department colleagues that diplomatically, there was little that could be done to eliminate them. For decades, Russia has been able to employ mercenary organizations, doing their nation's bidding, yet suffering none of the associated diplomatic consequences for their actions." The Admiral paused, letting that sink in.

"NISSASSA was not crafted idly. Senior members of the Defense Department, State Department, CIA, the Executive Branch and even Congress were aware. And more important, supportive. The problem became NISSASSA's leadership. Rightly so, Curt, you exposed their unethical training range. For that, I applaud your efforts. But the U.S. needs an organization like NISSASSA, now more than ever, given the ongoing war in Ukraine."

Smitty had heard enough. "I'm in." Curt shot him a scowl.

"Thanks, Smitty. I appreciate that," the Admiral replied. "Today, numerous Russian mercenaries are running around Ukraine and other places, doing things that, as a longtime war fighter, make me cringe. As the Chairman, I was unable to respond. Now, I can. I will share with you this. A few days ago, the President asked me to cancel my retirement and stay on as the Chairman in light of the Vice President's death. I refused. Not because I didn't wish to remain in office, but because I wanted revenge against the bastards that assassinated Steven Banks. And my best chance at that was via this path, not as the Chairman."

Buck jumped in, "Admiral, I'm in, but I don't know what you're gonna use an old pilot like me for." Again, Curt shot a scowl.

"Thanks Buck. I have big plans for you. We can discuss it later. Curt, that leaves just you. What do you say?"

"Admiral. I've listened, as I said I would. But I cannot be part of this. I don't believe the definition of combatant should extend beyond uniformed members under civilian control. It has long been a cornerstone of our military, and a good one that other nations emulate. We can't throw that away."

"I get your point, Curt. But we both know the U.S. military has not been the only department in the government that has wielded kinetic actions around the globe. Other agencies have done so, and in increasing fashion over the past few years. To be fair, Blackwater, a U.S. firm, stood up in 1987. Traditional definitions of warfare have been blurring for quite some time."

"Sorry, Admiral. I am still out. But I promise you this. If you keep to your word, and it remains ethical, by my standards, not yours, I will remain silent."

The Admiral's chest deflated. He truly wanted Curt in a leadership role. "Curt, I understand. I hope someday you'll change your mind."

As they were finishing talking, Allison walked out of the NCO Club and joined them. "Hey guys, did ya think it was wise to leave a girl alone in that bar of all places with a boatload of Marines?"

She walked up to Curt and slid her arm around his back. "Curt, we need to get back home." She turned her attention to the Admiral. "Sir, my apologies, but it is the first time we've left Baby Bo home alone with a sitter. At three months old, we were a bit pushing it, but we didn't want to miss your event. Not to mention, Noorullah is still struggling a bit and I'm doing all I can to get him integrated."

"Allison, I completely understand. I am grateful for your presence, even if for just a short while."

Curt spoke. "Yes, how about I take Allison back? Buck, you and Smitty stay and enjoy yourselves." Frankly, Curt did not wish to have a five-minute walk with either of them back to his house.

The group said their goodbyes as Allison and Curt, hand in hand, walked out of the barracks onto 8th Street. They walked down the bustling sidewalks, headed home.

"Curt, what did you guys talk about out there?"

"War stories and stuff. Nothing important." Curt tried to change the subject. "I hope Bo is OK."

"I'm sure he is." Allison wrapped her hands around Curt's arm.

The rest of the walk was quiet. Curt thought to himself. *'Am I wrong? What are Buck and Smitty thinking? How can they so easily agree? Don't they see the problem? Or is it me?'*

## *Chapter Nine*
# Follow the Evidence

Mark Flaherty was a fifteen-year FBI investigator. He'd been offered countless promotions but refused. He never wanted a desk job. Being outside, unanchored to an office desk and free to follow his own course was instrumental to his lifestyle. For the past few days, he'd been gathering evidence from the Mount Vernon crime scene. Mark had finished preparing to talk with Rachel Benson and share his findings. A ringing phone interrupted him.

Mark answered, "Detective Flaherty."

"Flap, can you come to my office?" It was Andy Ross, his chief. 'Flap' was Mark's long-time nickname among friends and colleagues. It was affectionately given to him when it was clear he was 'unflappable' when drunk.

"Sure thing, boss." Mark answered.

Within minutes, Mark Flaherty stood at Andy's office door and knocked twice.

"Good. You're here. Come in and sit down," his director said.

Flap did as requested. "What's up, Boss?"

"Hey, got a call from higher ups. Where are you on the Benson case, the one out in Mount Vernon." Flap could sense Andy was nervous by the way he spoke. That, and the fact that he rarely asked about a case update, usually waiting for Mark to provide one, were clear indications something was wrong.

Mark opened his small spiral pocket notebook. "Well, it appears two vehicles and four gunmen lit up this house like the 4th of July, miraculously missing the two individuals inside. The vehicles had USG (U.S. Government) tags, but they appear to either be fake, or some agency isn't playing nice in the schoolyard. If the tags were fake, they're good ones. I have solid video of the vehicles from neighborhood closed circuit security cameras. Also, we can make out some of the perps. If they weren't government agents, they sure dressed the part."

Mark paused long enough to flip to another page in his notebook. "The victim, Rachel Benson, is reportedly a cook at the White House with a clean record. Previously married. She has one child, Brooklyn, which was home during the shooting but unharmed. In their haste, the perps appear to have dropped an M-4 modified to full auto. Ran the serial numbers. Oddly, the ATF claims it was part of the Operation Fast and Furious weapons sent to Mexico. What's strange is that a U.S. government raid recovered nearly 750 weapons, but this weapon, along with a handful of other M-4s, were not in the seizure. It was reported as 'never recovered,' yet nearly all the other ones were." Flap took a pause as his boss was digesting the information. "I am going to go talk with Ms. Benson today. That's about all I have."

"Good. Good job, Flap," Andy said. "Thanks for this. Look. I need you to tread lightly on this one. The White House called and given this Benson gal works at the White House, they are shining a laser beam on this investigation. I don't know what Ms. Benson did to deserve this treatment or whom she's involved with but approach her with kid gloves for now. She is not a suspect until you can convince me otherwise. Got it?"

"Got it, boss. Different cranks for different ranks. I'll shift this one into high gear for ya." Mark's off-color comment was intended to sting a bit. He worked all his cases as hard as he could, and Andy knew it. Nonetheless, Flap hated when FBI top brass, or others, meddled in his investigations.

His boss ignored the comment. "Great. Let me know how the interview goes." Andy would feverishly type up a report on what he'd learned from Agent Flaherty. Once complete, it would get pushed all the way up to the White House.

Mark left the office and headed out to his car. He called Rachel, who was currently at work at the White House. She agreed to meet with Agent Flaherty outside the White House at The Hamilton, a trendy restaurant just one block away. Rachel knew the head chef there and felt comfortable.

As Flap approached, Rachel sat alone in a back booth. It was midafternoon, and the restaurant was relatively empty. "Ms. Benson, I presume. Hi. I'm Agent Flaherty." Flap pulled out his badge and Identification, letting her look at it for as long as she wished. Once satisfied, he placed it back in his pocket.

"Ma'am, I want to thank you for taking the time to meet with me today. To begin, I just want to clarify some key facts." Flap read through a document, requesting she verify the information he already had, her name, age, and address as well as her daughter's info. It was mundane, but Flap was meticulous, as if he were channeling his inner Mr. Bean. To him, every detail mattered.

"Great. Thanks for that." He paused. "May I ask, are you delinquent in any debts, legitimate or otherwise?" Flap asked.

"No. My home loan and car loan are my only debts, and they are paid automatically drafted from my bank account. I've never missed a payment."

"Do you know anyone who'd do this to you? Perhaps an ex-lover, an ex-husband? Perhaps even a current lover."

Rachel stared at him, shaking her head sideways. "No. No one. My ex-boyfriends are all on good terms and my ex-husband, Brooklyn's father, lives in Oklahoma."

"Great, and are you currently seeing anyone?"

The question regarding romances made her nervous. "Agent Flaherty. Why are you asking this? Everyone is blaming the government for this. You are the government. Tell me, who did this?"

"Ma'am, I just need to try to gather facts right now, but as soon as I…"

"This is bullshit. I'm calling the White House Chief of Staff. I won't be accused of this." Rachel pulled out her phone.

"Ma'am," Agent Flaherty said. "That won't be necessary. I'll answer your questions. Yes, there is some evidence this was done from within the U.S. Government. And while I am associated with the U.S. Government, I am not the entire U.S. Government. From my investigation, the plates on the vehicles appeared to be government vehicle plates, but they don't match the vehicles they were assigned to. Now, currently, I don't have enough information to solve this and hold those responsible to account. That is why I need to keep asking questions. I am not accusing you of anything. I am merely trying to find a motive, any motive, as to why someone would do this to you. Do you understand me?" It was the most 'kid glove' speech Agent Flaherty had ever given, and he hated every second of it. Normally in such a situation, he'd have matched her escalatory rhetoric and then some. But he was no match for Rachel Benson and the horsepower she commanded.

Rachel nodded. "Yes. Yes. I understand."

"Good," Flap responded. "Now, I need your utmost honesty here."

Again, Rachel nodded.

Flap continued. "Where did we leave off?" He looked at his notes and began questioning again. "Are you currently seeing anyone, someone who could have done this?"

Rachel may have been a great chef and a wonderful lover, but she was a horrid liar. She shook her head no, looking down, refusing to make eye contact. "No," she said, so unconvincingly not a soul would have believed her.

Flap paused. He wanted to press the issue, but given his discussion with Andy, he passed.

"May I ask, do you engage in any illegal activity?" Flap could tell she likely didn't, but he wanted to judge her answer.

Quickly, Rachel looked him in the eye and easily said, "No." It was now clear; her previous answer was a lie.

"Great, thanks. OK. Well, I think I have enough to keep tracking this down. Do you mind if I reach out to you in the event I have further questions?"

"No, not at all," Rachel responded. "May I ask? Am I going to get police protection?"

Flap thought about her question and decided just a hint of needling was warranted. "Well, currently, this looks like a 'one off' situation. I have no motive nor any idea why someone would do this. Until I can find something which would indicate protection is warranted, I won't likely be able to convince my bosses that there is a continuing threat against you. Have you asked this question to the local police authorities? I would imagine they could increase patrols but as for the FBI, I am sorry, ma'am, I don't believe there is anything we can do." He'd hoped that might get her to talk about her current relationship.

Dejected, Rachel answered, "Thanks, I understand." She'd not speak of her relationship.

Flap threw his business card and a $10 on the table to pay for the two coffees they'd drank. Rachel picked it up and gave it back. "Agent Flaherty, the coffee is on the house. I know the owner. Please, take this back."

"Much obliged, ma'am," Flap shot back. "And I thank you for your integrity." He meant it. Yet another minor fact about Ms. Benson he could file away for the investigation. "Keep the card and call me if you think of anything that could be of value in helping me solve this case for you."

With that, Mark Flaherty departed the restaurant. He stood outside for a brief moment, scribbling some more notes into his pocketbook. Rachel Benson watched him through the window. After he finished, he tucked the booklet into his coat pocket and strolled away.

Rachel sat there, not sure if she should believe Agent Flaherty or not. She wouldn't need to wait long to find out. A tall man in a dark trench coat approached her. "Ms. Benson?"

She looked up from her coffee. "Yes?"

"You don't know me, but I am a friend of the man who spoke to you from a limo in front of your house."

Rachel's heart quickened. "What do you want? How did you find me?" He could sense she was scared. He would not be offered a seat in her booth.

"Ma'am, I assure you. I mean you no harm. My friends and I are offering you help. Please, take this." He handed her a small piece of paper with a number written on it.

"Just what I need," Rachel said. "Another freaking phone number."

"Ms. Benson. That isn't a phone number. It's a serial number from an assault weapon one of the gunmen dropped out front of your house. I presume the FBI agent you just met informed you that weapon was seized by the federal government years ago and then went 'missing' in their inventory."

Rachel began to shake. The FBI agent hadn't told her that. "How do you know this?"

"Ma'am, you work in the White House. I am sure you realize there are many people who know many things. I apologize that I startled you. You have our number. I'm going to leave now. You have our number. I implore you, for your own safety, be careful, and be wary of the government. Your lover is not who you think he is." With that, the man put his hat back on and walked out of The Hamilton. Rachel sat there shaking. She needed to talk to her man, the President, immediately.

Rachel returned to work, telling Steve she'd met with the FBI.

"How did it go? Did you find out anything?"

Rachel shook and began to cry again.

Steve reached for a Kleenex, but it was of little comfort. Steve was an effective Chief of Staff, mainly because he drove the staff hard. Even Steve knew he lacked compassion and a leader's personal touch. "Is there anything I can do for you? What do you need?"

"I need to see the President again. I am one of his chefs and he understands."

"Rachel, look. You can't just keep seeing the President."

She began to cry even louder. Steve could not take much more. He knew the President's schedule for the remainder of the day was light. He also knew he did not want to further this precedent. Eventually, he caved.

"Look. Give me a few minutes. I'll see what I can do," Steve said reluctantly. Steve walked down the hall towards the Oval Office. The door was open, and the President was reviewing a speech he'd be giving the next day.

Steve knocked. "Mr. President, I hate to bother you, but it's Ms. Benson again. She's met with the FBI and...'

"Steve, please, send her in right away." The President demanded.

Steve did as instructed. "Sir, here is Ms. Benson, and I also have the initial report from the FBI Agent. An Agent Flaherty."

Steve escorted Rachel in and handed the document over.

"Thanks, Steve. That will be all." He looked down and scanned the report. Steve departed the room.

Rachel rushed to his side once the door was firmly shut. "Thank you, baby, for meeting me. I know how busy you are."

"Never too busy. This is important stuff. What did the FBI say?" Although married, he held a genuine fondness for Rachel. It was clear in his tone.

"That Agent Flaherty said there is a chance someone in the government is behind this. He asked if I was involved in any romances."

The President's pulse quickened. "What did you tell him?"

"I said no, of course. Why do you ask? Are you embarrassed by us? Have I run my course like your previous affairs?"

"No! No! Nothing like that. But we've discussed this. There are people out there that wish me grave harm and they'd use this information against me if they ever learned of it." The President was trying to rationalize with what was becoming a more and more irrational person.

"But now, people are trying to harm me, gravely! Don't you get that? He said the vehicles had government plates, yet no agency is clearly claiming them." She paused to look into his eyes, then spoke again. "And they said the serial number of the gun was from some ATF seizure years ago that went missing."

The President's eyebrows raised. He was surprised an investigator would share such details. "Yes, yes, I know. But the FBI Director and AG Reese both assure me they have our best men on this."

His confirmation of the gun serial number exacerbated her suspicions of the man she loved. It was mental torture. He gently grabbed her arms. The President said, "We are gonna get through this, I swear," as he tried to comfort her.

Slowly, she began to calm down. Then fell into his arms. Then began kissing him. Soon, he'd be ravishing her. Unhealthily, Rachel found more solace from a false safety in being with the President than from romance or love. Hastily, the President finished and soon they would both be dressed and presentable. The throes of passion with the President was the only place she found comfort.

## *Chapter Ten*

# Forging the Force

The next few weeks in D.C. were busy. Vice President Banks had laid in state in the Capitol Rotunda for three days. His two-hour funeral was covered by every U.S. television channel and most others around the globe. The United States was in mourning. Her allies offered supported and critics claimed it was the start of her great demise, a further erosion of the empire. There was little advance on who had committed the murder or how he died, but the investigation was a top priority.

Another priority was filling the void left by Vice President Banks' death. The President and others pushed Congress feverishly to fast track Vice President Crawford's confirmation. For the most part, Congress did as requested. The opposition party played their role perfectly, but given she was new to the political scene, there were few positions they could challenge. Somewhat humorously, this became their opposition strategy... to challenge Stacy Crawford on her 'lack of political decisions.' It presented her as a novice and an unknown entity. It was a weak argument but served its purpose. Opposition voters were pleased to see their elected officials saber rattle, albeit everyone knew she would be confirmed.

Agent Flaherty's investigation was another matter. He'd hit dead end after dead end. It was frustrating, but he knew it was all part of the process. A consummate professional, he knew if he just kept looking, another clue would surface. He was determined to find more.

\* \* \* \* \* \* \* \* \* \* \* \* \* \* \* \* \* \* \* \*

Conversely, Admiral Hershey's plans were progressing quite well. Don Denney had submitted legal paperwork, creating an LLC within New Jersey. The legal name of the new company would be The Valyrian Group, LLC, listing Eugene Hershey as the

CEO.  Unsurprisingly, Don was an avid *Game of Thrones* fan and the fictitious strength of Valyrian steel fascinated him.  Once the paperwork was complete, a bank account was created, and funds were wired in.  Over the past few years, Don had grown to admire Admiral Hershey.  So much so, he would become part owner in the company, as well as the key individual securing financing.  Given Don's D.C. relationships, he was perfectly positioned to both acquire funding and secure government contracts once the company began operating.  Eugene Hershey did not share the same level of fondness for Don Denney but was cognizant enough to know Don was a necessary evil in Washington.

Don's next task was to secure office space.  He would spend the next few days hunting out the right location.

Under Eugene Hershey's direction, Smitty was busy recruiting his first team.  He reached out to Jackal to serve as a sniper.  Smitty would never forget the shot Jackal took on Curt outside the White House.  If he could make that shot under such pressure, he would be good enough for their new team.  Smitty also knew Jackal had seen significant action in Afghanistan with a great reputation and eleven kills in combat.

Jackal was pleased to get the call and the offer.  He was currently working at a Jiffy Lube, making just over minimum wage.  The significant pay increase would be welcomed by his wife, Joy, and his son, Brandon.  After hanging up with Smitty, Jackal walked out of the Jiffy Lube and headed straight to the NY Army National Guard shooting range, where he was an instructor during his weekend guard duty.  He'd push over 100 rounds downrange through his favorite sniper rifle, working on his technique and breathing.  He felt alive again.

Next, Smitty reached out to Joel 'JT' Taylor.  JT had served as a Joint Terminal Air Controller and was one of the best Smitty had seen.  He had history embedded with Smitty's team and other U.S. Air Force Special Tactics Squadron personnel.

JT was now a civilian, forced to depart the U.S. Air Force because of an egregious error.  While in Afghanistan with Smitty, a U.S. Air Force intelligence officer failed to accurately report a threat to a team, causing them to fall under fire.  The team lost two members and JT was furious when he learned the withheld intelligence would have likely saved their lives. In front of most of the base staff officers and other military members, he screamed at the intel officer, berating her as well as blaming her for the death of the two fallen SOF members. She was enraged, angered that an enlisted member would dress down an officer in such a public fashion. Later that day, JT crafted a complaint, but before he could file it, the intel officer declared JT had sexually harassed her.

Within a day, the Air Force sent an overzealous investigator who interviewed most of the staff members present at the confrontation, to include the intel officer. By the time JT was interviewed, the investigator had been led down a baffling path. The sexual harassment investigation now included criminal charges. After being read his rights, JT lawyered up and given there were no lawyers on forward operating bases (FOB), he was flown away from his team.

Now hundreds of miles from his former team but with an attorney by his side, JT confronted the criminal charge. It was attempted bribery and clearly beyond the scope of a sexual harassment investigation. As evidence, the investigator stated that base personnel saw JT's checkbook on his desk around the same time he'd mentioned a local Afghan official needed money for an Afghan assistance program. This created the perception JT was trying to bribe Afghan officials.

JT exploded upon hearing the charges. After calming down, he told the investigator that the checkbook was out to pay his home utility bills. As a single airman, he had no one at home to perform the task and completed it online monthly. Growing more angered, JT then asked the investigator if he'd ever been off base and 'outside the wire?' The investigator, a reservist from Colorado, was a 'FOBBIT,' an unflattering nickname derived from 'Hobbit' given to personnel who never left the FOB or Forward Operating Base. confirmed he had never left the FOB. Again, JT grew irate, and his defense council had to calm him. Ironically, the prosecuting JAG saw opportunity in JT's emotional outburst and directly asked what it mattered if his investigator had been off any of the bases.

It was at that point JT could no longer contain his anger. He knew the sexual harassment charges were bullshit. All the charges were bullshit and likely an effort of the staff to protect their intel office from punishment for dereliction of duty and the deaths of his friends. JT jumped up and screamed. "Because! You idiot! There are no fucking banks in Afghanistan that take a U.S. check!" JT turned his attention to others in the room. "Even if I was to bribe an Afghan with a one-million-dollar check, where does this asshole think someone could cash that check?" JT's defense attorney attempted to contain his client and laughter, albeit poorly. As for the other side of the table, both the investigator and prosecuting JAG slumped down in their chairs. Neither had considered the issue, nor had any of those protecting the intel officer offered up this info. "Fuck this. I want an Article 15! If this is what you have, if this caused me to leave my team, I want trial in front of my peers. Now!" JT tossed the unsigned papers across the table and stormed out of the room.

Denying JT's wishes, the Air Force refused to let the case progress to an Article 15 under the Uniform Code of Military Justice. Air Force brass realized their case was weak. Instead, they issued JT a letter of reprimand (LOR). It was a cop-out by Air Force leadership, as an LOR allowed leadership to act as judge, jury, and executioner, void of trial. Per regulation, such punishment is not defendable, and per precedent, it is a career killer. Comically, the service allows a one-page rebuttal letter, but it is meaningless and few, if any, Air Force airmen can cite a situation when a rebuttal letter overturned an LOR.

The good news for JT was his operational record, at least on paper, remained unblemished. He exited the Air Force and was rebuilding his life in the civilian world. Their loss would be Smitty's gain. Smitty drove down to Virginia Beach and found JT working out with some Navy SEALS. JT remained in exceptional shape and would often find side jobs for the Navy helping the SEALS train.

"JT," Smitty yelled out. "What the fuck are you doing?"

Seeing Smitty was a sight for sore eyes. "Staying in better shape than you, that's for damn sure," JT belted. The two hugged. "Great to see ya, man! Hey guys, here is one of your own, Mark 'Smitty' Smith. He and I spent some time downrange."

Some of the other SEALS working out had heard of him, others hadn't. It didn't matter. All shook hands and greeted Smitty as if he were a brother... because he was.

"Hey, you got time for lunch today? It's on me," Smitty said.

"If you're buying, I'm in. Gimme a bit to clean up and I'll meet ya at the restaurant next door. The dude has the best soft shell crab sandwiches in the world." Such sandwiches were a staple for folks in the region. As a crab molts their old shell, they are harvested, battered and deep fried, then slathered in tartar sauce. Yet another American example that you can batter and fry anything.

Shortly thereafter, the two sat down and began to eat. "JT, question for ya. What are you doing for work?"

JT ate a French fry. "Odds and ends. Got 100% disability from the VA, so that's over three grand a month. I get by. Why?"

"How would you like to quadruple that?" Smitty responded. "We are putting together a team to go embed with Ukrainian Forces. First mission is just a week or two, establish contacts, and assess the need. From there, the sky is the limit. Come with me. Two weeks, twenty thousand dollars."

JT smiled. He loved being on a team, he loved being downrange, and he'd forever hold a grudge against the Air Force for taking that away from him. "I'm in. When do we start?"

"Come to D.C. tomorrow. Find a crash pad somewhere near Tyson's Corner."

"Too easy," JT said. "Now, tell me. How's your love life, Smitty? Are you still faithful to your right hand, or ya cheatin' with your left every now and then?" The two laughed and continued with small talk. With Jackal, Smitty now had three teammates minus Buck. It was a start, but he wanted one more.

Back in D.C., Admiral Hershey had spent a few days on his business model and meeting folks. Buck flew a few last missions with his employer before submitting his resignation.

\*\*\*\*\*\*\*\*\*\*\*\*\*\*\*\*\*\*\*\*

Earlier in the week, Admiral Hershey had asked Buck to meet him at the Smithsonian Air Museum near Dulles International Airport. The two met out front and walked in. As the former Chairman entered, the Smithsonian staff offered countless tours. Admiral Hershey politely declined them all. Eventually, the two were left alone, and they began walking.

"Buck, tell me what you see?" the Admiral said.

"Squirts, is that a trick question? They are airplanes."

"Yes, true. But let's talk about the designs. All the different fighter aircraft over the years. What story do they tell you?"

Buck stared at them for a bit and finally gave up. "Sorry, boss. Best I got is they all modernized throughout time."

"Good. That's correct. But why? Why didn't the U.S. Air Force just keep making F-86 Sabers and B-28 Hustlers?"

Buck answered. "They had to. As enemy air defense systems advance, so too did our combat fleet."

"Exactly," said the Admiral. "The fight for air superiority had been a long-standing cat-and-mouse game, but it's relatively similar in the land and sea domain. Every new offensive capability is eventually countered by a defensive one."

"Great boss, I get it. But what's your point?"

"Buck, what's the air threat today over Ukraine?"

"That's easy. Russian S300 and S400 missiles. They're freakin' lethal."

"Really? Are they?" replied the Admiral, as the two kept walking. "How do they work?"

"Basically, the system's acquisition radar finds the target, hands it over to a target tracking radar, which illuminates the target until the missile guidance leads the missile to finish the job."

"Perfect. But there's a problem with the S300 and S400 you're overlooking. Can I introduce you to one of my favorite aircraft?" They'd stopped walking. "Here she is. The CG-4A Hadrian."

Buck looked up. He'd seen the aircraft before and knew it. Built for WWII use, it was mainly fabric and wood, used as a glider to deliver special operations troops and supplies. They were quite successful.

"I get it boss, you think because they are wood, the S300 and S400 won't see the aircraft. I hate to tell ya, radar technology has advanced since WWII. They'll easily see this thing."

"Buck, that is where you're right... but you're wrong. As radar's ability to 'see' improved, the need to insert filters increased to help operators. Advanced radars see radar, flocks of birds, and even highway traffic. All of this becomes too overwhelming for radar operators to sift through to find actual targets. Today's air defense radars need filters to declutter an operator's screen or it would just be filled with hundreds of returns and a washed out scope. To solve this, radar engineers crafted 'Doppler notches' which eliminate returns below a certain speed. As fighter jet speeds increased, Doppler notches also increased. Today, many Doppler notches are over 100 miles per hour. And that 100 miles per hour is for a target that is perfectly perpendicular to the radar. As the angle away from the radar increases, the Doppler speed decreases, creating a blind spot. In today's modern air combat engagement, fighter aircraft turn to the 'notch' or put the threat on their wing-line, flying 'in' the notch. Is that correct?"

Buck was understanding. "Yup, Squirts. That's what we are taught."

"Great. Now, let's get back to the WWII Hadrian. Do you know what its cruise speed is?"

Buck looked at the plane for a bit. "80 knots?" he guessed.

"No. It was 73mph and it could carry a load of 13 personnel plus gear. I'd venture to say that given modern technology, even more weight could be carried. With Doppler blind spots in combination with the aircraft being mainly wood and fabric, I am confident this beast can beat S300s and S400s all day long, with the right pilot, of course." The last portion of that sentence was a clear challenge to Buck.

He smelled the bait. "OK, so for argument's sake, let's say a Hadrian could beat the missile systems. It's a glider. What are ya gonna do with it? Once it lands, it's useless."

"Buck, I thought you'd never ask." The Admiral smiled and continued his discussion. In the next few days, Buck, along with some aircraft engineers, would fly to Poland and begin construction of a modern day Hadrian. Buck was so excited about the project, he couldn't sleep. He was drawing sketches on dinner bar napkins or waking at 2AM and drafting concepts on a sketchpad next to his bed. It was exactly what the Admiral had hoped for.

## *Chapter Eleven*
# Cleansing the Soul

Like clockwork, Curt returned home from another workday at the Veteran's Affairs administration. It was a usual day, just like all the others. He reviewed and approved staff packages. He sat in meetings and voiced support or dissent for decisions in the administration. The halls of his building were filled with secretaries, clerks, interns, administrators, personalists, and many other 'office types' as he called them. What it lacked, and what he longed for, were patients.

As he walked into his home, he could hear Bo making noises upstairs. He also heard Noorullah yell, "Papa! Papa!" as he stood at the top of the flight of stairs.

Curt smiled to himself as he climbed the stairs up to the main level of the row home where the living room, dining room and kitchen resided. There, he found Allison on a rug with baby Bo, playing with a spatula. Bo loved it, waving it in the sky and yelling unrecognizable sounds.

Curt hugged Noorullah, then bent down and kissed Allison on the head, "Hey sweetheart. How was your day?"

Her hand reached back around his head, pulling his kiss tighter onto her head. "Hi baby. My day was good. Bo had about a two-hour nap and, as you see, he's now playing with my spatula. I don't get it, we spend serious bucks on toys for him, and he finds pleasure in a two-dollar plastic Safeway spatula."

As they looked at him and his spatula, baby Bo could feel the attention and waved and yelled even louder, laughing at himself. He'd grow to be a ham, much like his father. "What's for dinner baby? I'm starving."

"I made some curry chicken. I hope that sounds good," she said, just like she always said.

"That sounds perfect. I love it," Curt replied, just like he always replied.

"OK, Dr. Nover, you take your boys and I'll finish preparing dinner." Allison rose and went to the kitchen. Curt picked up baby Bo and placed the baby on his knee, bouncing him gently. Noorullah went back into the living room to watch TV.

"How was work today, baby?" she said.

"Eh. Same shit, different day," replied Curt.

"Curt, language please," snapped Allison.

Curt smiled. "Same stuff. Sorry, but how are our kids going to learn how to 'cuss like a sailor' if their sailor father can't cuss?"

Allison just stared at him a bit and said, "Sweetheart. Let's both be honest. You were a SEAL and hated sailing. In fact, Smitty said you were always the first to get sick on the boat. If anyone is going to teach our children about being a sailor, for their sake, I pray it isn't you."

Curt smiled. She was right, and humorous to boot. "Fair. Anyway, work was work."

Allison was walking a Yuengling beer from the refrigerator over to him, cracking it open and sipping it as she moved. "Well, it won't be forever. You'll move onward, upward, or laterally in a few years. It is the way of D.C."

Curt couldn't wait. "True." He noticed she drank part of his beer and was somewhat confused. "Hey, aren't you still breastfeeding? Why are you drinking my beer?"

"This is your question coming from the wanna be sailor's mouth?"

He chuckled again. God, he loved her. "Hey, I wanted to tell you. Do you remember when I was talking with Admiral Hershey and the guys at the retirement afterparty?"

"Yes," responded Allison.

"Well, it turns out that Hershey is starting his own security firm and asked all of us if we wanted to join."

Allison piped up quickly, "Define 'security firm.' You mean like NISSASSA?"

"No... and yes... Hershey knew about NISSASSA, oddly enough. He said where they went wrong was bad leadership and abandoning the ethics under which the organization was founded."

"Interesting," Allison said out loud. "What did you tell him?"

"I said no. But both Smitty and Buck are joining him."

Allison was now scooping rice onto the plates. "You would think after NISSASSA, neither of those two knuckleheads would go anywhere near a security firm, no matter how ethical."

"Fair, but the two of them are shipping out within the next few days to Poland and then into Ukraine. I don't know the details but seems like it's pretty good money."

Allison now was walking the plates over to the table, Curt lifted baby Bo up and put him into the highchair. "Curt, we have enough money. I sense you're considering this, and before you ask, I want you to know that I'm not comfortable with you going to combat. I thought you were not either. NOORULLAH, Dinner!" She yelled.

Curt stopped talking. The family sat down and began eating in silence. She was right. A part of Curt wanted to do 'something' for Ukraine. Something to thwart the efforts of Russia. Mentally, perhaps, he was too damaged to fight, not to mention he'd destroy his home life if he even considered it. Curt grew melancholy, realizing the exciting days of his life had long passed.

*********************

As Rachel and Brooklyn watched evening TV in their half-destroyed and boarded up home, a knock echoed from the front door. Rachel arose and looked through the peephole. Two well-dressed gentlemen, clearly looking like federal agents, stood at her door. Her heart raced. She opened the door far enough until the chain latch caught.

Peeking through the crack, she said, "May I help you?"

"Ms. Benson, we are Special Agents Dunford and McKay." The two flipped out their badges and ID. Rachel looked closely at them. The two were identical to the one Agent Flaherty had displayed.

After a thorough exam, she returned them. "Yes, what can I do for you?" Rachel still did not trust the government.

"Ma'am, we were sent by Agent Flaherty as he said you requested a security detail. If you no longer want it, please let us know and we can leave."

Rachel hastily unlocked the chain latch and swung the door fully open. "No! Please don't go. Come in. Please, come in."

The two agents entered, then stopped. "Ma'am, mind if we look around and evaluate the security situation we are dealing with here? It should only take a second."

Rachel agreed, "Yes, sure."

The two walked through the entire house, writing notes and taking photos. They then walked into the living room, where Brooklyn watched TV. One of the men began talking with her. Brooklyn clearly liked him and chatted up a storm.

"Ms. Benson, Brooklyn is a good child. You should be proud of her."

The mom in Rachel blushed, "I am. Thank you so much. I try so hard. It's tough as a single parent."

"Yes, ma'am," Agent Dunford replied. "I think we are done here. You'll see our SUV occasionally out front. Please do not be alarmed. Also, after we leave, feel free to call Agent Flaherty and let him know we were here. It will probably set him at ease."

Rachel began searching her purse for Agent Flaherty's card. "Yes, definitely. I will call him. So great he was able to arrange some security."

"Well, goodbye ma'am. Have a good night and sleep tight." Agents Dunford and McKay walked back out of the driveway to their SUV. Slowly, the vehicle pulled down the road about thirty yards, then stopped. The lights turned off, and the two sat there. Rachel was finally at peace.

Rachel Benson lifted her phone to her ear. She could hear the ring in her cell phone earpiece. It was Agent Flaherty. After the fourth ring, he picked up. "Agent Flaherty, may I help you?"

"Agent Flaherty, Hi. This is Rachel. Rachel Benson. We spoke before."

"Yes, Rachel. I remember. What can I do for you?"

"I wanted to call and just say thank you for arranging the FBI security detail. Special Agents Dunford and McKay seem great."

Agent Flaherty was confused. "Rachel, I didn't arrange any detail, nor do I know an Agent Dunford or McKay."

Rachel froze. "But they were in my house, they spoke to my daughter! They're out front in their SUV!"

Flap's voice grew serious. "Rachel, listen to me, go to the window. Are they still out front?"

She looked and did not like what she saw. Slowly, the black SUV crept by in front of the house, one officer waving his hand at her as they faded off down the street.

"They just drove by! They waved and are now driving away!"

"Rachel, lock your doors and call 911. Tell them an FBI agent directed you to call and your life is in danger. I'll be there in twenty minutes."

Rachel hung up and did as instructed. She locked all the doors and windows, checking a handful of times. When not checking locks, she and Brooklyn hid in the bathroom. Eventually, she heard the police sirens approaching and ran out to her front yard, dragging Brooklyn with her, screaming. Could she even trust the local police?

*******************

It was the end of the day at the State Department. A cable was hand delivered from the Russian Embassy. The document was quickly scanned for security, then taken to the Russia desk officer, who immediately opened it.

The signature was from Ambassador Anton Tarlov. Written in Russian Cyrillic, it stated that the twenty Russian diplomats that the President deemed Persona non grata had departed. Further, it included a list of twenty American diplomats assigned in Russia that Moscow deemed Persona non grata. They would need to depart in 48 hours. Of course, Moscow, being nine hours earlier than Washington, meant they really had 39 hours, and a good number of those hours would be at night. It was diplomatic gamesmanship, and Russia had mastered it akin to Kasparov and chess.

Roughly twenty minutes later, the courier handed a message of receipt from the State Department to the Russian Embassy, proof the cable was delivered. That paper was quickly rushed up to Ambassador Tarlov. He sat at his desk, drinking a glass of vodka, alone. His aide knocked on the door, holding the paper. In Russian, the Ambassador said, "You don't need to deliver that now."

"Sir, President Volkov. He is calling from London."

Ambassador Tarlov looked down at his watch. It was nearly midnight in London. Quickly, he scurried to pick up the phone. "Mr. President, Good Evening! I was not expecting your call."

"Ambassador Tarlov, it is good to still find you at work. I wanted an update on the plan."

"Yes, Mr. President. Today, our letter to displace twenty of their diplomats was delivered, just an hour ago, in fact. Also, as you likely know, the President selected Stacy Crawford for Vice President, as you predicted. She was just sworn in. Again, as you suggested." President Volkov clearly would have known this but offering it up as things the President predicted was a bit of good old-fashioned brown nosing. The Ambassador continued. "We have made progress on the other part of our plan, but our agents haven't flipped their target yet. Once they do, we can move to the next stage."

There was a pause in the line, and in the background Tarlov could hear a few different female voices. Tarlov spoke again. "Mr. President? Are you there?"

"Yes, Ambassador. Good work. Please let me know when the next phase can begin. It is the one I am most looking forward to." The line went dead before Tarlov could respond.

Anton hung up the phone and walked outside. His chauffer would drive him to his dinner engagement, a seat for one at Café Berlin, one of D.C.'s best German restaurants. He loved the place, as it reminded him of his first diplomatic assignment in East Berlin. How he longed for the old days. A bipolar world of superpowers, the U.S. and Russia. Someday Russia would again rise and surpass that benchmark, he thought. Someday, Russia will be the world hegemon.

## *Chapter Twelve*

# Downrange

Smitty's flight from Frankfurt into Warsaw was uneventful. He, Jackal, JT and Beef arrived as planned. A vehicle was waiting for them. It would take them to a hotel for the night. Beef's real name was Antonio Wormley. He was a large African American male and could have easily played professional football, but chose a path of service. Antonio served on a few different SEAL teams until a medical condition knocked him out of service. Beef never really talked about the condition, and few knew what it was. Smitty did not. It didn't matter. In the civilian world, Beef had served as personal security for celebrities, and he wanted the chance to, as he often said, 'crush some Russian skulls.'

The next morning, the team was met in the hotel lobby by Rob Farkas, the owner of a Polish company, PLUSOps. Years earlier, Rob served at U.S. Embassy Warsaw as a Defense Cooperation Officer. While there, he fell in love with a local, and decided to exit the service and stay in Poland. Requiring an income, he started a small company, which helped Polish defense firms compete for U.S. defense contracts and vice versa. His business exploded when Russia invaded Ukraine, as he was one of the few U.S. companies in Poland that had all the tickets punched to perform defense sales and transfers. He had been hiring, on average, five new employees a week for the past two months and could not keep up. Life had drastically changed for Rob, for the better.

"Gentlemen, welcome to Warsaw," Rob said in his warm, chummy voice. "Hope y'all got some sleep. Long day today."

Smitty was sitting in an overstuffed chair, drinking a coffee. He stood up as Ron approached. "Thanks. I'm Smitty," he said, offering his hand. "Bed was comfortable, but time zone changes messed with me bad. This is JT, Jackal and Beef." They all shook hands.

Rob motioned for them to follow him. "I have a van waiting outside. We can talk in it. Better than here in the lobby." They followed him to the van, loaded their personal luggage, the doors closed, and the driver pulled away.

Once the vehicle started moving, Rob laid out the plan. "It will be about a two-hour ride. We are headed southeast towards Ukraine, stopping at a depot base servicing the Ukrainian war effort in Jasionka, Poland, near Rzeszow, 20 miles from the Ukrainian border and about 45 miles from Lviv as the crow flies." Rob pulled a piece of paper out of a folder and passed it to Smitty. "I understand this is your Christmas list?"

Smitty looked at it. Admiral Hershey had forwarded exactly what he'd requested for each member, plus a few extra goodies. "Yeah. This looks good," Smitty answered. "How about our Terp? How well was he vetted?" If Smitty was going into Ukraine, he wanted to ensure he had not only a qualified interpreter but also a loyal one. He'd grown to trust Afghan interpreters. Ukrainian ones in a war with Russia were a concern.

"Relax," Rob said. "It gets no better. You'll be accompanied by Ukrainian Colonel Marko Taran," replied Rob.

"Retired or Active Duty?" inquired Smitty.

"Oh, he's active duty alright. He is a Ukrainian Special Forces officer. Seems your boss has some legit pull. Marko is a monster, and from my meeting with him yesterday, he'll be outfitted in country with comms gear linked to the Ukrainian Forces." Rob was clearly impressed with Marko.

"OK, how's his English?" Smitty wanted more. If the team was going to put their life in this guy's hands, he wanted every ounce of info.

"Guy attended Army War College at Carlisle Barracks in 2016 as a Lieutenant Colonel. The Ukrainians sent him after Russia invaded Crimea and they realized their only path to survival was embracing the West. You'll meet him later today. Trust me, he's the best I've seen, and I have matched terps to dozens of NGOs and other organizations into Ukraine."

Smitty was satisfied for the time being, as were the rest of the team. Admiral Hershey had come through.

The van pulled up to the entrance of the Polish depot base at Jasionka. Its nickname was 'Base U' for Ukraine. Rob showed his pass in the window, barely slowing at the gate. Once on the compound, they headed for an enormous hangar and stopped out front. "Well, this is it, boys. Come on in." Rob always seemed to be chipper.

The hangar door opened, and inside were about fifteen folks working on three aircraft. All airframes were similar, but at various stages of completion. On the other side of the hangar, four empty duffle bags lay neatly on the ground. In front of each was a bunch of military items, rifles, side arms, ammunition, medical kits, radios, laser designators, sleeping gear, food rations, and more. Given the number of items, it was hard to believe they'd all fit inside the duffle bags.

Smitty and the men started walking towards their gear when someone shoved Smitty from behind, hard.

"Hey, you fucker!" the familiar voice said.

Smitty turned around. It was Buck.

"Buck, you idiot. You're lucky I wasn't armed, or I'd have shot ya." The two embraced and laughed.

"Smitty, what do ya think of my new aircraft?"

Smitty was baffled. It looked like it was from the Wright Brothers era, wood, canvas, plastics. "Dude, you're jokin,' right?"

"Nope. Boss hooked me up with some kick ass aeronautical engineers. We pulled the old plans for a WWII era CG-4A Hadrian. Modified it with some plastic parts, adjusted the wing lines, streamlined the nose, and equipped her with a few extra toys. She's far more efficient and capable. The Hadrian could get a glide ratio of 12:1. We believe this aircraft can double that."

Smitty was not as savvy about glide ratios. "Dude, English please."

"OK. So, if they release the tow at thirty-five thousand feet, I can glide 168 miles. That's maximum range, unless I catch thermals or ride a good jet stream, but man, isn't that nuts!"

Smitty looked at him as if he had three heads. "You're gonna take this thing to thirty-five thousand feet? Are you out of your freaking mind?"

"Well, no. Not at first, but we think with supplemental oxygen and other structural integrity things, we could get her that high. Highest glider flight was over seventy-five thousand feet. This is less than half that. Cool, huh?"

Smitty was certain. Buck was an idiot. "Sure. Cool."

"What are you guys doing here?" Buck asked quizzically. "You going downrange? If you're wanting to ride with me, it will be a few more days before she flies, but you can be the first!"

Smitty chuckled. "Buddy, no offense, but we are gonna stick to ground transport until that contraption ever proves itself. Or should I say, 'if' it proves itself."

Smitty went to join the rest of his team as they were checking out their gear. Everything was as planned, and everything was new. For their first recon mission, if things went well, they'd need none of the firepower. If things didn't go as planned, they'd at least be prepared.

While they were unwrapping the plastic and boxing from their new gear and placing it in duffle bags, a large gentleman in a foreign uniform approached with Rob Farkas at his side.

"Gents, this is Colonel Marko Taran, your other team member," Rob announced. It seemed calling him a terp would have been a downgrade from his actual status.

Smitty reached out his hand. They were both about the same size, extra-large. They both also measured each other by the strength of their handshake, which could have squished an orange. "Nice to meet you, Colonel," Smitty said with a slight nod, silently acknowledging the handshake strength was to his satisfaction.

"You too, Mark. Call me Marko." Col Taran nodded as well.

"Great, but I'm Smitty. No need for too many Marks or Markos." Smitty introduced him to the rest of the guys. The team began to gel from the moment they met. Once the duffels were packed, Marko took the team to a small table, spread out a map and explained their scheme of maneuver over the next few days. In effect, this mission would be a 'meet and greet' for Smitty and the team, as well as area familiarization. The weather would be freezing cold, partially wooded terrain, partially open fields, all covered in deep snow. They'd fall in on a vehicle, provided by an unknown source.  Should this mission be executed well, the second one, Smitty knew, could change the outcome of the war.

As Marko wrapped up the meeting, Smitty pulled out his cellphone and shot a quick text to Curt:

> *'Just about to head inbound.  Miss ya buddy.  Wish you were on this one.'*

\* \* \* \* \* \* \* \* \* \* \* \* \* \* \* \* \* \* \* \*

Back in D.C., Secretary of State Baker sent Steve Lewis an email informing him of the twenty U.S. diplomats that would be returning to the U.S.  Of the twenty, two were able to secure moving companies before their witching hour.  The other eighteen would require embassy staff to pack them up and send their goods.  Additionally, given the short notice, fourteen of the families would not be able to fly with their pets, requiring additional flights of remaining embassy staff to accompany the animals on future flights.  Such was the way of diplomacy when dealing with Russia.

## *Chapter Thirteen*
# It's Radioactive

It was now early March and unexpectedly, the cherry blossoms had already popped, a few weeks early. General Gott's helicopter overflew the Potomac River on its way to the White House. He looked down at the Tidal Basin and Jefferson Memorial surrounded by the cherry trees. It was beautiful. A far more enjoyable event than he'd be encountering in the White House.

After touching down, the General walked across the lawn into the conference room. A national security council meeting was about to commence, and the topic would be findings from Vice President Banks' assassination. He had read the initial report findings and knew the meeting would not go well.

"Ladies and gentlemen, the President," announced Steve Lewis. Everyone stood as the President, followed by Vice President Crawford, walked in. It would be one of her first meetings in the role.

As the President took his chair, he said, "Please, take your seats. Proceed with the briefing, please."

The speaker presented the first slide on the screen and began to talk. "Mr. President, Madam Vice President, Secretaries, Generals and others, thank you for attending. I am Brian Aker, senior intelligence analyst for Russia under the Director of National Intelligence. The initial findings from Vice President Banks assassination are as follows. The Vice President appears to have been poisoned via his wineglass, as large traces of the poison, polonium-210, were confirmed in and on the glass. There were also traces of it at three different tables, one table showing the largest amount. Four other guests, to include Ukrainian Ambassador Ubyivovk and the Vice President's wife, fell ill from the poisoning due to contact with the Vice President, but all were able to make a full recovery."

Mr. Aker continued, "The polonium-210 has been tested by the Department of Energy and their findings have been verified by the International Atomic Energy Agency or IAEA. The poisoning agent is 90% likely to have originated from the Kostyantynivka nuclear power plant, also called the South Ukraine Power Plant." Brian paused for effect. Then continued.

"The South Ukraine Power Plant is located between Odessa and Kyiv and remains in Ukraine held territory. It has not fallen under Russian control. Regarding the investigation into potential suspects, I defer to the Department of Justice or FBI. Pending questions, ladies and gentlemen, that concludes my briefing."

There was a pause, waiting for questions. There were none. "Thanks, Mr. Aker, for the briefing," the President said, nodding to both Mr. Aker and his boss, Director of National Intelligence Greg Cromwell. Brian Aker stepped out of the room.

The President again spoke. "Clarence, how long will the IAEA sit on this info?"

Secretary of Energy Clarence Markham oversaw the department that conducted the test. "Mr. President, they've agreed to hold it for a while, but given the IAEA also has Russian scientists, Moscow will eventually find out. If they do, it's highly likely Russia will break the information."

Everyone in the room knew he was right. "Marleen, have we shared this information with Ukraine yet? What's the status on that front?"

Marleen Baker was prepared for that question. "Mr. President, our ambassador delivered the information a few hours ago, waking the Ukrainian President from bed. He was shocked, as we all are, and is ordering an immediate investigation and an accounting for all of their nuclear inventory still in their control."

"OK. Good. Not great. But good. Now, anyone have an idea how we frame this information to the public without completely upending our continued support to Ukraine, spooking fragile allies in the effort, as well as giving Russia a free pass from this assassination? I realize it isn't time for puns, but this information is the definition of radioactive."

The room remained quiet. Framing information to the public at the presidential level was clearly out of most of their wheelhouses.

"I didn't think so. OK, folks. This isn't good. My strategic communications team will come up with something. Until then, please refrain from commenting on this. We will handle it at the White House, and I pray we can come up with something before Moscow does." The President turned to his Vice President. "Stacy, I need you to get to Ms. Banks and share this information personally ASAP. I'll be damned if I let Russia be the first to inform her."

"Yes, Mr. President," she responded.

"Everyone is dismissed."

The room stood, and most cleared out. Stacy and Steve Lewis remained, and a few White House public affairs personnel were summonsed into the room. The new attendees were caught up on the intelligence report, and everyone began spit balling a plan to share this information with the U.S. public.

\*\*\*\*\*\*\*\*\*\*\*\*\*\*\*\*\*\*\*

Rachel Benson had enough. It had been days since she'd met with the President. Along with his normal events, he also was performing regional campaign fund-raising events with his wife. Steve was also of little help, offering no updates on the investigation. In reality, that was because there were none. As hard as Agent Flaherty tried to keep her informed, Rachel grew more and more suspicious of the U.S. Government.

It was time. She pulled out her phone and dialed the number given to her by the strange man in the limousine.

"Hello," the voice on the other end offered.

"Yes, this is Rachel. Rachel Benson. I want your help."

"Of course, Ms. Benson. Can we meet?"

"Yes. There is a Five Guys between Alexandria and Mount Vernon on Route One. I'll be there after work around six p.m. Can you meet me there? I want to be in public."

"I'll be there. And thank you for calling. You've made the right move. My name, by the way, is Lance. I'll see you then."

The two hung up.

Lance dialed another number and lifted his phone to his ear as the line rang.

In Russian, "Hello. Yes. Please tell the boss we have contact."

There was a pause as the other line spoke.

"Tonight. Near her house. We are getting close. I will call you after the meeting tonight at 1800Hrs."

Another pause, then "Dosvidanya," or 'Goodbye' in Russian. Lance hung up the phone. There was much to prepare before his meeting.

\*\*\*\*\*\*\*\*\*\*\*\*\*\*\*\*\*\*\*\*

Vice President Crawford's staff called the former Second Lady and inquired if a visit from the current Vice President would be OK. She agreed, and the Vice President's motorcade trundled through D.C., across the Potomac and up to Falls Church on the Virginia side. The vehicles meandered slowly up the driveway. There was no rush. The two ladies greeted each other, then went inside. The news was difficult for the former Second Lady to accept, but Stacy delivered it the best way possible.

As Stacy walked back to her motorcade and got in, one of her staff said, "Ma'am, that was close. News already broke the polonium-210 story."

She looked down at her smart phone. It was true. Media outlets were blaring the news, especially the fact that the radiation had ties to Ukraine.

*Chapter Fourteen*

# Services Needed

Smitty and his team woke from a night of sleep in the hangar alongside their gear. It wasn't luxurious, but it was safe, given all the weaponry and tech they were carrying. The group walked out of the hangar and over to a local mess hall. It was their only option at breakfast. Beef and JT woke much earlier and already had already run ten miles. They were hungry.

As they crisscrossed the base to get to the mess hall, a handful of Blackhawk helicopters began setting down in an open field next to them. Awaiting the helicopters were six individuals, dressed in medical gear. As each helicopter set down, no less than four wounded Ukrainian service members were slung off the choppers. The wounded Ukrainian service members immediately overwhelmed the six medical staff. Smitty and the team ran over and began doing anything they could do to triage the wounded and carry them into the medical facility next door.

Once inside, Smitty was stunned. There was nowhere near the medical capacity to deal with the number of casualties. He, Marko, JT, Beef and Jackal changed blood bags, dropped I.V.s, kept covers over sucking chest wounds, tightened tourniquets, and more until each patient either was serviced by a true medical professional or expired. Eventually, the medical staff caught up, and no longer required help.

Smitty and the team departed the medical facility and walked to the mess hall, covered in bloody clothes. "Marko," Smitty said. "Where is your medical support?"

"You saw it. We don't have much. NATO nations are working to provide more, but questions about facilities, operational capacity, funding, political liabilities, and other issues always surface. It is frustrating. Most of our medical assistance remains forward deployed in Ukraine. We do our best to save them in the golden hour, but after that, we rely on partner nations." The 'golden hour,' Marko referred to was well known to Smitty. Military professionals had long learned that if medical aid can be rendered to a wounded military member suffering battlefield trauma in the first hour, their chances of survival increased significantly.

The two continued walking with the others into the mess hall. They scrubbed their arms and hands. As they walked into the facility, everyone stared. Given the lifestyle each had led at one point, they thought nothing of their blood-stained attire. To the Polish conventional military members, it was a disturbing sight. Such was the difference between conventional and Special Forces. Given all the staring eyes, the team ate quickly and departed. No need to bring unwanted attention upon themselves.

\*\*\*\*\*\*\*\*\*\*\*\*\*\*\*\*\*\*\*

Back in D.C., evening was setting in and Steve Lewis was driving to a dinner engagement. Based on the invite, he presumed it would be less professional and more personal, likely a campaigning effort. His presumption would prove incorrect.

Ms. Becky Denney was overseeing the final touches for the dinner. Her staff would serve it and per Andrew's direction, it would be a table for three, a six-course meal, and most importantly, the staff were directed to be silent and unintrusive. As the hour approached, Andrew performed one reconnaissance pass through his dining room. It was perfect. Andrew continued to his study and poured a neat glass of scotch. Just then, the doorbell rang. The staff would answer it.

Roughly a minute later, Admiral Eugene Hershey walked in. "Good evening, Andrew. Thanks for hosting tonight."

Andrew shook Eugene's hand. "Of course, Admiral. Far better at a private residence than out in public." The doorbell rang again, and one more time, the staff would tend to it.

As Andrew and Eugene were engaged in small talk, Steve Lewis entered the room. "Gentlemen, great to see you both," he said, breaking up their conversation.

"Mr. Lewis," Andrew said. "Thank you for accepting our invitation."

"Of course," he responded. "You have an impressive home, Andrew. I hope this small gift is worthy of it and your bar." Steve had brought a bottle of Johnny Walker Blue Label, an extremely nice bottle of scotch.

"One of my favorites," Andrew responded. "It will fit right in." He thanked Steve, and hands were shook. "Our dinner awaits. Please follow me to the dining room." The three continued to the dining room, where staff professionally stood behind each seat. As the three entered, chairs were slowly pulled out. Each was seated, and the staff departed, never making eye contact.

"Andrew," Steve inquired, "Please tell me you do not eat like this every night."

"Truth be told, I'd eat a ballpark hot dog for every meal if I could. It's my wife Becky who pushes such meals."

"I see. Where is Ms. Denney? A pity she isn't joining us if this is her cup of tea."

"Very kind of you, but while she'd enjoy the meal, I suspect she'd get lost in the discussion."

"I see," Steve responded. "Well, in that case, let's try to drop the formalities. Please, Andrew. Can we just use first names?"

"Of course. As you wish," he responded.

Eugene had been quiet long enough. Tonight, he was the lynchpin of making this event a success. "Steve, I hope all is going well for you, and am hopeful Stacy is fitting in nicely up in the Executive Branch."

"Yes, Admiral. She is," he said.

"Steve, when I retired, the government gave me back my first name. Please, call me Eugene, or Squirts if you prefer."

It was awkward for Steve, but he'd comply. "Sure, Eugene."

"Great," Squirts responded, as soup was being served. "Steve, one of the reasons we wanted to talk to you tonight is to share some of our new efforts."

Steve sat, acting intrigued, but given the hundreds of sales pitches he received in a month, this would not be enjoyable. "Oh, great. Please, yes. Tell me."

"Post retirement, I teamed up with Andrew here, and we have established a new company, The Valyrian Group. We are crafting a new security firm, as we believe there are some opportunities in this business segment."

Andrew watched Steve closely. He could only imagine this was exactly how his deceased son, Don, likely had the same conversation just years ago.

As Eugene paused to ingest a spoonful of soup, he paused. Steve would fill the silence. "Interesting. I am not sure what opportunities you are referring to."

"Well, that's why you're here," Andrew said, bluntly. The scars of his son's death, and whom he blamed for it, were briefly exposed.

Admiral Hershey quickly regained control of the discussion. "Yes. Well." It was awkward. "We believe that with the demise of NISSASSA, there's opportunity."

There it was. The issue was on the table. Steve Lewis sat back. It was clearly not how he perceived the night to progress. "You're shitting me. Right?"

Admiral Hershey became serious. "No, I'm not. Please. Let me explain. There are three key reasons. First, NISSASSA's biggest failure was it lacked the leadership required for such an operation."

Andrew cringed, albeit conflictedly. He knew Don, his deceased son, had served as NISSASSA's Chief Operating Officer. He also knew Don had been in over his head.

"Second, the global landscape has changed. Specifically, there is an escalating war in Ukraine. Due to a handful of security issues, mainly nuclear arsenals, the U.S. government has extensive policy limitations on ways it can respond." Admiral Hershey paused to let that data point settle. Steve knew everything he had heard to this point was valid. As the pause took place, a hurried staff removed the empty soup bowls and quickly set down salads. They were done in less than thirty seconds and exited as quickly as they entered. During the exchange, no one spoke.

"Third, the heat associated with the NISSASSA exposure has settled, and even if it hasn't, U.S. citizens may be far more receptive to 'gray area' military efforts in Ukraine than they were before. So, to recap. Different leadership, different globe and different perceptions."

Steve's fork danced across his salad. He wasn't sure what to say. Prior to Admiral Hershey's retirement, he had sat in on National Security Council discussions on how the Defense Department could do more in Ukraine. Nearly every option that truly had teeth was deemed too risky. Admiral Hershey also attended those meetings. He shared enough of it with Andrew in an effort to convince Andrew that the Valyrian Group was a worthy cause.

"Admiral," Steve said; informalities were no longer acceptable in his mind. This was business. "Your points are not incorrect. Suppose the President were interested in your company's services. He's likely going to wish to move slow. I have two questions. First, what actual 'services' are you offering? And second, what assurances can you afford that the White House is insulated from any similar media explosions like the one of NISSASSA?"

Eugene took a deep breath. "Steve, as you are aware, I had a meeting where the President requested I delay my retirement. I refused. I did that because, frankly, there is little time to waste in dealing with Russia. Our company is already moving. We already have two separate efforts ongoing in Poland and Ukraine. One team is in Ukraine now, or soon will be, for an orientation effort and making contacts. We are moving, and I am hopeful the President joins our pace of effort. We can offer almost anything you can imagine. Expedited logistics efforts deep into Ukraine, key Russian military leadership removal, destruction of key Russian strategic targets within Ukraine. To be clear. We will not target Russian political or civilian leaders, nor will we push teams into Russia. Lastly, our efforts will adhere to the Geneva Convention and Laws of Armed Conflict, even if such agreements do not protect our operatives. As for the second part of your question, I'll let Andrew answer that."

Steve swung his head around to look at Andrew, as he wiped his face clean after completing a bite of his salad.

"The Valyrian Group is a U.S. company, much like NISSASSA was, and it will operate in the same gray zone like many other security firms around the globe. Russian security firms today are operating unimpeded by the Russian government, or international laws that govern conventional warfare. Arguably, they are secretly assisted by the Russian government, receiving logistics, intelligence and other. Much in the way those companies do little to no damage to the Kremlin, The Valyrian Group would also do nothing to our White House."

Andrew waved his hand in the air and the group paused the discussion one more time. Salad dishes were removed, and a perfectly cooked duck à l'orange was set in front of the three. Again, another hasty retreat by the staff.

"Gentlemen, why me?" Steve asked. "Either of you have more than enough clout to engage the President directly."

"That's true, Steve," the Admiral answered. "And eventually, we will get to that point, but we believed that he's likely to be far more receptive to the idea if key staff members are onboard."

Steve nodded, then turned away from Eugene. "Andrew," Steve said. "I must confess. I am a bit speechless. This is the last thing that I expected to find you involved in... especially given your personal history."

Andrew knew the comment was coming. He could not avoid it. "Steve, let's not kid ourselves. I hold little love loss for our current president, as well as his staff. That should not shock you, as we both know my campaign contributions stopped long ago. When Eugene approached me regarding this proposal, I was completely against it. But over time I realized, the chance for miscalculation between two nuclear powered political leaders in the world ending human existence was increasing. As little faith as I have in the President, I felt the need to act. Know this. The Valyrian Group is a business venture I most disdain. It is perhaps also the one that is most important."

As Andrew finished his comment, he looked at Admiral Hershey, a partner of necessity, not one of desire.

The conversation had progressed as far as Admiral Hershey wished, at least for the evening. "Gentlemen. May I suggest we take a break? The duck looks amazing, and I believe desires our full attention. Perhaps we can shelve our current discussion and engage in a lighter topic." Both men welcomed the notion. "Might I suggest the upcoming baseball season?" The three spent the rest of the evening talking about myriad subjects, and occasionally, they'd fall back into the primary topic. Both Andrew and the Admiral knew Steve had taken the bait and would discuss it with the President. The second half of the dinner was far less tense and much more enjoyable than the first.

As Steve prepared to depart, Andrew handed him an envelope. "Steve, please pass this campaign contribution to the President. It is the first of what we hope are many from The Valyrian Group."

Steve took the envelope and thanked both Andrew and the Admiral. He chuckled to himself as he walked to his car. *'Well, at least I got the contribution I'd hoped for,'* he thought to himself.

## *Chapter Fifteen*

# Contact

Rachel entered the Five Guys restaurant, unsure if she was making the right move. As she walked in, she immediately noticed a well-dressed man in a booth. He appeared out of place, and once he saw Rachel, he stood up and politely greeted her.

"Rachel, hello. I am grateful you contacted us," he said.

"Thank you. Yes, are you Lance?"

"Yes. Yes, I am. Please, let's sit. Can I get you anything to eat or drink?"

"No thank you," Rachel responded. Her nervousness was palpable. "Please, can you tell me anything more than the FBI."

"Actually, yes I can," replied. "Rachel, what I am going to share with you is going to be difficult for you to accept. But it is the truth."

Rachel nodded. "OK."

Lance took a deep breath. "Rachel, there are some very powerful political people in the U.S., and they've learned of your affair with the President."

Rachel's first reaction was to deny it. She'd not get far.

"Rachel, please. We need to trust one and other. On the dark web, a video of you and the President having sex is circulating. It is only a matter of time until it makes it into the public eye." Lance tried to remain compassionate, yet convincing.

"I. I. I don't know what to say." Rachel stuttered.

"I understand that." He offered to reach across the table and hold her hand, trying to comfort a scared woman. She recoiled. "Rachel, it gets worse. The President's people have decided you are expendable."

"Expendable?" she inquired.

Lance looked straight into her eyes. "Rachel. They're planning to kill you."

Rachel's eyes widened. "No. It can't be true. He loves me. None of this can be true!" She got up and ran to her car, started it, and began driving away.

After roughly five minutes, she noticed a small, old iPod laid in the center of the passenger seat. It wasn't hers and it wasn't there when she entered Five Guys.

As Rachel pulled up to a red traffic light, she grabbed the iPod and turned it on. It was unlocked, and as soon as it opened, the video of her and the President having sex began playing. She dropped it, horrified.

A car horn behind her broke the silence. She failed to notice the traffic light turn green. Rachel turned the car around and sped back to the Five Guys, running in.

Lance was still sitting there. "YOU!" she screamed. "YOU! Put this in my car." She waved the old iPod in the air, standing at the table and intimidatingly hovering over him.

"Rachel, please, sit down. Please. You realize the way you're reacting is exactly what they want." He paused, then continued. His voice was soothing, as if he were a professional at dealing with humans and their emotions. In actuality, he was. "Rachel, I truly only want to help you."

She kept breathing rapidly. "I don't know who to trust."

Lance dropped his head. "Rachel, I have nothing more to give you to gain your trust. I understand, though." Lance, slowly raised from the booth, stood fully erect, and began walking, passed her as he headed to the door.

"Where are you going?" She demanded.

"Rachel, you don't trust me, or those that work with me. We can't make you trust us, and until you do, this won't work. I am sorry I failed to convince you. I only wanted to help you. Please be careful, and if you ever believe you can trust us, please call."

Lance walked out the door and headed to his car. Rachel stood there alone in the Five Guys holding an iPod with an amateur sex video of the President and her. She not only didn't know who to trust, but she was also overwhelmed with a sense of loneliness. She rushed out into the parking lot. "Lance!" She screamed. "Please. Can we keep talking?"

Lance saw her run out. He returned his car to its parking spot and shut it down. Her reaction was exactly as he expected. "Of course, Rachel. Anything you wish."

The two would go back into the restaurant, and Lance laid out what he believed to be the best way she could save her own life. It involved being proactive, and should she execute his recommended course of action, it would shake the world.

\*\*\*\*\*\*\*\*\*\*\*\*\*\*\*\*\*\*\*\*

Buck sat in his glider's first prototype, roughly one hundred meters behind a towplane. The first flight would be without a load and in safe Polish airspace. The towplane's propeller engine revved, and the two trundled down the runway. In mere seconds, Buck was airborne, well before the heavier towplane. A grin washed across Buck's face. He loved it. After climbing to approximately three thousand feet above ground, Buck released the towline, and he was on his own.

A host of sophisticated instruments began collecting and recording everything about the flight. Engineers would thirst upon this information, much like a drunk on booze. Buck didn't need any of the data. The plane flew like a dream. He scanned his instrumentation with glee. Closely watching his vertical velocity indicator, (VVI) he watched it jump from a sink rate of one hundred feet per minute to a climb of 300 feet per minute. Quickly, Buck swung the plane back to that location and, as he suspected, he had found a thermal pocket of warm, rising air. Buck maintained a lazy left-hand turn in the thermal, and in a matter of minutes, he had climbed to five thousand feet. Simply by flying in an updraft, Buck had gained two thousand feet from his tow plane release altitude.

Many birds instinctually locate thermals and effortlessly 'climb' in the sky. In actuality, the updraft pocket of air they are flying in rises faster than the bird's glide sink rate. While birds are able to leverage instinct to find such thermals, humans must rely on VVI instrumentation and also a bit of luck. This is how

94

many glider pilots stay aloft for extended periods of time. In fact, the longest flight on record is 56 hours and was completed over the French Alps in 1956.

Buck eventually flew a pre-briefed sequence of maneuvers requested by the engineers, then brought the aircraft back in for a landing. Quickly, the engineers downloaded the data. It was impressive. The air loads on the wings and fuselage were far less than anticipated, and the engineers felt confident they could increase the max speed to 200knots. Additionally, the glide ratio was far improved from the WWII era Hadrian design of 12:1. It was even greater than engineers' desired goal. If the sensors were working accurately, Buck's new ride had a glide ratio of over 50:1 unloaded. Tomorrow, they'd again fly and learn what the aircraft could do, but most quick calculations suggested a fully loaded aircraft could achieve 35:1 if not 40:1. Either way, it would be enough to meet mission requirements.

Buck sat there watching the engineers read the metric data and extrapolate the aircraft's abilities. "She's awesome, right?" he said.

"She's amazing," one of them replied.

Buck looked at the other aircraft in the hangar. He smiled, taking it all in. Buck would soon have a fleet. Just then, a smack hit him hard in the back of the head. "Hey dickhead, whaddya doing? Day dreamin?"

Buck spun around. It was Smitty. Buck raised his left arm as if to hit Smitty in the head. As he did, Smitty raised his arms to block it, just as Buck planned. Buck's left arm swung low and smacked Smitty in the groin, buckling his knees and bringing him to the ground.

"Dude!" Smitty said. "My junk? Out of bounds! Seriously?"

Buck had no regrets. "Look, chuckles. I'm not a Special Forces snake eater. I'm a pilot. I need every advantage possible. Perhaps you stop smacking me on the back of my head, and I'll stop playin' marbles with your nuts."

Smitty regained his composure. "Well, that's a hell of a way to say goodbye to us before we head into Ukraine."

Buck was caught off guard. "Smitty? You're going in? Now?"

"Yup. Departing in about ten minutes," Smitty replied as he began to climb back up to his feet. "Good luck with your Wright Brothers contraption. I have no clue how you think that thing is combat air worthy."

Buck ignored the second part. His primary concern was for his friend. "Hey, you be safe, alright? Russians don't play fair."

"Will do. Gonna send a quick note off to Curt here in a bit, then turn my phone off. Will you hold on to it for me? I'm taking a burner downrange."

"Sure. I'll be in the hangar for a bit longer. Just bring it by when you're done writing Curt. Tell him I said hi."

Smitty sat down on the hangar floor and feverishly 'thumbed' in the email.

> 'Curt,
>
> Hope all is well. Getting ready to head in. Wish you were here. Understand why you're not, but man, Ukraine could use some skilled medical hands. Had three die in my arms today on a med evac. Short staffed here in Poland, bad.
>
> Miss ya buddy.
> Smitty'

## *Chapter Sixteen*

# Recon, and Then Some

The team had been traveling for most of the afternoon, riding in the truck Colonel Marko Taran secured earlier in the week. It would be a long ride, continuing well into the night. The vastness of Ukraine was not lost on the passengers. They crossed over the Polish-Ukraine border, passed through Lviv in the northwest corner of the country, and continued west on highway E50. After a brief stop in Khmelnytskyi, the team transitioned to a two-lane country road, H03, and headed straight south. With check points and stops, it would take them nearly another half a day.

As they neared the end of their ride, the driver began to slow. The team was now within twenty kilometers of the fighting. Weeks ago, Russian forces gained a small section of terrain near Odessa. Ukrainian forces fought heroically, launching tactical counteroffensives, attempting to push back Russian forces. Most efforts were fruitless. The front had devolved to a stalemate. The driver pulled off the main road onto an unmarked dirt path that led into a wooded area. Deep in the forest was a heavily camouflaged bunker. It was near the town of Podilsk, but far enough away to keep the villagers safe from Russian fire. The location was fairly close to the border with Moldova. In this region, the Ukrainian strategy included leveraging the border to their advantage as they took the offensive. Moldova had little love loss for Russia, especially given their long-standing grudge over the region of Transnistria.

The vehicle parked near the bunker, and the team pulled out their gear. Once offloaded, the truck would depart. The driver had no interest in sticking around and risking his vehicle, which was his livelihood in the war.

As Marko walked into the bunker, his chest swelled out. He was home again with his warrior brethren. After a few handshakes and man hugs with the staff, Marko walked up to a tall burly man and saluted. General Shevchenko, the Ukrainian Southern District Commander, offered Marko a quick update in

Ukrainian. He was clearly weary from a lack of sleep. He also appeared he could keep up such a pace for years if needed. Marko and the General spoke in Ukrainian. While none of the team understood, it appeared Marko was explaining why he'd brought a handful of Americans into the command bunker. When General Shevchenko spoke, he used his hands often, pointing at a chart hanging on the wall, as well as singling out some of the staff while talking. Smitty and the team stood there, realizing some things in combat were more important than immediate introductions. After roughly a minute discussion, Marko transitioned to English and turned towards Smitty. It was time for an introduction to Brigadier General Shevchenko. "Smitty," Brigadier General Shevchenko said, "It's nice to meet you. Welcome to Russia's version of hell."

"Brigadier General Shev... Chenk... Ko," Smitty replied, stumbling through the pronunciation of the General's name. "It's an honor to meet you."

"Smitty, please call me 'Chevy.' None of my American friends from National War College could pronounce my name either. After a week, they just called me Chevy. It works. Let's go into my office and talk."

"Yes Sir, General Chevy. Sounds good. Thanks," Smitty gratefully responded. Chevy led Marko, Smitty, and the team into his office. It was far from what a civilian would refer to as 'an office.' It was in a tent, heavily protected on each side by a wall of sandbags, three bags thick. There was a running generator, camouflaged by both netting and plywood, masking the visual and heat signatures from wondering Russian collection assets. During winter and spring months, infrared collection systems could easily identify uncamouflaged heat signatures, especially against a cold snowy ground cover. In the middle of the tent was a long table for briefings and at the end was the General's desk, where paperwork would be accomplished. It was field conditions in combat, just as any warfighter would expect.

They all took seats at the long table under the request of Chevy. Coffee and water were served. Even in war, commanders garner some privileges. Chevy began to speak, pointing down onto the tabletop map of the combat region. "We've been fighting the Russians along this line for weeks. They are dug in and seem to be happy with the terrain they've taken. At this point, they don't seem inclined to advance further north... for now. We've expended a large amount of resources to just hold this line. We anticipate orders and resources soon to launch another counter offensive in order to push them out of their dug in locations. I'm hopeful we will have better luck on this next counteroffensive, but I am not optimistic. My leadership offers no different strategy other than a head on push, through an area that we've suffered massive losses."

He stopped to take a drink of his coffee. Smitty was reviewing the map, containing his excitement to once again be neck deep in combat operations and planning. "This threat you keep running into. Is it artillery, trenches, or a multiple rocket launcher?"

"Nope. Actually, just old school. The area is somewhat residential, and Russia has emplaced one of their best snipers who moves around every day in different buildings. He has proven quite a worthy adversary, targeting and eliminating our strategic pushes from long range. We've launched efforts to counter this sniper with no success. Last time, we were close to having a successful offensive. But again, this sniper took out our strategic supply of fuel. It blew up and in three seconds, our offensive was stopped."

"Sniper, huh?" Smitty said. "Sir, it seems the best way to take out a sniper is with another sniper."

Chevy nodded. "Agree. And we keep trying to get ours close, but we can't. Lost four of ours to this guy. He's good."

Smitty smiled. "My guy is better," as he looked at Jackal. Jackal grinned and nodded.

Chevy looked at Jackal. "You're a sniper?"

"Yes, Sir," Jackal responded.

"Want a shot at this asshole?" Chevy asked.

Jackal looked at Smitty, who nodded, then took over the conversation. "Chevy, how about we show you our sniper's ability as capabilities display? Kinda like, 'the first one is on us.'

If you and the Ukrainian government like what you see, we can discuss future missions."

Chevy was elated. He had absolutely zero concern about bringing a nontraditional combatant onto the battlefield. He just wanted the Russian sniper killed. And given this group of fighters were escorted in by Marko, so much the better. Marko was under direct orders from the Defense Ministry in Kyiv. If he said they were good, then they were good. "Deal."

"Good. Here is what we need. I want Marko on a radio, listening in on the Russian force's channels. If that's not possible, I need him to have comms to your intelligence cell for real-time updates. If they find us first, I want to know ASAP, and get our asses out. I'm a fan of helping you. I'm not a fan of dying."

Chevy butted in. "You can have a radio pack. Russians are not speaking on secure channels. They talk openly. There is so much talking as well as jamming, no one is sure which force is jamming or talking on which channels."

"OK, but an hour before we take the shot, you direct your forces to stop jamming. Understand?"

"Sure," Chevy said.

"I need two good vehicles as well. Ones that can take my team. Marko, me, Jackal, Beef and JT." Smitty was done, other than getting a few logistic issues sorted out like food, fuel and others. Jackal, JT and Beef studied the chart. They could clearly see where the Russian sniper, nicknamed Ivan, was setting up. Ironically, that wasn't a name given by the Ukrainians, but rather the Russians, who spoke of him on the radios, taunting their enemy. Russian forces knew they had an excellent sniper and enjoyed boasting about his kills on Ukrainian radio frequencies. It was all part of phycological warfare that forces in contact employed.

Jackal grew fond of a ridgeline on the crest of a small hill which looked southeast into the town. It was mostly corn fields, but now just stalks that sprouted out of the snow. Additionally, it was not a likely place Ivan would be surveilling. For most snipers, it would be too far for a shot. Jackal, however, wasn't most snipers. It would be an 1800m shot and one that only the most elite marksmen would even consider. Jackal was confident he could make the shot.

Smitty and his team racked out for the rest of the day. At 2100Hrs, they'd depart, moving under the cover of darkness to get in position.

\*\*\*\*\*\*\*\*\*\*\*\*\*\*\*\*\*\*\*\*

Back in D.C., Steve and the President were receiving an updated briefing on the Vice President assassination. Other key players were also in the White House conference room. Sitting next to the President was his new Vice, Stacy Crawford.

Brian Aker began. "Mr. President, Madam Vice President, Secretaries, Generals and others, thank you for attending. I am Brian Aker, senior intelligence analyst for Russia under the Director of National Intelligence. We have worked hard over the past few weeks regarding the Vice President's death. I want to thank the FBI, CIA, DIA, DOJ, State Department, and others. This turned out to be a true interagency effort, and I think you'll appreciate our hard work."

He changed to the next slide, which displayed three photos. One was a side shot from a closed-circuit television where the person was in motion. Another was a front facial shot and on some sort of identification card, the third was a mug shot. All three appeared to be the same men. "Mr. President, meet Victor Petrov. From our exhaustive analysis, we believe he is the assassin who poisoned Vice President Banks."

Again, Mr. Aker changed slides. "Sir. Here is a feed from a video camera in the ballroom where the fund-raising event took place. You can see the Vice President, sitting at his table, giving a speech and his toast. Staff are noticeably not moving at this time. As the Vice President finishes, there is an applause, and all the staff begin moving, clearing plates and refreshing drinks." Mr. Aker paused for a moment, then said, "Stop." The video froze.

"Mr. President, in this frame, you can see a man approaching from the left, moving to the right in front of the Vice President's table. He is carrying a tray with only one glass of wine on it. He sets it down at the Vice President's table from the front and begins stacking plates and silverware on the tray. Run it." The video ran again. "Stop. Notice, he takes the wineglass from the tray and swaps it for the Vice President's glass, as the Vice President turns to stand up. Run it." The video kept running. The switch was so obvious to everyone watching. It was unbelievable no one noticed. "Sir, there is one other piece of evidence in this video. The man who switched out the wineglasses is also the only server wearing gloves. White gloves." The video cycled back and then played again. It was true. None of the other servers wore anything on their hands.

"Sir, this video was the best display of the assassination, but we do have other video and other closed-circuit systems around the hotel if you wish to view those." Brian paused and was prepared to show others. The President waved his hand as if to pass on the offer.

Brian continued. "We also discovered the company hired to perform the catering and vetted by the White House Secret Service had an unreported security breach. One of their employees lost their badge and failed to report it. We believe this is how Victor Petrov gained access to the event." Brian had paused again to change the slide.

"Mr. Aker," the President interrupted. "Forgive me for wanting to get to the punchline, but please tell me he's not Ukrainian."

"Correct, Mr. President. He's not. He's Russian. But he does not work for the Russian government. Or I should say he doesn't work for them directly. He is not in their military, in their secret service, or in their intelligence branches. He is, however, a senior level member of one of Russia's largest and most revered private security firms. Here is a clip of Russian President Volkov praising the work of this company." The video played for roughly a minute with English subtitles. Most in the room were aware of the firm, as it was just one of many private security firms Russia funded. Eventually, the video stopped.

"Since the event, CIA and State Department believe Petrov has returned Russia. Sources have reported he received a large promotion in the firm and is now commanding some of the Russian operations in Ukraine. Analysts believe he's assumed a hybrid role in the war. He's in charge of his security firm's forces as well as Russian military forces, brigade level down."

"OK," the President interrupted again. "How do we get him?"

"Sir, that's not my lane," Brian replied and went silent.

Eventually, Secretary Baker addressed the group. "Mr. President, we have communicated with Embassy Kyiv, and they are prepared to engage the Ukrainian government. I do, however, caution this course of action. Sharing this intelligence with Ukraine in hopes they help us target Petrov could also be used by them in an information campaign that we can't control."

The President nodded.

General Gott had remained quiet long enough. "Mr. President, Ukraine's ongoing war makes it unlikely they'll be able to dedicate the resources and effort needed to capture or kill Mr. Petrov. Even if they wanted to assist, I am not sure they could."

Again, the President nodded. He was furious. Not at the answers, but rather this assassin's ability to complete his task and exit the United States in what appeared to be an effortless manner. He executed the Vice President in the nation's capital under the nose of every U.S. security and intelligence apparatus!

An awkward silence fell upon the table. Mr. Aker, began feeling out of place as merely the briefer, and spoke up. "Are there further questions?"

Director of National Intelligence Greg Cromwell, Mr. Aker's boss, spoke up. "Belly (Brian Aker's nickname), thanks for pulling this together. Mr. President, getting to Petrov now is going to be nearly impossible. He's a hero in President Volkov's eyes and safely out of our reach. We still have the breadth of our intelligence agencies trying to pin him down for anything actionable, but it's proving impossible."

"Thanks," the President answered. "So, we can now put to bed the Ukrainian tie to the polonium-210 and pin this to Russia publicly. They'll deny it. What can we take forward in the way of intelligence to demonstrate to the American people as well as the world, this was Russia?"

Greg Cromwell answered. "Sir, the images I showed at the beginning and the closed caption video are unclassified. They can be shared at your discretion."

"Good. Let's get these to the Press Secretary and help him build a story for the press pool. I don't want to be the one to share this." He turned to his Vice President. "Stacy, again, can you get to Ms. Banks and let her know soonest, before it comes out in the Press?

After wrapping up that meeting, Steve and the President went back to the Oval Office. It would be their usual weekly one-on-one meeting, going over the upcoming schedule and other more personal subjects. At the end, Steve pulled out an envelope and handed it over. "Mr. President, I thought you'd be interested in this."

The President smiled. Steve would never pass negative news in such a way, thus, it had to be good. He looked at the outside and quizzically said, "The Valyrian Group?"

"Yes. It's Andrew Denney's new company. I didn't open it. How much is it?"

"Impressive. It's $10,000. Old Andy, he couldn't stay away forever. Good for him." The President was pleased.

Steve offered, "Sir, there is more. The Valyrian Group is a security firm, much like NISSASSA. It's a joint venture between Andrew and Eugene Hershey."

The President's eyebrows rose. "Squirts? Now that is interesting. What on earth are they doing that for? Don't they remember what shit show NISSASSA turned into?"

"Yes, Sir. They do." Steve went on to explain everything from the dinner. The President was briefed to the best of Steve's ability. It was just as Andrew and Eugene wanted it... perhaps even better. Valyrian Group was presented to the President just minutes after he was presented an impossible task for the U.S. Government.

## *Chapter Seventeen*
# The Grind

Curt was returning from his early morning run.  Living on 7th Street Southeast by the Eastern Market Metro stop facilitated a perfect three-mile run to the WWII Memorial.  Just a bit farther was the Vietnam Veterans Memorial.  At least three times a week, he'd visit his grandfather's name inscribed on the memorial's black granite memorial wall.

Curt was tired, but pumped with endorphins.  He climbed the steps of his row home and found Allison sitting at the dining room table, feeding baby Bo.  Noorullah was still asleep.

"Morning baby," he said to Allison.  "Bo didn't want to sleep in today, huh?"

"Nope.  Woke right after you left."

Curt leaned in and attempted to kiss Allison.  She accepted it, begrudgingly.  She was not angry, but rather had aversions to the sweat and funk covering her lover.  "OK, I'm going to run upstairs, shower, and get ready for work."

"OK.  Once his highness Bo is finished with breakfast, I'll bring you some coffee."

Curt smiled.  "Awesome.  Thanks, sweetheart."  He headed upstairs to the bedroom, grabbed his phone from the nightstand and unplugged it from the charger.  There were no immediate fires from work requiring attention.  At the Veteran's Affairs administration in his department, there never were.  Then he saw Smitty's test message and read it.

*'Be safe, buddy,'* he thought to himself.  Part of him longed to be with Smitty.  Another knew exactly why he couldn't be.  Such was the life of an old warrior.  What really stung, however, was the part of Smitty's text that reported three killed because of insufficient medical care.  As a doctor, any suffering and death was mentally anguishing, but un-cared for warriors tore him apart.

Curt showered and prepared for work.  Within a half hour, he was out the door and on the way to the VA Medical Facility on North Capitol Street near Trinity Washington College.  The facility was so far north in D.C., there was no convenient Metro stop to use. When the weather was poor like this day, he drove. Now that spring was coming and, more often than not, he'd ride his bike to and from work.

Throughout the day, Curt sat at his desk, took some calls, and sent some emails. His efforts were halfhearted. He'd also sit in briefings, and instead of focusing on the issue at hand, he could not stop thinking about Smitty and his team. They were likely stalking through the Ukrainian countryside, hunting Russians. He'd also casually check around to see what U.S. medical assets could be moved to Poland or Ukraine to assist. He now had firsthand knowledge regarding the lack of medical care. As a doctor and a warrior, he was determined to address it.

*********************

The weather at Poland's Jazionka airfield was cold, albeit sunny. Buck again hooked up to his towplane, a Cessna Sky Courier. It was a twin prop, over wing design, with good flight characteristics at slow speeds. This time, Buck would also have a parachute in his seat. He'd be pushing the limits of the aircraft, and if things went wrong, he wanted options. This takeoff was far different from his previous one. With a fully loaded aircraft, it took the glider much longer to get to rotational speed and begin flying. Eventually so, however, the glider was aloft well before the Sky Courier tow plane.

Slowly, the two aircraft continued to climb in large circles over a piece of ground that was rarely traveled by other aircraft. Passing 10,000ft, Buck put on his supplemental oxygen. It would be another thirty minutes until they reached their ceiling, 25,000ft. The plane grew cold inside, far colder than it was on the ground, but Buck had dressed for the occasion. The Sky Courier continued its climb at an airspeed of 180knots. It was what the engineers deemed to be the maximum load for the glider. After a long ride up, a few creeks and other strange sounds, as well as a few "Come on, Old Girl" comments from

Buck, his glider made altitude. Buck disconnected from the Sky Courier, which immediately began a descent back down towards the airfield. That pilot had no desire to remain at 25,000 any longer than he had to. He expedited his flight down to 15,000ft, keeping Buck in sight.

As the Cessna flew further away, Buck's glider grew to an eerie silence other than a cold, whistling wind. He flew her on a flight profile, just as the engineers requested. A few stalls at various altitudes and a few 30-degree bank turns with the nose down to keep enough speed on the aircraft.

At such an altitude, the flight window, or the parameters that would keep the aircraft flying, was quite narrow. The wings could not roll more than a few degrees without departing controlled flight. As for speed, too slow and he'd stall, too fast and he would over-speed the aircraft. Such was a common trait of all high-flying guilder type airframes and purist pilots loved such a challenge.

At 25,000 feet over a flat terrain and with cold weather, there would be no updrafts to catch, similar to the ones Buck enjoyed on his first flight. Perhaps at a lower altitude he might find some, but even so, they'd only offer marginal assistance for an aircraft carrying 2.5 tons of cargo.

As Buck continued his journey down to lower altitudes, the air grew thicker and the flight characteristics of his 'old girl' were vastly improving. He flew with more and more confidence and was beside himself with enjoyment. Buck was a modern-day cowboy, sans horse, but rather a wooden, plastic, makeshift aircraft. It was his calling.

After touching down, a truck came out to meet the aircraft and tow it back to the hangar. A few onlookers snapped photos of the strange-looking aircraft. It wasn't uncommon.

Buck provided a verbal debrief to the aerospace engineers who'd overseen the building of the aircraft. They feverously scribbled down everything but yearned to download the flight recording information. Buck's words were fine, but hard numbers from precision instruments were the benchmark.

The team of mechanics would closely evaluate stress points on the aircraft for even the slightest cracks or hints of damage.

They were paid well by The Valyrian Group and were experts at aviation structures. Perhaps more importantly, they'd grown fond of the funny character, Buck. If he was crazy enough to fly this contraption, they were gonna do everything they could to ensure it wouldn't be their fault he didn't make it home.

As the ground teams worked, Buck left to grab a bite to eat. When he returned to the hangar, a cloth covered the nose of the aircraft. Engineers and mechanics were huddled around it.

"What happened? Did she break?" Buck asked.

"Mr. Thiessen, nope." The lead engineer responded. "But we have a problem."

Usually such words wouldn't phase Buck, as he'd been in some seriously dangerous situations in his life. This, however, was different. He'd spent so much effort on his new aircraft, and, from his perspective, they were so close. He feared a significant problem now would upend the entire effort. "OK," he said cautiously. "What is it?"

"There was an issue with the flight data recorder. Specifically, the audio," the lead engineer said grimly.

"Flight recorder? Seriously? That can be fixed, right? Can't you just swap it out?" Buck asked.

"Mr. Thiessen, I don't think swapping it out will fix the problem. Do you mind if we play the audio capture which has us concerned?"

"Yes, please! Play it. I want to know the problem," Buck demanded.

"OK. I think we isolated the issue. Here are the snippets we've merged together."

With that, one of the engineers began playing the audio through a loudspeaker in the hangar. Other than the crackling of the audio, the place was dead silent.

Then a voice cracked over the speaker. It was Buck. "Come on, Old Girl... That's it you Old Girl. Come to daddy, Old Girl..." The phrases just got worse from there. He said 'Old Girl' with some associated verbiage at least twenty times. As each one played, members of the ground team laughed in a crescendo that at the end had everyone in stitches.

Buck was embarrassed but found the whole event somewhat humorous. He even laughed at a few of the clips. When the audio stopped playing, the cloth draped over the nose was pulled away. Freshly painted on the aircraft in fancy lettering was 'OLD GIRL,' with a hastily crafted nose art sketch of a haggish, yet endearing elderly woman.

Buck loved it, and the crowd began clapping. "Old School Aviation!" Buck shouted out loud. This is what it was all about.

\*\*\*\*\*\*\*\*\*\*\*\*\*\*\*\*\*\*\*\*

It was late in the afternoon back in D.C. An official courier dropped off a letter at the Russian Embassy. A signature was provided, and the document was carried up to Ambassador Tarlov's awaiting hand. It was an official Note Verbal from the U.S. Secretary of State demanding the extradition of Russian citizen Victor Petrov. The charge was murder, and he was to stand trial for the assassination of Vice President Banks.

Ambassador Tarlov chuckled as he read it. "Impressive investigating. You found the right man, but you'll never have this man," he said to himself out loud. Within the inner sanctum of the Russian political elite, Victor Petrov's stock was climbing fast. In time, Anton thought, Victor could eventually be a revered hero of the nation.

Ambassador Tarlov held the message up to the light and examined it one last time. There was no need to send it to Moscow. They all knew Petrov committed the assassination. What was the point of sharing already known information? As he held it in the air, he slowly moved a cigar lighter to the corner and set it ablaze. As the fire grew, he tossed it into a metal trash can and watched the fire grow, then extinguish. There was an odd sense of enjoyment from such things for Tarlov.

## *Chapter Eighteen*

# Your Trigger

Within two miles of the Russian front line and just a few hours before dawn, Smitty and the team were confident the planned location for Jackal's shot was a good one. Through the night, they had 'glassed' it with their night vision and thermal binoculars for hours, looking for any type of activity. Other than a handful of remaining wildlife in a war region, there was none. Slowly, the team moved closer. Jackal and Smitty would traverse slowly to the crest of the hill and set up for the shot. Beef and Marko would move to a flanking position along a tree line, watching for enemy activity. JT would do the same, although on the other side. His location was a bit more challenging, as he was the one closest to a public road. It was an old farming dirt road, with little traffic, but it was also where they had pre-positioned their vehicles. Without transportation, the trip back to safety would be extremely challenging.

Each team member was in place. A few low-cut corn stalks provided meager cover for Smitty and Jackal, who were both laying on the ground dressed in snow camo, blending perfectly. The barrel of his gun was masked, to a degree, by a few natural clumps of dirt that had been kicked up during harvest. Slowly, the two scanned the buildings. They looked in broken windows and holes. Searching for any movement. Anything that may indicate life. According to Chevy, Ivan often set up in Stoyanove. It was a tiny village that led into a far larger city of Zakharivka, the primary location of Russian forces, and Chevy's objective. In the early morning, all three groups of the team could see smoke rising out of Zakharivka structures. The town was coming to life, albeit from Russian occupiers.

"There. Movement." Smitty whispered.

"Where? Talk me on," Jackal said, calmly.

"Follow the road into town. Do you see the second structure on the right-hand side of the street with the flat roof?"

"Visual," Jackal said calmly.

"OK. From there, continue on that line of structures to the right, three over. It's a two-story structure and the front door is missing."

"Visual," Jackal said again.

Smitty provided the final puzzle piece. "Second-floor window on the left."

Jackal set his scope on the window and watched for movement. Eventually, he saw a silhouette cross the broken-out window frame. "Got it," he said calmly.

Jackal watched the window for a while. There was a chance this wasn't their guy, but as he observed the building, he was growing confident they'd found their target. That window offered a wide field of view out towards the Ukrainian front line. It also blended with the surrounding buildings exceptionally well. He again spoke. "Smitty. You got a range on that window?"

Smitty shuffled to grab his laser range finder. He lifted it and waited a second for the range to display on the screen. "1776," he said. "Damn, that's ironic. It's like the founding fathers even want you to take the shot."

Jackal smiled as he methodically dialed that distance into his high-tech scope. With each turn of the knob, the barrel of Jackal's sniper rifle rose just a bit further, compensating for the massive distance. Jackal's movements were slow, knowing in that building there was a man doing the same thing... hunting the hunted.

"I see movement again," Jackal said. He'd watch for the next fifteen minutes, silently, almost lifeless. Then he spoke the words Smitty had hoped to hear. "I see a gun barrel. I think this is our guy." Jackal was right. It was Ivan who had exposed the barrel of his gun, protruding from the window. It appeared Jackal wasn't the only sniper hunting on the battlefield this morning.

Smitty jumped on the team radio. Each member was using sophisticated PRC-152 JTRS radios or Joint Tactical Radio System. Within the U.S. military, these devices were highly controlled items and were not available for public sales. Clearly, Admiral Hershey had his ways. The comms were secure and clear.

"Marko. Have your guys stop jamming now and start random chatter on their radios."

Marko called back on his Ukrainian radio and did as instructed. Within minutes, the chatter on the Ukrainian radios was active, just like any other day, and the Russians began jamming, then talking on their own radios. Communications discipline was apparently not a training course in Russian military schools.

Beef reached down alongside his leg and pulled out a small, handheld drone. Attached to it were two packages, each the same: a cell phone, a small weather sensor. From the tree line, he launched the drone and then jumped back into the brush. As the drone flew, a few sporadic shots were taken somewhere along the front and Marko, hearing the shots, stumbled and fell out from the tree line. Quickly, he rose back up and again secured his hiding spot against a tree. *'Fuck,'* he thought. *'That was embarrassing.'*

Unfortunately, it was more than just embarrassing. Marko had caught Ivan's attention. Ivan swung his scope to the area, looking for his next kill. As Ivan searched for movement, he unfortunately found it in the tree line. Unbeknownst to the team, Ivan had found Marko, somewhat exposed in the tree line. 'Another recon team, I presume,' Ivan thought to himself. It wouldn't be a huge strategic win, but he was bored, and it was all the battlespace was offering today. He'd prepare to take the shot.

Beef flew the drone parallel to the enemy front, nearly right over Smitty and Jackal, then turned it straight towards the town of Stoyanove. The drone was not very sophisticated. It was loud and flew only 50 feet above the ground. Eventually, it would get noticed by Russian forces, but that mattered little on this operation. The drone was expendable.

"Now," Smitty said, and the first package dropped. It was roughly a thousand meters from Ivan. The drone continued again towards Ivan. "Now," Smitty said for a second time, and the second package was released at about five hundred meters from Ivan. After releasing its second payload, the drone kept flying south. It would soon overfly the small town. Gunfire erupted from Russian guns and the drone was struck within minutes. Soon, it came crashing down.

On the Ukrainian military radio channels, the Russian forces intruded. They jeered the Ukraine soldiers as amateurs while cheering their downing of another useless drone.

Almost robotic, Jackal said. "What are they?"

Smitty looked down at a small handheld computer screen. The weather sensors were pushing wind info through their connected phone and then wirelessly onto Smitty's screen. He replied, "At a thousand meters, you have 285 at 5 and at five hundred meters winds read calm." With a shot of 1776 meters, every bit of info was welcome to help improve the accuracy of a shot. Terminating Ivan's existence on this earth was a no fail mission.

Jackal absorbed the info shared by Smitty, he then took a long look at a small piece of string that hung at the end of his barrel. It faintly moved to the right. *'About two knots. Nothing a little Kentucky windage can't fix,'* he thought. Jackal made the final adjustments to his rifle. He then said softly, "I'm ready."

Smitty took a breath and said, "Take it. Your trigger."

As Jackal was calmly taking his last few deep breaths, Marko, as well as other Ukrainian intelligence assets were listening to the Russians. They were laughing and taunting the Ukrainians about how they'd just shot down, yet again, another one of their drones. They were rejoicing and singing.

"CRACK!" The ground around Jackal shook, and the snow lifted then settled. Smitty kept his binoculars on the window, as did Jackal, but he was confident it was an excellent shot.

Inside the window, Ivan was slowly dialing in the final settings of his rifle. Ivan's reticle set squarely on Marko's chest. It was the perfect situation. An enemy attempting to stay as still as possible to avoid detection. A sniper's dream. Ivan's right hand slid slowly from the scope calibration knob down the side of the weapon. Calmly, his index finger curved into the trigger well. Ivan took one last deep breath before he'd pull the trigger.

It would prove to be his last breath. Jackal's bullet screamed through the window. Ivan's left eye stared through his rifle scope, and for a millisecond he saw a blur. It would be the last thing he'd see. Jackal's bullet ripped through Ivan's closed right eye, exploding his eye socket then plowing through his brain. Since Ivan was in a prone shooting position, the projectile traversed through a decent portion of his neck and back until exiting around the base of his ribcage. He was dead instantly.

Smitty and Jackal expeditiously slithered backwards until the crest of the ridgeline hid them. Once there, they hastily packed up and shuffled back at a hasten pace. No need to stick around a bunch of furious Russians. Both support teams monitored their exit. Beef and Marko withdrew from the tree line in concert. JT watched the road, hoping no traffic would come. Faintly, he heard the sound of a vehicle engine approaching and quickly recalled that 'hope' was never a good course of action in warfare.

Russian radios began to report Ivan was shot. There would be calls for medical support, but it was pointless. Given this news, the Russian rejoicing stopped. Taunting comments rapidly transitioned to rage, anger and threats. The Ukrainians just listened; gleefully satisfied Ivan had fallen.

While the radios were full of chatter, an unmarked vehicle, which appeared to be a modified civilian truck, raced north out of the town. JT watched as it continued towards him on the main road. A few empty farm fields were considered no-man's-land between the two warring factions, and this truck was entering it. JT hoped it wouldn't turn down his dirt road. Another worthless hope. The vehicle turned and approached. Now roughly four hundred meters away, JT was able to get his binoculars on it. The truck had four doors and had at least four occupants. They were not civilian, but rather Russian soldiers. In the bed, a manned machine gun stood on a tripod.

Slowly, JT reached into his cargo bag of goodies and pulled out a javelin missile. Such a weapon against a civilian truck would be overkill as javelins normally destroyed tanks. But JT didn't care. He knew that one against five wasn't a fair fight, and he wanted as much certainty as possible that no one was surviving his shot. Their sniper mission was almost a success. They just needed to get out of harm's way. There was no need to take chances. JT lined up the Javelin crosshairs and fired. The projectile immediately tracked the vehicle. The driver noticed the missile coming directly at him, but far too late. A meaningless swerve was all he could muster. Within milliseconds, the truck exploded, then transitioned into millions of metal fragments and bits of human remains.

"Nice shootin', Tex," Smitty said as he observed the explosion from a distance.

JT's radio cracked to life, "Yeah. Thanks. No need to carry shit back to camp if you don't have to. Those javelin missiles are heavy." JT smiled at his own joke and began transitioning back to the vehicles. By now, Russians were hastily lobbing artillery and mortars into the area, but given their rush, the targeting solution was horrible. It would take minutes to dial it in and by then, the team would be gone.

Jackal was throwing his gear in the back of the truck when Marko and Beef arrived. Smitty had driven ahead to get JT. The team was now in both vehicles headed north. In under a minute, they were safe from enemy fire. Ivan and five bonus Russians were dead.

*********************

The engineers and ground crew could not have been more pleased with the glider aircraft they built. The data collected from Buck's last flight clearly showed the platform was more than they'd hoped for. They debriefed Buck, who stated he had 'no doubt' and that night, he'd be clear to fly. There was only one more hurdle.

"Mr. Thiessen," the lead engineer said to Buck. "We just want you to be familiar with all the systems. Are you sure you understand them?"

Buck was certain, but there was no need to be a showoff. He chuckled, and said, "Please, let's go over them again."

The engineer looked at Buck, puzzled. "Mr. Thiessen, I'm sorry. Did I say something funny?"

"No," Buck quickly replied. "Your offer to teach me all the systems reminded me of a funny story."

Buck looked around. The engineers and team were far too serious. He wasn't sure if it was because they'd just built a test platform he'd take to war, but he was growing concerned. The team needed something, and Buck knew exactly what it was. "Look," he said, "You guys gotta start calling me Buck. And, I'm gonna tell you a story."

Buck brought all the engineers and maintainers around and they took seats. Buck brought over the cooler and placed it in the middle of them. "Grab a beer. Seriously, all of you," he said. They were hesitant but obliged.

Buck sat down after everyone had a beer and began telling his story. "Years ago, I was flying off the coast of Croatia on a long duration mission. Our C-130 was outfitted with some special sensors, and we were just observing what was going on in the Balkans. After thirteen hours, one of the aircrew, a captain who was a sensor operator, needed to take a shit. It would be his first time using what we called 'the honeypot.' In this case, it wasn't a hot espionage chick, but rather a flimsy toilet seat with a trash bag to catch the waste. On that mission, the aircrew member responsible for the aft portion of the C-130 was Technical Sergeant Garrison, I believe. As the captain approached the honeypot, Technical Sergeant Garrison, asked if the captain needed any instruction on how to use the honey pot. The captain replied 'No' and that he knew how to use a shitter."

"Well, the C-130 honeypot is very far aft along the side fuselage and fairly high up the ramp. The young captain hiked up the ramp, dropped the honeypot standing platform, and climbed on. Once on the honeypot platform, he pulled the modesty curtain around himself."

Buck looked around, the engineers were listening intently. He was an exceptional storyteller. "His first sign of trouble should have been the modesty curtain. It hung about four feet down from his feet to the floor of the C-130, and his head stuck out about three feet over the top of the curtain rod. How he didn't realize there was a problem, I do not know. No matter, he began going about his business, assuming it was just one of the many poorly designed U.S. Air Force acquisition programs." A few engineers scowled a bit, realizing some of them were responsible for more than a few of such designs.

Buck continued. "Just to ensure the captain was OK, Technical Sergeant Garrison went back to the ramp. As he approached, the two made eye contact." Buck chuckled. "They were both surprised. Get this… in his fifteen years as a loadmaster, Technical Sergeant Garrison witnessed something he'd never seen on a C-130 before. A person attempting to shit on the honeypot while it was in the 'up and stowed' position. The captain never lowered the toilet to the ground before he began relieving himself."

"Technical Sergeant Garrison called up to me on the intercom and said, *'Aircraft commander, loadmaster. You're not going to believe this. The captain is back here taking a shit on the honeypot in the 'up and stowed' position.'* I laughed out loud right on the intercom." Buck paused and noticed the engineers were smiling, some even chuckling with him.

"Well, I couldn't let this opportunity pass. I decided it might be fun to slowly oscillate pressure on the rudder pedals. As you likely know, this would make the tail of the aircraft sway significantly from side to side. Over the next minute, I increased the distance I was tossing the tail, the entire time laughing with my copilot, navigator, and flight engineer. Technical Sergeant Garrison kept peeking around and was watching the captain holding onto the top of the curtain rod. I think my favorite description was the captain looked like a rodeo rider sitting on an angry bull in the release pen. To this day, I still remember those comments from Technical Sergeant Garrison and smile." By now, the engineers were laughing, drinking beer far more loosely. Buck was achieving his intended effect.

"Well. It seems I may have been a bit too aggressive on the rudder pedals. Unbeknownst to us, the small metal retaining pin holding the honeypot in the 'up and stowed position' could not support the captain's weight, and the g forces I was inducing. Without notice, it snapped. Once it did, Technical Sergeant Garrison's eyes rapidly widened. The captain raced down the honeypot modesty curtain tunnel as if he were on Disney's

Space Mountain ride. Unfortunately for the poor captain, the honeypot rails were only so long. The honeypot rapidly came to a stop on the floor of the C-130 ramp. The captain, however, had far too much inertia to rapidly stop, and tumbled off the honeypot, out through the modesty curtain, and out onto the cargo bay floor of the C-130. There, naked as a jaybird and partially covered in blue toilet fluid, the captain laid. Technical Sergeant Garrison wisely chose to avoid any effort to help and acted as if he saw nothing. It was the only chance our fearless captain could retain any resemblance of dignity." Buck's engineers and team were in hysterics.

The story was over, but the moral of the story needed to be shared. "Now, the reason I share that story is twofold. First, no matter who offers to teach me something, I'll never say no, especially in the aviation world. Second. Aviation is inherently dangerous, but it can also thrill and be hilarious." Buck was right. Aviation is life and death. The 'between,' is a rarity. Buck continued. "You guys, please... lighten up. I know the risks of the career I chose and wouldn't change a thing. You're scaring me, and I'm supposed to be the one in danger." Buck finished.

"OK, Mr.... well, Buck," the lead engineer said. Over the next fifteen minutes, Buck would again learn how the makeshift radar warning receiver worked on the aircraft. He also was taught how to expend the small number of decoys should he truly face an enemy radar-guided missile. Engineers were confident he'd avoid radar, but there was no use taking chances.

Next, they briefed the other piece of technology. "Buck, one more time. Let's go over how you're gonna get Old Girl back to us."

"I'm all ears," Buck replied.

## *Chapter Nineteen*

# A Freebie

It was late afternoon back in the Ukrainian command bunker when General Shevchenko received a debriefing on Ivan's death. He was elated at the news and had served a few shots of gorilka to the team. Gorilka (sometimes spelled horilka) is nearly identical to vodka, however often flavored with a spicy pepper, honey, or berries. While similar to vodka, but Ukrainians are adamant about the difference… especially after the 2014 invasion. The team loved it. After the toast, Smitty stepped outside of the tent, pulled out his burner phone, and placed a call.

"Hello?" the party answered.

"Sir. Team lead here. Good news. Mission one in the books. Ukrainian brigade commander needed a sniper eliminated. Our boy rocked it at 1776 meters. Funny stuff, eh?" Smitty still couldn't get over the distance. "We are at the brigade command now and just finished the debrief. About twenty klicks from the front line."

Admiral Hershey was a stickler for communications discipline and would not use names while his teams were downrange. "Thanks 'team lead.' Great news. When are you back to a safe area for a full download of everything that happened?"

"Sir, I think we will spend the night in Ukraine, near a place called Uman. Tomorrow late morning, we will drive back west. We were in the field all night and need some rack time."

"Roger. Keep me posted. And please, pass along my regards to the Ukrainian commander," Admiral Hershey said.

"Will do, boss. Out." Smitty hung up his burner phone, snapped it in two, then threw it into a fire, burning slowly in a large oil drum outside the command post.

He returned into the command bunker and rallied the team. Before he left, he addressed Brigadier General Shevchenko one more time. "Chevy. Thanks again for the opportunity. I just spoke to my boss. He wanted me to again reiterate, this one was a freebie. He also asked me to give this to you." Smitty handed over a business card. It was of top quality. On one side, a U.S. phone number with a 703 area code in Northern Virginia. On the other side were three letters. T.V.G.

Shevchenko graciously accepted the card and examined it closely. He didn't need to know what the three letters meant. All he needed was the phone number. When the team left, he'd funnel that number up the chain of command to headquarters. "Please, tell your boss thank you again. You're welcome in my A.O.R. (Area of Operation) anytime."

The two shook hands, and the team departed. They would trek another fifty miles back northwest into safer territory to sleep. It was only midday, but the team had been up all night and was beat. They'd deservedly sleep for quite a while.

Meanwhile, back in D.C., Admiral Hershey called Andrew and relayed the good news. As expected, Andrew was elated, and now ready to take the next step. After hanging up with Eugene, he took a deep breath and dialed the phone, placing a call to Steve Lewis.

"Steve, Andrew Denney here. How are you?"

"I'm well, Mr. Denney." Steve was pleased to get the call, then quickly recalled a small faux pas. "Hey, I owe you a minor apology. I meant to reach out earlier. The President received your campaign donation and wanted me to thank you personally."

Mr. Denney smiled. The money had served its purpose. "That's great news, Steve, no apology necessary. Perhaps the President can thank me in person. I think the time has come for a meeting if you can arrange it. Perhaps four of us, the President, you, Admiral Hershey, and I. There's been some recent developments that I am certain the two of you will find valuable. When can we come by? I also have another check."

Steve couldn't say no if he ever expected another donation. Looking at the calendar, there was a small opening in two days, nothing earlier. Andrew would take it. "Thanks, Steve. We will see you then. Please ensure the meeting is just the four of us."

"Absolutely, Mr. Denney. It's on the calendar."

"I don't believe the Admiral, or I need to send our personal information. Your security team should still have us in their records, correct?"

"Yes. I'll arrange everything. Have a great day, Mr. Denney." Steve hung up. He wasn't sure where this endeavor would lead, but there was progress. For months, Andrew Denney withheld donations from the President. Those had started again, and the campaign season was coming. Whatever Mr. Denney wished to discuss, the President could handle it.

\*\*\*\*\*\*\*\*\*\*\*\*\*\*\*\*\*\*\*\*

Old Girl was packed up to her load of 2.5 tons. While such a load seemed impossible for a glider, such was far from the case. In fact, a later version of the Waco called the GC-10 could carry nearly double the load, roughly five tons.

On this mission, Buck would be delivering war material: ammunition, weapons, food stores, medical supplies, and more. Most were critical need items as convoys were being sabotaged by Russian operatives behind enemy lines. The sun was setting over Poland and soon Buck would be airborne, flying on night vision devices.

The slack in Old Girl's tow cable grew taunt, and as the towplane's engines revved, the two began rolling. Just like last time, Old Girl lifted off before the tow plane. This time, however, the Cessna would not make circles climbing directly up over the airfield. Rather, the two would fly east towards the border between Poland and Ukraine.

The sun had now set, and the tow plane was almost at 25,000 feet. Buck, wearing his supplemental oxygen system and night vision device, looked at his GPS. The two adjoined aircraft were directly over the border. It was go time. Buck flashed his lights once. As he did, the Sky Courier initiated a lazy left banking turn back as Buck disconnected the tow rope. The hum of the Cessna's engines faded away. The only sound was wind whistling by the glider. Buck pointed the nose directly to his intended landing point, deep into war torn Ukraine.

At such a high altitude, Buck flew with extreme finesse to maximize every ounce of flight duration, mitigating erroneous or drag inducing flight inputs. It was pure flying, and Buck loved it. Ironically, nearly any other military member flying at such an altitude in Ukraine would be heavily focused on the Russian ground-based air defense systems such as the S300 or S400. To traditional fighter aircraft, these systems were widow makers. But Old Girl was anything but a traditional fighter, and such systems would struggle to find her.

Buck checked his ground speed. It was slightly faster than he'd planned, but he knew he had a prevailing tail wind. Across Europe, the traditional winds flowed west to east. That was a bonus for his flights into Ukraine. They'd serve as a hindrance on his way out.

As he flew, there was little to concentrate on. There were no radios to monitor, no data-link systems feeding him an air picture update. Just Buck and his radar warning receiver. He watched it intently. For now, the device remained silent, which was a good thing. The device was programed to only alert Buck if a Russia radar was locking up on him. Again, hoping his radar signature was low enough and that his slow airspeeds even further exacerbated any radar that might find him. Aviators, at times, would question such systems. On one hand, it was reassuring when they remained silent, meaning enemy radars were not attempting to search and find your aircraft. On the other hand, such silence could be due to a system fault, and the enemy was mere seconds from shooting the aircraft down. On the third hand, if it was working and reporting enemy radars, that too presented its own challenges.

As for heat-seeking missiles or enemy anti-aircraft artillery, Buck was fairly safe. The aircraft had no heat source for an IR missile to lock on, and without emitting lights, it would be almost impossible for ground artillery to find him.

Buck continued his slow descent. If he could achieve a glide ratio of 40:1, he'd easily make his landing strip. It was a small military field operation on the outskirts of a small town called Uman.

A flash in the distance caught the right corner of Buck's eye. He saw it again. Rockets or artillery fire on the ground well off in the distance. It was a stark reminder that Buck was once more a combat pilot. He focused.

Well into the flight and now down to five thousand feet, he could make out houses and lights of villages below him. It was only another thirty miles to the airstrip, and Buck's quick calculations ensured he'd make it. Uman was on the 'safe' side of the combat line, but resupply had proved challenging. Long range Russian fires were disrupting Ukrainian traditional supply lines. Admiral Hershey's solution for a glider, if it worked, would be a tremendous help to the Ukrainian forces.

Buck was now at 1000 feet, and he could see the makeshift runway. As directed, he flashed his lights twice. The airfield lights sprung to life and Buck removed his night vision devices. He lumbered Old Girl onto the ground, and she rolled to a stop. Quickly, three military trucks raced out to the aircraft. A group of Ukrainian soldiers frantically shook Buck's hand and started offloading the cargo. Once offloaded, Old Girl was towed into a nearby hangar. After everyone left, it was just Buck and Old Girl, alone in the hangar. He realized he'd just flown through a substantial Russian air defense system unscathed and unnoticed. Buck smiled, pulled out his burner phone, snapped a few photos of Old Girl, and then sent them to Admiral Hershey. As he laid down on a cot next to Old Girl in the hangar, he typed out a text message as well.

*'First half of the mission, complete. – Buck.'*

Admiral Hershey got the message and soon thereafter called Andrew. "Hey. More good news. Buck's mission also delivered. Literally."

"Excellent, Admiral. Thanks for the update. I also have news for you. We have a meeting at the White House in two days. Get all the facts you can. We'll need them."

"Will do, Andrew. Thanks." The two hung up.

Buck was asleep on his cot next to Old Girl when he was approached by a well-dressed soldier. It was the regional logistics officer for the brigade, a full colonel. He introduced himself, stating his name, but for the life of Buck, there was no way he'd be able to repeat it.

"Sir," the Colonel said. "On behalf of my government, thank you for your delivery and for the risk you took. Our skies are far from safe."

As directed, Buck reached into his pocket. "Colonel, I'm glad you appreciated our work. On behalf of my boss, he wanted me to remind you this one was a freebie, and he also wanted me to give you this. It was another business card, just like the one Smitty had. A phone number on one side and the letters TVG on the other.

"Thank you, Mr. Thiessen. You are welcome to sleep in our barracks if you wish."

"No. I wanna be right here. Thanks though."

"Sure. May I have some food brought to you? Perhaps some vodka."

"Well, if you're offering food and vodka, I'd be much obliged."

The Colonel looked at him, confused. "A blidghed?" he said, trying to repeat Buck's last word. "Forgive me, what is a blighted?"

"Ha. Sorry. I'd be grateful. Yes. Please. Food and some vodka."

As Buck ate and drank, he was unaware Smitty and the rest of the team were also on the Uman barracks, sleeping through the night. Admiral Hershey's teams were both safe, and the day was a huge success.

## *Chapter Twenty*

# Friction

In a decent sized room in the White House, a muted yet festive group sat and ate. It was a small working lunch for the senior most members of the Transportation Department. The event was a gift from the President given their hard work on rolling out and successfully implementing his recent infrastructure bill. Part way through the event, the President walked in to make his brief appearance.

"Hey everybody," he said as he passed through the door. "Please! Please! Keep your seats and enjoy the food! You earned it, and I know my staff worked tirelessly to make sure it tasted perfect." As he said this, he glanced at Rachel. She would make no eye contact and clearly was not smitten to see him.

The Transportation Secretary ignored the President's request to remain seated. She stood and greeted the President, having the rest of her staff stay seated. She was a rotund lady and charming to a fault. In her younger days, she won the Southeastern Southern Bell beauty pageant. Later in life, she went on to be runner-up in the Ms. Georgia competition. "Thank you so much, Mr. President, for our working lunch. It truly is a wonderful event, and I must say, the food is almost just as good as mine." The room let out a soft laugh. She was cracking a joke, but as always, there is a hint of truth in every joke and the Secretary took great pride in her southern culinary skills.

"Well, I'm glad you like it. Unfortunately, I won't be able to eat with you today." There was a sigh among the crowd. "Let's get a photo together though, and I'll have my staff bring my food to the Oval Office. Frustrating being the President. I sometimes get stuck in overdrive. Trust me, I'd rather be eating here with you folks." It was a lie. He had no pressing work, but the look that Rachel had shot him was concerning. He hoped to smooth things over and then perhaps relieve some of his presidential stress with her on the Oval Office sofa.

The photos were taken as Steve helped Rachel quickly transfer the President's meal to his office. The President said his goodbyes and then progressed to his office. As the President walked in, Steve and Rachel were finishing up.

"Rachel," he said. "I was wondering how you're doing with this whole FBI case. As you know, we've worked hard to ensure we've investigated and ensured it was not a U.S. government entity that caused that horrible damage. Right, Steve."

"Yes, Mr. President," he responded.

Rachel coldly nodded and remained silent.

"Rachel, please, why don't you stick around and tell me how you are doing and what's going on from your perspective on this investigation? Steve, please leave us."

"Mr. President, Sir," Rachel said, almost shaking. "I'm sorry. I'd love to stay, but I can't leave the rest of my staff to deal with the other luncheon. Perhaps later?"

The President was stunned. Steve was a bit surprised, too. He hadn't seen a staff member decline such an offer in years.

"Yes, sure. I understand," responded the President, as if recovering from a body blow. "Steve, perhaps you can stay back and chat." He said it, looking directly into Rachel's eyes.

She almost froze. While the comment was innocent, she was certain the following discussion would be a plot which led to her demise.

Steve answered immediately. "Of course, Mr. President."

As Rachel walked out of the office, she looked back. Both Steve and the President were staring at her. She closed the door and scurried down the hall. Alone, she placed a call to Lance.

"Lance, I think they are onto me. I'm in trouble."

"Rachel. Where are you?"

"I'm in the White House." Even Rachel's voice was trembling.

"OK. Stay in a group of people. Don't be alone. Get out of there and we can again meet tonight."

"Lance, I don't want to meet. I want to be safe. Can you have some people guard my house?"

"Sure. I will have them there by five this evening," Lance said. Ironically, the two goons who'd camp outside her house were two of the gunmen who shot up the place just weeks earlier.

"Thank you, Lance." She was feeling a bit more at ease for both Brooklyn's and her safety.

## *Chapter Twenty-One*
# Reset & Refit

The sky glowed softly from the pending dawn.  Sunrise was getting earlier and earlier in Poland as the northern hemisphere crept closer to summer.  Smitty was already awake, still juiced by the adrenalin of the mission.  It was strange.  When working for NISSASSA, he dreaded going on missions, but with this organization, Smitty had a renewed sense of warrior spirit.  Perhaps it was because the fight was with the long-standing enemy.  Perhaps it was because it was the force construct was more familiar.  Smitty didn't know why.  He just knew he wanted to fight again; demons be damned.

After a short jog around the camp with Marko, the two grabbed a coffee and a quick breakfast.

"Marko," Smitty asked, "You said you attended U.S. military school.  Where was that?"

With a sense of pride, Marko replied, "Carlisle Barracks, in Pennsylvania.  I graduated in the class of 2018.  It's been a blessed but crazy career for me, my friend."

Smitty was puzzled.  "How so?"

"Well, I joined the Ukrainian army at a young age, roughly in 1985.  My initial training was alongside Russian forces, as Ukraine was part of the Soviet Union then.  In the 1990s, communism crumbled, and many of the nations once behind the Iron Curtain shifted loyalties to NATO.  But not Ukraine.  We remained loyal to Russia.  We shared a history."

Marko took a sip of coffee, then continued.  "I watched the color revolutions over the years.  Then I watched the frozen conflicts develop; Transnistria, South Ossetia, Abkhazia, Nagorno-Karabakh and others.  Russia was attempting to regain its control.  They literally carved off pieces of Moldova, Georgia and Azerbaijan.  Russia's fingerprints were all over these efforts, and likely, with the unmentioned assistance of Ukraine.  What happened here in 2014, I would suggest, was just a matter of time.  Crimea did not break away.  Russia invaded, but the news somehow overlooked it.  Our Oblast in the West didn't seek independence, they were taken over by Russia.  Again, the media narrative somehow overlooked that."

Marko was getting frustrated.  The way he told the story, it was if Ukraine should have prepared better for the anticipated Russian actions.  He then continued.  "In 2014, I was a Lieutenant Colonel.  Once at war with Russia, our Defense Ministry made a drastic shift to learn western styles of warfare.  To be fair, there never would have been the inertia within such a large organization if Russia hadn't invaded.  They made it easy for our military to change."

Another sip of coffee.  "Notice I said it was easy for the military, not for me.  Lieutenant colonels are set in their ways.  I had to relearn everything, just like our lieutenants.  My training, however, had to be at a strategic level.  I had to learn it with a deeper understanding.  I'll forever be grateful to the United States for bringing me to Carlisle.  There was no question, I was the dumbest student when I arrived, but I'd like to think I was... I guess you guys call it 'the most improved player' in your sports.  Yes.  That was me."

Smitty was fascinated.  How hard would it be for an old warrior to not only completely learn a new war-fighting doctrine but also lead others under that construct?  "Wow, Marko.  That's a bit of a wild ride.  I bet you have some amazing stories."

"You are correct.  Perhaps someday, but not now.  I and others must all fight for our homeland.  If we don't, it will be gone.  And it will only be a matter of time that Poland, Czechia, Slovakia and others fall."

The two got up and walked outside.  Daylight had finally truly broken over the horizon.  It was no longer dawn.

Off in the distance, a high-pitched whine was revving.  It was a strange sound, one that neither had heard nor could place.  They were far from concerned, though.  It was a military installation and one in peaceful Poland.  Anything was possible.

Soon the pitch of the noise increased and then they could hear it was now moving.  Marko looked up and saw a mid-sized aircraft with what appeared to be something protruding out on the top of the fuselage spine, centered over the wing line.

"Hey," Marko said. "Isn't that similar to your buddy's glider? The ones we saw at Base Uniform?"

"Marko," Smitty replied. "I'm gonna guess it's not like Buck's airplane, but rather it 'is' Buck's airplane. I just don't know what the hell that contraption is on the top." Smitty smiled and then said out loud. "Go get 'em General Buck Turgidson. Fly that fucker like you're frying chickens in a henhouse."

Marko looked at Smitty as if he'd lost his head. "What did you say?"

"Eh. Nothing. Just quoting a famous movie in the U.S. It's from *Dr. Strangelove*. Ever see it?"

"No. What's it about?"

"It's a dark comedy from the 50s or 60s about a miscalculation between two superpowers that leads to nuclear war."

Marko smiled. "Timely."

The two chuckled.

********************

Minutes earlier, Buck ordered his glider to be towed out of the hangar to the end of the runway. It was empty, and more importantly, without a towplane. Buck pulled back on a large black lever. As he did, a door on the top of the fuselage opened. Then he pulled a red lever that made a ratcheting sound. After multiple consecutive pulls on the lever, a small, 175lb jet engine locked into place on top of the fuselage.

This was no ordinary jet engine, however. It was a DGEN380, a lightweight composite design with exceptional ability. Along with impressive performance metrics, the engine was wrapped in carbon and glass fiber to reduce its radar signature. Given the lightweight of an empty glider, the technologically advanced jet engine could easily lift the aircraft into the air. She had over 550lbs of thrust, roughly three times her actual weight.

Buck revved up the engine and rolled down the runway, beginning to fly at roughly fifty knots. He would have no problem getting her airborne, but he needed to be careful. The engine burned nearly a hundred gallons an hour, and Old Girl only carried 25 gallons, basically 15 minutes of useable engine time.

In combat, the engine would serve as both a blessing and curse. When exposed, Old Girl became far more vulnerable to enemy air defense threats. The carbon and glass fiber would eliminate some of the reflective energy, but not all of it.

As Old Girl climbed off the runway, Buck aimed her wing line right on the last known location of the nearest S400 Russian surface-to-air missile system. Doing so meant that Buck's flight path would be tangential to the air defense system, creating a velocity null or Doppler notch. The unbreakable laws of physics would serve as his security blanket. Once at altitude, Buck would stow the engine, both masking his radar signature and improving aerodynamic performance. Heading west, Old Girl and Buck would slowly lumber to her home base.

Flying Old Girl back to Poland was a dream for Buck. Now empty, she was light and nimble. He'd fly over Ukraine, find a few thermals, and lift back up. When a thermal wasn't available and he was low, he'd deploy the engine and light it for a minute or two. It was more than enough to get him a few thousand feet.

After a little over two hours, Buck was rolling to a full stop on Base Uniform's runway. Cheers arose from all the engineers that worked on her. The program funded by Eugene Hershey and Andrew Denney was not cheap. But if Buck could make that run a dozen times, the program would break even. Then it would be all profit.

## Chapter Twenty-Two
# Landing a Big Fish

Another day had passed, and the White House schedule would include a meeting between the President, Admiral Hershey, and Andrew Denney. In the official log, there'd be no reference to The Valyrian Group. The meeting, on paper, would appear far less innocuous than reality.

As usual, Steve and the President privately discussed the day's meetings. Oddly, the President skipped what Steve perceived to be the President's key talking points for his meeting with Andrew and Eugene. Steve, realizing the history between the President and the other two men, presumed it merely an oversight. There was no genuine concern about 'getting the meeting right.'

Near the White House, in a plush leather booth, both Andrew and Eugene were casually going over their talking points. The booth was in the Duck Bar of the famed Old Ebbitt Grill. One of a handful of bars in the restaurant, the Duck Bar, was beautiful. Dark wood and leather were the décor's base, with ornate duck hunting paraphernalia and old hunting shotguns. The last items often made D.C.ers chuckle given the city's longstanding 'no guns' policy.

"Andrew," Eugene said, "I made a few changes to the talking points for Smitty's mission. I think the overall message flows better." Admiral Hershey handed over a piece of paper. "The changes are highlighted."

Andrew looked at the sheet with his reading glasses for less than five seconds. It mattered little to him. In his world, 'talking points' did not accomplish business in D.C. It was a checkbook, and an arm twist or two... for lack of a better term, leverage. "We're good. This is going to go well. I have no doubt," Andrew replied. He also changed the subject. "Where are we on cost for Thiessen's operation? The flying cardboard box?"

"Just over five million right now, but the majority of the cost has been paid. The three gliders are built. We are cutting back design engineering and ramping staff to maintain the existing aircraft. Also looking for a few more pilots to increase the mission rates."

Andrew looked over his glasses. "Five million? That's a hell of an expensive flying cardboard box, no matter if there are three or three hundred."

"I agree," the Admiral replied. "But a good number of those aircraft parts are one of a kind, generated on a state-of-the art 3D printer in high-tech plastics. Not to mention the salaries of the engineers that crafted this thing. Luckily, we did it in Poland which has few restrictions on defense industry builds and civil aviation oversight. Had we done it in the U.S., the cost would have doubled."

Admiral Hershey paused to evaluate Andrew. After all, it was Andrew's money funding the effort. Eugene was certain he was being judicious, but that didn't matter nearly as much as Andrew believing it. "For each 2.5 ton run we make into Ukraine, we get one hundred and fifty grand. Daily costs are around twenty-five thousand per flight. That's a profit of one hundred and twenty-five per flight. Once we start running two flights a day, that's a quarter mil. Then three flights... well, you get the picture."

Andrew's face calmed. It always did when the discussion shifted from costs to revenue. "OK. Good. I like those numbers. Let's get the bill and head over to the White House. I don't wish to be late."

The Admiral settled the tab of $50 for two iced teas, two waters, an appetizer plate, taxes and tip. 'Jesus,' the Admiral thought, 'D.C. is far too expensive.'

The two exited Old Ebbitt Grill and walked over to the White House visitor entrance. Within a minute or so, both were cleared through the metal detectors and met by a young, energetic staffer that Steve had sent to the gate. Five-digit campaign contributions had their perks.

The staffer escorted the two towards the Oval Office, where the President and Steve were standing, awaiting their arrival.

"Andrew, Squirts," the President said. "It is great to see you two again. It's been far too long."

"Mr. President," the Admiral said. "I agree." The two shook hands.

"Yes. Mr. President. It is good to be back in the White House. I missed this old drafty building." Andrew's comments were somewhere between a joke and a jab. Often difficult in D.C. to differentiate the two.

"Please, both of you, sit." The President sat first on a sofa and the other two followed. Steve would sit in his usual chair, a bit off to the side. "Can I get either of you a coffee or tea?"

Eugene responded, "No, but thanks, we just had some water and tea at Old Ebbitt and my teeth are nearly floating."

Andrew looked at Admiral Hershey sternly, then turned to the President. "I'll have a cappuccino if you don't mind."

"Yes, of course," the President said, and the staff quickly scurried to fill the order.

"So, gentlemen," the President continued. "Steve here tells me you shared an informative evening together and explained your new business venture. I look forward to hearing more about it."

"Yes, well, since that time, we have executed a few missions in Ukraine. A few logistics runs via radar evading cargo aircraft and an elite forces hit on a Russian sniper," Admiral Hershey boasted. "Here's the details if you are interested." He offered two folders, one taken by the President and the other handed over to Steve.

The President reviewed them closely and quietly, for what seemed like nearly two minutes. "Damn, Squirts. Good stuff here. Looks like you're already on your way. What do you need me for?"

It was an intentionally obtuse question. The President knew exactly why they needed him. "Yes, well, Sir. Ops like this do not happen for free. We were hoping you could help us secure funding for further operations."

"Interesting," the President replied. His reaction in diplomatic circles would be clearly unsupportive. "But who's funding your operations now?"

"Well, the logistics runs are being paid by the Ukrainian government, but that won't last forever. The sniper hit remains unpaid, but we consider it more of a capabilities demo."

Andrew had grown more and more uneasy as he listened to the conversation. He was certain he knew what the President wanted to hear, and it was not a capabilities sales pitch. He'd agreed, however, to let Eugene make his full presentation.

"Mr. President. I understand I am asking a lot. I also know from our many discussions that you often wished the U.S. could do more in Ukraine. That, however, was impossible due to political risk or limitations by congressional legislation. You may recall when I declined your offer to remain as the Chairman. This is why. I wanted the same thing. Now I am offering it to you on a silver platter."

Steve sat in the corner. His interest was piqued and was fairly certain it would be at least marginally enticing to the President. "Squirts, I hear ya. And again, I am extremely happy you guys are getting some of our boys in the fight, but I just don't see how I can fund this."

Andrew was done remaining silent. "The same way you funded NISSASSA. You know, my deceased son's former security firm."

The comment was harsh but was a helpful reminder for the President to understand Andrew's angle. "Yes, Andrew. I realize such funds were used in the past, but Congress exposed that loophole once NISSASSA was outed. We no longer have unlimited access to that funding."

"Mr. President, if I may," Admiral Hershey attempting to regain control of the conversation. "I've done some research. Based on what we found, I'd like to bring your attention to this funding line," handing over a piece of paper. He continued, "It belongs to the Executive Branch and has under executed over the first half of this year. If it continues to under execute, there will be nine million dollars available. This line is earmarked by Congress for the Executive Branch with wide discretion. With these funds, we can negotiate a fair price for us to continue to operate through the rest of the year and demonstrate our value." The Admiral had done his homework. His numbers checked. Steve didn't need to see the paper. He knew about the funding line as well. Even if it didn't exist, there was always money if the President wanted it.

"Yes, Squirts. I see. Well, I tell ya what. Let me talk to my inner circle about this, and I think I need to look at it with the Vice President, and perhaps the acting Defense Secretary."

That line right there said it all. Alone, the President may have agreed. Announcing an intent to bring others into the discussion was like inviting two 'no's' to a vote of three.

Andrew looked at Eugene. "May I?" Eugene nodded.

"Mr. President, I realize we've had our differences, but I think this here will help smooth things a bit and at least get us off on the right step. We have about three other elite missions ready to go. All we need is your discrete funding." Andrew handed over another envelope.

The President took it and opened it. He stared for a few seconds at the check, a campaign contribution.

"Fifty thousand dollars," the President said out loud. "Impressive." He paused between each thought, and was choosing his next words carefully. "Andy. Let me ask you something. At what point does your spine present itself?"

The room went silent.

The President continued. "Do you recall riding in Marine One back from a campaign event with the former Defense Secretary? The two of you squeezed my balls in a vice. Do you remember the fall out I endured from the financial racket the two of you swindled in the pharmaceutical industry? Not to mention the dark clouds your son and NISSASSA brought over this 'old drafty house' as you put it."

The President handed the check back. "Andy, I have never, nor do I know a politician who has, handed back such a substantial campaign contribution. That said. Keep your money." He reached into his pocket and pulled out another check. "You can keep the one you gave to Steve to secure this appointment, too."

Steve's pen stood still, hovering over his notepad. His jaw locked open. He'd never seen such a display and although he was a professional at containing his emotions, this time it broke through.

As for Andrew, steam could visibly be seen shooting from his ears. Slowly, Andrew stood. "You self-righteous fuck. You have the nerve to talk to me about right and wrong, dark clouds and fall out? In a normal world, you'd have no right to speak such crap. I was wrong. This isn't an old drafty house. It's a glass house, and you are clearly chucking stones unabashedly."

Andrew walked out of the room, his checks in hand. Awkwardly, Eugene arose and followed.

The Oval Office door closed. Steve looked at the President. "Sir, you just let sixty thousand dollars walk out the door. I hope you know what you're doing."

"Steve. I know exactly what I am doing," the President responded firmly without reservation. "Thanks. Who's next on the schedule?"

Outside the White House, Admiral Hershey had caught up to Andrew. He was muttering and cussing under his breath.

"Hey. Andrew. Slow down. We will figure something out."

"I already have." Andrew bellowed as they arrived at his car. "Get in. We have two meetings to arrange. First, we are going to see Ukrainian Ambassador Ubyivovk. Later we will meet with Congressman Donegan."

Jack Donegan was a former Navy SEAL and a longtime friend of Smitty. In fact, Jack's kids referred to Smitty as 'Uncle Smitty.' Jack and Eugene also shared a friendship from their time together in the Navy. They had served together. If anyone would understand their plight, it would be him.

\*\*\*\*\*\*\*\*\*\*\*\*\*\*\*\*\*\*\*\*

Like clockwork, Curt arrived home after another day of work. Although he hadn't admitted it, a desk job was killing him. For dinner, Allison had ordered take-out from the Banana Café on the corner of 8th Street and E Street. It was a famous Cuban restaurant, but sadly would soon be closing. The owner was selling it and somehow it would be renovated into something else. For many in the Eastern Market section of D.C., this closure would be a travesty. Banana Café was an unofficial landmark for locals.

"How was your day, Curt?" she asked.

"Hell," he said, without flinching. He kissed her and Bo on the head. Noorullah threw his arms around Curt, interrupting his ability to set the table. Curt didn't mind at all. "Hey Noorullah, how was your day?"

"Good, papa!" Noorullah paused, then continued. "I finished reading my first English book today!" He was proud and sought a father's love.

"Noorullah!" Curt said. "That's Great! I'm proud of you." Curt held Noorullah for just a bit longer... proud of his decision to extract the boy from Afghanistan. "Now, son, please go wash your hands for dinner," Curt asked. Hygiene remained a constant reminder for Noorullah. Breaking Afghan habits was not easy.

As Noorullah ran off to the bathroom, Allison spoke up. "I'm sorry work was so bad. What happened? Did one of the political appointees blow up again, or did Congress meddle again in the VA?" These two events were the most common that would send Curt or other D.C. governmental employees into a hell day.

"Nope. Nothing like that. It was just hell. Like it always is."

The two sat down and put Bo in his highchair. Allison prepped Bo's puree and began feeding him. "Curt, I don't understand. I thought you liked your job."

Curt put his fork down and stared at Allison. He needed to tell her. "Sweetheart. Look. I am not sure I ever loved the job. When Squirts offered it to me, I truly thought I was going to be able to make sweeping changes for the better within the VA. I've been there for a long time now, and the biggest success I've had is moving my desk from the wall to the window. The entrenchment in D.C. is overwhelming."

Allison had never heard such comments from Curt before, but she knew.

He continued. "I stayed on for this long because I also know this job feeds my family and is caring for us. But it's not me. I'm losing myself and dying inside."

Allison remained silent. From the day she met Curt in that African village, she knew of his thirst for adventure. To believe he'd somehow resolve his life to a desk job was foolish. Part of her was upset with herself for not seeing it earlier.

Curt continued, "When Smitty and Buck were approached by Squirts to go to Ukraine, a part of me was busting to join them. I know it would be unwise to go into Ukraine, especially after Afghanistan, but damn, I'm exploding inside when I think about them being there."

Allison heard enough. She finally interjected. "Go." She said.

"Excuse me?" Curt responded.

"Curt, I saw the text from Smitty come in on your phone. Go. There is a need for you in Poland, and I know you can do good things. Just promise me you won't go into Ukraine."

Curt's eyes widened and began to water. "Really?"

"Curt," she said. "Why did you go to Africa? If I'm not mistaken, it was to heal people, and yourself. NISSASSA got in the way, and you never really ever completed that mission. Noorullah and I can care for Bo. I hate it, but I love you. And I know this is what you need. But know this. I said go to Poland, not Ukraine."

Curt stood and walked over to Allison. He hugged her tightly and said, 'Thank you,' over and over and over. Noorullah leaned into the hug as well and blurted, "You're welcome, Papa." His English was getting better, but he clearly had no idea what he was commenting on.

Later that night, Curt called the Admiral.

"Hello?" the party answered.

"Admiral Hershey, hey, it's me Curt Nover."

"Curt. Great to hear from ya. It's a bit late. What can I do for you?"

"Yes, Sir. I'm sorry. I'll keep it short. About a week ago, I got a message from Smitty. He said there is a need for mobile / semi-mobile surgical hospital style support in Poland for wounded Ukrainians in transition to Landstuhl."

"Yup. That's accurate," the Admiral said.

"If there is any interest in your organization, I want to set it up. I can help find doctors and maybe through international orgs, I can find some equipment."

"Curt. Medical is a big-ticket cost for combat operations. I am not sure."

"Sir, please. I'll ensure you turn a profit. Get me to Poland, I'll do the rest. I'm not sure if you heard, but in Ukraine, there are serious medical challenges."

The Admiral hadn't heard and was curious. "Please, explain."

"In the past few U.S. wars, we've maintained Air Superiority. This allowed medevac helicopters to operate freely, enabling them to pick up wounded and get them to care within the golden hour." Curt paused, then continued. "In Ukraine, Russian air defense systems blanket the whole country, even the part still controlled by Ukraine. That means wounded Ukrainian soldiers are only able to be evacuated via ground transportation. Survival rates are far lower than what the U.S. enjoyed in Iraq and Afghanistan. I know if I can get there, I can help solve this problem."

"OK. Slow down, Curt. Tomorrow, we meet with Ukrainian Ambassador Ubyivovk. Let me see what options for funding might be there. I need to tell you, we took a big financial hit today. Not the best time to approach us with a new start."

Curt froze. "Is Smitty and Buck OK?"

"Oh, sorry. Yeah. No, they are fine. The hit was closer to home. The D.C. business world is far different from the governmental world. I'm learning quickly. Have a good night, Curt. I'll be in touch later." The Admiral hung up. It was the best Curt could do. Tomorrow, he'd submit his two-week notice. Rarely did one rejoice at the notion of giving up a $185k a year job. Curt couldn't have been happier. He also knew going to Poland would eventually pay better. Far better.

## Chapter Twenty-Three
# Wartime Diplomacy

As the Admiral had told Curt, there would be a morning meeting with the Ukrainian Ambassador. It would take place at the Ukrainian Embassy in D.C., near the Francis Scott Key Bridge, as it enters Georgetown, just next to the park. It was prime real estate in the upscale section of the city. Ambassador Ubyivovk was a well-educated man with a demanding job. While many ambassadorships are reserved for political friends or nepotism, ambassadors to the U.S. were polished diplomats. His name could not have been better, either. Ubyivovk's literal translation was 'Wolf Killer,' and Russian President Volkov's name literally translated to 'Wolf.' The narrative of this was often relished within the Truman Building offices. State Department personnel loved such things.

Andrew and the Admiral arrived in front of the Ukrainian embassy five minutes before the appointed time. Uniformed D.C. police stood out front, and there were likely a handful of plain clothed officers also pulling security. The threat posture ever since the Vice President's assassination was elevated.

After entering the Embassy, the two were greeted by a polite secretary. Ambassador Ubyivovk was busy, and she politely asked the two to wait in a greeting area. Foot traffic through the embassy was light, but everyone walked with a sense of urgency. It was just as you'd expect from a nation at war.

Eventually, a well-dressed man approached. "Gentlemen, I apologize for keeping you waiting. I am Ambassador Ubyivovk. Please, will you come into my office?"

The group shook hands and were all soon seated privately in the Ambassador's office.

"Mr. Ambassador," the Admiral said. "It is an honor to meet you and, if I may say, from a very honed military perspective, your nation has some amazing warriors putting up one hell of a fight." Before being Chairman, Admiral Hershey had served as a senior officer within U.S. SOUTHCOM. He met countless defense ministers, chiefs of defense, and ambassadors, just like all his predecessors. He was well trained in pumping up allied diplomats.

"Admiral, I thank you greatly, and I too am honored to be in your presence. I want to thank you for the work you did for our nation as the Chairman. I know our Defense Attaché attended your retirement, but if you'll allow me, I have a small gift for you." The Ambassador reached down and there was a hand carved wooden box.

The Admiral took it and opened it. Inside was what appeared to be an extremely expensive bottle of vodka. "Mr. Ambassador, this is too much. You are too kind. We too have a gift for you."

Andrew did a double take. There was no discussion about a gift before they arrived.

Patiently, Admiral Hershey opened his papers and neatly took out an 8x10 image of Ivan the sniper with red letters over it that said, 'K.I.A.'

The Ambassador took the photo and smiled. "Yes, I heard about this. It was your warrior who took the shot?"

"Yes, Mr. Ambassador. It was our guy."

"Well, I guess I will need to get him a bottle of Vodka too!" The Ambassador bellowed. They all chuckled.

"Mr. Ambassador, as you know, our company is also the ones doing aerial logistics to your front lines. We appreciate that business, but hope that perhaps the Ukrainian government may have some other missions they'd like to employ our elite team with."

The Ambassador was intrigued at the idea. He also already knew about The Valyrian Group, about Jackal, Smitty, and the entire team. If there was one thing the Ukrainians learned from Russians, it was how to perform intelligence gathering. He was bluffing when he acted like he didn't know.

"Interesting," Ambassador Ubyivovk said as he rubbed his chin. "Might I ask how much these missions are?"

"Ambassador. There is no fixed price, but if you give us a task, we will quote you a price. For clarity. We will not operate in Russia, and we will not target political leadership. Those are two of our main 'out of bounds' issues. Do you understand?"

"Yes, yes… of course," the ambassador responded. "I tell you what, let me meet with my defense attaché and have him inquire as to what our Defense Ministry might want."

Andrew had observed enough of the diplo show. "Ambassador, if I may."

The Ambassador turned his attention to Andrew, "Yes, please."

"Your defense attaché doesn't have any idea what your MoD wants to target, and even if he did, it wouldn't be a mission for us. The aerial supply runs we fly are a significant benefit to you, but the margins are small, and the initial investment to build the aircraft was substantial. Financially, our company won't survive on these missions alone. Further, I suspect you already knew who we were and if you didn't know who killed Ivan before we walked in; you need to fire someone in your Ministry of Foreign Affairs. Our company doesn't have time to pussyfoot around. I have an elite team, sitting in Poland with their thumbs in each other's asses. If they don't have a mission in three days, I'm pulling them out and putting them in another country that wants them."

The Admiral winced at every sentence, but Andrew was footing the bill, and it was hard to argue against money.

The Ambassador sat there, staring at Andrew. "Andrew, might you have any Ukrainian blood in you?"

"No. I'm 100% Irish," he responded, curtly.

"Yes. Just as stubborn as us Ukrainians," the Ambassador responded as he smiled. "OK, Mr. Denney. We do it your way. I will talk to the President this evening when Kyiv awakes. If he is interested, we will have a mission for you within forty-eight hours. If he has no mission for you, I am sorry. This is the best I can do."

Andrew grinned, "Clear speak. I appreciate that, Mr. Ambassador. Thank you. One last question. We have a Special Ops trained emergency room doctor who's looking to come help. I understand your survival rates are low due to lack of rotary wing lift to evacuate your wounded."

"That's true, but I think we'd rather have a few crazy helo pilots than a doctor."

"I've already given you one crazy pilot and am getting you another. How about 300k for the year for our medical guy. If he works out, great. Then we can talk about further costs."

"What's $300k when we are talking millions? Sure, please send him. I know our government will support this."

The three wrapped up the rest of their conversation and the two departed. Lunchtime was approaching and the two would head to Café Milano in Georgetown. They hailed a cab and were at the restaurant within minutes.

As they approached the table, Congressman Jack Donegan stood up to greet them.

"Admiral Squirts!" He said, chuckling. "Great to see ya, you old warrior!"

"You too, Jack... or should I use your nickname too?" Jack's nickname was 'Noff,' for perhaps obvious reasons.

"Ah... ya got me. No nicknames. How about first names? What do ya say?" Jack was a great guy and a fast talker. Years ago, he and the Admiral served on the same SEAL team for a short stint. It may have been long ago, but they were still brothers in arms.

"Jack, this is my partner, Mr. Andrew Denney."

"Andrew, it's great to meet you. Your name precedes you in this town. I think I am the only unlucky politician that hasn't benefited from your generosity." Jack chuckled as he shook Andrew's hand. It was a slight jab and an attempt to secure a campaign donation.

Andrew took no offense to the comment. It was how D.C. worked. "Consider yourself lucky, Jack. Everyone I've given money to has sold their souls to the devil." Andrew shot back. It was perfect.

The three sat down and made small talk as they ordered drinks and food. Eugene and Jack shared updates about their families and Jack inquired into Andrew's family, albeit lightly. He clearly remembered the tragic suicide of Andrew's son, Don.

After the small talk, Jack cut to the point. "Gents, I appreciate the casual chatter, but I am presuming you didn't invite me here to discuss my family. What can I help you with?" The line was textbook Congressman. Given their term is two years, a congressman is always campaigning, always trying to help, and always seeking donations.

"Well, Jack," the Admiral responded. "I'm glad you asked. We've started a security firm. I'm overseeing it. There is nothing that will get us sideways, ethically or otherwise. We are looking to help allies, like Ukraine, with efforts that, due to U.S. law, limit overt governmental endorsement. On a positive note, our company mitigates governmental risk as well."

It was perhaps the last thing Jack thought he'd hear from Eugene, especially after the NISSASSA issue exploded a year ago. And if it was surprising from Eugene, it was an utter shock to learn Andrew was financing the effort, given his son's involvement in NISSASSA. "You're pulling my leg, correct?"

Andrew's face showed no comical look. "No. We are serious. And, Jack, I have a campaign contribution for you. Should you help us, my contribution will put others to shame."

Jack wiped his face with his napkin. The bruschetta appetizer was amazingly tasty, but not the easiest to eat. "Well, I admit, such comments get my attention."

"Jack," the Admiral chimed in. "This isn't NISSASSA. I cannot go into details here, for obvious reasons, but know this. I have placed boundaries on our operations. Given our history, I'd like to believe you'd be supportive of our efforts once you learn these limits."

"OK, Squirts," Jack replied. "How far along are you?"

The Admiral looked Jack in the eyes and said just one word. "Operational."

Jack nodded in interest. "Anything of interest."

"Yes, a very successful Russian sniper recently was forced to plead his case to Saint Peter."

Jack nodded again. It was farther than the Admiral wished to talk in an open forum, but money was on the line. Jack spoke. "Have you discussed your efforts with the acting Defense Secretary or with SOCOM? Squirts, you have a good relationship with General Etcher. I'm sure he'd listen to you."

The Admiral's relationship with Etcher was good. But Eugene had already cashed a large check with the effort in Kosovo. He was hoping to avoid going to that well another time. "Yes, I do, but we are in D.C. right now, and you're a far closer target than he is." The Admiral smiled, as did Jack. It was true, with a hint of humorous military jargon.

"Gents. I'm not saying no, and I'm not saying yes. Any chance you can meet in my office this evening with a few of the Congressional members I'd like to invite? Congress is a massive beast, and nothing gets done by a lone member. I'll need support."

The two nodded. "Deal," Andrew said. "We will be there."

Jack was satisfied. "Good. I think we can get some traction. Ukraine is a popular topic. Just need to be clean on how all this works." The main course was being placed on the table as Jack finished his comments. "Now, let's eat. I'm starving. And Andrew, please don't forget that check. A Congressman cannot live on bread and water alone." They all smiled. It was D.C., after all.

## *Chapter Twenty-Four*
# Lights, Camera, Action

The famed entertainment lawyer, Matt Yospe, ESQ, sent out an email to the main media stations. It was midafternoon and one of his clients would be making a bombshell statement. Matt was not cheap, but he was one of a very few attorneys who could rapidly cast a large net and ensure all the right fish were ensnared. Nearly every mainstream media news outlet showed. Some of the smaller outlets promised to go live. The larger ones were there, but producers were not convinced the story was worth interrupting the already scheduled programming. They would be proved wrong, but in fairness, it wasn't their fault. For such situations, Matt would normally hint at the topic or share some juicy bits of info to maximize exposure. This time, Matt was as tight-lipped as it got, just like his client demanded.

It took Lance four attempts to secure Matt as legal counsel. Eventually, after wiring a substantial amount of money, Matt returned Lance's call, and he was happy he did. Lance, however, had substantial demands, all of which Matt promised to fulfill, once he learned Rachel's story.

The tower of microphones stood over the podium, and as Matt walked out, camera lights shot up. "Ladies, gentlemen. I am grateful you chose to be here and accept my invitation. My client, Ms. Rachel Benson, has a statement which will be followed by a release of a video which is only for your producers. You will all sign agreements. The video will NOT be shown to the public. You can see it, you can describe it, but the actual video will not be made public. Do you understand?"

Like a gopher infested field, heads in the audience bobbed up and down.

"Great, OK, Rachel, please come out."

From behind a screen, an attractive, yet scared woman emerged. "Folks, this is my client. Ms. Rachel Benson, who works as a government employee at the White House as a culinary expert and dietician for the President. This is her statement. There will be no questions."

Matt turned his attention to Rachel. "OK, Rachel, it's time." He was gentle and supportive.

Rachel stepped to the microphone and pulled out a piece of paper. She'd read it as written. "My name is Rachel Benson. I have worked at the White House for the past two and a half years. During my employment, I was approached by the President and seduced by him into a long-term romance, lasting well over a year." Gasps from the crowd went up and still camera flashes exploded across the room. Reporters for the large media outlets were texting as fast as they could to producers to interrupt broadcasting.

"Roughly six months ago, former Defense Secretary Gerzema confessed at an attempt to create a deep fake video that would embarrass the President. His statement was a lie, and the video he was referencing is real. It is a video of the President and I having..." She paused, almost sobbing at his point. She would change the words 'having sex,' to, "making love in the White House private residence. I am coming forward now, as an attempt against my life was made by what I believe to be U.S. government agents trying to silence me. My house was shot up by federal agents. I fear for my daughter's life and my life." Rachel broke down, and Matt was there to hold her, sideways in his arm, like a supporting father.

She was done. Questions were shouted and Matt waved them off. Rachel was shuffled back behind the curtain as Matt turned back towards the microphones. "I have put Ms. Benson into a private hiding program. I'd ask you not to try and find her. Further details will be made available at a later date. The questions you have should be submitted in writing to my office. Good day."

The news broke like wildfire across the globe, on television, radio, the internet and social media. The President, at the time of the announcement, was standing in a small farm field in Maryland on the outskirts of the National Capital Region. He was touting one of his prized small business programs for farmers. It was supposed to be a vanilla event until the media exploded. Steve, standing off to the side, watched the President speak while looking down at his phone. His face grew white as a ghost. *'That son of a bitch'* he thought to himself. *'He's been fucking her this whole time.'*

Steve tried to rush up to the President and swoop him away with 'urgent Executive Branch issues,' but the press corps phones were also exploding. The questions rapidly shifted from farming to infidelity.

"Mr. President, does the First Lady know of your affair?"

"Mr. President, are you in love with your personal chef?"

"Mr. President, how long has this relationship been going on?"

"Mr. President, is this your only affair?"

The questions shot out in rapid fire, far faster than the President could answer. He now faced a potential career ending scandal.

He froze, attempting to ask reporters where such outlandish claims were originating from.

Eventually, Secret Service and Steve shoved him into The Beast and the car drove away. Video of this also splashed across every media outlet. It was clearly the President's darkest hour.

"Steve," he said once in the Presidential limo, "What the fuck happened?"

It was just the two of them in the back of the limo and the soundproof wall was raised. Steve let loose. "Sir! You've been fucking her this whole time! Haven't you!? Every 'oh, let me talk to her alone' was a bullshit excuse to pound your cook? Are you Fucking God Damn stupid? For Christ's sake!"

The President sat there, about as alone as he had ever been. His limousine was driving to the White House, where he would have to face his faithful wife of thirty-two years. Would she kick him out, he wondered? Was that even possible in the White House? He didn't know. It was all uncharted waters.

Every media outlet was signing waiver forms, committing to not releasing the sex video, and should they broadcast it, the fine was a staggering ten million dollars. Few even considered sharing the contract with their legal department. They wanted that video... immediately.

Over the next few hours, political pundits from the President's party conjured up excuses. They'd attack both

Rachel's and Matt's character, doing whatever they could to mitigate the damage. Pundits from the other party tasted blood in the political waters and seized on it. This was a political gift from heaven, and they'd not let it silently pass by. The polarized broadcasting would last well into the night.

In the sparsely filled Trusty's Restaurant on the corner of Pennsylvania Ave and 14th Street Southeast, Lance and Ambassador Tarlov sat at the bar. Trusty's was a perfect location. A neighborhood dive bar, far enough from the 'be seen' locales of the Capital. There, they watched the breaking news unravel. Their staff were pushing direct messages and emails as fast as they could. As if by magic, Russian bots were leveraging social media protocols to boost the circulation. There was nothing U.S. Cyber Command could do to prevent it. The optics of suppressing such a scandalous news story had far worse implications than the story itself.

The President arrived back at the White House and slowly walked up the stairs to his private residence, dreading the discussion he'd have with his wife. Luckily, he wouldn't have to worry about it. She had taken a suitcase and departed with her security detail. The First Lady was on her way to Camp David. *'She would be safe there, at least,'* he thought. The President collapsed in his bed.

Downstairs, on Steve's desk, was a plain envelope, right on top and in the middle. He opened it. The letter was from the law firm of Matt Yospe, ESQ. It was both a resignation letter from Rachel as well as a notification that both Steve and the President could be subpoenaed at any time, and a demand they not destroy any evidence pertaining to a potential case of sexual harassment as well as sexual assault. Steve fell back into his chair. *'What a fucking day,'* he thought.

\*\*\*\*\*\*\*\*\*\*\*\*\*\*\*\*\*\*\*

Three miles from the White House, Ukrainian Ambassador Ubyivovk grew quite concerned over the news about the

President. American support for the Ukrainian war effort was vital, and a media circus like this could easily disrupt the momentum Ukraine had made. A phone call from Kyiv arrived as he sat in his office. It appeared officials back in the homeland shared his fears. A directive was placed on the Ambassador, and he would fill it. Ambassador Ubyivovk picked up the business card left by Andrew and called.

"Mr. Denney. It's Ambassador Ubyivovk. Can you come to my office tonight? I have a job for you."

"Ambassador, please hold on." Andrew covered the phone. He and the Admiral were in a cab on the way to the Capitol building to meet with Jack and other Congressional members. "Eugene. It's the Ukrainian Ambassador. He has a job for us."

The Admiral didn't think twice. "Driver, change of plans. Georgetown. I'll get you an address in a second."

Andrew uncovered the phone. "Ambassador, we will be there in a half hour."

"Perfect. I look forward to it."

The Admiral quickly dialed another number. "Jack. Hey, Squirts here. We have a small issue and need to reschedule. I greatly apologize but let me get back to you tomorrow or later this week."

"Squirts. No worries. All of us are waiting around for a midnight vote and are glued to televisions, watching the demise of the President. Tell Andrew he still owes me a check." Jack snickered at the end of the statement. It was a joke, with significant overtones of truth slathered into it.

· "I will. Thanks for understanding. Yes, it seems our President has really put his foot in it this time," Admiral Hersey said.

"Eh, I'm not sure it was his foot," Jack said, chuckling again at his humor. "Take care, Squirts. Catch ya later."

The Admiral hung up and looked at his companion. "Andrew. I think this thing with the President has changed the game."

Andrew was slowly nodding. "I agree. I don't see him surviving this. He's fucked. What do we know of Crawford? Will she be supportive?" Andrew was referring to Vice President Stacy Crawford.

Admiral Hershey had never really given it much thought as to Stacy assuming the U.S. helm. During his time as Chairman, the two had an excellent working relationship at the Pentagon. Eugene was aware of Stacy's occasional frustrations on an overly cautious administration. This also extended to the support for Ukraine, but would that be enough for her to support The Valyrian Group? He didn't know.

The cab pulled up to the Ukrainian Embassy, and a staffer was there waiting to escort them in. There'd be no waiting this time, and the Ambassador was standing in the lobby ready to greet them. All the signals were clear. There was business to be done.

"Gentlemen. Congratulations, Kyiv has a mission and would like to know your cost."

"Great," the Admiral said. "I'm all ears."

"There is a decent sized rail yard in a town called Izvaryne, near the Russian border of our Luhansk Oblast. It is where Russia is staging the vast majority of their logistics supplies. We want the tracks destroyed, and all existing cars there destroyed as well."

Andrew would do no calculations. "Ten million dollars."

The Ambassador chuckled. "Andrew. Please, do not insult me. That sum of money is foolish."

"Mr. Ambassador, eight hours ago when we originally met, that sum was foolish. The landscape has changed. If I were Kyiv, I'd have great concern about the current status of the United States' domestic issues overshadowing international efforts. It's why you called us. Ten million is roughly the same cost as three Patriot PAC 3 missiles. Last night, Ukraine launched over a dozen at incoming threats. If you want this facility destroyed, the price is fair."

The Ambassador had no real response. It was three times the amount that Kyiv authorized him to spend. He also knew there would be no budging Andrew.

"Please, let me make a call." The Ambassador made the call right in front of them. He spoke in Ukrainian, and it was clear the other party was not pleased with the number. Eventually, he hung up. "We have a deal."

Andrew and the Ambassador worked out payment arrangements. Part, of course, would need to be up front.

During the discussion, the Admiral pulled out his smart phone and Googled Izvaryne. The town was small and dominated by its rail yard. It was also quite deep into the heart of Russian-held territory. Most of the town was north of the rail yard, with just a few buildings to the south. It appeared to have eight parallel tracks in the yard, each funneling down to entry / exits to the west and east. The overhead imagery in Google showed the tracks abandoned, but Andrew was certain it would be well protected. For any further analysis, current satellite imagery would be required.

The Ambassador and Andrew shook hands on the deal as they stood up. Of the ten million received, at least a quarter of that would be needed for the mission. Andrew and Eugene had long ago made an agreement there would be no shortchanging mission requirements, especially funding.

Later that night, the Admiral sent a secure email via the Defense Department's 'Drop Box' to Rob Farkas, the CEO of PLUSOps in Warsaw. The program was a somewhat secure means to transfer files across the internet. It wasn't the most secure system, but it would be enough.

Rob received the files, printed them off, and hopped into his car. He would personally deliver the target package to Smitty on Base Uniform.

Smitty was about ready to fall asleep in his quarters. The entire team was given individual staterooms, nice ones, especially for Poland. A knock at his door and a file slid under it. Smitty slowly got up and grabbed the packet, then opened the door. He saw Rob's vehicle slowly driving away. Smitty wasn't sure why Rob didn't stick around. Perhaps Rob had seen too many spy movies.

Smitty opened the package and read the mission directive. He grinned, and oddly, his saliva glands grew active. A note from the Admiral accompanied the package,

*'Funding secured, $10M. This is a paid mission. No skimping. Tell us what you need.*
*Stay Safe, Squirts'*

Smitty cleared his table and began planning, alone. The next morning, Beef and JT knocked on his door for the morning run and work out. Smitty answered, still awake and planning. He looked like a wreck, pulling the two into his room. After sharing the packet, the three began planning together, supporting some ideas and criticizing others. There would be no hurt feelings from critical comments. This wasn't a business strategy. It was potentially life and death. Every detail had to be right.

## *Chapter Twenty-Five*
# The Morning After

The next morning, the President walked calmly downstairs from his residence into the working part of the White House. As he passed staffers, some awkwardly nodded, offering a resemblance of support. Others could barely look at him.

He continued towards the Oval Office, greeting Steve as he passed.

"Good morning, Mr. President," Steve responded, as he always did. The President thought to himself, '*It was at least a step.*'

"Steve, please come into my office when you have a second."

Steve put down his paperwork, slowly arose, and walked behind the President into the Oval Office. There was no point in delaying the inevitable.

"Steve, close the door." He did as instructed and remained silent. It was not his turn to speak. "Yes, the affair is legitimate," the president continued. "I was stupid and I'm embarrassed, but now we need to perform damage control. Christ, Clinton survived a freaking blow job in the Oval Office. I can survive this. I know I can. I need you to get me the best damn PR firm in D.C. and secure private counsel."

Steve was furious, but anger and rage will get one nowhere in Washington. And the President was right. None of them were perfect, some were more imperfect than others. Steve also could sense the President was up for the fight. At least he was not giving up. And if the President didn't give up, neither would Steve. "OK, Sir. Will do."

There was a knock on the Oval Office door. "Come in," the President directed.

The door opened, and it was Vice President Crawford. "Stacy, please, come in."

"Sir, you wanted to see me?" She asked awkwardly, as such meetings rarely took place, especially after such publicly salacious and damaging information.

"Yes, please, sit down."

The two sat on the opposing sofas. As she sat down, Stacy wondered if one or both of the sofas had been props for the President's frolics. She was also fairly confident he wasn't the first President to indulge in such activities.

"Stacy, I need to know your thoughts on this information about the affair."

Stacy looked at him for a bit. "Mr. President, I guess my first thought is that I'm curious if it's true?"

"It is, but let's spare the details, please. You should know, I have no intention of rolling over. Someone put Rachel up to coming out, and to me, that's far more concerning than the affair. Someone is meddling with the U.S. government at the highest levels, and we need to be concerned."

"Sir, I am your Vice President. You hired me to do a job and I will. You hired me to support your agenda, and I will. I think it is best, however, if we refrain from any discussion regarding my personal feelings about you or deflecting the issue of the affair towards some nefarious actor's grand strategy."

The President wasn't pleased with her answer, but there was little he could do. After such a recent hire, dismissing her as his VP would be suicide, especially facing an affair. "Well, I see," he commented, searching for more words.

"Mr. President, if I may," Stacy Offered. "I plan to keep up my efforts as the Vice President. Should I be asked about the affair, I will simply respond that's an Oval Office issue. I will not comment on it. Do you and Steve support this course of action?"

Both Steve and the President nodded at each other. There was some disappointment that the Vice President wouldn't cheerlead for the President. But they took solace in knowing she would not be a loose cannon. It was a fair trade.

"Yes, Stacy. That's fair, and thanks for stopping by. I appreciate it."

"Mr. President, since I am here, there are some other items I'd like to discuss, if you…"

The President cut her off. "Stacy, I hate to admit this, but we are in a bit of crisis mode here. I don't have time right now for other issues. You made it clear you don't want to help bail out the boat, and I accept that. But at this moment, that is my task, and I can't stop bailing out the boat."

Stacy nodded, albeit frustrated with his answer. Prior to accepting the job, the President had assured her that she'd have a strong portfolio. That she would assume ownership of key issues for the administration. Until this point, that proved to be false. Now, when he needed her for a key issue, it wasn't for policy or platform, it was to save his sinking ship. She had no intent to jump in and bail. "Yes, Mr. President. I understand. Will that be all?" she tersely said while gently glaring at him.

"Yes. Thanks." The President responded, begrudgingly.

Stacy walked out of the office as Steve prepared to search for an attorney. Just then, the President's secretary knocked on the open door and said, "Mr. President, Secretary Baker is on the line, and claims it is fairly important."

Marleen Baker would also be disappointed by the President's actions, but she was a long time Washington politico. She'd seen this rodeo before. More importantly, Marleen knew the President's concerns about nefarious actors had merit based on the information she intended to share.

Steve stood up and pressed a few buttons on the President's desk phone. Immediately, Secretary Baker was on the line. "Madam Secretary, Steve here, you are on speakerphone with the President."

"Mr. President, I apologize for the intrusion, but I felt you'd want to know this information immediately. Our staff received a phone call from Ambassador Tarlov. In the course of the discussion, he intimated he had some information that would be beneficial to your administration. Specifically, he claims to know who encouraged your cook, er, uh, Rachel, to go public."

Steve couldn't retain himself. "For fuck's sake. Of course he does. It's his people!"

The President gestured for Steve to calm down with his hand, a communication kept hidden from Marleen. "Marleen, say nothing of the interruption, and you're right. This clearly is something of a priority for us right now. Thanks for sharing it. Did Ambassador Tarlov share anything further?"

"Sir, he claims he wants to meet with you, but I strongly urge you not to do so."

"I'll meet him. Alone. In my office." The President responded rather hastily. Of the three, he was the only one who knew the sex tape that had caused him such grave trouble over the past year was the product of Ambassador Tarlov.

Steve glared at the President, clearly indicating his disapproval for such a meeting. He would, however, remain silent.

Secretary Baker also knew better than to challenge the President. She had offered her best advice. He declined.

"Yes Sir. I'll work with Steve to get him on your schedule."

The President responded. "Today. Thanks, Marleen. We must go now."

Steve's eyebrows raised, but again, he didn't say a word.

The phone line went dead.

"Sir, if there is nothing else?" Steve offered.

"No. Please ensure Tarlov is in my office today," the President responded.

Steve departed the Oval Office for his own. There was much work to be done.

*********************

As Buck sat in Poland, things were far less stressful. To this point, he'd made six supply runs into Ukraine and Old Girl was performing perfectly. Additionally, intelligence reports suggested Russian S300 and S400 surface-to-air missile systems were being destroyed by Ukrainian forces.

The second glider was now also finished. Buck performed all the compulsory flight tests, just as he had on Old Girl. She was just as good, albeit nameless.

Later that afternoon, Buck was relaxing out front of the hangar, soaking up some of the midday sun. Rob Farkas' SUV slowly approached, then parked. The passenger door opened, and someone jumped out. Buck immediately recognized him.

"Jughead!" He shouted.

"Buck, you ugly fucker. How are you?"

"Never better buddy. Thanks for taking the job."

"Hell, thanks for offering it. If I had to fly one more MD11 ferry flight for FedEx, I was gonna slit my wrists. From what you discussed, your missions sound far more intriguing. And the pay is exactly what I'm looking for. Short duration flights, plenty of risk, and even more pay."

Jughead's real name was John Souza. Any other military aviator with such a name would have been a shoo-in for the nickname, 'Philip' following the famed D.C. composer. Given John didn't end up with Philip was a testament to how horrifically dis-proportioned his nogging was, hence, the name Jughead. Jughead had flown EA-6B Prowlers for years, and then transitioned to commercial aviation. He met Buck years ago at an FAA flying convention and the two hit it off. Both had a passion for aviation that extended far beyond commercial pilots, and both missed their respective days in the military.

"Love it, buddy. Let me introduce you to your aircraft," Buck said.

"What? You're shitting me? I have my own aircraft? What is this? World War II?"

"Close," Buck responded. "Follow me."

Jughead was introduced to his aircraft, and on the other side of the hangar, Smitty and his team were rehearsing their next mission. It wouldn't be long before they'd execute their challenging and dangerous effort.

## Chapter Twenty-Six
# Deals with Devils & Ugly Bed Fellows

Ambassador Tarlov arrived punctually at the White House. This time, there'd be no casually late intent. His unspoken messaging was clear. Tarlov had been awaiting this meeting for quite some time. He walked through the White House security scanners and was patted down. Regardless of his diplomatic status, little trust remained at this point in the ambassador.

Steve escorted Ambassador Tarlov into the Oval Office. The President stood there, alone. Motionless, he gazed out at the Rose Garden. It was far from beautiful. There were no flowers to be seen. The rose stems stood empty, with barely a hint of leaves and only the slightest indication of buds.

The President heard the door close and could sense the ambassador was in the room. "Well, Tarlov. It's an impressive play. I gotta hand it to you."

"Mr. President, I don't know what you speak of. Nor do I know what eavesdropping technology you have in this room. Please don't play me for a fool."

"Fair enough, Tarlov. Let's walk."

"No, Mr. President, not until I pat you down like your gorillas did to me."

It was humiliating, but the President indulged him. After the vigorous pat down, the two stepped out of the office and began walking through the rose garden.

"OK, Tarlov. You have my attention. What do you want?"

"Mr. President, I have the entire world's attention now. As for desire, my nation's requests haven't changed. We want you out of Ukraine. No more military support."

The President had expected such a request. Tarlov had been interviewed by many press outlets. Aside from his disingenuous shock and surprise over the Rachel affair, Tarlov was adamant the U.S. should mind its own business. Specifically, it should not meddle in Russia's affairs in Ukraine.

"You and I know that is political suicide. I can't just stop supporting Ukraine. You must give me something."

"OK, Mr. President, I'm listening." Tarlov was pleasantly surprised the President was at least contemplating an end to Ukraine support.

"My request is simple. I want Victor Petrov extradited to the U.S. and to stand trial for the assassination of Vice President Banks. If Russia does that, I can shape a narrative the U.S. and Russia are mending relations and cooperating. In conjunction with a guilty verdict, I believe I can convince NATO as well as the American public that support for Ukraine is no longer warranted."

"Mr. President, what you ask, I cannot deliver. Mr. Petrov is a private citizen with strong ties. We both know he is not an operative of the Russian Government. He works for a private firm. I need something else."

The President gently bit his lip. Every nation in the world knew Petrov was an FSB operative. To claim he wasn't an operative was an outright lie. Unfortunately, Petrov was the only card the President felt he could play. He didn't have anything else to offer. Then the President realized, he actually did.

"What if I told you there is a U.S. private mercenary group fighting in Ukraine? And I can give you the contact information. Think of it as a good faith offer."

The Ambassador grew interested. "This organization, is it sponsored and paid for by the U.S. Government? If so, the deal is off."

"No. It is not. In fact, I told them to walk when they approached me for money. And I know this. It was their guy that took the shot on your somewhat famous sniper."

The Ambassador wasted no more time. "Give me their names and I will inquire about Petrov to the Kremlin."

"OK. But the other issue is that video never sees the light of day. Understand.?"

"What video, Mr. President?" Tarlov said smiling. He had waited months to deliver this line. "I thought it was a deep fake?"

The President ignored it. "Deal, or no Deal?"

"Deal," Tarlov responded.

"One last question," the President couldn't help himself. "Where is Rachel?"

Tarlov smiled. "Mr. President. You must learn to let women go when you are done with them. If I were to guess, I would suspect she is safe for now. But I do not believe you will ever see her again. I'd strongly advise you to stop asking such questions. They'll only lead to more trouble."

There would be no polite coffee or small talk. The President had Tarlov ushered off the grounds once the discussion was over. As promised, the President provided Tarlov the Admirals and Andrews phone numbers, as well as all the information he had on The Valyrian Group. For political survival, the President just sold out one of his largest donors and his former Joint Chief. He didn't think twice about it.

Within hours, Tarlov had bugs crawling all over The Valyrian Group's communication systems. Russian GRU spies were also pulled off less important targets to follow the Admiral and Andrew. It was only a matter of time before they would learn about Smitty and Buck's efforts in Ukraine.

## Chapter Twenty-Seven
# Movin' Out

Smitty, Beef, JT, and Marko packed up their vehicle and would soon be heading into the jaws of the Russian military. As they packed up, Jackal sat alone, watching. He would not be part of this mission. Smitty had made the decision, much to Jackal's protests. Mission requirements did not call for a sniper, and Smitty saw no reason to expose Jackal to danger. After packing, Jackal man hugged each. He desperately wanted to be on the mission.

As their up armored Land Rover pulled out of the base, Jackal watched them depart, waving his hand with an odd sense of guilt. The vehicle was loaded down with weapons, ammo, and detonators. For explosives, the team had come up with an ingenious plan.

Marko had called ahead to ensure Ukrainian military checkpoints would not be a problem. With ease, the vehicle proceeded eastward. Once they were within forty miles of the eastern front, Beef drove the vehicle off the highway, following Marko's instructions towards an old farmhouse. Slowly they approached, as an elderly Ukrainian farmer stood outside. He looked weathered but strong. Gray hair, but in fairly good shape. As the vehicle came to a stop, Marko jumped out and hugged the man. The team would soon be introduced to Marko's uncle, Symon.

Symon swung open the barn door. Inside was a BTR-80 Russian armored personnel carrier that had been abandoned when Ukraine thwarted Russia's first attacks on Kyiv. Next to it was a large, old flatbed truck, loaded down with what appeared to be bags of grain or seed. It was exactly what Smitty had asked for.

Smitty walked over to Symon and unfolded a large wad of bills. Marko acted as the interpreter and the deal was struck. Soon, the Land Rover, along with their two newly acquired vehicles, would depart the farm. The small convoy moved cautiously towards the Ukrainian brigade headquarters near the front line. The drive would take less than an hour.

Again, Marko provided directions and slowly, the three vehicles approached a well-armed checkpoint. JT drew the short straw and was driving the Russian BTR-80. He was the most uncomfortable in the bunch, for obvious reasons. Even though the BTR's Russian 'Z' symbol was painted over, the vehicle stood out like a sore thumb on the Ukrainian side of the battle line.

After a brief exchange between Colonel Marko Taran and the gate guard, the three vehicles lumbered forward and entered the compound.

As they approached the parking lot, a large, stocky man stood out to greet them. His uniform was somewhat disheveled, a common trait for military members in field conditions. "Marko!" he belted out as if he had the lungs of an opera singer.

"General Khmeleva!" Marko returned as he saluted. The two shook hands heartily, like old friends.

The General had noticed the other vehicles arrive. "What is this, Marko? You bring me a Russian BTR-80? It is a gift?"

Marko smiled. "General, it is only a small part of our gift for you. We came on orders from Kyiv. It is a special mission that we must brief you about. My friends here are former Special Forces from the United States. They now work for a private military company, and we have a plan to make your life much better."

The general was intrigued. "Please. Let's discuss it in my tent."

Within a few minutes, the group was in the general's tent and Smitty was explaining the entire plan on a large map. After a few questions, the general was satisfied and loved the plan. He told his operations officer immediately to hand deliver slips of paper to their front-line forces. There would be no electronic communications about this mission on the radio. It was too important to risk. The general stood up from the table. His English wasn't great, but understandable. "Tonight," he said "We feast. Tomorrow, we fight!"

The few Ukrainian staff officers standing in the tent clapped and pounded the table. Smitty and the others followed, somewhat out of peer pressure.  Clearly, the Ukrainian morale at the front line was high.

As the meal was prepared, Smitty stepped out of the tent. He unpacked a burner phone from his pack, inserted a temporary SIM card, and placed a call.  "Admiral," he said. "Good afternoon."

"Good to hear from you," the Admiral replied; avoiding using Smitty's name.

"Sir, everything is a go for tomorrow.  I'll be comm out for about three days."

"Copy.  God Speed, my friend.  And good luck."

"Yes, Sir.  Out here."  Smitty hung up the phone, pulled the SIM card, and destroyed both.  The call lasted less than a minute.

Thousands of miles away, sitting in the Russian embassy of Washington, a young Russian intelligence officer transcribed the entire conversation.  While the call was too short for pinpointing an exact location, the cellular tower, which the call originated from, was easily located.  The mere presence of English being spoken that close to the front was high priority intelligence.  The Russians were getting closer, thanks to a president fighting for his political life.

********************

At Dulles Washington airport, Curt stood next to Allison outside their car in the departure flights drop off area.  He was excited about the journey but tried desperately to contain the excitement in front of Allison.

"I will miss you," he said as he held her tightly as cars, taxis and buses whizzed by.  "Us too," she said with a pause, then continued.  "Curt, please.  Stay safe.  Noorullah, Bo and I need you."

Curt hugged her tight.  "Sweetheart.  You three are my world. I will stay safe.  I promise, I won't cut myself with a scalpel, which is perhaps the greatest danger I face on this mission."

His joke made Allison crack a smile. She also knew there was risk, of some sort, that Curt may face. She just wasn't sure what it would be.

"Remember, you promised. Nothing risky. We need you, Curt. More than Ukraine."

"I know. I know. I promise," he again committed.

They hugged one last time and Allison watched Curt walk into the airport, standing there as a tear fell down her cheek. She wanted to believe his promise but never forgot the words of her father months ago. The man she married was an adventurist. Attempting to contain him was a fool's errand. She prayed Curt would stay safe, no matter what he did.

Curt's departure out of Washington was uneventful, and he unsuccessfully tried to sleep through the night. It was useless. Even seated, his adrenaline was pumping. He'd finally broken free from the chains of a desk job and again would be in the operational world.

After a brief layover in Frankfurt, Curt caught the second leg of his journey onto Warsaw, Poland, where he'd meet up with Rob Farkas. The Admiral and Andrew had agreed, having Curt in theater was far more beneficial than having him in Washington. Working in a field hospital in Poland would provide some revenue for The Valeryan Group, but it was far from the underlying reason they sent him. Should a need arise for his skills on a combat mission, there was hope Smitty could convince Curt to go. None of this, however, was shared with Curt. As far as he knew, he'd be merely performing life-saving medical treatment in field conditions.

*********************

Curt's plane slowly descended out of the sky towards Warsaw International Airport. At the same time, Smitty's team was loading up their three vehicles and prepared to start the shaping phase of their operation. The first phase of the mission was crucial.

Roughly two kilometers away back from the line of contact, the three vehicles were staged, ready to go. Marko made the first call on a Ukrainian radio channel. In a frantic voice, he screamed, "The Russian pigs have stolen our grain, and the pigs are escorting it with a BTR-80!"

As expected, the once silent radio channel cracked to life. Numerous transmissions began breaking the silence of the Ukrainian military radios, demanding to know where and how. Then, as scripted, the General transmitted. "This is General Khmeleva! If you see these vehicles, shoot to kill!"

On the other side of the battle line, Russian eavesdroppers heard everything. With every transmission, they grew more and more excited, immediately reporting the situation up the chain of command.

The time had come. Marko was dressed in a shabby Russian military uniform taken from a war prisoner. The others were oddly dressed in New Zealand military uniforms as per the plan. They began driving towards the line of contact. Again, as scripted, gunfire erupted from the Ukrainian Army, but not one round would hit the convoy. As directed by the paper notes sent by Gen Khmeleva the day prior, all Ukrainian units were to merely 'fire for effect' and intentionally miss the vehicles.

Simultaneously, JT manning the BTR-80 gun would fire aimlessly back towards the Ukrainians.

After five harrowing minutes, the three vehicles were on the Russian side and speeding towards the Russian line of contact. Marko changed radio frequencies and in his best Russian accent was chanting proudly of his conquest and begging them not to shoot.

Soon, the convoy was flagged down by a squad of Russian soldiers. If there was a critical moment of the plan, it was now.

Marko jumped out of the BTR-80 with his hands up, but also with a smile and a sense of excitement. In Russian, he kept screaming, "We did it! We did it! We stole from those Ukrainian Nazis!"

Eventually, a young Russian soldier was able to calm him down. "Keep your hands up," he commanded, pointing his gun at Marko. "What did you steal?"

"Look! Look here! We recovered a BTR-80, and we also stole a large amount of seed and fertilizer. We can now plant crops in our recovered lands and the money will go to Mother Russia!"

The Russian soldiers evaluated the cargo. Marko's comments checked out. "And who are these men? Why are they with you?" The other men, also pulled from the vehicles were on their knees, heads down, with their hands in the air.

Marko turned and saw them face down, "NO!" he screamed in Russian. "Let them up! These are privately funded mercenaries from New Zealand. They were hired on a Top Secret directly from Moscow to perform infiltration special operation missions!"

The lead Russian soldier was not convinced. "Where are their papers?" he asked. Because in Russia, there were always papers.

Marko paused and stared at the young soldier with glaring eyes. "Soldier, let me ask you this. Should we just take back the BTR-80 and the seed? These men risked their lives for Mother Russia, and this is how you repay them? Enough with you! Where is your commander?"

As those comments sank into the young soldier's skull, another Russian vehicle came racing towards them. A captain, the company commander, jumped out of the vehicle and demanded to know what was going on. The young soldier, clearly fearful of his superior officer, stuttered and stumbled as he provided recent accounts.

The captain then looked at Marko. "Who do you work for?" The captain demanded. Marko looked at him and without blinking, responded. "Rasputin Firm." The firm was one of the most well-known mercenary organizations in Russia. They had been active for years in Africa and Syria, performing numerous missions in support of Russian interests. The name maintained historic ties to the famed Russian historic figure, Rasputin, who, ironically as a non-state actor, was able to wield significant influence over the Russian Empire. The name Rasputin Firm also resonated with others, given the initials of the company 'RF' mirrored that of the Russian Federation. Russians loved the coincidence. Rasputin Firm's global reach was impressive.

Secretly, they also employed Victor Petrov, the man who recently assassinated U.S. Vice President Steven Banks.

The captain looked at the others on the ground. "And these men?"

"Also, Rasputin Firm." Marko slowly withdrew papers from inside his flak vest and passed them to the captain. They were exceptional forgeries based on previously acquired Rasputin Firm documents from a CIA raid in Syria. Marko continued, "And I will tell you this. We paid a hefty price to get them from New Zealand. We needed native English speakers in order to infiltrate Ukrainian forces. New Zealand was about the only nation where we could get them. Harming these men will come with consequences. Killing them will come with a prison term." Marko's comments were perfect. Much like everything in Russia, military command structures decisions were often based on fear and repercussions from higher command. Militarily, the fear was partly based on reality. Stories of soldiers being punished for wrong decisions permeated Russian forces structures, especially across the lower ranks. Over time, some of such stories were amplified into near folklore, much like any long-told military story.

"OK," the captain said, "Get the vehicles, round up the men, and let's go back to the battalion."

"Captain," Marko said. "I have two requests. First what is your name, and second, do you mind if I make a phone call? My leadership wanted to know how our mission went, and I'd like to tell them we've made it across the line of contact but are being held up by you."

"What do you mean by held up?" the captain responded, refusing to provide his name, especially considering it could be reported adversely to a senior command.

"Captain, we are on a tight timeline. The seed must be planted immediately, and the fertilizer needs to get processed. Frankly, the BTR-80 was luck. The Ukrainian Nazis left it unattended. We don't want it. If you do, it's yours. Do what you wish with it. But I implore you, either let me call my leadership or let us continue on our mission." Marko paused and closely watched the Russian captain attempt to process the information. He then continued, "Look comrade, you seem like a very good officer, and I'd hate to see anything derogatory happen because you held up this special mission. You are clearly a great captain, entrusted to be on the front line of our best units, fighting for Mother Russia."

Between fears of retribution and flattery, the captain folded. He was just offered a BTR-80 of great value. All he had to do was let this mission continue. His battalion commander would surely be pleased. In the back of his mind; however, he also began calculating how much he could fetch on the black market for such an item. Corruption was commonplace in the Russian military, and this captain was as common as they came.

"Let them up," the captain ordered. Smitty, Beef, and JT stood and brushed the dirt and grass from their Kiwi uniforms. "You say I can have the BTR-80, for free. Correct?"

Marko was close to victory. "Captain. I am giving it to you because you are the highest-ranking officer at this location. It is intended for Mother Russia to be victorious in this fight against the pigs of Ukraine. When I get back to my leadership in the Rasputin Firm, I will tell them I handed it over to your unit for immediate use on the front lines. They will be pleased with this."

The captain's eyebrows raised. His name would pass the lips of the Rasputin Group and leadership in Moscow. It was more than he could have dreamed of. A free BTR-80 and his name shared with an organization that paid four times a regular Russian military salary was more than he could imagine. "Sir, I thank you for this gift. Please tell your leadership my name is Captain Dmitry Mazur. And yes, we shall use it for victory. Take your other vehicles and proceed."

As if on command, the officers under Captain Mazur lowered their guns. Marko nodded to his other teammates as they were clueless as to the Russian exchange that just took place. Once the guns were lowered, Smitty and the others nodded to the captain. The nod was far from appreciative, however, and clearly in keeping with that of an angered mercenary for hire.

Slowly, the team pulled away, continuing deeper and deeper into the Russian-occupied territory of Ukraine. As they continued, they saw fewer and fewer Russian forces. Once they were over twenty miles from the front lines, Marko pulled out a cell phone and sent a single word text message to General Khmeleva:

*'Tak' ('Yes' in Ukrainian)*

Within minutes, artillery began raining down on the Russian captain and his team. Unbeknownst to them, a small beacon transmitter affixed to the bottom of the BTR-80 was reporting its exact location to Ukrainian forces.

The captain and others in his company drove the BTR-80 hastily back towards battalion headquarters, deep into the wood lines. As they continued, the transmitter continued to report their location.

Eventually, the artillery ended and the captain finally made it to his battalion headquarters. There, a dozen battalion staff officers came out to see the newly gained war booty. They climbed on it and checked the tires. High fives and chants of victory circulated among the team.

Unbeknownst to the Russian battalion officers, a remote-controlled detonator and claymore charge sat deep in the vehicle hidden in the ammunition bunker. A small unmanned aerial vehicle hovered over the BTR-80 transmitting video of the Russian's activities back to General Khmeleva headquarters. He looked at the drone operator and casually said, "Now."

The operator pressed a button on his control console. A signal transmitted up to the drone, which relayed the command down to the remote detonator. It traveled nearly instantaneously and was a command to activate the detonator.

A massive initial blast threw most of the Russian soldiers from the vehicle. Those not killed instantly would soon be dead as ammunition in the bunker began to cook off, sending large pieces of shrapnel and BTR parts across the area. General Khmeleva smiled and said quietly, "Great work, Marko. God's speed. Slava Ukraine."

## *Chapter Twenty-Eight*
# Homing In

Providing ever so gentle flight inputs to Old Girl, Buck gently landed his glider back onto Polish soil. The flights had become somewhat old hat, and Buck was becoming more and more comfortable with the silence of the radar warning receiver. It was clear Russian air defenses were either unable to target him or unaware of his activities. Either way, Buck was safe and grateful. He loved the mission, and the money was great. After landing, he pulled out his phone and reported back to Admiral Hershey that another run had been successfully flown. Once relayed, payment would soon be processed for The Valeryan Group.

What Buck did not know was that two Russian GRU agents were getting closer. Based on earlier phone intercepts, the two agents had cloned the Polish cellular tower nearest the airfield. In effect, they created their own cellular tower that enabled them to manage any cellular calls transmitted in the area. From their cloned tower, they easily pushed the traffic onto the real tower, all of this oblivious to the user. Not only had they captured Buck's transmission, they also snapped photos of Buck's aircraft, Old Girl, as it was landing. At this point, they weren't certain of Buck's missions, but within days, Russian intelligence would fuse together enough data to figure it out. Unfortunately for Buck, once that happened, it was just a matter of time to concoct a plan to eliminate Old Girl... and Buck.

Orders for more and more logistics flights filled the Valeryan Coffers. Later that night, Jughead would be flying. He'd completed his functional check flights and was growing more and more comfortable with his aircraft. Jughead was walking around his aircraft and double-checking the tie down straps over his large cargo load. As he did, Buck approached.

"Hey Juggie, you ready for tonight?"

"Buck. Hey, didn't see ya there. Yeah. I think so. Just doing some last checks. Trying to keep busy. Haven't flown an aircraft without a real engine for a long time. And never did it in combat."

"You'll be fine. I've made over a half dozen runs. It's cake. Hey, I saw the name on the side of your aircraft. You named it SBD Dauntless II?" I'm lost. The Dauntless was a massive, heavy World War II aircraft, nicknamed 'slow but deadly.'

"Yeah. I know. It's a double entendre. My Dauntless is not 'slow but deadly' rather it's 'silent but deadly,' like the well known acronym 'SBD.' As you know, a glider is silent. Regarding the deadly part, it has to do with my digestion tract. Given our cabins are unpressurized, the gas in my intestines must have expanded to five times its normal volume up in the sky. I must have farted about fifteen times during the functional altitude ceiling flight."

Buck busted out laughing. It was true. For a few of his flights, Buck was grateful he was on supplemental oxygen, as the cabin reeked of his flatulence. "Fair enough. I love it. Try to get some sleep and don't stress. It will be fine."

The sun began to set over the airfield as SBD Dauntless II climbed out behind her tow plane, lumbering slowly up into the sky. Finally at altitude, Jughead said a small prayer and disconnected from the towline. With a gentle bank of the wings, he turned east, into the conflict zone of Ukraine.

The first hour of his mission, things were fairly quiet. Then, inside his headset, he began hearing a sound he'd heard many times flying in the Navy. The makeshift radar warning receiver was picking up the faint sounds of an acquisition radar, scanning the skies. The sound was distinct, as the radar spun slowly in a circular pattern. It emitted a long warbley sound until the main beam pointed directly at the glider and into the makeshift receivers, making a loud 'whamp' sound. Jughead quickly deciphered the scan of the radar. A full rotation of the radar was around five to six seconds, suggesting it was most likely a more advance acquisition radar, and not an older, slower spinning model. He also knew, and hoped, it could very well be a Ukrainian radar as well.

Unfortunately, his hopes that the radar was friendly quickly faded. Missiles off in the distance lit up the night sky, and climbed rapidly into the air. They were launched from Russian-held territory and began heading in his general direction. Given the heat signatures of the missiles, Jughead could see the flight tracks, and it was clear none had locked on him. His radar warning receiver also provided no indication a threat or tracking radar had locked on his aircraft. If one had, the blare of a 'missile lock' tone would blare in his headset, to the point of being overwhelming.

Jughead's combat aviation experience kicked in and he did exactly what he did years ago. He whispered to himself, *'If they ain't found ya, no reason to make a bunch of moves and help 'em. Keep it straight and level. Press on buddy.'*

A few searchlights also popped up from the Russian side, which clearly wouldn't be strong enough to find him. But he'd be sure to tell Buck once he returned. Something had clearly caught the attention of Russian air defense. Perhaps the Ukrainians had launched a strike that evening, or perhaps Russia was getting wise to their little operation.

As he kept flying, Jughead noticed something which made him quite happy. Multiple missiles and artillery from the Ukrainian territory launched in a counter battery effort, and began targeting the locations of the Russian missile launches. Soon thereafter, the alpha scan radar he heard in his headset vanished. Jughead knew it either blew up, or the radar operator grew scared and decided it was a far better life choice to turn off the radar and stop transmitting. Either way, Jughead was content.

After a few minutes, activity in the airspace subsided. The night returned to quiet darkness, and Jughead smiled. His aircraft truly was difficult for Russian radars to find. The wood, plastics, and other components didn't provide enough of a return for Russian radar systems. Additionally, the slow airspeeds were filtered out of modern radar systems designed to track and target faster combat aircraft. Advancing technology always held a bit of advantage on the battlefield, but it never lasted forever. For now, Old Girl and SBD Dauntless II were safe, but balance would eventually return, and Russia would find a way to target these aircraft. The question was when.

Jughead eventually landed without incident at the forward airfield, offloaded his cargo and then took off the next morning. His flight back to Base U was far less eventful than his flight into harm's way. Jughead rather enjoyed deploying the jet engine and zooming back up into the air. For an aviation enthusiast, these gliders offered the spectrum of flying aspects. Power to rapidly climb and the ability to glide into thermals and milk out every foot of altitude. Jughead had no regrets leaving FedEx for such an opportunity.

Jughead flew his glider to short final, nearly done with the mission. With extra fuel in the tank, Jughead wanted to have some fun. He deployed the jet engine, fired it off and climbed out for a beautifully executed 'go around,' showing off for the ground crew.

After his small air show, Jughead gently set his glider down on the runway. Those on the base weren't the only appreciating the short airshow. GRU agents disguised as locals were rapidly taking photos and video of SBD Dauntless II, especially with the jet engine extended and operating. That information would rapidly be pushed back to the Kremlin. It was another piece in the puzzle, and eventually Moscow would find a weakness to exploit.

Upon landing at Base U, his glider was towed into the hangar where Buck was waiting.

"Twenty-three hundred feet, Buck," Jughead said.

"What?" Buck replied.

"That's how much altitude I was able to put on SBD II catching thermals back home. How much have you gotten?"

It was the classic tale of two pilots attempting to figure out whose dick was longer, and Buck fell for it hook, line and sinker. "I think I've gotten more, but I hadn't tracked it that closely. I will tomorrow. I'm sure I'll eat your lunch."

Jughead smiled. "Fifty bucks?"

"Deal," Buck said. "But I'll hate taking your money."

"You see, Buck," Jughead responded. "That's where you and I differ. I'll love taking yours."

Another voice chimed in, "Can I get in on this action?"

175

Buck turned around. It was Curt, standing there with Rob Farkas.

"Curt!" Buck screamed in excitement as he reached out and gave his old friend a proper bear hug. "Great to see ya, man! Welcome to the fight!"

"Easy, Buck. I'm here to fix folks. I'm not going downrange."

"Sure. Whatever," Buck said. "Hey, this is one of our new pilots. Jughead."

"Hey Jughead, nice to meet ya," Curt announced.

"Yeah. You too. And good to see ya again, Rob. How are things going for you?" Jughead asked.

Rob was swimming in taskers while raking in massive amounts of money. In war, there are winners, losers, and those that become wealthy. Being the latter, Rob was a product of the right place, right time. The Ukraine war broke out quickly, and he was one of only a handful of qualified U.S. companies in Poland to manage defense contracts. "Life couldn't get any better," he said, smiling as he was mentally calculating his swelling bank accounts.

Jughead, after sizing up Curt, asked, "Dr. Nover, what did you mean by you're here to fix folks?"

"Jughead, I'm a former SEAL and now a medical doctor. I wanted to cage Buck's expectations before his head spiraled into fantasy land about what I might be doing here." Curt then looked at Buck as they both grinned, realizing had he not framed his efforts, that was exactly what Buck would do.

Jughead then responded, "Cool. Clearly there's a need for more medical staff. On my last run, I learned three of the doctors down in Uman, Ukraine have fallen ill. Indications suggest they've been poisoned. That medical facility could really use some help."

Rob echoed the comments. "That's true. I got the same intel earlier today. Dr. Nover, I know you are here for rear echelon medical support, but if the wounded arriving are already dead due to lack of triage, that doesn't make much sense."

Curt bit his lip. He promised Allison he'd not enter Ukraine. "Thanks for sharing, Rob. Hopefully, others can fill the requirement. As my company relayed, I will be patching up folks in Poland, not Ukraine."

"Suit yourself, but I hope you're a voodoo magician, or your workload is going to be light." Rob was right. Over the past two days, the survival rate of those arriving on Jasionka's Base U was low.

Buck, being Buck, thought there'd be no harm in trying to nudge his good friend into the fight. "Curt, if you want, you can fly with me into Uman tonight and fly out tomorrow. I've been there. I assure you it's far enough back from the front lines. You won't see any action. You'll be fine."

"Buck, no disrespect, but if I even consider going into Ukraine, it will be on land. I've heard too many stories about Russian anti-aircraft missile systems."

"Well, as Rob said, suit yourself, but I've flown a bunch of times in and out. Up to you. I fly at 8pm tonight. I'd love to show ya."

Curt had received enough pushing. "OK. Let me talk to the medical team here and see what's going on. For fuck's sake, Buck. I just got here."

Buck nodded. "Hey, let's at least grab dinner before I go fly? Deal?"

"Sure, Buck. Just like old times back in Africa." The two smiled fondly, reminded of their lunches in Akjoujt, Mauritania.

Rob led Curt away, as they headed over to the medical unit for Base U. The news Curt received was discouraging. He had traveled halfway around the globe to save lives. Unfortunately, at least for the time being, that would be nearly impossible on Base U, Jasionka. The information that Jughead and Rob shared was accurate. Deadly accurate.

After dropping off Curt at the medical unit, Rob headed back to Warsaw, the headquarters for PLUSOps, Inc. His signature was required on seven new contracts with the U.S. Government, all intended to receive more and more war supplies. They'd total over fifty million dollars, and his cut would be healthy. Rob's wife had already started investigating private school options for their two children and new home shopping. After a few more contracts like that, money would no longer be an issue for the Farkas family.

\*\*\*\*\*\*\*\*\*\*\*\*\*\*\*\*\*\*\*\*

Smitty and the team had cautiously driven across the Russian-occupied territory for well over three hours. The travel was challenging. A significant amount of mines and GPS jammers had been deployed across the area. The former to kill Ukrainian forces, the latter to protect Russian forces from precision-guided munitions. However, GPS jamming didn't just affect precision-guided weapons. It denied all GPS systems in the area, forcing Smitty's team to navigate old school style with maps, charts and compasses.

Eventually, they would arrive in the vicinity of Izvaryne's rail yard. As they neared, they planned to perform recon efforts, attempting to find a location to serve as their base. Finding a location where they could avoid engagement with locals was important; however, that effort was arguably not required as nearly every villager had abandoned their houses, or what remained of them. Heavy artillery had irreparably destroyed eighty percent of the town's buildings. On the outskirts of town, artillery divots littered the countryside. The apocalyptic landscape presented little signs of life. All this damage was at the hands of Russian forces as they invaded the area.

Smitty quickly realized recon efforts were less concerning than moving around the village. Given the situation, moving and surveying the area was riskier than just hunkering down. Finally, the team agreed to hole up in an abandoned house just over a kilometer away from the rail yard. Once inside, they unloaded gear, set up a makeshift security perimeter and began scoping their objective. What they saw was frustrating. In stark contrast to the destroyed village they were occupying, the rail yard was in excellent condition. It was also extremely well protected. Large flood lights swept around constantly with a significant amount of vehicle activity. It was easy to see why the Ukrainian government wanted the rail yard destroyed. This location served as a top logistics hub for feeding the Russian fight. Destroying it would be a challenging task.

Through the night, the team observed the Russian activity, taking notes on every little movement. When cars drove around the perimeter, the timing pattern of surveillance lights swept the ground or when guards passed. After a while, they would begin to establish the Russian's pattern of life around the base. Eventually, they would find a weakness.

Over the night, the team had gathered nearly three pages of intelligence. As the sun rose, another shift rotation was in order, and Smitty assumed the watch. Off in the distance, a train horn blared and Russian forces and rail yard personnel scurried around.

The train slowed as it pulled into the yard, creeping to its assigned location, then stopping. After the engineer set the brakes, a cloud of steam gushed from the wheel assemblies, accompanied by a loud hiss. The load was exceptionally heavy, and the train's hiss expressed a sigh of relief, pleased the task was complete.

The rail cars appeared identical, as they laded the train with a specific type of military vehicle; something Smitty recognized on instinct. The vehicles were brand new T-90 Russian tanks, some still in their protective wrapping. They were so new they lacked Russian military insignias, or the commonly identifiable 'Z' marking. Looking down the length of the train, it was clear the number of tanks approached triple digits. After the tanks, there were roughly twenty other unique vehicles. Military versions of dune buggies were stacked on the rail cars. To Smitty, this meant one thing: Special Forces. He'd used such vehicles in Afghanistan. They were exceptional for SOF units, but had no purpose for conventional forces. Smitty looked down at his notebook and scribbled down details about the new train load. As he looked back up, Smitty saw a man exit the train's engine compartment and his heart nearly froze. He knew that face. Nearly every American did. It had been splashed across television sets, newspapers and the internet media outlets for weeks. Just one kilometer from Smitty stood Victor Petrov, the

man who had assassinated U.S. Vice President Steven Banks. In a soft whisper, Smitty said, *'Mother Fucker…. I found ya.'*
Petrov's presence at the rail yard presented a dilemma. Was capturing or killing Petrov the new priority mission? A destroyed rail yard would fetch ten million dollars. Petrov's head would fetch far more than that amount. Petrov walked along the rail line, stopping at the dune buggies and inspecting them. While Smitty couldn't be certain, the impression was these assets were not for conventional Russian forces, but rather Petrov's men in the Rasputin Firm.

As Smitty tried to process the new information, he realized there was a problem, pounding his fist against the wall. *'What a time not to have a sniper,'* he thought. His risk adverse decision to leave Jackal back at Base U was now more than just regrettable. It was infuriating.

Smitty snapped a few photos of Petrov with a long-range camera. He then woke the others and showed them. Unanimously, they all agreed it was Petrov.

Smitty also began to discuss options with the team. "With this new intelligence, I think we need to consider transitioning to either a hit or a grab and go."

"We stay with the plan," Marko immediately demanded. Marko was under orders to help them destroy the rail yard. As a Ukrainian, he had no business or beef with Petrov. It wasn't his Vice President that was assassinated.

"Marko, the rail yard isn't going anywhere. We can come back and get it next time. Petrov is mobile. We need to take him out now," Smitty pleaded.

Marko steamed. "Do you have any idea how much it cost and what bridges we burned to get our team this deep into enemy lines? For us, such things are not commonplace. We stick to the plan."

There was no changing his mind. Eventually, Smitty had only two options. The first was to continue with the original mission, and the second was to go over Marko's head and gain approval to alter the mission. The latter would require a fairly dangerous phone call back to Admiral Hershey. Petrov's head was what every American wanted. He had to take the chance. Smitty pulled out his last burner phone and called.

"Hey boss. Can't talk long. I'm eyes on the Vice President killer, but our local national doesn't want to deviate from the plan. Please advise."

Admiral Hershey knew exactly what Smitty meant. Without delay, he said, "Can you get him?"

Smitty was slightly embarrassed to admit he had no sniper on this mission, especially since Hershey had funded Jackal's trip into the operating area. "Sir, I'm minus Jackal. We can try, but I need approval to deviate from our mission or I lose my local national."

"I'll work it. Surface again in twelve hours," Admiral Hershey replied.

"Wilco. Out." Smitty hung up and looked at a furious Marko who had heard every word.

"Buddy, I owe my life to you, so I'm not gonna fight ya, but catching this guy changes everything. The Rasputin Firm gets exposed, and Russia's best fighters become vulnerable."

Marko thought about it and slowly relaxed his pursed lips. "I see your point. But look at that," as Marko said, pointing towards the rail yard. "Roughly one hundred new combat vehicles means more death for my comrades. It's my fellow Ukrainian warriors that keep me committed to our mission. Not my leadership, not your leadership, and not you. I've lost too many already."

Smitty would not argue against Marko's point. It was valid, and debating against dead warriors was a losing effort. "Alright, Marko. Let's come up with a new plan. Perhaps there is a way to achieve both objectives with a bit more risk. Frankly, I'm willing to assume it if I can secure Petrov's head is on a spike."

The two nodded and continued discussing options. Unfortunately, given the rail yard's extensive security structures, viable options to achieve both objectives were few and far between.

\*\*\*\*\*\*\*\*\*\*\*\*\*\*\*\*\*\*\*\*

Outside Admiral Hershey's Washington D.C. residence, an indistinct van sat in a row of parked cars. Inside, a Russian field intelligence officer intercepted Smitty's call. He did not completely understand the full details of the conversation, but he understood Vice President killer. He rapidly transcribed the words exchanged and sent off his report. It would rise to higher-level units who could analyze the intercept. Russian military analysts would eventually determine enemy forces were close to Petrov; however, their primary concern was locating Smitty and his team, not saving Petrov's life. The Russian Army and the Rasputin Firm were separate entities. Eventually, someone would inform Victor Petrov of his danger, but that would take time. The danger to Smitty and the team would manifest much faster, and to a far greater degree. Time was not on their side.

\*\*\*\*\*\*\*\*\*\*\*\*\*\*\*\*\*\*\*\*

After Admiral Hershey hung up with Smitty, he quickly called Andrew. The two agreed this new situation warranted an immediate meeting with Secretary Baker and Ukrainian Ambassador Ubyivovk. After a few phone calls, the late-night crew at the State Department began scurrying to coordinate the meeting details. Much like New York City, Washington D.C. never slept, albeit for different reasons.

The next morning, Admiral Hershey and Andrew expeditiously grabbed cabs to the State Department's Truman building. Ukrainian Ambassador Ubyivovk's car slowly pulled to the front of the building. A State Department staffer met the vehicle, expediting his entry into the building.

Outside the conference room, all the attendees placed their phones and other wireless devices into a Faraday cage, following security protocols. Once inside, the participants took their seats, and the Admiral began. "Madam Secretary and Mr. Ambassador. I truly appreciate your willingness to take this meeting on such short notice, but I'm confident I have information of vital interest to all parties."

"Admiral Hershey, good morning," Secretary Baker responded. "I hope so. If you weren't the former Chairman, there's not a snowball's chance in hell I'd have accepted. Even with your former status, I confess, I hesitated, given what I've learned of your current efforts."

"Ma'am. I understand. And yes, our company, the Valyrian Group, is taking on some level of activity in Ukraine. In fact, I have a team in place and prepared to destroy a rail yard logistics hub under contract from the Ukraine government."

Secretary Marleen Baker looked at Ukrainian Ambassador Ubyivovk, who merely shrugged his shoulders. Hiring a U.S. mercenary company was not illegal, no matter how distasteful the State Secretary may have deemed it. "Well, Eugene, it seems you have your business. I don't see how, or more importantly, why, I would want to be involved?"

"Marleen," Eugene Hershey responded, "Because my team currently has eyes on Victor Petrov."

There was a noticeable silence in the room, and both Marleen's and Ambassador Ubyivovk's eyebrows raised. The Admiral said nothing more, awaiting a response.

"I need to communicate this to the President," Secretary Baker said.

"Ma'am, you are welcome to share this with the President, but that's not why I'm here. To be clear, I am not seeking U.S. approval for any operation against Petrov. I'm here today asking for another favor. I am hopeful you can help me convince our friend the Ambassador that a mission to either eliminate Petrov or exfil him to stand trial is the priority. If you can do that, then we can discuss further options."

Ambassador Ubyivovk said nothing, remaining unphased by

the request. The cards in his hand had significantly improved, as far as he was concerned. There was no need to engage at this point.

"Admiral, we have tools in the DoD arsenal, as you know, that can target Petrov. You don't need to risk your team."

"Marleen, as the former Chairman, I am aware of the tools, thanks. I also am not giving you Petrov's location. I'll give you his head, dead or alive, but that's going to cost you."

Secretary Baker gazed harshly at the Admiral as if he'd said something inappropriate. "Admiral, the U.S. does not pay mercenary organizations to do its bidding. I presume you remember this as well from your time as the Chairman." Her words were intended to sting. They didn't. She directed her next comments to her staff and the Ambassador. "May I ask all of you to step outside? I need to remind the Admiral how the U.S. does business." The Ambassador smiled and Marleen's staff scurried away. The tension in the room was not lost on anyone.

Now alone, the Admiral, the Secretary and Andrew sat in the office. "Eugene, don't bullshit me. Do you have Petrov?"

"My best guy says he's eyes on."

"OK. What's it going to cost?"

Andrew had waited for this moment. It was his turn to speak. "Forty million."

Secretary Baker chuckled. "Be serious, Mr. Denney. That's not practical."

"Madam Secretary, I believe it's absolutely practical. Here's why. Currently, my team is on another mission, paid for by the Ukrainian government. I'll need to refund their money should the mission change. That will cost me twenty million. For my second point, your party has a president who is on the ropes, given the news of his affair. At this point, a re-election is suspect, if not unlikely. Of course, unless he can deliver a massive win... such as the Vice President's assassin. And to be fair, your party's campaign war chest could easily fund $40M. The price stands."

"Mr. Denney, as you know, those funds are not mine. I am not the party chairman. You've clearly come to the wrong office."

Andrew sat back and smiled. "Have I?" He would say no more. Marleen and he both knew she was a political appointee with direct ties to the party's leadership. They also knew her job was on the line should the President lose the next election. Power in D.C. is everything. The coming election would either keep Marleen as a member of the National Security Council or teaching at a private college. Clearly, the former was far more desirable.

"Madam Secretary," Admiral Hersey engaged. "Perhaps we have come to the wrong office, but time is of the essence for me. I have four more hours until my team lead checks in again. At that time, I tell him to capture or kill Petrov, or just let him go. I don't have time to coordinate a meeting with the party chairmanship, nor am I as powerful as you to coordinate such an effort." Eugene paused, as he slowly began to stand. "Marleen, I do hope you'll share this opportunity with the right folks. We were both fond of Vice President Banks. Let's do this for him."

Andrew followed the Admiral's lead and stood. They were done.

"Gentlemen," Secretary Baker said, "Before you go, don't you need Ambassador Ubyivovk to reenter and secure his approval?"

Andrew chuckled. "For the ambassador, this was a show. He knows we can take Petrov. In under an hour, he'll report this to Kyiv. He'll perform just as we expect. Ma'am, you have four hours. Good day."

The two walked out of Secretary Baker's office as if they'd been on the receiving end of a massive scolding. Ambassador Ubyivovk, along with the State Department staff, smiled as the two walked by. Incorrectly, they presumed Marleen had emphatically informed the two that the U.S. does not engage in funding mercenary activities. Such were the ways of the highest levels of governance in Washington.

As they walked out the Truman building front doors, Admiral Hershey said, "Forty Million? And twenty of that for Ukraine? That's ten million more than we actually charged for the rail yard mission."

Without breaking stride, Andrew's face smirked as he said, "Yes. I know. Consider the other ten million a processing fee."

Andrew held a PhD in supply, demand and opportunity costs in the world of politics as well as national security.  He had the bull by the balls and was not about to let go.

## *Chapter Twenty-Nine*
# Coffin Nails

After everyone departed the State Department, Marleen cleared her calendar and scrambled to deal with this opportunity. For months, the Algerian ambassador had lobbied for a meeting with Secretary Baker. In a matter of seconds, those efforts were squashed. Marleen contacted her party's political leadership as the sun climbed over Washington.

*******************

Across town, the Russian Embassy to Washington also showed signs of morning life. Ambassador Tarlov sat in his office, answering his secure phone for a scheduled discussion with Moscow.

"Yes," he replied as he received the Kremlin's instructions. "I agree, the President has served his purpose. He's of little value to us now and we've taken too many steps to put Ms. Crawford into place."

He paused again, listening intently. The other party on the line was clearly superior to Tarlov. "Yes, Sir. It will happen today, in a few hours. Good day, Sir." Tarlov hung up.

He placed another call to Moscow. This time, it was to one of his longtime friends, the producer at the news outlet *Russia Today International*. A brief exchange took place and the two men said goodbye.

In D.C. through the day, Secretary Baker worked feverishly to secure the forty million, communicating with the President and other power players within the party. Much like Andrew Denney argued, they all realized Petrov's head was a prize they could not afford, but also could not afford to pass up. Begrudgingly, money was shifted around party accounts and billionaire donors were quietly engaged. After a few hours, forty million was secured and passed along to Andrew Denney. The Valyrian

Group was having a rainmaker year. As for the President, he at least had hope and a possible way out of his mess. On the other side of the world, however, other folks were scurrying at *Russia Today*. Unbeknownst to the President, their efforts would quash any hope he'd garner through the day.

\*\*\*\*\*\*\*\*\*\*\*\*\*\*\*\*\*\*\*\*

Ambassador Tarlov stood from his desk and barked orders to his secretary, demanding his car and driver. Once inside, he relayed his desired destination, Joe's Seafood, Prime Steak and Stone Crab. It was a restaurant he rarely frequented, but it was only two hundred yards from his residence and had plenty of televisions in the bar. Watching the news would be his primary requirement for the evening.

By the time he arrived, the news channels were merely regurgitating the day's stale information. He sat there, drinking vodka and eating raw oysters, like a child in anticipation of Christmas. Eventually, the major news outlets began reporting. Almost like clockwork, news began to break. CNN, Fox News, MSNBC in near unison cut to share the 'unconfirmed' information.

"And just in, sources from the Russian state sponsored media outlet *Russia Today* have released a video," the CNN reporter announced as if he'd stumbled upon the holy grail. "We cannot verify this video's authenticity and warn our viewers as to its mature content. While we at the network have seen the video, we are awaiting approval to share it with you, our viewers. According to *Russia Today*, this is a video of a romantic interlude between the President of the United States and his personal White House chef, Rachel Benson."

"We are trying to confirm the people in the video are actually the President and Ms. Benson," the CNN anchor stated, albeit pointless. The faces in the video were clear, although the private areas were blurred. The anchor's statement was a lie in an effort to buy time. CNN producers and other U.S.

mainstream media outlets begged *Russia Today* to play the video. An empty request until this point.

While *Russia Today* was banned in the United States due to misinformation and other allegations, the video spread like wildfire across the rest of the world. Even if they wanted to, U.S. mainstream media outlets could not bury the story. Until garnering *Russia Today's* approval, they also could not share the video. Quickly, media outlets raced to capture reaction to the video's existence.

A mobile camera crew rapidly set up outside the Russian Embassy gate. Standing there in a perfectly pressed suit and a hint of makeup was Ambassador Tarlov's spokesman, Victor. The news crew caught him, as if by chance, shoving a microphone into his face. When hearing the question, Victor acted just as surprised as everyone else, shocked the U.S. President would engage in such a scandalous affair. Upon further questioning, Victor, as if on script, lamented the U.S. government ban on *Russia Today*, clearly a violation of free speech. Given the breaking news, Victor was certain the outlet was worthy of being a credible news source, if not for the U.S., at least for the rest of the globe. As if the video wasn't scandalous enough, Russia extracted further blood, questioning the validity of American liberties.

Eventually, *Russia Today* authorized release of the video, under a singular demand that the *Russia Today* logo be visible and credited. Soon, U.S. news outlets were broadcasting the video and social media outlets facilitated its exponential spread. This, too, caused a kerfuffle. Leadership at the various social media outlets contemplated blocking the video. Some did, others did not. Social media outlets blocking the video were quickly labeled vassals of the current administration. For the next twenty-four hour media cycle, U.S. mainstream media would repeatedly play the video.

Rachel's lawyer, Matt Yospe, immediately filed a ten-million-dollar lawsuit against *Russia Today*. Within days, they'd settle privately for eight million dollars, both parties agreeing to a nondisclosure agreement. Rachel would get half of the total which was a substantial sum to help her and Brooklyn fade away. Matt Yospe was no fool. He quickly realized this was Russia's plan all along. Matt won the case for his client, but he felt angry. Matt couldn't help but feel manipulated like a pawn in a grand game. He was one of the best lawyers that money could buy, and yet, he was merely a small piece on a global chessboard.

In the White House, there was little the President could do. He was already under attack from the opposition party. Now, members of his own party began turning on him, especially those up for midterm reelections. Remaining silent about a presidential affair was political suicide. They had to turn on him. Political survival was the key to the party. The President's options grew even further limited.

At Joe's Seafood, Tarlov was as happy as the clams he was devouring. Now deep into his fifth martini, he was drunk, lavishing in the news. Soon, his phone rang.

Tarlov made a poor attempt to wipe his fingers clean from all the seafood, then answered. "Ambassador Tarlov," he said.

The party on the other end of the phone screamed. "You fucker! You promised that video would not be released." It was the White House Chief of Staff, Steve, who was livid.

"I'm sorry. Who is this?" Tarlov responded.

"You know EXACTLY who this is! It's Steve Lewis! Don't play fucking coy."

In the background, Tarlov could hear the President faintly say, "Steve, hang up." Tarlov smiled and remained quiet.

"But, Mr. President," Steve said, holding the phone in his hand.

"Steve, did you really expect the Russian Ambassador to Washington to keep a promise?" It was a valid point. Hope was the only option the President had when it came to Tarlov's promise. And 'hope' is a pipedream in such affairs.

Tarlov held the phone as close to his ear as possible, attempting to hear every morsel of information. His efforts, however, were short-lived, as Steve hung up the phone, then continued to speak. "Sir, how do you want to play this?"

The President sat there for a while. He didn't say anything.

"Mr. President. We have options here. Should I get the staff together?" Steve paused, staring at a dejected man. "Sir, the video was released by *Russia Today*. We can attack the source which is clearly far from a reputable outlet."

"Steve, the reputability of *Russia Today's* is not the one at stake. It's mine."

Steve was not willing to roll over. "Sir, you're human. You fucked up. We can survive this."

"Steve, my wife moved out of the White House. My children won't return my calls. And I will never see Rachel again. Perhaps things will look differently tomorrow, but for now, please go home to your family. I am going to retire to my quarters."

Steve looked at the President. Until this point, he'd never seen the man disconsolate and pessimistic. "Yes, Mr. President. Sleep on it. Things will look better tomorrow." Steve walked out of the Oval Office and closed the door.

*********************

Across the entire globe, there were few places unaware of the presidential affair. One such place was the war-torn house where Smitty and his team hunkered down. It was night in Ukraine. Smitty had waited longer than Admiral Hershey's mandated twelve-hour recall. At the prescribed time, a two-man team of Russian soldiers had walked towards the town where the team was hiding. For hours, the Russians walked the village, kicking over rubble and scavenging for anything of value. Silently, the team sat in the basement, praying the two scavengers would not stumble into their death.

Eventually, the two started a trek back to the rail yard, with a prized bounty in their possession. Some scraps of food and a few personal effects of the former villagers were all they could find.

Finally, Smitty pulled his burner phone from his pants cargo pocket and turned it on. Before he could dial the Admiral, a text message popped into the screen. It read:

*'Get VP, D or A.  Priority 1.  UKR concurs.'*

Smitty turned off the phone, pulled the sim card and snapped it in half.  As he did, he couldn't help but find it interesting that Victor Petrov and Vice President shared the same initials.  *'Dead or Alive'* he thought to himself.  Smitty's personal hopes were the former.

## *Chapter Thirty*

# Fireworks

It was 1800Hrs on Base U as Buck waited for Curt outside the base chow hall. Eventually, Curt showed up, and the two entered. After signing in, they grabbed their trays, proceeded through the line, and then took a seat at an empty table.

"So, how are things with the family?" Buck asked.

"Pretty good. Man, baby Bo is a freakin' blast. Every day there is something new he does. I love it. And Noorullah's English improves all the time. It's hard for him, but I'm proud that he is really trying to fit in. There are still hurdles, but I think we will be able to iron them out."

"Cool, man. I'm really happy for you. It's crazy though. You went from zero family to a full nest in about six months, man." Buck was right. The addition of little Bo and Noorullah at the same time was a bit much.

"True, but Allison has been a rock star. Not to mention, the Afghan community in D.C. really has stepped up to help Noorullah adjust. We are very lucky."

"Cool. And the job? How's the job?" Buck asked, making small talk and catching up.

Curt smiled "I quit."

Buck's head shot up. "Dude. You were making bank! What the fuck?"

"I was. And I was miserable. Buck, I can't work behind a desk in a bureaucracy which literally has zero movement. One of the newest and cutting-edge roll outs for the Veteran's Affairs administration this past month was an effort started fifteen years ago. Hell, we couldn't even find the first action officer who began the project to have him at the announcement. For all I know, he's dead. I can't work in an organization which functions at that pace. It's why Allison agreed to let me come to Poland to help out."

"Uh, you getting paid?"

"Yes, Buck, I appreciate you being concerned over my financial viability," Curt sarcastically replied. "It's currently not as much as I was making, but that's not the point."

"Buddy. I'm not trying to get into your money issues," Buck said. "I just want you to know. You and Allison never need to worry about money. I'm still sitting on a literal mountain of cash from NISSASSA. Just let me know."

It was a nice offer, and Buck likely truly was sitting on the cash. The guy was a true aviator, stingy to the core. "Thanks, Buck."

Both their bellies were reaching max density and there was a long pause in their conversation. Buck could not help himself and asked one more time. "Curt. The guys in Uman need you. Are you coming? I'm telling ya, it's about as safe as it gets. And that's where the current action is... or at least the medical action."

"Buck, no. I promised Allison," he responded.

"Buddy, I get that. But if you don't go to Uman, go home. If the front-line MASH units can't stabilize the wounded, you're just going to be performing autopsies. If that's what you came to do, fine. But I don't know how many times one can write, 'Death due to untreated combat wounds within the golden hour.'"

Curt both hated and loved Buck's bluntness. "I hear ya, Buck," was all he'd respond with.

"Fuck you and your promise to Allison," Buck said. "We both know she's not here and has zero understanding of the situation. If she did, she'd want you to go. You're a fool if you don't see that. Just go home and reconsider that VA job." Buck got up from the table and began walking away.

A fire grew in Curt's chest that wanted to challenge Buck's harsh words. The problem was, Curt's soul wanted to go to Uman, and he also knew if Allison were present, he thought he would have a 50/50 chance of convincing her. Begrudgingly, Curt relented. "Buck!" he screamed.

Buck stopped and looked back. "What?" he replied as if in disgust.

Curt exhaled and said, "What time do I need to be at the airplane?"

Buck smiled. "About 15 minutes before eight. It's a glider dude. You'll love it!"

\*\*\*\*\*\*\*\*\*\*\*\*\*\*\*\*\*\*\*\*

Smitty had already started thinking through a plan on how to capture or kill Petrov. He hadn't, however, told Marko the mission had changed.

"Hey," Marko said as he walked into the room where Smitty was sitting.

"Marko. Hey," he replied. "I'm glad you're here. I need to show you something." Smitty turned on the phone and showed Marko the Admiral's text message. Marko grunted in minor disapproval, but he knew the message was likely accurate. The Valyrian Group may be new, but they were led by the former Joint Chiefs Chairman. He had strings.

"Buddy," Smitty said as he turned off the phone and put it away. "As we discussed, we can still try to execute both missions. But I can't even do one without you. We need you. Without you, Marko, there is no chance. I need to know. Are you in?"

Marko looked at Smitty. "Sir, without your nation's help, my nation didn't have a chance. I hate we are this close to destroying Russian supplies, but I am with you." The two shook hands.

Smitty rallied the team together. He laid out his plan on how to get Petrov. He briefed it, then briefed it again. On the floor, the team made a makeshift sand table, rehearsing the mission over and over. Once everyone was comfortable with the plan, Marko began putting on his Russian uniform one more time. According to the pattern of life gleaned by the team, Victor Petrov would walk along the rail cars in one hour on his way back from dinner. Accompanying him would likely be one other unknown Russian soldier.

JT and Beef finished loading seed and fertilizer into a truck left abandoned in the village.

Marko got into the flatbed driver's seat and slowly pulled out of the abandoned house's garage. He drove away from the village, then turned towards the rail yard, as if he were approaching from the front lines. Nearing the facility, Marko slowed the vehicle, stopping at the first checkpoint.

"Identification," the Russian soldier said.

Marko's face appeared overly tired. Acting frustrated, he responded in perfect Russian, "I don't have it anymore. I've been driving this fucking truck for hours trying to find this place." Marko turned off the engine and threw the keys at the soldier. "You drive it the rest of the way. This is seed and fertilizer to go back to Russia. I'm done."

As Marko opened the truck door, the Russian soldier ordered him to stay in the vehicle. With his AK-47 rifle at the ready, the soldier slowly circled the vehicle, inspecting it. In the back were large containers of seed and fluids, exactly what Marko claimed. It looked nonthreatening enough, and he wanted no part of having a truck just sitting at his entry point.

"OK. Go ahead in." The soldier ordered.

"Fine, but I'm getting some sleep after this," Marko demanded. He started up the truck and drove into the yard. The closer he got to the railhead, the greater the activity and his blood pressure. Marko realized, though, it seemed everyone moved with purpose around the facility, as if they were all fixated on their task. Marko followed suit, and as if he were on a specific task, pulled the truck up behind others sitting in a loading/unloading stockyard. Once parked, Marko got out and cautiously unsheathed his knife. After a quick scan to ensure he was not being observed, Marko casually bent down as if to inspect the vehicle, then stabbed the tire. After standing back up, he casually walked towards the other tire and performed the same act. Within a minute, they were both flat. *'Slava Ukraine'* he thought to himself.

Marko sheathed his knife and meandered towards the part of the rail yard with the Rasputin Firm dune buggies. Once there, he took out a cigarette and lit it, leaning against a power-line pole. Appearing as if he were merely a soldier taking a break, Marko looked out to the north. One hundred meters away, out in the vastness of a dark and unattended field, a light flashed in three quick bursts, then it flashed again. Smitty and the team were in place. Marko casually tossed his barely smoked cigarette on the ground and snuffed it out with his foot. After taking one last deep breath, he climbed up into one of the dune buggies and sat in the driver's seat, pulling an empty bottle of vodka from his jacket. He poured some of the vodka onto his uniform and then untucked his uniform to offer a disheveled appearance.

In the distance, Marko heard voices approaching and looked out to where Smitty and the team indicated their presence. There was nothing, and his heart raced. Marko was alone. He slid down in the seat and remained still. Based on the planning, Marko presumed whoever was approaching, it was not Petrov.

Within a minute, his assumption would prove correct. Three Russian soldiers were walking along the train cars of dune buggies. They were in deep conversation, debating when they'd be able to see their families again. Marko remained motionless, and the three failed to notice Marko, who could have passed for dead. Just as fast as they approached, they departed, and Marko could finally breathe again.

For a second time, Marko heard voices approach and again he looked in the field. This time, a small light flashed three times in two sets. Petrov was approaching, and the team was in place. Far from a religious man, Marko said one last prayer, then began singing softly, old Russian military songs he'd learned as a lieutenant. Never did he believe they'd come in handy again.

As Petrov neared, the singing drew his attention to Marko. Once close enough in the darkness, Petrov and his companion saw a drunk Russian soldier sitting in their new vehicle up on a rail car. "Hey! You! Get down from there!" Petrov demanded.

In a drunken stupor, Marko replied, "Who? Me? Hey, it is comfortable here. Look at the stars. There's so many!" Marko paused, then held out his bottle of vodka. "Relax, comrade. How about some vodka with me?"

Petrov's colleague grew far more frustrated than Victor and began climbing up the side of the railcar to grab Marko and pull him out. "Come on, you fucking drunk. Let's go." As the man attempted to corral Marko, the two struggled.

Marko was far stronger and again held out the bottle, "Hey! Leave me alone, comrade! Come on! Sit and drink with me."

His assailant attempted to pull the bottle from Marko's hand. As he did, Marko slowly exposed a fresh box cutter razor with his other hand and, with exceptional precision, cleanly sliced the man's jugular and vocal box. There'd be no scream as the man quickly released Marko's vodka bottle arm, futilely grasping at his throat. Marko returned to singing his Russian military song, masking the flailing and muted screams of a dying man.

It was too dark for Petrov to see the swift attack or the blood. In under half a minute, his now dead colleague collapsed into the dune buggy onto Marko's chest. Petrov stood below attempting to understand what was going on.

"Hey," Marko said. "I think your comrade is sick or something?" Looking down at Petrov with a drunken demeanor. "Maybe he had too much vodka, too." Marko laughed for a few seconds.

Petrov had enough. Frustratingly, he began climbing up the side of the railcar to get to the dune buggy. Once his hands were firmly on the railcar, Smitty and Beef sprung out of thin air. With a powerful swing, Smitty landed a flashlight blow to the back of Petrov's head, instantly knocking him unconscious. Quickly, they drug him away, into the brush and then towards the abandoned house they'd used to hide out. JT sat approximately 100 meters away, he and his machine gun camouflaged in the grass. If things went south, at least the team would have a chance. Smitty, Marko, and Beef took turns carrying Petrov for the full half mile until they were in the safe house. Once there, they tied him up. Soon, JT followed and the five of them got into the Land Rover, with Petrov tied up in the back.

There was little time left. The team was forced to ditch a significant portion of their gear. They needed to start driving immediately.

Slowly, they pulled out of the garage and casually drove away, headed west. After driving for twenty minutes and making it ten miles away, they heard and felt the repercussions of the blast.

Minutes earlier, a nearly unnoticeable action began taking place on Marko's long abandoned truck. The ammonia nitrate barrels began mixing with diesel fuel from the gas tanks, along with other components. The makeshift system was crafted by Beef, who was somewhat of a bomb hobbyist. The bomb was massive and would create similar effects as the one Timothy McVeigh used on the Oklahoma City FBI building in 1995. Ironically, it was that bomb which sparked Beef's interest in explosives. Both bombs were crafted from similar substances.

As the detonation shook the earth, the night sky lit up as if it were daytime for a few seconds. From a distance, a soft glow emanated from the Izvaryne rail yard along with wails of sirens. The team continued away with Victor Petrov in their mitts. On one hand, Petrov was lucky he'd been identified by Smitty. Had he not, he'd likely be dead. On the other hand, Petrov was now a captive.

Smitty and the team drove for another fifty miles until they found a small lake near Klyuchove. The lake was surrounded by a significant wooded area in which they could hide. They'd need to lie low for a bit. The forest and lake would provide everything they needed.

*********************

Up in the Ukrainian sky, Buck and Curt were peacefully gliding eastward. Buck had heard another alpha scan radar but chose to ignore it and not startle Curt. After hearing a handful of such radars, Buck's concerns began to ease. With every mission, he'd grown more comfortable in the notion Russian radars could not find him.

As both were looking out the front window, off in the distance, they saw the explosion. "Jesus Christ! Was that a nuke?" Buck said.

"I don't think so, but it was a monster. I'd hate to be anywhere around that place. Wow."

Seconds later, a rumble similar to thunder pierced the silent air. It was the bomb's concussion wave, radiating away from its epicenter. Old Girl shook a bit as she flew through the wave. She then lumbered slowly and uneventfully into Uman.

The Russian leadership had been dealt a significant blow this evening. A primary rail hub was in ruins and the man accused of Vice President Bank's assassination was apprehended.

\*\*\*\*\*\*\*\*\*\*\*\*\*\*\*\*\*\*\*

In Izvaryne, the scene was utter chaos. Seventy-five percent of the military vehicles in the yard were destroyed. Another portion was damaged, but neither of these were the key issue. It would take months to repair the railhead, dealing a massive blow to Russia's strategic logistics.

Social media quickly reported the explosion. As they did, the Russian Defense Ministry would report only a handful of soldiers were killed and roughly twenty with injuries. In fact, the number of dead neared fifty. The deaths were fast as the explosion incinerated most of the victims. As news permeated Moscow, a call between the Kremlin and the Rasputin Firm took place.

"Good evening, President Volkov."

"I presume you've heard about the explosion in Izvaryne," the President queried.

"Yes, Sir. I understand the explosion destroyed our new dune buggies. It's a pity, but we will get more. Our new tactics with these assets will prove very beneficial," the Rasputin Firm leader offered.

"How many men did you lose? Do you know?"

"Mr. President, at this point, we don't know. Our lead man on the ground is not answering yet, but we are confident he's

200

safe.  According to our sources, he's not near the explosion and is many kilometers west of the rail yard.  Once we can reach him, we will let you know."

"Please do.  And get ahold of someone on the ground in Izvaryne.  I don't want any public images of your vehicles."

"Understood, Mr. President.  Good night."

Back at the Rasputin Firm, Stefan Balakin, the chief operations officer, hung up the phone, then ran his fingers along the rim of his cognac glass.  As he did, another man observed him from across the desk.

"Petrov still has not called?" Stefan asked.

"No, Sir."

"This is a pity.  When you make contact with our team in Izvaryne, I need someone to go to where Petrov's tracker is active.  I fear Mr. Petrov's usefulness may have run its course."

## Chapter Thirty-One
# Cats and Mice

Morning arrived in Ukraine. At the base in Uman, Curt began meeting the medical teams he'd be working with, as well as evaluating the forward MASH units. He was nervous, but Buck was a calming soul. It would prove to be far more helpful than Buck knew. Eventually, it was time for Buck to depart and with the screechy whine of his jet engine, his glider climbed into the sky, heading west into the morning air. Curt watched, somewhat in awe that such a tiny motor could lift a glider, even if it was empty. In the distance, Curt heard ambulance sirens faintly. The noise increased, and he knew they were coming onto the base. There was no time to waste.

Curt jogged to the medical facility and scrubbed up. From patient to patient, Curt removed shrapnel, stabilized limbs for later evaluation, pulled bullets, stitched up those that he could and for others, said a small prayer as he pulled a sheet over them for the last time. After hours of work, he'd saved seven Ukrainian soldiers from gunshot wounds and lost two. It was the two losses that would eat at him the rest of the day. He was exhausted, but he derived more sense of accomplishment and personal satisfaction in those hours than he had in his entire time at the Veteran's Affairs administration.

Roughly a hundred miles away from Curt in the forest near Klyuchove, Ukraine, Smitty and the team were all awake. In the night, they had set up a perimeter and partially camouflaged the vehicle. They took turns on the watch and also prepping an escape route out of the camp.

Beef was poking the hot coals of a small fire, heating up a small metal cup to make some coffee. JT quietly snuck away from the group with his weapon. He not only wished to not wake others, but was somewhat bashful and didn't want to explain why he was leaving. Like clockwork, JT needed to partake in his morning constitutional and was hoping to keep the campsite from knowing and stinking.

Victor Petrov was awake, remaining still. Although he was in excessive restraints, he was somewhat content with his predicament. Smitty brought him a plastic container of water and kicked him hard enough on his side to garner Petrov's attention. "Here, drink," Smitty said as he tipped the plastic bottle over his Victor's head. There would be no untying his hands. Victor Petrov was as dangerous as anyone Smitty had ever dealt with. Intentionally, Smitty made Victor's drinking a challenge, spilling water down his face and onto his chest.

Off in the woods, a lone man decked out in heavy camouflage watched Petrov drink. Slowly, he placed a call and in Russian said, "He's captured," into a discrete microphone near his mouth.

The voice on the other end simply said, "You know what to do," then hung up. The words tunneled into the man's ears via a small headset. With the precision of an expert assassin, the man readied his rifle.

Back in camp, Victor Petrov sarcastically said, "Thanks," as he finished drinking. "Do you have some food?"

"Later," Smitty said. "I see you speak English."

"Well, without perfect English, it would have been nearly impossible to get near your Vice President, now wouldn't it?" Petrov smiled.

Before Smitty could answer, a single gunshot pierced the air, hitting Victor in the shoulder. The shooter intended to hit Petrov's heart, but luckily for Victor, the bullet glanced off of a branch. Victor fell to the ground. Smitty, Beef and Marko rapidly drew weapons and sought cover. The forest and brush were dense. They never saw the shooter.

Seconds later, two more shots. The team and Petrov flinched with each shot.

Then JT yelled from out in the forest, "Shooter Down!" Awkwardly, JT approached his downed target; his pants around his ankles. Earlier, JT's sneaking off to take a shit was so stealthy, even the now dead shooter had been unaware of his movements. Merely thirty meters away, JT was leaning against a tree when the first shot rang out.

JT found the Russian shooter head down in a large thistle bush. He'd rolled roughly five meters down an embankment.

JT's first shot entered the victim's ribcage, the second into his skull. He was likely dead before he hit the ground.

"Beef! Marko! Scan for more," Smitty demanded. The two cut off out into the forest, but experience told them all this was likely a lone shooter. If there were more, they'd have targeted the entire team.

Smitty then looked down at Victor. Victor sustained injuries, but he would survive, Smitty confirmed. Nonetheless, Petrov gently clutched his shoulder in pain, oddly more reminiscent of someone with arthritis than a gaping gun-shot wound.

The team all converged on the campsite. JT had taken the dead sniper's radio, wallet, and other valuables. "Fuck. We gotta get out of here. Let's load Petrov into the Land Rover." Smitty ordered.

Smitty and JT broke down the camp while Beef and Marko pulled overwatch. Once packed out, Smitty helped Petrov into the vehicle while JT began evaluating the dead gunman's personal effects. Based on the quality of his gear, JT quickly determined the man was not Russian military, and clearly had indications of working for the Rasputin Firm. His smart phone screen was locked and there was little time to screw with it. Smitty swiped down on the iPhone and placed it in airplane mode, turning off any incoming or outgoing transmissions. There was no reason to give the enemy further opportunities to track them.

Once packed up and in the vehicle, JT and Marko dumped the dead shooters body into the back of the vehicle. Smitty wanted to leave no traces. The vehicle engine roared to life and quickly stormed out of the woods. Once on the main road, they slowed.

"How the hell did they find us? How did they find Petrov?" Smitty demanded. "Check him again for a phone or a transmitter. There is no fucking way they were that lucky." Smitty was furious. "Beef, did you cover our tracks into the woods like I asked?"

"Yes, boss. It wasn't our tracks."

Marko patted Victor down, extensively, looking for any electronic device. He especially concentrated on the fresh shoulder wound. Clearly, there was little likelihood a transmitting device was in his open wound, but it was quite pleasurable searching the area as Victor winced in pain. As Marko induced more pain, Victor smiled to the point he began laughing. Marko would find no transmitter. "Smitty, there's nothing on him," Marko responded.

"OK, God Damn it. How did they find us?" Smitty double checked the iPhone he'd pulled from Victor. It was off. Smitty drove for another ten miles, searching out another hideout. They were not ready to cross the border, nor did they really have a plan at this point. Victor Petrov was proving both a worthy bounty, but also a deadly liability.

\*\*\*\*\*\*\*\*\*\*\*\*\*\*\*\*\*\*\*\*

In the U.S., both Andrew and the Admiral awoke to the news about the Izvaryne rail yard. Andrew saw dollar signs, and the Admiral made a small fist pump. Both Andrew and Eugene had planned on refunding the ten million to Ukraine. Now that the rail yard was destroyed, that money was Valyrian Group profit.

The two also knew the mission was far from over. They both prayed for Smitty and the team. As much as the two wanted to know details and if the team was ok, there would be no contact until they were safe. If they were safe. Andrew scheduled an appointment with the Ukrainian Ambassador for that morning. He wanted the remainder of his money.

As Andrew walked into the Embassy, he noticed many of the embassy staff huddled around a television. They were watching what little video Russia released from the rail yard. It was truly destroyed, and the smiles around the room clearly indicated the Ambassador was not the only one who knew about the deal.

"Andrew," the Ambassador said. "It is a good day today. Don't you agree?"

"I do believe for you; it is an actually a great day. Perhaps soon, it will be great for both of us." The subtle insinuation wasn't lost on the Ambassador.

"Yes, yes. Please come with me." The ambassador escorted Andrew into his office, where a laptop computer sat open. On it, there was a wiring order for the remaining $7.5M to be sent to the same account that the first $2.5M went to. With a mere mouse click, the money transferred. A text message popped into Andrew's phone from his bank. The transfer was successful.

"Thank you, Mr. Ambassador. It was nice doing business with you." Andrew stood up and began to turn towards the door.

"Andrew, Andrew!" The Ambassador hastily called out. "Why are you running off so quickly? I would like to think we have more to discuss."

Andrew slowly sat back down, confused. "We do?"

"Yes. I believe you are looking for more opportunities to make money. Yes? Well, from your first mission, you have convinced Kyiv that you are more than capable of delivering."

Andrew was conflicted. Yes, he wanted more money, but the one team he had was still deep behind enemy lines, perhaps dead, or perhaps with Victor Petrov. He didn't know, and as a man who was often in control of things, the silence from Smitty was deafening. "Mr. Ambassador. I'd love to entertain more options, perhaps once I am able to commit to performing them."

"OK, I understand," said the Ambassador. "You get your team out and prepared again. They are just as valuable to us as they are to you."

"Yes. They are very special," Andrew said. Then he paused. "Mr. Ambassador. May I ask you a question?"

"Sure, Andrew. Anything."

"I didn't tell you the status of my team, but you clearly said 'get your team out.' How do you know they are still behind enemy lines?"

The Ambassador's voice changed, noticeably, before his answer. "Oh, Andrew. Well, I just presumed they were still in combat. The explosion was just hours ago. Surely they couldn't get back so quickly." He was as unconvincing as an unfaithful preacher.

The hair on Andrew's neck stood up. "Ok. But if you know something about my team and are not telling me, we will never do business again. And that's merely the start of the pain my company will press upon you."

Andrew may not have served in the military, but he'd grown fond of his personnel. In part, they'd somewhat morph into his now deceased son, Don. He was a West Point graduate and had taken his own life just the year prior.

The Ambassador nervously responded, "No! No. Of course not. I was just worried about them. Sorry. Have a great day."

The two shook hands and Andrew walked out. *'Where the fuck was Smitty? The Ambassador knows something I don't. But what?'* he thought to himself. Andrew, now in his cab, placed a quick call to Admiral Hershey and relayed the strange exchange.

Hershey replied. "Son of a bitch, Andrew. I think our guys got him."

"Petrov?" Andrew asked quizzically.

"Yup. He's not only a prize for the U.S., but he would be a massive catch for Ukraine as well. I'm not sure how Ukraine knows, but we need to talk privately. Let's get together as soon as possible."

The two hung up after establishing plans to meet. As they did, Russian intelligence units in the Washington, D.C. area finished transcribing the conversation. They quickly sent it back to the Russian embassy via secure communication systems and with that, Russian Intelligence learned Victor Petrov was in enemy hands. But where?

\*\*\*\*\*\*\*\*\*\*\*\*\*\*\*\*\*\*\*\*

Across D.C. in the White House, the President was meeting with the chair of his national political party. For hours, the White House staff and political party strategists worked through options on how to survive this devastating blow. As they did, opposition party members were pounding the airwaves, ordering Ms. Benson to testify. They sought an impeachment inquiry. And if legal, they would have demanded the President's head on a spit.

For the President, there was no way out, and that said a lot given the numerous times he and previous presidents had performed Houdini acts. The video was too clear, too perfect, and too damning.

"Mr. President. I truly do not see a way out of this," the party chair said.

"I realize that. At this point, we need to focus on how I step away and who assumes the position." The President paused, then started again. "Is there any precedent for some sort of special election? As it stands, if I step down, Crawford becomes the President. I'm not comfortable with that course of action."

A stately attorney for the national party responded. "Mr. President. The Twenty-Fifth Amendment is very clear on the chain of succession. There has never been a special election, nor a need for one. Bluntly, offering one would undermine all the trust and confidence you exuded towards Ms. Crawford when you selected her."

The President's face grew red. "Well, fuck you very much. Do you somehow think I care about that? Do you somehow think I plan to salvage my reputation and again run for office?" Silence fell upon the working group. Not one person wanted to be in that room.

Steve Lewis broke the quietness. "Sir, with all due respect, we are in a situation which was not considered by the framers. The succession is Veep, House Speaker, and then President Pro Tempore of the Senate. Of those three, at least the last two have faced elections. If the President steps down, the Vice President, a political no name, assumes the highest seat in the free world. Given the other two were selected by the people, would it be possible to bypass the Vice President?"

The President sat, listening. While he may be a dead man walking, he would do everything possible to ensure his party remained in power. Vice President Crawford had political value when he nominated her. Now, she was a liability that had to be eliminated.

The constitutional attorney again spoke up, this time a bit more timidly, "Mr. President. If the Vice President was to resign before you did, it would create the opportunity for the House Speaker to be next in legal succession."

The room was quiet, and eventually the President spoke up. "We have a few options. Stacy was brought on because she had a strong sense of listening to reason. Perhaps she'll agree that she shouldn't be the President. If that doesn't work, perhaps we can use the Ninth Amendment."

"Excuse me, Sir," Steve said.

"The Ninth Amendment states if a certain right is not explicitly stated in, or forbidden by the Constitution, it belongs to the people. A special presidential election could be one of these rights. While the Twenty-Fifth Amendment clearly describes succession, it states no claim, for or against, a special election. I realize this is a stretch, but if we can get the House Speaker and the Whip to generate enough Congressional objections to an unelected Vice President assuming office, there is perhaps a chance."

The party chair looked at his constitutional lawyer, who said, "It's possible, but the President is right. It is a stretch. The people would have to demand it."

It was the second-best option on the table behind Vice President Crawford offering her resignation. Aside from that, it was the only option on the table. The national party chairman stood up. "OK. I'll meet with the Speaker today. We will find a way to stoke the messaging if you're unsuccessful with the Veep. That leaves one last piece. Sir, when will you stand down?"

All eyes in the room were on the President. "Within the next 48 hours, I will relinquish my position."

The answer, as bitter as it was, satisfied the audience. The crowd departed, except for Steve, who stayed back.

"Steve," the President said. "Please have Ms. Crawford come to my office."

"Right away, Sir," Steve answered. Within minutes, the Vice President was standing at the Oval Office doorway.

"Mr. President, you wanted to see me?" she inquired.

"Yes, Stacy, please, come in."

As she entered, the President motioned for her to sit on one sofa as he sat on the other. Steve, as usual, sat in his chair off to the side. "Stacy. I want to thank you for all your support."

"Well, you are welcome, Mr. President, but I am not sure I like where this is starting."

"Well, I wanted to let you know that I am considering stepping down and since you were somewhat thrown into this Vice President thing, I wanted to give you the chance to get out of here before the whole thing explodes. Of course, I'd like to get your thoughts on this."

Stacy looked across the Oval Office sofas, sizing up the President. Part of her wanted to scream in rage at his patronizing comment. With every fiber, she suppressed that urge and responded. "Mr. President. I am sorry to hear you're considering stepping down, but in light of the damning video, I think you are right in that such a move is perhaps best for our nation."

Her words stung. She didn't have to mention the video, but she did... intentionally. "Yes. I appreciate that, and I don't disagree. But Stacy, the Senate appointed you via confirmation. The people never voted you into office. I'm concerned as to how that is perceived by the American public. Many will be angered. I am not sure it makes sense for you to assume the office."

Stacy was stunned. "Mr. President, the order of succession is very clear. If you didn't wish to have a Vice President, you should have waited until you ran on the midterms with another candidate." She was angry but calmed before the rest of her answer. "As for an angry American public. Our nation has grown so bifurcated, half of the nation would be upset with whoever is in the seat, elected or appointed via succession. In fact, one could make the argument an appointed President may actually garner less anger given no voter 'lost' in their selection of President."

"Stacy," Steve said, trying to calm the waters.

She immediately interrupted, "No, Steve. That's Madam Vice President to you. I know exactly what you're trying to do. I will not be politically beneficial one day and then a liability the next."

She stood up and began to walk away. Before departing the Oval Office, she turned back to the President. "Mr. President, if you choose to step down is your decision. Who replaces you is not. Good day." Stacy stormed out of the office.

"Well," the President said. "That didn't go very well."

"No, Sir. It did not." Steve was beginning to also realize that as the President stood down, his chances of remaining the Chief of Staff were rapidly diminishing. His loyalty to one master was clear. Stacy would never bring him on. *'Well, there's always K Street lobby firms,'* he thought to himself. Lobby firms paid top dollar to hire former high-level staff. It was great money, but it couldn't hold a candle to the power Steve currently possessed.

Back in her office, Stacy closed the door and picked up the phone. After a brief request to the White House Communications staff, her call was connected.

"Hello?" a male voice answered.

"Ryan, hey babe. It's me," she answered.

"Hey, Stac. What's up?"

"I think he's stepping down. He asked me to step aside and let the Speaker assume the position of President."

"No!" Ryan answered. "What did you say?"

"Well, in professional political speak, I told him to go fuck himself."

"That's my girl. What do you want for dinner?" Ryan asked. He cooked nearly every night for her, and he enjoyed it. They were in love, and although they never had planned for it, the two were less than two days from assuming the most powerful house in the world.

## *Chapter Thirty-Two*
# A Little Help from My Friends

The hour was late in Ukraine. Smitty and the team had found another hole up site and, now on the run, prioritized over watch. JT and Beef were both on an unstable roof, monitoring the near nonexistent vehicle traffic. The town they would hunker down in was Merefa, south of Kharkiv. Like other towns in Russian-occupied areas, Russian forces had destroyed it to moonscape status through intense, indiscriminate shelling. Nearly every structure was rubble. Luckily, such locations served as excellent hiding spots behind enemy lines.

Smitty had patched up Petrov's shoulder the best he could. The bullet shattered Petrov's shoulder blade, making his shoulder unusable, but he'd live. Petrov showed no emotion through the entire triage, smiling at Smitty, as if he were numb to the pain. Smitty could only sense evil in the man's eyes.

Their Land Rover sat in a makeshift garage of rubble. Marko had opened the windows to air the vehicle out as the other dead Rasputin Firm mercenary was beginning to smell. Eventually, they would dispose of the body, but for now, that wasn't the priority.

Marko set out all the personal effects they'd pulled from the shooter. "Let's see what we have here," he said out loud. "Seems our dead friend is named Boris according to his identification card. He also doesn't seem to be suffering financial hardship." Marko held up a wad of rubles. Other than these two facts, Boris presented nothing out of the ordinary.

Smitty knew they were being tailed, but he did not know how. The risks of communicating behind enemy lines was now outweighing remaining silent behind enemy lines. Smitty opened his backpack and pulled out a Thuraya IP+ satellite broadband router system. Thuraya, a United Arab Emirates firm, built out one of the larger and modern commercial global satellite communication systems. For Smitty, it was the best of numerous poor options. The IP+ was small, lightweight, was extremely expensive, and most importantly, was rare in Ukraine.

On the downside, once turned on, it was a beacon transmitter. If Russian surveillance systems were monitoring such systems, they could quickly geolocate his position. Luckily, SpaceX's Starlink satellite communication system had flooded Ukraine, and it was likely the primary collection target of Russia. Smitty hoped his choice of a unique and extremely expensive system would fall outside the Russian collection priorities. It was a chance he had to take.

Once operating, Smitty fired up WhatsApp on a small tablet. If his timing was right, Buck should have landed about a half hour ago in Uman. He placed the call. It rang a few times, then Buck picked up. "Smitty?"

"Buck! Thank God. Dude. I can't talk much. I need your help. ASAP. Are you in Uman?"

"No. Jughead had the run today. I'm in Poland."

"Damn it! Are you flying tomorrow?"

"Yes. Tomorrow is my run."

"OK. Tomorrow night, I need you to pick us up in that contraption of yours."

Buck was curious. "Where? In Russian held territory?"

"Yes, in Russian-held territory. What the fuck? Do you think I'm drinking Mai Tais in the Maldives?"

Buck's pulse quickened. He wasn't comfortable with the idea, but Smitty was a brother in arms. "OK. What's the plan?"

"Right now, I don't have one. I'm working on that. I'll send you info somehow, something more secure. But tomorrow, after your Uman run, can you fly in and get us?"

Buck took a deep breath. "Send me the details. If I can make it, I'll be there." It was the best he could offer, but he also knew, he'd take every risk in the book to get his friend.

"Thanks, Buck. I owe ya." Smitty hung up and turned off the network.

His unique choice of communication systems paid off.

Russian forces had not intercepted the conversation.

********************

Back in Moscow, a private line into the Rasputin Firm rang. A large man sitting in an oversized Italian leather chair answered. "Hello?"

"I've learned Petrov has been captured," the other party offered. The voice was familiar. It was Russian President Volkov's personal assistant.

"That is correct. But do not worry. We have things under control." The reply came from Stefan Balakin, the Rasputin Firm's operations officer. He was a powerful figure in Moscow, not from wealth of his own doing, but rather marrying President Volkov's sister.

"Do you know where he is?" Volkov's assistant asked.

"Yes. And by tomorrow, he will be disposed of," Stefan responded.

"The repercussions of his capture are unacceptable for the President. This must end. Just tell us where he is, and we will take care of it."

Shifting in his fine leather chair, Stefan grew angered. "That is not our deal. From the very beginning, my brother-in-law (the President) demanded Russian Forces and Rasputin Firm never mix. Neither he nor you get to make such a request. This is our problem. I will fix it. Please give my best to President Volkov." Stefan hung up and placed another call.

The other party answered, and before friendly greetings could be offered, Stefan demanded, "Are you tracking him?"

An operative for the Rasputin Firm looked down at his smart phone, watching a small blip blink on a map. "I show activity in Merefa."

The leather chair swung around, and Stefan glared into his computer screen. It also showed Merefa, but instead of one beacon, there were two. "Yes. But it is not just one target. There are two. It appears he's with Boris. They are on the run

214

or captured.  Either way, they have become too much of a liability.  If they are being held, both must to be terminated."

"Yes, boss," the operative answered as he drove slowly through the night towards Merefa.


\*\*\*\*\*\*\*\*\*\*\*\*\*\*\*\*\*\*\*\*


Smitty's team rotated through lookout responsibilities.  It was not easy work, given the rare movement.  Every now and then, they would see stray animals, and the rare locals who refused to leave and lived in their Flintstone rock rubble house.  Early in the morning, JT noticed an SUV slowly drive towards the village, then stop roughly a half mile away.  Given the rare activity, it wasn't difficult to identify.  It was the first vehicle he'd seen on his shift.  Oddly, neither the driver nor passenger exited the vehicle.  They just sat there.  JT then noticed the distinctive glint of binoculars flicker through the dashboard window.

"Smitty, I think we have company." JT said on his team radio, explaining what he saw.

Smitty, down in the main portion of the building's remains, stormed over to Petrov and grabbed him by the shirt.  "Look, you son of a bitch.  Tell me how they're finding us.  We haven't been here more than one God Damn day.  If you don't, I'll fucking kill you myself."

Petrov smiled, "Perhaps they are just lucky."

"Bullshit.  This is beyond luck.  How are they tracking us, and why do they want you so bad?"

Petrov laughed.  "You idiot.  They are not trying to find me to recover me.  I suspect they are trying to kill me.  So please.  Don't just threaten to kill me.  Do it and leave my body here.  You'd be far safer."

JT watched the SUV doors slowly open.  One man pulled out a massive pelican case container, likely containing a rifle.  The other grabbed two large bags and then the two walked into another abandoned building.  JT watched intently, reporting

215

everything over the team radio. There was no longer any doubt. Their new location was compromised.

Smitty grew concerned. If it was this easy to find them, the chances they'd stay safe until Buck arrived were slim. "Marko, go get the dead asshole out of the Land Rover and bring him up here."

Marko nodded and within a few minutes Marko arrived with the dead operative slung over his shoulder. He'd stopped bleeding, but the rotting and other excretions were beginning to smell. Marko tossed him down onto the floor.

Smitty rifled through the man's pockets again. They were empty. Smitty then rummaged through Boris' personal effects that Marko had already evaluated. Boris' wallet had a decent amount of cash, but all the ID cards were of little help. He grabbed the man's iPhone. The screen was locked, but the indications at the top still showed it in airplane mode and not transmitting. *'What else? What else does he have,'* Smitty thought. "JT, when you shot this idiot, did you find a radio or any other devices?" Smitty said on their secure comms."

"Nope boss. And I scoured his hole up site. Just him and a gun."

Smitty grabbed the man by the back of the hair, lifting his face. With the other hand, he held up the iPhone, attempting to open the device via facial recognition. Unfortunately, Boris was now sporting a large air-conditioning vent where his left cheekbone used to be. The phone wouldn't open. Smitty set the man down and began cleaning his face, attempting to patch the hole. Petrov watched in utter amusement. Eventually, the face was cleaned up, mitigating the hole to a degree. One more time, Smitty tried. It worked, and the phone opened. "Marko! Look," Smitty said. Some of the apps were obvious, but that was all Smitty could make out. All the text was in Russian Cyrillic.

Marko took the phone and began opening and closing apps, trying to learn anything he could. Eventually, he stumbled on an app that looked like a gun site reticle. The name was simply 'FindMe' in Russian. As he attempted to open the app, a banner popped up in Cyrillic, stating the phone was in airplane mode and would only display local members.  Marko selected the 'ok' button, and a map opened.

As soon as it opened, a map displayed with a small blue dot in the middle, similar to other iPhone apps which show the phone's location.  Within seconds, two additional blinking dots popped in, right on top of the phone's location.  Next to the blinking dots were two names in Cyrillic.  One said 'Victor' and the other said 'Boris.'

"Smitty," Marko said as he turned the phone's face towards him.  "This is how they are finding us."

Petrov smiled.

## Chapter Thirty-Three
# A Gentleman's Grip

Smitty took the phone and with two fingers shrunk the map to expose all of eastern Ukraine. Map details didn't fill out, and only the two beacons remained, Boris and Victor. He then took the phone out of airplane mode, activating the phone's network connection. Within seconds, beacons across eastern Ukraine all the way into Russia began popping up on the screen. Smitty's eyes widened. "Got you, you fucker," he said. It was a gold mine of information, and both Marko and Smitty knew it. "Alright. Let's find those beacons." Smitty stripped Boris naked. Somewhere on, or in, him was a transmitter and Smitty was hell bent to find it. He tossed Boris' filth ridden clothes out a window, on the other side of the building from the two Rasputin Firm mercenaries tracking them. The clothes fell to the ground roughly fifteen yards away from the building.

Smitty said to Marko who was holding the phone now, "Did the location change?"

Marko looked closely, the beacons did not move. "Nope. It wasn't the clothes."

Smitty grabbed Boris by a hand in an effort to roll him over. With his other hand, Smitty pulled out his knife, ready to filet Boris apart if necessary. As Smitty pulled hard on Boris' hand, he felt an odd object inside the back of the man's left hand. Smitty inspected the hand and began pushing the embedded object around. It appeared to be a small capsule, approximately the size of a perfume tester vile. Smitty cut the object out. As it protruded from the skin, it was clearly an electronic device. Smitty completely removed the capsule. Handing it to Beef, he said, "Run this down to the car." Beef took the device and did as instructed.

"Marko. What's on the phone now?"

Marko watched the screen. Within seconds, the blinking dot began to move. Marko smiled as he said, "Boris is moving!" It was perhaps a dark joke, implying Boris had returned to the living.

Smitty immediately turned to Petrov, who's smirk had vanished.

Smitty dropped Boris' hand and scrambled towards Petrov. He tossed Petrov onto the floor, face down, with his hands tied behind his back. Petrov struggled, but it was of little use. In Petrov's left hand, Smitty discovered another capsule embedded under the skin.

"Got ya, you fucker!" Smitty proclaimed. He pulled out his knife and cut open Petrov's hand without mercy. Petrov winced in pain as Smitty pushed the capsule through the newly formed hole. This time, Smitty examined the capsule further than the one he'd retrieved from Boris. On the outside, there was a serial number. Smitty thought for a second, then hatched a plan. It wasn't perfect, but it would buy them time. The tide was turning.

"JT," Smitty said on the radio. "Are you still eyes on the two dudes tracking on us?"

"Yup, boss, they are on a roof setting up for what appears to be a sniper shot. I'd stay away from the windows down there if I were you."

"OK. Here's what I want you to do." Smitty laid out detailed instructions for JT, who was to remain on the roof. Beef and Marko packed the Land Rover, preparing to depart. Smitty butchered away Boris' left hand from the arm. Given the many wrist bones, the task was a bit more challenging than he'd imagined, but eventually, the hand was freed.

Once the team was in the Land Rover, Smitty transmitted on the radio, "JT, your show. Take the shots."

JT was not a sniper, nor did he have a professional sniper rifle, but he did the best he could.

"Copy, boss," he said on the radio, as he began squeezing the trigger. A few shots rang off the front of the building where the Rasputin Firm mercenaries were set up. As anticipated, they dove for cover, realizing they were now exposed.

JT slowed his breathing. The next two shots needed to be perfect. Slowly, he applied pressure to the trigger. BANG! The first shot hit the target. '*One down*,' he thought. Again, he slowly squeezed. BANG! The second shot missed. "Damn it!" JT said out loud. Another deep breath, another settling of the reticle and another slow squeeze. BANG! The third was a bullseye. JT's job was done. He scrambled off the roof with his rifle in hand. In under a minute, he was at ground level and jumped into the Land Rover. Once safely inside, the vehicle sped away.

The roof line where the two Rasputin Firm snipers remained still. After a few seconds, one head, then the other popped up, cresting over the roof ledge. The two looked out to see the Land Rover fleeing. They too rapidly gathered their gear and scrambled down from the rooftop. They were close and did not want to let Petrov get away. Quickly, they tossed their gear into the vehicle, jumped in, cranked the engine, and hit the gas. The vehicle lurched forward; however, there was an intense pull towards the left. Confused, the driver stopped the car and got out. He immediately realized the problem. The Rasputin Firm SUV was not going anywhere with two flat tires... JT's targets.

Smitty and his team had bought a little time. They would drive for twenty minutes to make sure no one was tailing them. Eventually, they found another destroyed village with an abandoned building west of their last location. The village's name was Verkhnya. Not only did this village provide suitable cover, Smitty selected it with Buck's pending mission in mind. Although Smitty wasn't an aviator, he knew Verkhnya was an excellent location for an aircraft landing.

\*\*\*\*\*\*\*\*\*\*\*\*\*\*\*\*\*\*\*\*

A lonely presidential podium stood in front of a large White House press corps. The contents of this speech would not be surprising. There was no secret. The President would be stepping down. While everyone knew the actual reason was his affair, many were curious what excuse the President would offer. It was morning in D.C., and all the news outlets were prepared to go live to the White House. To fill the time, pundits and analysts were splashed across the screen in efforts to buy time until the President began to speak.

Cameras shuttered and flash bulbs strobed as the President emerged. Just as confidently as ever, he walked up the hallway towards the podium. Once behind the podium, he was flanked by Vice President Crawford on one side and House Speaker Karen Petroski on the other. He began to speak.

"Good morning. As many of you know, Russian state-owned media released a video, claiming it is Ms. Benson and I. This video is not only an attack on me. It is an attack on the American people. While my staff and supporters have demanded I fight this, I must confess, I no longer possess the strength to fight these continual inappropriate and personal attacks. I confess, they have worn on me, and I know Americans need someone who still can robustly fight back. Because of this, I am stepping down as President of the United States."

As the President made the announcement, even more cameras flashed.

"To make sure American remains strong and well represented, I've had our team clearly examine the rules of succession laid out within the Twenty-Fifth Amendment. As most know, the normal succession would be the Vice President of the United States, as done in our past a handful of times, most recently after the tragic assassination of President Kennedy." He paused for impact.

"However, what was clearly different in all those cases versus the one we face today is that all those Vice Presidents were part of an elected ticket. They had run on a successful campaign and were chosen by the people."

Stacy Crawford's blood began to boil, but she was on national television. While her insides raged, externally, she showed a sense of interest and inquisitiveness towards the President's comments.

He continued. "I want to underline that I stand by my selection of Vice President Crawford, who has performed remarkably in the short time she's been here." He paused and turned to Stacy with a big political smile. "Thank you, Stacy. I mean that sincerely."

Stacy smiled and nodded, again wanting to punch the President square in the jaw.

He turned back towards the cameras. "To me, though, I just can't help but think the American people deserve the chance to select the replacement, and Ms. Crawford was never part of a campaign ticket. She was never selected by the people. As we all know, however, House Speaker Petroski is a long-standing politician. She has faced countless campaigns, continually being selected not only by her district but also by the Congressional majority as their elected Speaker. I'm not suggesting an effort to usurp the Constitutionally mandated chain of succession, but clearly, there are some serious questions as our nation moves forward."

The President turned toward Congresswoman Petroski and smiled. In true political form, she lovingly returned the gesture.

After the interlude, the President continued. "What is perhaps of interest to the American people, the Ninth Amendment of the Constitution states, 'The enumeration in the Constitution, of certain rights, shall not be construed to deny or disparage others retained by the people.' Now, that may not make much sense to anyone other than a lawyer. Heck, I don't really understand it. But according to many constitutional scholars, James Madison ensured this text so that the rights within the Bill of Rights were not limiting. In other words, if a 'right' is not defined in the Constitution, it belongs to the people. Given the unique situation we are currently in, I can think of no better time for the Ninth Amendment to be considered. Should Americans be denied the right to have selected by vote a Vice President by an electoral college vote? If so, and I think there's merit here, perhaps an immediate special election be held to choose the next President of the United States."

Again, the President paused for effect. The clear difference in the reception of these comments between Stacy and Karen standing next to him grew ever more prevalent. Karen smiled as her chest bowed out with pride. Conversely, Stacy now realized she'd been set up. The President's request for her to accompany him onto camera was a hit job in the making. She had no choice but to stand there as stoic as possible, supporting the man she wanted to attack.

"Because of this," the President continued. "I've asked the other two branches of government to rapidly evaluate this issue. A decision to invoke the Ninth Amendment should not be mine alone, it should be a decision of those who have skin in the game, which makes sense. Frankly, it makes sense in a similar fashion as to why I think it's the right thing to do, just like to give the American people the chance to select their true chain of succession. Thank you. May God Bless you, and the United States of America."

Screams of questions rose from the Press Corps, but the President ignored them all. He turned to the Speaker first, shaking her hand and nodding. He then turned to Stacy, shaking her hand and squeezing it tight, overly tight, in fact.

While still on camera, Stacy smiled as she stepped towards him, and behind the podium dug the heel of her shoe into the top of his foot. "You have fucked with the wrong woman," she said to him, all the while smiling politely for the cameras.

His eyes open wide. He knew he was still on camera and could not react in the way he desired. He smiled and stepped away from the podium. As he did, Stacy Crawford stepped behind it, unscheduled, and without prepared remarks.

The Press Corps hushed as Vice President Crawford lowered the microphone to her height and calmly cleared her throat.

"Mr. President, Madam Speaker, and American people," she began. "While the sun shines brightly outside this building, today is a gloomy day for America. Make no mistake, however, bright days will again soon shine down on us. As the nominated and Senate confirmed Vice President of the United States of America, I wanted to be the first to thank you, Mr. President, for your unwavering and stalwart service to our nation. You've helmed our nation courageously and it would be an injustice if I was not afforded the chance to be the first to thank you on behalf of a grateful nation."

Stacy finished her comments while intentionally slowly pulling away from the microphone. As she expected, a journalist screamed out, "Madam Vice President, do you agree with the President regarding the Ninth Amendment?"

Quickly, she re-assumed the podium. Much in the way she was forced to endure the President's comments, she now would return the favor.

"Well, thanks for asking that. I must confess. Much like you, this is the first-time I am hearing about this. So, I really would need to do some responsible research before answering off the cuff. What is somewhat puzzling, however, is this notion that I was not selected by the people? Frankly, I was nominated and confirmed by the Senate of the United States. Senators that face elections every six years and are responsible to their constituents, the American people. True, I didn't run a national campaign as Vice President. But, I would point out the American people have not, in fact, ever selected a president by popular vote. It's always been by the electoral college, or a group of representatives for each state. This is quite similar, if not exactly the same thing as Senators voting for and approving a nomination." Stacy paused to let the thought resonate.

"All that said, I think both the House Speaker and I agree. This issue is extremely important. As the immediate line of succession, I humbly accept the Office of the President of the United States for now. Leaving our nation rudderless until a decision on the Ninth Amendment is made would harm our nation. As Congress and the Supreme Court evaluate the merits, I will lead. Should they, and the American people, decide a special election is warranted, I will stand by that decision."

Stacy stepped away from the microphone and immediately shook Speaker Petroski's hand, who looked like she'd been hit by a truck. Stacy then shook the now former President's hand, quite professionally, then began walking away from the podium down the hallway from which the President emerged, leaving the two standing there.

For the former President as well as the presidential staff, it was a PR nightmare. Now, President Crawford had snatched the reins of leadership and was running off with the keys to the White House. This was not how the press conference was supposed to end.

Standing there, awkwardly, the former President and the Speaker talked and waved to audience members until the cameras cut away.

Within hours after the press conference, Marine One's rotor blades began turning. The former President walked across the south lawn one last time, waving to onlookers.

Standing off to the side, President Crawford and her husband, Ryan, a former Marine, watched with stoic sincerity. As he boarded Marine One, Ryan slowly lifted his right hand to a salute. The image was captured by the press. The new President, along with her husband, who was rendering military courtesies to a disgraced President. It would be on the cover of every media outlet in minutes.

Marine One lifted off and, at roughly fifteen feet above the South lawn, slowly turned its nose towards Camp David. It was the agreed location where he would remain through the transition.

Without delay, White House staff were rapidly cleaning up the Oval Office. They would not complete the task.

Stacy approached her new office, opening the door to find staff scurrying. She had startled them. "No, please. Keep doing what you're doing. Don't mind us."

Stacy and Ryan looked at the office. It was hers. "What do you think?" she asked her husband.

"Eh. Not bad. I'm just not a fan of a room without a corner. Technically, there's no place to hide in a shootout." It was the Marine in him answering.

Stacy chuckled. "Sweetheart. I think that's the point."

## Chapter Thirty-Four

# Friends & Foes

Smitty and the team were safe, or at least safer. Tracking them down had just become a far greater challenge for the Rasputin Firm. Additionally, with Boris' phone, they could easily see when other Rasputin Firm members were closing in on their location... at least the ones who'd been chipped.

Smitty looked up Rob Farkas' number on his personal phone, which remained in airplane mode. He transcribed the number into Boris' and dialed the number.

"Hello?" Rob answered. It was odd to see a Russian number calling.

"Rob. Smitty here. Need your help. Gonna give you some info and need you to write it down and hand deliver it to Buck before he flies tonight."

Rob knew Smitty was on a mission deep in Ukraine. If he was calling on an open line, it must be important. "OK, standby. Let me get something to write on... And, go."

"Pick up point is Verkhnya. Approach from the south. There is a straight road leading into the village, treelined on either side with no overhead wires. Also, good cover to the north at the end of the road. IR sticks will mark the road. Five pax."

Rob read it back.

"Correct. Rob, this is critical. Please, only a hand delivered piece of paper. Nothing digital on this. Please. I've already taken chances just sharing with you."

"Will do. But I gotta run. I'm in Warsaw and need to drive to Base U."

"What are you waiting for then? Go!" Smitty hung up. He was concerned that the message was in the clear. Using Boris' phone likely meant the line would not be intercepted, but one never knew. It was the best of many poor options.

Rob sped to Base U and hand delivered the message, just as Smitty requested. As Buck examined all the information and the local area map, he was impressed. Smitty had done well. The road Smitty identified was long enough to land, and then once on the ground, treelines would provide a decent amount of cover from any potential small arms fire. The landing roll would be slightly uphill, a dual benefit. First, it would slow the aircraft faster on landing and when turning around, it would help accelerate the takeoff roll. With 5 pax and gear, Buck wanted all the takeoff help he could get. He had never tried to take off with an extra thirteen hundred pounds with just the jet engine. All of his takeoffs with gear were from a towline and with a monster aircraft tugging him into the air. Buck calculated one thousand for the pax and another three hundred for fuel. It would be tough, but he felt confident he could do it. As for getting there, there was only one option. A take off from Base U with no cargo and an extremely high-altitude release. He'd need to glide a long way.

Back in Verkhnya, Smitty had pulled out Petrov's phone and opened it via facial recognition. Handing it to Marko, he said, "Marko, send the following text message translated in Russian to the top three numbers you can find associated with Rasputin Firm:

> *Comrades!*
> *I've snuck onto my phone. They're holding Boris and I. You need to send more than just one or two operatives. Come tonight. Boris on main level. I'm in the basement. They sleep from 2AM to 4AM. Do what you must. Tell my family I love them.*
>
> *Victor*

Marko did as requested. Smitty was laying a trap. Whether it worked or not, Verkhnya, Ukraine, was about to have one of its most exciting nights in a long time.

*********************

The cleaning crews were finished in the Oval Office. Stacy entered and slowly walked around. She wanted to soak in every ounce. Her hand gently drug across the top of one of the sofas.

Slowly, she moved to the window overlooking the rose garden. It was a lovely view. Turning back, she looked down at the desk. It was spotless and nearly empty, minus one yellow sticky note placed in the center. *'No doubt a last jab from her former boss,'* she thought.

As she got closer, she learned she was wrong. It said:

> *Baby,*
> *You got this!*
> *Love,*
> *Ryan*

A soft knock thumped from the thick Oval Office door.

"Yes." Stacy said.

It opened, and Steve Lewis, the Chief of Staff stood there. "Madam President, you wanted to see me?"

"Yes, Steve. You were the first on my list, in fact. Please come in and sit down."

Steve slowly walked in. He was certain he knew the logical outcome of this conversation. As far as Steve was concerned, he was the future former Chief of Staff. He slowly sat down.

"Steve," Stacy said. "Where do you think I believe your loyalties lie?"

"Ma'am. I assume that answer is with the former President."

"Steve, this is where you are wrong. Please do not assume anything. We both know the old saying about assuming."

"Yes, ma'am," Steve replied.

"Steve," she continued. "I believe your loyalties lie where you tell me they lie. And I will trust you until you prove otherwise. Let me tell you something. When we learned of the President's infidelity. I could clearly see you were unaware. To me, that was one of the most telling traits about you."

"Ma'am?" Steve replied. "Yes, it's true. I did not know, but I am lost."

"Steve, as the Chief of Staff, the President has the choice to share information with you or keep it from you. Clearly, from his judgement, his affair was something you'd not approve of."

She was right, and Steve was grateful for her awareness. "Thanks, Madam President."

"Steve, do you want to stay on as the Chief of Staff or should I expect your resignation letter?"

Steve was somewhat stunned. He wasn't getting fired. "Ma'am..." He stuttered. "I just assumed you'd plan to use your Vice Presidential Chief of Staff."

"Steve, no more assuming. Please."

"Yes... yes, I'd like to remain the Chief of Staff."

"OK. Here's my rules. First, your loyalty is to me. You will have no conversations with the former president, or party officials without my prior knowledge and approval. Is that clear?"

"Yes, Ma'am."

"Second. You are in a probationary period. You are correct, I could easily bring up my former Chief of Staff, but I'd rather find him a position within your staff, for now. We possibly have an election to prepare for, and I believe it's far better to keep as much of the ship's crew intact. You are an integral part of that."

"Yes, Ma'am."

"Third. I want meetings with the acting Defense Secretary, and Chairman ASAP..."

"I'll schedule them immediately," Steve responded.

"Good. One last thing. Look me in the eye and tell me where your loyalty lies."

Steve found it an odd request but didn't' question it. "Madam President. My loyalty lies with you."

"Great. It's settled. Now, I..." The President was interrupted by a knock at the door.

"Yes?" she said.

The door opened and Major Buckhout, the Presidential Military Aide said, "Madam President, I am sorry to bother you, but Russian President Volkov has called three times and demands to speak to you."

"Well," Stacy said as she looked at Steve. "What do you recommend I do?"

Steve didn't need to think twice. "Ma'am, it's your call. Making him wait or taking it immediately, either sends a message.  I guess my answer is, what relationship do you want to build with Russia?"

"Excellent answer, Steve. Thanks."  She turned to the major.  "Major Buckhout is it?  Please, put President Volkov through."

Steve got up to turn the speaker phone around.  As he did, Stacy grabbed his arm and said, "I can do that."

Before Steve could respond, Volkov's voice boomed over the Speaker.  "Madam President.  Please pardon my interruption, but I wanted to be the first to congratulate you on your new position."

"President Volkov.  I am grateful for your message.  Yes, things are quite busy, as you can likely imagine.  I do want to assure you, though, the United States leadership across all three branches of government remains strong.  Transitioning Presidents is something we are quite good at.  In fact, I think we've done it far more times than Russia in the past forty years."

President Volkov chuckled.  Stacy was correct, but Volkov could not care less.  "Very true, Madam President.  Very true.  I am curious if there is anything Russia can do to help ease your transition, and perhaps a meeting with our ambassador to discuss the west's inappropriate assistance to Ukraine is warranted."

Stacy would not take the bait.  "Mister President.  I am grateful for your offer and yes, I plan to meet with as many ambassadors as possible but for now, I am extremely busy.  Perhaps we can talk again later."

"Madam President.  I am not sure what could be more important than the issue of Ukraine."

Stacy shot a small grin at Steve.  "Well, to be honest, Mr. President, I could think of about half a dozen."  Steve returned the grin.

There was a pause on the other end of the line.  Then Volkov spoke again.  "I see.  Well, to ensure you are aware of our position.  Russia...."

Stacy cut him off.  "Mr. President.  I confess, I have yet to be briefed by my security council on numerous issues, and clearly, the war in Ukraine is key.  But unless some dramatically different information surfaces, I, together with the American people, am inclined to believe there is nothing just in the Russian position and your invasion was illegal if not unethical and immoral."

"Madam President," Volkov responded immediately. "This is perhaps not the way you should start your presidency. There is likely information you do not know. I'd ask you to meet at your earliest opportunity with our ambassador. He will have things you likely find... shall we say... interesting."

"President Volkov, I will meet with your ambassador soon enough. As I will meet with many others. Again, thank you for your call. I understand these conversations are challenging, but open, and more importantly, honest dialogue between our nations has never been more vital."

"I agree, Madam President. I shall leave you to your affairs. Good day." The line went dead. Volkov grinned. A clueless, unelected female was at America's helm. The plan had taken years, but it finally worked.

Back in the Oval Office, Stacy looked at Steve. "Well, that was interesting."

"Yes, ma'am. Should I schedule a meeting with Ambassador Tarlov?"

"No. Let's get the acting Defense Secretary, Chairman and Marleen Baker one on ones first. Thanks, Steve."

"Madam President. If I am going to work with you, I do have one request."

Stacy's eyebrows raised. She hadn't expected a man who just had his career spared to have demands. Intrigued, she responded, "Yes?"

"Ma'am. When I spun the phone around for you and you stopped me. I'm the President's Chief of Staff and would do that for a man, a woman, or a Bohemian transexual if they were president. I promise I will never 'mansplain' anything to you, but you must let me do my job. You are a very determined woman, and that's likely why you've achieved the status you have. I assure you, I'll let you do your job, but please let me do my job."

Stacy reflected for a short time on Steve's comment. He was right, and she'd have to work on that. "Deal. But Steve..."

"Yes, Madam President?"

"Thirty years of being a determined woman doesn't flip off like a light switch. You gotta give me a few passes every now and then." She grinned again at him.

Steve smiled back. "Sure thing, boss." Steve walked out of the office and began arranging her meetings for the next day. As he walked out, Ryan, Stacy's husband, waited just outside the door.

"Ryan, get in here." She said as if she was ordering a young Marine private around. Ryan, a retired Marine major, followed the order with precision, scurrying into the office.

"Yes, Madam President," he said. Then he embraced her, giving her a hug and a kiss. "Stacy, I'm so proud of you. You're gonna do great."

"Thanks. How are things going upstairs in the private quarters? Are you getting our things settled in?"

"I'm trying, but I think we are gonna have to sleep on the floor tonight. There just isn't really enough time."

Stacy kissed Ryan on the cheek. "Nah. How about a nice night in a hotel?"

Stacy raised her voice just a bit and faced the door. "Agnus," she said, addressing the President's secretary. Stacy knew Agnus quite well. Ever since Stacy was a senior member in the Defense Department, she'd seen Agnus when visiting the Oval Office.

"Yes, ma'am," a gentle but weathered voice responded.

"Do you think we could make arrangements to stay in the little White House this evening?" The little White House of President McKinley was an old historic residence just outside the main White House. For years, it had been part of the U.S. Federal court, located just next door, and extremely powerful federal employees held high-level meetings there. During Stacy's first few years in D.C., she'd passed it countless times, attracted by its charm. Never in her life did she imagine she'd have the chance to spend the night.

"I'll coordinate it for you, ma'am." Agnus shot back. Special Agent David Griffin was the head Secret Service agent on Stacy's detail. He overheard the conversation and had already started putting security protocols in place.

## Chapter Thirty-Five
# The Hunters & The Hunted

Darkness had fallen over the small Ukrainian village of Verkhnya. In an abandoned house, the team was placing the finishing touches on their trap. Over a small fire, Smitty melted down three of his lead bullets into a small glass. As the molten lead began to cool, he dropped Boris' tracking capsule into the metal, then melted another bullet over the top. Now trapped inside a makeshift Faraday cage, the transmitter would be masked to any receivers.

Once complete, the team slowly crept up to the top of the hill, placing infrared glow sticks along the two-lane paved road. To the average eye, they were undetectable, but through night vision devices, they stood out like a powerful flashlight.

At the top of the hill, Smitty watched the tracking app on Victor's phone. Roughly two miles away, a team of twelve Rasputin operatives were holed up, likely preparing for their mission. Victor's beacon was performing perfectly in the house down below. Boris' beacon was nowhere to be found, but latency indications showed it last in the same house.

The road was well camouflaged by the western tree line. JT scanned the eastern tree line and down to the town. Conversely, Beef was in the eastern treeline, performing the same function to the west.

Roughly fifty miles away, Buck was gliding towards them, in five miles, he'd cross into Russian-held territory. The fighting on the ground was fairly intense that night. As he closed the line of contact, he witnessed massive artillery barrages being lobbed between the opposing forces. His headset had the distinct sounds of acquisition radars spinning and looking for air targets. The indications of a target tracker still had not blared into his headset.

Now twenty miles away, Buck took a slight offset from Verkhnya to the south. His GPS was only partially reliable, and it faded in and out, likely affected by ground-based jammers. Luckily, as an air asset, he was able to reacquire a signal every now and then between the jammers. He would fly to a point three miles south of the town. Once lined up on the extended runway / road heading, he would turn 90 degrees to the left for the landing. Normally, with an unfamiliar airfield, a pilot would hope for a much longer approach, but this was enemy territory. Being 'low and slow' for a long time was far too uncomfortable for Buck.

As he continued to his offset point, Buck saw very few lights emanating from the village. What little light did shine were the stubborn Ukrainians who refused to leave their homes under Russian occupation. Most faked their loyalty to Russia, just waiting for the return of Ukrainian forces. Even on his night vision devices, there was little activity. Almost into the turn to final, Buck still couldn't see any infrared markers. He said a small prayer, hoping Smitty and the team had not been captured. Preparing for the worst, he also deployed his jet engine into the airstream. Prayers were good, but if he received no indications that Smitty was there, Buck had no intention to land.

Gently turning the glider north, the two tree lines separated and eight glow sticks lit up the small road. "Hell yes, Buddy!" Buck screamed. He silently flew in for the landing, setting Old Girl onto the road right at the first glow stick marker. The plane rolled uphill, slowing fairly quickly. He'd stay off the brakes as much as possible to get as far up the hill as he could. Given the anticipated takeoff weight, he'd take every inch of runway he could. As he crested onto the top of the hill, Buck plunged the brakes to the floor and the aircraft stopped.

Quickly, Smitty and Marko drug Victor onto the plane while JT and Beef ran up the road, jumping onboard in the back left and right cargo doors.

"Hey Smitty! Bernard Fisher at your service!"

"Who the f... what the? Dude. Shut up and fly!" Smitty screamed.

Buck was somewhat hurt. He'd come up with Bernard Fisher analogy and really believed it was a good one, hoping Smitty would ask.

"OK, turn me around boys!" Buck commanded. JT and Beef

jumped off Old Girl, and pushed the tail around until she was facing down the road, and more importantly, downhill.

With a few flips of a switch, the small jet engine began to whine. Buck applied full power, then released the brakes. Old Girl began rolling down the hill. With the weight, Buck calculated a takeoff speed of 72 knots. Slowly, the gauge climbed. 40 knots. 50 knots. He was halfway down the road by now. 60 knots and the tail lifted off the ground. Old Girl was now feeling light on the road, bouncing just a bit. 70 knots and Buck slowly pulled back. Old Girl lumbered slowly into the air. She'd clear the houses in the village of Verkhnya by a few meters. The rest of Ukraine's terrain heading south towards the Black Sea was flat. Buck had a positive rate of climb and was growing more confident by the minute. He was airborne and flying away, albeit still deep in enemy territory.

Five miles south of Verkhnya, a Russian air defense team sat with their 9K34 Strela-3 shoulder launched ground to air infrared missile, also known by its NATO designation, the SA-14 Gremlin. It was a fairly advanced missile and Russian intelligence had placed them in the area based on tips derived from 'unidentified sources.'

In the distance, the Russian air defense team heard a strange noise. Over time, it grew closer. Querying each other, none were familiar with the noise. It wasn't the typical fighter jet engine or military grade helicopter. It was too high pitched. They were right. It wasn't a traditional military aircraft. It was Old Girl, and she was headed right for them.

The missile operator coolly turned on the missile computer, activating power from the battery to the infrared seeker and the identification friend or foe system. He sat there looking in the direction of Old Girl, just waiting for the missile to lock onto the engine.

Now less than 800 meters away, a Russian lieutenant was on night vision and could see Old Girl. He screamed, "It's right there! Shoot it!!"

Now 600 feet, the operator could see the aircraft silhouette in the lens, but the missile would not lock.

Old Girl flew over the top of the air defense operators at

roughly three hundred feet. Desperate, the Russian lieutenant raised his AK-47 and began firing. It would be the last bad decision he made. Beef, sitting in the back cargo door, witnessed the sporadic small arms fire and returned in kind from a Squadron Automatic Weapon M249. Within seconds, most of the air defense team was lying mortally wounded, dead or dying.

Beef leaned into the aircraft and screamed. "Dude's had a MANPAD! (Man Portable Air Defense Missile). Dunno why they didn't whack us."

Buck laughed. "Poor dudes. Probably couldn't lock us. Old Girl's engine exhaust is about 350 degrees Celsius. That missile was likely designed to seek out aircraft with far hotter exhaust systems. As MANPADs advanced in design, they naturally advanced to counter their specific targets, modern jet fighters. Fighter jet engines have become hotter and hotter, thus the seeker for the MANPAD 'looks' for that heat range, roughly around 800 degrees Celsius. We were probably never in its seeker's temperature limits or field of view. Eh, live and learn. If they wanna shoot us, they'll likely have to go pull out their older missiles with a larger temperature field of view. But I ain't gonna tell 'em. Some of their air defense missiles could also have a contrast mode as well. Even with that though, it would be extremely hard to lock us up against the backdrop of a dark sky." Buck paused. "Ain't technology a bitch!"

For minutes, he'd been talking to Smitty, who didn't react to any of his comments. Finally, he looked over. Smitty was holding the side of his abdomen, and there was clearly blood. He'd been hit by a golden BB from the Russian lieutenant's AK-47.

"Shit!" Buck yelled. "Smitty's hit!"

Marko jumped up and ran to the front, pulling Smitty out of the copilot seat and laying him down in the cargo bay near Petrov. Both JT and Beef closed their cargo doors. Small arms fire would provide no further challenges for the flight. After laying him on the ground, they could see Smitty had suffered a gut shot. There was a clean entry wound, but no exit. Petrov sat on the side of the aircraft, his hands zip tied to the side of the plane, smiling at Smitty. "It seems you will die before I do.

That's a pity. Until we meet again in hell."

"Fuck you!" Smitty yelled.

JT opened his medic bag and pulled out a HemCon bandage, opened it and slapped it on the wound. Within seconds the bandage began to swell, causing clotting, at least externally. The bandages were a modern wonder. A complex carbohydrate from shrimp shells called chitosan was discovered to create a webbing effect and caused blood to rapidly clot in under two minutes. It saved countless U.S. service members in Iraq and Afghanistan.

JT then ran up to Buck. "Dude. I don't know how much time he has. Do full throttle or whatever the hell this thing has."

Unfortunately, Old Girl didn't have much. She never was intended to. Buck climbed slowly into the night sky heading West. He'd have enough fuel to make it to Uman, but no further.

Buck pulled out his phone and began typing a text message to Curt.

> 'Curt,
> Smitty took a round to the gut. Flying to your location. Be there in just over an hour.
> Buck'

As Buck hit send, his heart sank. For the next thirty minutes, Buck would try to get a cellular network and then rapidly hit send. Each time he did, an error message displayed, *'Message failed to send.'* Eventually, he'd give up.

Slowly, Smitty's belly began to swell. At first, it looked like he'd eaten too much food. After another ten minutes, he almost looked pregnant. The internal bleeding hadn't subsided. The pain was excruciating. The only positive sign was the external bleeding had stopped.

Smitty's eyes began rolling back. He wanted to sleep. JT screamed, "Stay with me, Smitty! Come on, man. Stay with us!"

Buck could hear the entire conversation in the back. He looked down at his airspeed indicator. It read 110knots. There was to getting Old Girl any faster. Given the head winds, he was possibly getting 80-90 knots of ground speed. A tear welled up in his eye. He was hopeless to do more.

Smitty's alarm on his watch began beeping. "Gimme the fucking phone! Gimme it!"

JT handed Petrov's phone over. Smitty opened the tracker app and watched.

*********************

Back in Verkhnya, twelve operatives were poised around the house. After a few minutes, they rushed in from three different sides, two through front and back doors, and the other through a window. Inside, they found Boris, laying naked on the ground, with a blanket over him, covering his torso, legs and arms. Quickly clearing that room, the team lead stormed into the basement. As they did, they saw a lone table with a plate on it. On the plate, a severed hand stood upright on top of a round dish. Next to the hand was the Rasputin Firm transponder once inside Petrov. It was the only thing in the entire basement. "Stop!" The team lead screamed. Realizing it was a trap. Unfortunately, he was too late. His next step tugged a tripwire which knocked the hand off of the table, fully exposing the dish and hand was sitting on. The dish was hiding a circular anti-tank mine. The hand and additional weights had held the detonator down. Once removed, the plunger released, and the device exploded. Instantly, five members of the team were killed, and the other seven were seriously wounded.

Smitty watched as five beacons stopped moving and seven scattered slowly from the house. "Die you fuckers," he said as he winced in pain.

## Chapter Thirty-Six

# Not Today

It was late at Uman and Curt had gotten up to take a leak. As he returned to bed, he checked his phone. One of Buck's messages had gotten through. Curt rapidly dressed and then ran to the medical tent. There was a skeleton crew working in the tent, most of the other medical staff had retired to bed. Through the night, they'd worked on countless patients who kept arriving from a battle between two brigade sized elements. Wounded totals were extremely high for both sides.

Slowly, Buck began descending into Uman. Back in the cargo bay, he could hear JT and Beef talking to Smitty, trying to keep him alive. In response, all Smitty could muster were some horrid sounding moans due to his excruciating pain. Old Girl's fuel tank had about three gallons remaining.

Curt stood on the side of the runway with a team and a gurney. Inside, a surgical doctor Curt had befriended was rustled from bed. His name was Michael Cohen, a former Army surgical doctor who'd married a French-Ukrainian woman. Because of her ties to Ukraine, Michael was volunteering to help in a MASH unit. It was the least he could do.

Old Girl slowly settled onto the runway, Buck could see Curt on the side of the runway and biased the landing roll towards Curt's side. It was all he could do.

Expeditiously, Smitty was placed on the gurney. Curt feared the worst. His liver was possibly pierced open. "Hey buddy. Looks like it's my turn to save your life," he said to Smitty.

"Doc, just fix it, now! Or kill me. Either way. I can't take the pain."

Curt and the staff wheeled him to the medical tent. Doc Cohen was standing by, as was an anesthesiologist who went by the name 'Ludes,' which was short for quaaludes.

Quickly, Ludes placed a mask over Smitty's mouth while the team began ripping off his clothes and scrubbing him down. His stomach was massive now, but the HemCon had done its job. The external bleeding had all but stopped.

Smitty began to fade away under the watchful eye of Ludes. He'd feel no more pain, or at least he would not be able to complain about it. A blood pressure sleeve was affixed to his arm as well as a temperature and oxygen level sensor to his finger. The team was moving as fast as they could. Curt was directing traffic as if he were on his first patient back at Cook County Medical Center in Chicago.

Doc Cohen looked at Curt as he held a scalpel over Smitty belly. "You ready?"

"Yes. Cut. Let's go," Curt replied.

As Doc Cohen cut into the belly, a blast of blood, bile and other fluid spewed across the room. Medical technicians worked to clean off Smitty's stomach as well as clean the wound. The vacuum was working nonstop, literally buried in a pool of blood in Smitty's stomach.

"Losing him," Ludes said, as Smitty's blood pressure instantly dropped after the cut. Evidently, the pressure from internal bleeding was holding up his blood pressure. Once that wound was exposed and opened, the pressure fell.

Ludes immediately provided a medical cocktail to bring the blood pressure back up, but it wouldn't last long, especially if Doc Cohen didn't find the wound. As the blood pressure stabilized, Ludes again called out. "O2 falling. Get more blood now." Two bags of red blood sat next to the table. They were the last two that matched Smitty's needs. After another five minutes, one of them was already empty.

"Gimme the empty one," Curt commanded. He reached down on the medical tray, grabbed an IV needle then stabbed the vein of his left arm, quickly connecting the bag.

"What are you doing?" Dr. Cohen asked.

"I'm saving my fucking friends live. Keep working," Curt replied.

Within minutes, Smitty would have pure whole blood from Curt who was O negative, a universal donor. "Hang on, Damn it Smitty!" He said aloud.

Dr. Cohen worked feverishly inside Smitty's stomach. Curt's first bag of blood was filled, just as the second bag of blood affixed in Smitty's arm expired. Curt disconnected his bag and

240

gave it to the nurse. She traded out the empty bag with Curt who started filling that bag as well. Eventually, Curt heard the magic sound. A piece of lead smacking against the bottom of a metal container.

"Found the bullet. It's a liver shot. Packing it now. What's his O2 levels?"

Ludes called out, "Good for O2." Curt was squeezing a rubber ball in his hand and releasing as quick as possible, doing everything he could to keep filling up his donation bags of blood. Again, Curt had filled another in a matter of minutes. He and the nurse exchanged bags for a second time.

Dr. Cohen cleaned the wound. The liver was pierced and was seeping bile. Once clean, he began packing it.

Then, they heard the tone no medical staff wants to hear. A steady tone. "Flat line." Curt pulled out the paddles, yelled, "Clear," and shocked Smitty. There was no response. Again, he yelled, "Clear!" still no response. Curt threw down the paddles and pounded on Smitty's chest. And with that, Smitty's heart started back up. "Keep going, Mike! You're doing great!" Curt said.

For a third time, Curt's bag was full, and he again exchanged it. Curt's eyes were getting heavy, and he was getting lightheaded, as he tried to fill a fourth bag.

"Slow down, buddy," Ludes said to Curt. "I don't need two patients at this table."

"Ludes, keep him alive. Don't worry about me. You do you, man. You do you!"

Dr. Cohen was stuffing the wound with perihepatic packing. It was the best he could do in the field hospital. The bleeding would at least be controlled... not stopped. Smitty would need surgery, soon, to repair his liver. If that couldn't happen, Smitty had no chance at survival.

Curt fell to the floor. Passed out. A few nurses drug him out and withdrew the IV needle. They checked his vitals. His blood pressure was low, but he was fine. He was placed in one of the patient beds.

"Can't believe that guy," Ludes said to Mike. "That's some of the craziest shit I've seen."

241

"Yeah," Mike responded. "It likely saved this guy's life. At least for now. Sutures," he called out as he began sewing up Smitty's belly.

As all the commotion was going on in the medical unit, another circus was on display outside of it. JT, Beef and Buck were holding Victor Petrov as Marko was talking to Ukrainian police, who were trying to take him. It was a Mexican standoff.

Buck began fueling his aircraft again, readying it for a flight to Base U. As he did, more and more Ukrainian military police arrived at the scene. Quickly, the three were outnumbered. Victor rather enjoyed the attention. A black sedan with flags signifying some high-ranking official pulled up. Before the driver could open the back passenger door, a well-dressed man in a military field uniform emerged. Marko and all the others sprung to attention, saluting immediately. The man returned the salute and bellowed something in Ukrainian. Marko responded.

"Yes, Sir. I am the Ukrainian most in charge."

"Fine. What is your name, son?"

"Marko. Colonel Marko Taran."

"Marko, I want you to take Victor Petrov from the Americans and come with me to Kyiv."

Marko hesitated at the order.

"Do you have a problem with that?"

"No Sir, it's just." Marko stumbled. He cleared his throat and continued. "Sir, we have Petrov on our base. He is surrounded by police officers and not likely getting away anytime soon. This mission was executed by a U.S. company with the knowledge of the U.S. Government and our leadership. Before we seize him, wouldn't it be wise to allow Washington D.C. to awake and speak to our ambassador there?"

Everything Marko said made sense. But the commanding General didn't care.

"Put him in the car. Right fucking now."

Buck had finished fueling the aircraft and, as if without a care in the world, walked right up to the General. "Sir, excuse me. What's your name?" he said in English.

Incensed, the man said in a commanding voice. "I am Lieutenant General Andre Aleksandar! Land Forces Commander for Ukraine!"

"Great!" Buck said, "Hold on." Buck turned his head and lifted the phone back up to his ear, which he'd been carrying. "Guy says he's Lieutenant General Aleksandar." Buck listened for a bit then turned back to the General. "General, this guy wants to talk to you."

"Who is it!" The General demanded.

"It's Admiral Eugene Hershey, former Chairman of the Joint Chiefs of Staff."

With that, the General's eyes widened. He had met Admiral Hershey many times, especially since the initial invasion of Russia into Crimea. He was far from prepared for this call, especially in an audience of which he commanded attention.

"Admiral," he said, as the decibels behind his bark reduced by half. "Good morning to you."

"Good morning, Lieutenant General Aleksandar. I understand there is a problem at your base."

"Sir, there is no problem. Some leaders in Kyiv would like to question Mr. Petrov, and then we shall return him to you. You have my word."

"General. I appreciate that. But if any of my team lose sight of Mr. Petrov before I have a chance to speak to your Ambassador, I can assure you, the consequences for your country will be unimaginable. My pilot tells me your colonel helped capture Mr. Petrov, and I am grateful for that. I also believe your colonel helped ensure the destruction of a key Russian logistics hub, a mission my men also executed for your nation. Your colonel, as I understand, has recommended everyone wait until Washington wakes up. I believe that is also a fine recommendation. What do you think, General?"

Magically, when the recommendation came from the former Chairman of the Joint Chiefs, it was a fabulous recommendation that the General could easily support. "Yes... yes, Admiral. There is no rush. We shall wait here."

"Great. Thank you, General. Can you please put my pilot back on the phone?" The General handed over the phone.

"Hey, Admiral. It's me, Buck."

"Buck. OK. I bought you some time. Where's Curt?"

"Sir, Curt has passed out in a hospital bed. He gave Smitty somewhere between three and four bags of blood."

"Well, that answers my next question, 'Where is Smitty?' Let me change that question to 'How is Smitty?'"

"Sir, not good. Liver shot. He's patched up and I guess they say they 'stuffed' the wound, but without true surgery soon, his chances are grim. Jackal is sitting by his side. Hasn't left him."

"OK. Keep me posted. I'm gonna work from Landstuhl back to you. You work to get him there. Hopefully, we meet in the middle." The Admiral was determined to do what he could.

"Will do, Sir. What about Petrov?"

"Keep JT or Beef on him. I need you to pack up Petrov and fly him to Poland as soon as the Ukrainian government released him to your custody."

"OK. I presume that's when General Aleksandar says OK."

"Yes," replied the Admiral.

"Sounds good. Looks like it will have to be Jughead flying him, though. I found some damage to my aircraft. Do you want this mission to take priority? Jughead's aircraft is here, and we are unloading it from the logistics flight."

"Yes, Petrov is the priority. He flies out today. Once at Base U, Rob Farkas will take Petrov into holding."

"Easy day, Boss."

"OK. Keep me posted."

The phone line disconnected, and Buck walked over to Jughead who was preparing the SBD II for the flight back to Base U. "Juggie, hey. Looks like you'll have two pax on this flight back."

"Pax? Dude, I know you brought out pax, but man, that little engine is far too stressed for such missions."

"Aww, you can do it. Easy day. You're flying over friendly territory."

"Alright. I give. Who's the pax?"

"You're taking Beef and Petrov to Base U," Buck replied.

"Well, what are we waiting for?" Jughead wanted to get going. It had been a long night already for him, flying in another cargo load. He was antsy to get back and relax.

"I'd love to help you out, but the wheels of diplomacy are

spinning slowly. Can't go until we get him released.

Jughead nodded. "OK. I'm gonna rack out in the SBD II for a bit. Just let me know when they are ready."

*********************

As Smitty was fighting for his life, others were as well out on the other side of the battlefield. Within a half hour of the attack, Russian deployed in Kharkiv would recover their dead and wounded Rasputin Firm operatives from Verkhnya, flying them back to a medical unit. One operative named Roman, suffered only superficial wounds and, upon reaching the medical base, placed a call back to Moscow.

"Sir, sorry to call so late. Mission failed. We took casualties. It was a setup."

Groggily, Stefan Balakin responded, "Tell me everything."

"Sir, we moved in on the objective. There was no movement above ground as expected, given the message said Petrov was in the cellar. Upon entering, we found Boris, dead and naked. His hand was cut off, likely to get the transmitter. As the first team pressed down to the basement, someone yelled it was a trap, then an explosion. It was massive. Everyone on the first team entering the cellar was killed. Those near the stairwell were injured."

"OK. And where are you now?" Stefan inquired.

"Sir, we are at a Russian military field hospital. When the explosion detonated, Russian forces from nearby found us. They called in medevac helicopters for us."

Stefan grimaced. He knew he'd hear this again from the Kremlin soon enough, and in a far less friendly tone. "OK. I got it. Call me again tomorrow afternoon with a status report."

"I will, boss, but the guys are a bit concerned. All of us have these fucking capsule trackers in us and it seems the entire system is exposed. Do you know if that's true? How did these guys set up such an ambush? Why cut off Boris' hand if it wasn't to recover the tracker?"

"I understand your concerns. Please tell the men the system is safe. Even if Petrov's or Boris' phone or transmitters were compromised, there are protocols in place to keep you safe. While I don't know the status of their devices, tell the men I will implement the protocols now. Within a day, those two phones will be useless." Stefan needed to assure Roman and the rest of the men everything was fine.

"Thanks, Sir. I will relay that. Again, sorry to wake you."

"It is not a concern. Thanks, Roman. Wish the men well, goodbye."

"Goodbye." The two hung up.

Stefan wiped the sleepers out of his eyes and stood up, plodding to his home office. It was far less impressive than the one in his swanky Moscow office building. He sat at the desk and placed a call to the Kremlin.

"Yes. Hello sister." There was a pause. "Yes, I know it's late. This is urgent. I need to speak to your husband."

Within seconds, President Volkov was on the phone. "What is it?" He said, frustrated he was awoken so late.

"We didn't get Petrov. He got away. Also, my team took casualties and Russian military helicopters flew them onto a Russian military field hospital where they are undergoing lifesaving surgery. My men did not ask for this, and it was beyond our control. Once my men are medically able, I will transition them to a civilian hospital."

There was a pause. President Volkov was furious, but at this point, rage would do little to contain the problem. "Who knows about this?"

"Mr. President, likely only your units that have assisted my men, and us. It is not in the media. Local emergency teams may know, fire brigades and police, but I doubt they'd take notice," Stefan replied.

For the President, containing the disaster was the lesser of his two concerns. "And what about Petrov?"

"Sir, he's gone. We have no tracking on him and the aircraft has flown into Ukrainian held territory. I have a few informants in the Ukrainian military. According to one of them, there is a significant commotion at Uman. I don't have confirmation yet, but if that is true, Petrov is likely there. I will need funds to make this problem disappear, but I have a plan."

"Brother, you are getting no more money for Petrov. You've failed at killing him. Why would I continue to throw good money after bad at you for failures?"

"Mr. President, suit yourself. But if Petrov is not eliminated before he reaches the U.S., there will be serious consequences for both the Rasputin Firm and the Russian Federation. Your choice."

There was a pause. "OK, one more payment. And this time, Petrov dies. Do you understand?"

"Yes, Mr. President. Good night. And please pass my best regards to your wife. Tell her I am sorry to have woken her."

Both lines went dead. Stefan leaned forward at the desk with his elbows on top of it. Holding his smart phone, he scrolled through his contacts until he found the one he was searching for, then executed the call.

"Hello?" the other party answered sleepily.

"Get up. FindMe is compromised."

Within seconds, the other party was far more alert. "Yes, Sir. Should I implement the protocols?"

"Yes. First, I need phones number seven and number twenty-three bricked. They were the ones that were compromised."

"Yes Sir. I'll start that process. What about the app?"

"Please, tell me again in non-computer terms what you will do?"

"Yes, Sir. It's actually fairly simple. I will create a new app, let's call it 'FindMe 2' and reroute all the transponder locations away from the first app to the second one. I can have that app installed on all the phones remotely within a day or two. Think of it like taking all of the Twitter inputs and routing them away from the Twitter app over to Facebook. It's relatively easy. Just will take some time."

"OK. Do it. And soon. We lost men last night due to an ambush that was based on a compromise of your app."

There was a delayed response. "I'm sorry to hear that. I will work on it right away."

"Thank you.  Please call me once you've destroyed the two phones.  I will need to share this information with others."

"Yes, Sir.  I will.  Goodbye."

Both parties hung up.  Stefan had one more call to make.

"Hello again, it's me," Stefan said.

"I have secured money for you.  If you can accomplish what we discussed, you will be handsomely rewarded."

Standing off to the side of an aircraft hangar at the military base in Uman, a young Ukrainian soldier held the phone to his ear.  "Yes, Sir.  I think I can."  In the background, Buck, Petrov and General Aleksandar stood.  "I am standing about thirty meters away from Victor Petrov.  He's here.  I see him."

"Good.  I wish you luck."  Stefan hung up and went to get a shower.  The morning sun had risen.  There'd be much work to do today.

## Chapter Thirty-Seven
# First Hour, First Day

President Crawford awoke early in the Little White House master bedroom. She rolled over to seek out Ryan. He wasn't there, but her nose would quickly assure her that he was close. Slowly, she got out of bed and found him in the kitchen, whipping up a breakfast fit for a queen... or a president.

"Ryno. You're the best," she said, kissing him gently.

"You're gonna need energy for your first full day. Need to keep ya healthy. Your coffee is on the table."

Stacy sat down. Her coffee was piping hot. "Hey. You know, we never talked about what you'd do as the First Man. You know, many of the former First Ladies took on numerous campaigns or efforts. Do you have any idea to do something like that?"

"Sweetheart. How about you get through your first day and we can talk about that later?" Ryan set down a plate of eggs, bacon, sausage, toast, and fruit. Cooking made him happy, which also made Stacy happy... she was a horrible cook.

As she began to eat, a knock at the open kitchen door disturbed them. Special Agent Griffin stood in the door frame. "Madam President, good morning. I am very sorry to interrupt your breakfast, but Secretary Baker is already at the White House with an item she deems a crisis."

Stacy looked at Ryan. "Well, I guess my first one on one will be with Marleen." She took one last bite, wiped her face and stood as she chewed.

Stacy went upstairs and cleaned up for the day. As she did, Ryan packed up her breakfast so she could take it with her, even though the walk would only be a few hundred feet. She also had a full team ready to cook whatever she wished.

Eventually, she was ready for her day. As she walked to the Little White House front door, it opened without her touching it. On the outside, a Marine Guard stood in a perfectly pressed uniform. "Good morning, Devil Dog," Stacy said as she passed by.

The Marine said nothing, and merely nodded with full respect. Agent Griffin and others stood nearby, all communicating the President's movement. It was nearly double the secret service detail she had as the Vice President.

Steve Lewis stood patiently, prepared to brief her as she walked across the North square of the White House. A few people were mulling about at that time. When they saw her, most yelled supportive comments. Others were less supportive. She would quickly learn to ignore the bad ones.

"Good morning, Steve. What's so important that Marleen decided to disrupt my breakfast?"

"Ma'am. I have good news for you. We kind of captured Victor Petrov."

"Great news, for my first day! Steve, I like stuff like this. Keep going."

"Ma'am, I said, 'kind of.' There is an international tug of war, and Secretary Baker is going to ask for your help."

The two passed by through the White House security gates in full stride. Some of the security staff saying "Good morning, Madam President." To each, she was polite to a fault, either responding or nodding.

"OK Steve. On a scale of one to ten, how hard is this going to be?"

"Honestly, ma'am? If you were in the office for months, I'd give it a seven. First day? It's an eleven."

Stacy grinned. "Great. I love a challenge." Stacy passed by Agnus just outside the Oval Office, wishing her well. She also greeted Secretary Baker, who was patiently seated on a beautiful antique sofa in a waiting area out front. "Marleen, please, come in. I guess we have some work to do."

"Yes, Madam President." The two walked in, followed by Steve. Stacy sat on one sofa as Marleen sat on the other. Steve pulled a chair from the side and prepared to write.

"Marleen, what's going on?"

"Madam President, there is an issue in Ukraine that demands your..." the President cut her off.

"Steve. Why are you sitting way over there? Come sit with me."

"Ma'am?" He said.

"Did I stutter? Steve, you're my Chief of Staff. This sofa is large enough and you're my teammate. Come sit with me."

Steve got up and sat on the sofa.

"Sorry, Marleen, please continue."

"Ma'am. The good news is, Victor Petrov is in custody on a Ukrainian military base."

"Great. But I presume you were not here at seven AM to ask me if we should extradite him?"

"No, ma'am. I wish it was that easy. It appears, Petrov was captured by a private U.S. security firm named The Valyrian Group. It is a recent start up, owned by Andrew Denney. The Chief Operations Officer is retired Admiral Eugene Hershey."

The President nodded. She had heard rumblings about Hershey's future efforts. As she chewed on the information, President Crawford was surprised. For a start-up private military company, capturing the world's most wanted man was a bit shocking. That said, 'shock and surprise' were two reactions unhelpful for a sitting President to display.

"Ma'am," Marleen continued. "The Ukrainian government officials claim they have extradition rights and wish to take him from the Valyrian Group."

"OK, Marleen. And please help me. From what I know, there is still some bad eggs in the Ukrainian government. Right?"

"Yes, Madam President. If TVG is forced to release Petrov, we likely will lose him for good."

"TVG?," President Crawford asked.

"Sorry, Madam President. The Valyrian Group," Marleen replied.

"Impressive. They already have their own acronym," she openly lamented, as if chuckling inside. "Anyway, who is the current Ukrainian ambassador? What's his name? What is he saying?" Stacy asked.

"As expected, he's trumpeting Kyiv's position, demanding we release him immediately, and promising the U.S. will get their pound of flesh later."

"And, at the end of all this. Who actually 'holds' Petrov? Is it TVG?" Stacy feared the answer.

"Yes, ma'am."

Stacy turned her attention to Steve. "Steve, can you get me Andrew Denney or Squirts on the line?" She always loved Admiral Hershey's callsign, using it even in the most inappropriate situations. She meant no disrespect, and if Admiral Hershey was present, none would be taken.

Steve jumped up, "Yes Madam President." He departed the room.

"So, how do we play this, Marleen? Did you know about TVG?"

"Ma'am, between you and I, yes. They are one of a handful that are friendly to the U.S., although we don't condone or support them. Most popped up after Russia began using them years ago, companies like The Rasputin Firm. When the NISSASSA scandal was exposed, a good number went away or went quiet. This is the first time a significant issue arose."

"Marleen, consider this our initial one on one. Also know this. For now, Steve will remain onboard, as I believe keeping the same crew in the ship right now is critical. I only have one rule more important than keeping the same crew. I demand trust. One more time. Did you know what TVG was doing?"

Marleen's face did not hide her emotion. To a degree, she was set back by President Crawford's suggestion of untrustworthiness. "Madam President. My first answer to you will also be my last answer. Because it will always be the truth with as much information as I have on a subject. I will hold nothing back... no matter how hard it is to say, or how hard it may be to hear. If you don't want me to remain as Secretary, I can accept that, but please don't question my integrity."

Stacy was taken aback. Then smiled. "Marleen. I think we are gonna get along just fine."

Steve reentered the room. "Great, Steve, please put them on the speakerphone," she replied; smiling as she 'let' Steve push the phone buttons.

"Ma'am. There is no need. They are standing at the security gate, waiting to come in. They'll be in your office in minutes."

"Well, that's convenient," Stacy replied. "OK, Marleen, if these security firms are all about money, what's this gonna cost us?"

"Madam President, I have never spent U.S. funds on questionable actions of mercenary organizations." She was correct. State Department funds under her watch had never done such a thing.

"Great, Marleen. Who has, and who does?"

Marleen squirmed a bit. She was in way over her head. Just days before, she'd offered Andrew $40 million for Petrov. That was under the former President and was an effort to shore up his image. Now, the last thing the party would want to do is spend $40M for Petrov when a special election was about to take place. She didn't know what to say. Her first answer was honest, but as a political appointee, she knew full well that political parties funded such efforts.

"Marleen. Never mind. Steve? And before you answer, please remember our conversation yesterday."

Steve didn't hesitate. "Ma'am. There are a few ways. The most common is through the political party via political donations and Super PAC funds."

"OK. Thanks, Steve," she said as she looked at Marleen. "And based on your experience, how much is Petrov gonna cost me?"

Steve shrugged. "Anywhere from $25 million to $50 million. It all depends on how important his capture is to your political position."

"Thanks, Steve," she said as a knock came from the office door. "Come in, please," Stacy said.

The door opened and in walked Andrew and Eugene. "Good morning, Madam President," they both said in unison. Admiral Hershey, based on his former friendship at the Pentagon with Stacy further said, "Might I say, Oval looks good on you."

Stacy chuckled. "Gentlemen. Please sit down." She paused and looked at Secretary Baker. "Marleen, I think that will be all. Let's circle back later and further discuss your resignation letter."

There was a slight pause from the awkward comment. Marleen attempted to speak, "Madam President, I think..." before she could finish, Stacy jumped in.

"I'm sure you do. I think I have this. Thanks."

Marleen departed. Angered... mostly at herself. She had just swore unswerving loyalty and then stumbled on how private military companies are funded.

"So, gentlemen. Today is my first day, and I got a bunch of stuff to do. What I understand is you have Petrov, kind of, on a Ukrainian military base. You want to bring him here but need my help insuring the Ukrainians will release him back to you and let him leave the base with you. How am I doing?"

"So far, ma'am. 100%." Eugene Hershey answered.

"Great. Here's what I don't know. Who paid for this? I can't imagine a for profit security organization took on this mission out of the goodness of their heart or for patriotic love. I'm gonna guess someone plans to pay and you need to deliver Petrov for the payment. Am I still on track?"

"Ma'am?" Andrew said, somewhat puzzled. "We presumed you knew. Through Secretary Baker, the national party chair secured funding to pay us for Petrov's head, preferably alive, but dead was also OK."

"Can you be more specific? I want a number."

Andrew hesitated for a moment. He didn't know Stacy very well and was unsure if she actually did know the number and was testing him. Now was not the time to get greedy and risky. "Forty million, ma'am."

"OK. Here's the new offer. Four Million." Both Hershey and Andrew choked. "Ma'am. That's one tenth of the original offer," Hershey said.

"Yes. That's true. But here is how I see it. Your original deal is with an entity which is likely going to alienate me in the possible term special election. They are no longer going to pay a penny for my team to get a political victory. I might be able to get some funds together, I imagine I can get four million, but that will take me time. I won't use USG funds."

Andrew crossed his arms over his chest. "Ma'am, is that your final offer?"

"Yes, Mr. Denney. It is. Gentlemen, I understand the Ukrainian government also may provide a greater offer. If they do, I suggest you take it. Of course, we all know... Possession is

nine-tenths of the law. Petrov is on their soil, not ours." Stacy
was right, and extremely matter of fact. Her offer wasn't
intended to sting, although it did. It was her honest answer, and
the best she thought she could do.

"OK," Andrew said as he stood and began making his way to
the door.

"Andrew," she said. "Where are you going?"

"Madam President, no disrespect. I think you're going to
make a great president. You're still ethical and not poisoned
yet." He paused. "But I have been long poisoned by the D.C.
drugs. If you don't wish to pay us, that's fine, but, as you said,
the Ukrainian Ambassador will pay far more than that. As much
as I'd like to help the United States, my organization doesn't
operate on handshakes and smiles. Currently, one of our best
men is fighting for his life and I need money to get him
immediate medical care."

Stacy hated it, but she knew Andrew was right. As far as the
U.S. was concerned, Ukraine was still a corrupt government that
would easily pay greatly for Petrov. Her moral high ground
standing was noble, but the top of that proverbial hill was scarce
on available funds. In international politics, money was very
susceptible to gravity. Most of it settled in the low ground, no
matter how dirty it got. If that's where international leaders
wished to operate, funds were always plentiful.

Ironically, many nations see the U.S. government as corrupt
for openly accepting political donations, a criminal act in a good
number of other nations. Corruption, at the senior most levels,
is not black and white. It is shades of gray and only the shades
an individual can live with.

Stacy spoke up. "Twenty Million, and I'll get your guy
airlifted and to our best medical teams in Landstuhl. I imagine
he's in Europe?" As soon as she said it, she felt dirty and in need
of a shower.

Andrew looked at the Admiral. Both nodded. "Deal." They
said.

"Great," Stacy responded. "Steve, get the Ukrainian
Ambassador on the phone."

Steve opened the Oval Office door and directed Agnus to

complete the task.

"Gentlemen, I do ask one favor though," President Crawford offered.

"I'm listening," Andrew replied.

"I'll get you your money. But I will need a little time. I think we can both agree that twenty million on my first day is a bit of a heavy lift. Give me one quarter."

Andrew nodded. The money from Buck's missions was filling company coffers. Additionally, the ten million from Ukrainian for destroying Russia's logistics hub would erase most of the company's start up debt. More importantly, Andrew knew the strategic value of a good relationship with the U.S. President, especially for a U.S. private military company.

The speaker on the President's desk phone crackled to life. "Ma'am, Agnus here."

They all smiled at each other in the room. "Hi, Agnus," Stacy responded. "What's up?"

"Ambassador Ubyivovk is on the line. Mr. Ambassador, the President of the United States." Agnus disconnected herself from the call.

"Madam President! Good morning. Congratulations on your new appointment. I am honored to be one of the first diplomats you wish to engage with. My President sends his best wishes and wants you to know Ukraine is one of the United States' best allies."

"Ambassador Ubyivovk, am I saying that right? Thank you very much for your well wishes."

"Yes, yes. You are correct. Madam President, I presume you are calling about Victor Petrov. I appreciate your concern, but he is currently on Ukrainian soil, and he is a wanted man in our country for war crimes."

"Ambassador. I understand your position. But I must confess, I am very concerned with that course of action. When the American public discovers Petrov is in your country on trial, they'll likely learn it was a U.S. operation that secured him. They will grow angered that Ukraine was able to extract first blood, not the U.S. Mind you. They won't be angry at me, they'll be angry at Ukraine." She paused to drive that point home.

Then continued. "If my poll numbers are correct, 70% of Americans support the war in Ukraine. That makes it easy for the U.S. government to keep feeding weapon and supplies to your ongoing war. If that number falls below 50%, I cannot promise you any more support." The connection, while not explicitly stated, was clear.

The President continued. "So, I guess if you are close to winning the war, I can understand the decision to keep Petrov, but if Ukraine needs long term U.S. support, you may wish to let us have him. I once heard a wise U.S. flag officer tell me, 'Wars are not won on battle lines but rather shipyards and assembly lines.' We both know the U.S. and NATO are those very assets supporting your war."

Ambassador Ubyivovk paused. "Madam President. Long ago, a friend told me how to recognize an excellent politician. They are the ones that can tell a person to go to hell in a way the individual looks forward to the ride." The Ukrainian Ambassador chuckled at his own joke.

He then spoke again. "I get your point and I will relay your comments to my President. I'll have an answer for you later today. May I call you directly or should I pass it through Secretary Baker?"

"Ambassador, I'm flattered by your comment, and yes, please call my Chief of Staff, Steve Lewis, directly. I wish you luck conveying our important message to your President."

The two hung up.

"Steve, I believe the acting Defense Secretary and the Chairman are waiting. Things today somewhat messed up my calendar, and I'd like to try to get back on track." President Crawford paused and turned to Andrew and Eugene. "Andrew. 'Squirts,' if I can still call ya that. Please excuse me."

Admiral Hershey smiled. "Ma'am, as long as you don't call me a four-letter word, we're good."

"Great! I always loved your callsign." Stacy turned back to her Chief of Staff, "Steve, can you take these two gentlemen into your office and get the details about their injured member? We will need to pass that to DoD soon to get him the help he needs."

"Yes, ma'am," Steve said as all three gentlemen stood up. The Admiral and Andrew shook Stacy's hand. It was cordial, as if it were the beginning of a good partnership.

Steve led them out of the office.

Stacy stared out the Oval Office window into the rose garden. Softly she whispered under her breath, *"Stacy Crawford, what the fuck have you gotten yourself into?"*

## *Chapter Thirty-Eight*
# Transition to Traitor

Thomas Agnew had served for three years as the national party chairperson. Before the President's untimely departure from office, he was considered a shoe in for a cabinet level position if he wanted it. Another option would have been a cushy ambassadorial position, somewhere in the heart of Old Europe.

That was before the President's torrid affair was exposed. Now, he was scrambling to do whatever he could to steady the ship. Stacy Crawford would not have been in his top five presidential candidates. Not because she wasn't qualified, but because she hadn't been leveraged and committed to the party's causes. She was too new without skeletons that could be used against her. Large donors have expectations for presidents. Stacy had not committed to any of them.

Before the President stepped down, he'd at least started laying the groundwork for a special election. Since the President's speech, Thomas had worked with every PR firm trying to generate support. As he was working on his computer, his phone chirped. He looked down and saw the following message.

> *Tom –*
> *Call me. I think I need a job.*
> *Marleen*

Thomas quickly called. "Marleen. Tom here. What's up?"

"Tom, hey. So, the President just said she wished to further discuss my resignation letter."

"Damn. What else did she say?"

"She said she's keeping Steve on as her Chief."

"That's good," Thomas said. "At least we will have a mole."

Marleen shot that down. "I wouldn't count on that. From the atmosphere of the meeting I was in, he's committed to her."

"OK. Another issue. Have you spoken with Andrew Denny about the forty million for Petrov? The dynamics of that deal have drastically changed, and we have no intent of honoring that payment."

"Thomas, I didn't talk to him. But Crawford did. She likely has made her own deal. I worry far more about her getting the political win of bringing Petrov to the U.S. before a special election than keeping your $40M. To overcome that win, you'll need $400M."

"Would I?" Thomas replied with a grin.

"Well, what do you have in mind?"

"I want to expose TVG to the public and pin it on her. There's no way Denney is going to deliver Petrov for free. She'll have to pay for something. When she does, I want to know where the money came from and expose TVG. The key will be keeping you and others out of the collateral damage."

"Thomas, I'm not sure I like that plan. I am tied fairly deeply to TVG. Exposing them puts me at risk."

"Marleen, I can protect you. The priority is having a primary election in a few months. Current polling is almost at 30% and with a few more million invested in mainstream media outlets' talking heads, I think we can get to 50%. Once there, we are good."

"Alright. I'll work on my resignation letter."

"Eh, it's not that bad. In a few months, you could be sitting in Crawford's chair. Keep your head up," Agnew said. Marleen knew the chances of that were nearly zero, but if Crawford was gone, she'd at least get some senior position in the new administration. That was incentive enough.

\*\*\*\*\*\*\*\*\*\*\*\*\*\*\*\*\*\*\*

General Aleksandar was none too happy as he hung up the phone. He walked over to Buck. "Seems Petrov is yours. You have an hour to get him off my base and out of my sight."

Buck nodded. And thanked the General. The timing

stipulations were added by the General and not Kyiv. He needed to maintain some form of control over the matter. It was his only option, and being a General, he held a PhD in being an asshole.

Buck turned back to his teammates and said, "Beef. You got Petrov. Go wake up Jughead and get the SBD II outta here. I'll call the Admiral and let him know."

As General Aleksandar was walking away, Colonel Marko Taran stopped him. "General. You will not walk away empty-handed to Kyiv. Please. Look at this." Marko showed the General Petrov's phone, and specifically showed him the 'FindMe' app. "Sir, we found that a good number of Rasputin Firm operatives have embedded communication capsules. This map shows all their current location."

The General's eyes lit up. "Are you sure?"

"Yes. This is Petrov's phone. We discovered embedded capsules on Petrov and another dead operative named Boris. In fact, we used one of the capsules to set up an ambush as we flew out. I'd imagine Moscow is eventually going to realize it's compromised, but until then, you have all the information."

The General seized the phone and jumped in his car. If he couldn't deliver Petrov to the Ukrainian President, he could at least deliver his phone. His black sedan raced away.

Inside the medical tent, Jackal sat next to Smitty, watching over him. Smitty mumbled a bit, and his eyes flickered opened. He saw Jackal and could recognize him. "Well, hell. You're not the blonde I was dreaming about."

"True, Smitty. I'm not. Glad to see you awake. You OK? What can I get you?"

Smitty adjusted in the bed, wincing as he did. "I'm good. Thanks. Did you get debriefed on our mission?"

"Yeah. Crazy times out there. Glad you all made it out safe," Jackal responded.

Smitty paused, "Hey. I'm sorry I didn't take you. Turns out I needed a sniper and didn't have ya."

Jackal was touched, but it wasn't the time to gloat. "Nah. Buck told me one more dude in that plane and he'd never gotten off the ground. And I sure as hell wasn't gonna stay on that side of the battle line."

Smitty tried to chuckle, but as his abdomen muscles contracted in pain.

Jackal spoke again. "Hey, you want more meds?"

Another voice said from behind Jackal, "He's already loaded up with meds. Not sure his liver could process anymore."

Jackal turned around. It was Curt, looking weary and weak, but standing. "Hey Doc. How you doing?" Jackal asked.

"I'm good. Seem about ten pounds lighter." Curt and Jackal smiled. Nover was weak and his skin stretched tight over his skeletal frame. He needed fluids badly... mainly blood.

"Hey Curt," Smitty said. "Thanks for the medical support."

"Ah, that was nothin'," Curt replied. "It was the four pints of blood I gave you that really set me back."

Smitty paused. "You mean I got Nover blood in me?"

"Four pints," Curt smiled as he spoke.

Smitty stared at the ceiling of the tent. "Shit. Kill me now. I'll never be the same."

The three smiled. "You're not dying on my watch buddy," Curt said. "I'm glad you're alive. It was a close one. We need to get you some rest and then onto Poland. OK? Get some sleep."

"Thanks Doc," Smitty said, rarely ever calling Curt by his medical professional title. "Oh Shit! Curt. Where's my clothes?"

Curt looked at him, puzzled. "Buddy, you're not going anywhere."

"No. My pants, in the zip up cargo pocket of my tactical pants!"

Jackal and Curt looked around, and soon found the clothes in a pile behind the cot. Curt lifted the pants and zipped them open. A clod of lead fell out into his hand.

"That!" Smitty said. "Dude. Don't fucking lose that and don't open it up until it gets back to the Admiral or Andrew."

"Aw, thanks Smitty. It isn't even Christmas. Can you tell me what it is?"

"Nice sarcasm, dickhead. Inside the lead is a high-tech capsule, about the size of a perfume sample. In that vile is some sort of transmitter. We cut two of these from the hands of both

Petrov and another Rasputin Firm operative. I used one to set up an ambush. This is the last one. Somehow, the devices transmit the locations of Rasputin Firm operatives." Smitty winced and coughed, then continued. "You can't turn it off. I had to melt down a few rounds and encase it in a makeshift Faraday cage to mask its transmissions. Get Marko and look at Petrov's smart phone. You'll see the app that shows all of them." Smitty, in his excitement, began to cough and wince.

"Easy buddy," Curt said. "I got it. Please, get some rest. You're not out of the woods yet. I need you strong for the trip to Poland."

Curt reached out and grabbed Smitty's hand, squeezing it firmly. Smitty laid his head back and tried to sleep. "Jackal, stay with him, please."

"Not going anywhere, boss." Jackal said.

Curt put the lead blob in his pocket and walked out of the tent. Marko was sitting at a table, alone, watching Jughead and Beef prepare to fly out Victor Petrov.

"Hey Marko, how's it going?"

"It's war, Curt. For us, fortunes and fatalities are made and lost every day."

"I've never heard it put that way, but I guess you're right," Curt said.

"How's Smitty?" Marko asked.

"He's conscious, but his liver needs to be fixed soon, and we need to get him to Poland. Once Buck's aircraft is repaired, I'm hoping we can load him up on that flight and get him to Base U. Hey, Smitty said something about Petrov's phone. Can I see it?"

Matter of factly, Marko answered, "No. It's gone."

"Where did it go?" Curt asked.

Deflecting from the question, Marko responded, "Curt, America will get Petrov. The least Ukraine can get is his phone. General Aleksandar took it with him to Kyiv. We are partners in this war. We must not forget that."

Curt knew it wasn't Marko's place to determine possession for the phone, but there was little point arguing at this point. "OK, fair. Can you tell me what you saw on it?"

"Sure." Marko began to explain the 'FindMe' app. As they

263

spoke, SBD II's jet engine extended up and began to whine. With Jughead at the controls, she taxied out with Beef and Petrov on the aircraft. Soon, Victor Petrov would be one step closer to U.S. possession.


\*\*\*\*\*\*\*\*\*\*\*\*\*\*\*\*\*\*\*\*


Tucked along a tree line, a young, plain clothed Ukrainian stood next to his old and rusty car. He was nervously smoking a cigarette and fidgeting. His name was Yuri, a child from a struggling Ukrainian family, much like many other kids and families in the nation. They were poor; he had a girlfriend and a child with her. He was barely able to provide a roof over their heads, let alone figure out where the next meal was going to come from. Unable to join the Ukrainian military due to a medical issue, he was shunned by others. Today, however, his financial burdens would ease.

Yuri felt horrible about his agreement with Stefan Balakin, but there was no backing down. In the distance, he heard the whine of the aircraft's jet engine. Yuri opened the back of his truck bed and pulled out a rocket-propelled grenade launcher, inserting a grenade into the tube.

In the distance, Yuri saw SBD II. She was slowly climbing out of the base in Uman. Lazily, it turned north, just like it always did, and began flying directly towards Yuri. The flight path of SBD II and Old Girl became well known to the locals. Yuri's parents owned a farm in the area and had witnessed nearly every flight. With little to do when farming wasn't busy, Yuri, his parents and other villagers actively speculated what these aircraft were for.

The SBD II struggled to climb with the extra weight. Jughead was doing everything possible to keep the aircraft steady. Today's climb rate would be far less than all the previous missions with an empty aircraft. Beef and Petrov sat along the fuselage wall, looking at each other.

Closer now, Yuri turned the safety off and raised the

launcher. He'd lead the aircraft, but not by much, and then squeezed the trigger. Now, with SBD II locked in his sights, Yuri pulled the trigger. The grenade wooshed from the tube, traveling straight at the aircraft.

Jughead saw the smoke trail, but there was no time to react. He was fucked. The grenade struck the aircraft between the fuselage and left-wing root, ripping it from the airframe. The grenade traveled so fast that it exploded above the aircraft. It mattered little. The damage was done.

Jughead wrestled the controls, he still had elevator and rudder. What he didn't have was time. He was only 100 feet above the ground. SBD II banked drastically towards the damaged wing as it had lost lift. Instinctively, Jughead yelled out "Raise the dead," which was pilot lingo from his days in the Prowler. It was a reminder to 'step' on the rudder pedal of the dead engine or the damaged wing. As Jughead said it, he mashed the left rudder pedal to the floor. The roll rate was staved, but there was no way to get the wing back to level. SBD II could not manage such a bank at that speed and weight. Soon, she had lost her lift, and the nose began to fall. Jughead instinctively pulled back on the yoke, but knew it was in vain. Seconds before crashing nose first, he reached up and tighten his shoulder straps and screamed.

Instinctively, Beef jumped across the aircraft and onto Petrov. His special forces training had kicked in. Saving the 'package' was always the priority.

SBD II impacted nose low in a left bank. What remained of the left wing struck the ground first, causing the aircraft to cartwheel, before the nose struck the ground. At roughly 100 knots, Jughead was pushed forward in his straps. His ribs cracked and his neck could not handle the G forces. Head thrown forward, his neck snapped, which killed him instantly.

In the back, Beef had grabbed hold of Petrov and as the aircraft impacted, Beef was thrown against the bulkhead, holding onto Petrov. The weight of Petrov crushed Beef against the bulkhead, his chest cavity collapsed, as did part of his skull. He, too, was quickly lifeless.

Petrov's good hand, the one that had not been cut open to

remove the transmitter, had been zip tied to a fuselage rib. At impact, the zip tie ripped the skin from his hand and crushed the wrist bones. His legs flailed, and both femurs broke. The pain was excoriating to the point he would pass out. Ironically, Beef's efforts to protect Petrov's head and vital organs would enable Petrov to be the lone survivor of the crash, at least for the time being.

The aircraft, made of light materials, broke apart, throwing Petrov and Beef clear of the wreckage. The heaviest part, the engine and fuel tank rolled another fifty feet, then the gas caught fire.

Yuri watched the airplane crash, then drove away. He'd not be the only witness. As Marko was explaining the 'FindMe' app, he and Curt watched the SBD II lumber away from Uman like an elephant struggling to stand up. As the SBD II passed behind a set of buildings, obscuring their view, they heard the grenade explode, causing Marko to stop talking. Seconds later, they saw the plume of smoke rise from the crash site. They both immediately jumped into a vehicle driving out.

Upon arriving at the crash site, Curt quickly learned of Jughead and Beef's fate. There was nothing to do for them. Petrov, unconscious, still had a pulse, but his legs were mangled, and his hand was crushed. Marko and Curt lifted him up, trying to place Petrov into the back of the vehicle. As they did, Curt, still low on blood, fainted.

"I got him," Marko said, slinging Petrov over his shoulder, opening the trunk and tossing him in. Curt, still extremely weak, had fallen to the ground.

Next, Marko picked up Curt, and laid him in the back seat. Marko started the car and raced back onto the base at Uman. Petrov could not die.

## *Chapter Thirty-Nine*

# By Other Means

Marko sped up to the medical tent. A group of nurses rushed to the car and opened the back seat to find Curt laying there, partially conscious.

"No!" Marko yelled. "In here!" He opened the trunk. Petrov looked like a jigsaw puzzle that was not put together properly. The medical staff also was perplexed a patient was arriving in a trunk, but it was war, and stranger things had happened. They pulled Petrov out, placed him on a gurney and rushed him into the tent.

Curt was slowly coming around, fighting to get into the medical tent to save Petrov's life. As he struggled to get out and stand, he fell flat on his face. Curt was in no condition to work. Jackal rushed outside, hearing all the commotion, to find Curt face down on the sidewalk. He'd broken his nose from the fall, and under his eyes blood was turning his cheeks beet red.

"Come on, Doc," Jackal said. "You will live to fight another day."

Jackal carried Curt into the hospital, set him in the chair next to Smitty. Once stabilized, Jackal cleaned up Curt's nose and put an ice pack on it. Hours later, another doctor would reset Curt's nose. There were far more pressing issues in the medical tent. Specifically, saving Petrov.

At the crash site, first responders from both the local community and the military base were putting out the fire and dealing with the catastrophe. Buck and JT had raced out separately to the crash site. They each found black plastic tarps covering Jughead and Beef. For years in their military career, JT and Buck had lost comrades, but it never got any easier. Buck kneeled next to Jughead and JT next to Beef. Separately, they both said a small prayer as their hands rested over the top of the plastic. Both could still feel warmth emanating from the bodies below. Tears welled in their eyes, but both would quickly wipe them away. There was work to be done. They could grieve later, alone, when there was time.

Buck pulled out his phone and placed a call. "Admiral," he said. "Jughead crashed about a minute after takeoff." He was sobbing a bit.

Jughead's fate was clear to the Admiral. He asked anyway. "Fatalities?"

"Yes. Jughead and Beef are KIA."

"Damn it. I'm sorry Buck. Any word on the crash?"

"Sir, we heard an explosion and then the plane crashed out of our sight. Dunno yet."

"OK, Buck, but until you find out, no more flights. Got it? You're grounded until we know what happened."

"Yes, Sir. Old Girl isn't ready to fly yet, anyway. Still getting repaired."

"Buck, you only mentioned Jughead and Beef. What about Petrov? Is he dead as well?"

"Not yet," Buck answered. "Supposedly, he survived and is in surgery now. Curt would know better."

"Copy. Please, keep me informed. And I'm sorry Buck. Truly I am."

Buck wiped away another tear. "Hey boss. JT and I have a favor to ask. Don't just call Beef's and Jughead's family. They deserve better than that. Give them the dignity and honors they'd have received if they were active duty."

"Buck, I promise you that. I shall." This promise meant the Admiral would need to don his uniform and travel to both residencies. It was time consuming, but both he and Buck knew it was the right thing to do.

"Thanks, boss. They were great dudes." Buck hung up. He didn't want to talk anymore in that condition.

Jackal pulled up to the crash site in another car. He'd heard from Curt what had happened. There was no rush to his arrival. From the passenger seat, he pulled out a medium-sized package and walked over to where JT and Buck were standing. Reaching inside, he pulled out one item and handed it to JT, a second item was handed to Buck. The two items were new American flags. JT and Buck opened the flags and laid them over the top of the black plastic.

As they did, the activities around the crash drew to a standstill. All the Ukrainian soldiers and local first responders watched as the American flags slowly billowed down over the bodies. In near unison, the entire crowd took off their covers, be them helmets, or hats, holding them close to their chest. Those without covers placed their hands awkwardly over their hearts, as if they were Americans. A sense of quiet fell over the area. Most had been unaware the two lives lost were American. Now they knew, and accurately suspected, the two had been in Ukraine to help fight Russia.

*********************

At an intelligence processing center on a Russian military installation, somewhere near Moscow, an intelligence collector typed the transcript from Admiral Hershey's phone. At the top of it, he placed a small synopsis which read.

*'Two dead Americans (Jughead & Beef – actual names unknown) from a plane crash near Uman, Ukraine. One survivor, Victor Petrov.'*

The name, 'Petrov' had been flagged by many senior intelligence analysts, and as the message entered the Russian intelligence computer system, it immediately arrived upon dozens of desks, to include those in the Kremlin. Within an hour, President Volkov would read only the headline. His blood pressure rose, and his fist slammed the desk. He whispered to himself, *'Petrov must be a fucking cat. No man has this many lives.'*

While not part of the Russian intelligence apparatus, the same message would arrive at Stefan Balakin's desk. He, too, would express anger.  There was little more he could do other than just keep trying.

\*\*\*\*\*\*\*\*\*\*\*\*\*\*\*\*\*\*\*\*

Buck slowly drove back onto the military installation.  He parked, then walked in to check on Smitty.  Curt was sitting there with an icepack on his face.  "What happened to you?  Did you get too frisky with Smitty?"

"I fainted and fell.  You OK?" Curt asked.  He knew Jughead's death would be a tough on Buck.

"Yeah.  I'm OK, thanks for askin.'  The Ukrainian military is working a plan to get the bodies back to Base U via land transport."

"Oh.  I presumed you'd fly them," Curt said.

"No can do.  Squirts grounded my operation until we determine the cause of the crash."

Curt's heart sunk.  "Buddy.  We need to fly Smitty out of here in the next few hours or he's not gonna make it.  And there is no way he'd survive a multi hour road trip across Ukraine to Poland.  None."

Doctor Cohen had overheard the conversation.  "Doctor Nover is correct.  If Mr. Smith can't fly to Poland, we need to get him loaded right now in an ambulance and starting to move ASAP."

Curt looked at Mike, "Dr. Cohen.  I think we both can agree, Smitty is not ready yet to travel."

Mike could see the emotion in Curt's eyes and knew what Smitty meant to him.  "Curt.  I get it.  But you have two choices: start driving him now and hope he can survive the trip, or he dies here.  Sorry.  That's the truth."  Mike put his hand on Curt's shoulder for a brief moment, then walked away.

"Buck, please tell me you can fly."  The desperation in Curt's eyes was overwhelming.

"Let me go look at the crash site.  If I can find it was caused by a malfunction, I'll try to convince Squirts to let us fly.  Deal?"

"Deal, but hurry."

Buck ran out and jumped in the car. The drive to the crash site was less than ten minutes and the emergency responders were wrapping up. Now it was police detectives taking photos for when the national crash experts arrived and began combing over the wreckage.

Buck checked the control cables from the cockpit. While they were mangled, they were still connected. Jughead was flying until the end. He then walked over to the engine and the fuel tank. Both were together, and while ruptured, the fuel tank clearly had not exploded into numerous pieces. *'So much for my sabotage theory from Petrov,'* Buck thought. It was understandable he'd consider this first given his crash in Kosovo was caused by a saboteur. He then walked over to the fuselage and wings. Most of it was broken apart, but after a few seconds, he'd see the telltale signs. The half of the left wing that was remaining had numerous little holes in it and some black charring. *'Fuck,'* he thought, realizing someone shot Jughead down. He took a photo with his phone, got in his car, and drove back to the base.

Without saying anything, Buck showed Curt the photo. Words weren't needed. Clearly, the Russians had figured out a way to shoot down the gliders, even in friendly territory. It was warfare, and as in all warfare, unique advantages only last so long. Eventually, the enemy will figure out a way to mitigate any advantage if it wishes to survive.

Tears welled up in Curt's eyes as he looked at Smitty sleep. Without a plan, Curt was staring at a dead man.


*******************

Across the medical tent, the final efforts to save Victor Petrov were taking place. He would live, with two massive casts on his legs, up to his hips. Eventually, the bones would need to be professionally reset along with a significant amount of physical therapy, but he'd live, for now.

Buck walked out of the tent, finding Marko smoking another cigarette and sitting at the table outside the tent. "Hey, Buddy," Buck said.

"Hey, Buck," Marko said as he exhaled his cigarette smoke.

"Any chance we can get an ambulance or vehicle large enough to transport Smitty to Poland?"

Marko looked at Buck, confused. "Why don't you fly him in your aircraft? It would be much faster."

Buck showed Marko the photo. "You see that damage? That's shrapnel and char markings from some kind of explosive out on the wing. Not much of a chance they took off with a bomb out there, so the most likely scenario is they got shot down."

Marko looked at the photo and immediately knew Buck was correct. "Buck, please send me this photo. I will talk to General Aleksandar and see what I can do about a vehicle."

"Thanks," Buck replied, "But we need to leave soon. Both Doc Cohen and Curt are saying Smitty's chances to live are about zero."

"I'll do my best effort," Marko said. He put out his cigarette and grabbed his phone. Soon he was speaking in Ukrainian... Buck understood none of it. At the other end of the line was General Aleksandar.

"Colonel," the General said. "What can I do for you?"

"I need a favor, Sir. Can we get a vehicle to take the American to Poland? Not sure if you heard, but one of the Valyrian Group planes was shot down about an hour ago."

"Yes, I heard. Didn't know it was shot down. Are you sure?"

"Fairly certain, General. They won't fly the gliders anymore until they figure out how it happened, hence the need for a vehicle. And currently, one of their Special Forces guys is clinking to life."

"I will do what I can. By the way. Petrov's phone was interesting. I showed it to our tech team, who quickly cloned it. Within five minutes of cloning, the phone went blank and no longer works. From the clone, we are learning amazing things. Kyiv is thrilled."

"Good, General.  A victory for the good guys.  I am going to go grab dinner.  Please get back to me by this evening about the car.  We need it desperately, along with an escort to get through roadblocks."  Marko was correct.  The drive was long enough, but the checkpoints and roadblocks could double the amount of time.

"I will try, Colonel."  The General hung up.

## *Chapter Forty*
# Bulls and Horns

President Crawford's meetings with Acting Secretary Lincoln Shurr and General Gott went well. The Acting Secretary was an unconfirmed political appointee with aspirations of greater responsibility. His loyalty would be to President Crawford. As for General Gott, he was in the military. His loyalty was to the nation and the constitution, both of which Stacy was more than OK with.

During her meeting with General Gott, once again, President Volkov called the White House. Steve ran interference on the call, but Volkov once again demanded President Crawford at a minimum meet with Russian Ambassador Tarlov. Stacy relented, telling Steve to relay she would do so before the end of the day. Steve and Agnus coordinated through the State Department and before long, a meeting was arranged to take place at the White House for later that day.

At the State Department, Marleen had finished up a draft resignation letter. She'd present it at the end of the day. She typed it, a bit angered that the Russian Ambassador would be meeting the President without her. That was not the norm. No matter, the letter was still flowery, and grateful... just as one would expect from a person vying to be a future president. Anger and resentment were unflattering characteristics in a candidate or senior level appointee, no matter how valid the feelings were.

********************

Across D.C., Andrew and the Admiral were in a secure room that the Valyrian Group had constructed. It was the closest thing they could use until accredited to have a USG certified secure facility. The two discussed the recent tragedy alone in their newly established offices.

274

"Andrew," the Admiral said. "Buck says the aircraft was shot down. Not sure how or by what, but I've ordered him to stand down until we figure it out."

"I agree with that. And it appears we are no longer acting with impunity in Ukraine. Someone is onto us... understandable, given we are trying to land a big fish. Eugene, I want you to do something. When we step out of the vault, I want you to call me and tell me you've just gotten word through a third party that Victor Petrov is dead."

The Admiral looked at Andrew confused, then figured it out as he grinned. "I can do one better." Andrew went to his desk and with his Secure Voice Over Internet Phone, he placed a call to Rob Farkas, "Rob. Need a favor. Close hold. Via discrete means, I need you to get a note to Curt Nover and have him call me. Specifically, I need him to clearly state Victor Petrov is dead. Have him message my cell phone and then Andrew's phone. Do you understand?"

"Too easy, Admiral. I have secure comms with a guy in Uman. Expect a call in a few minutes." Rob hung up his SVOIP in Poland and called down to Uman, relaying the message to one of his employees.

Curt had gotten the message. He'd do one better, however. He went over to Petrov, who was unconscious on a heavy morphine drip. Curt pulled Petrov's head back and snapped a photo. To any observer, it appeared Petrov was in fact dead.

The Admiral's phone pinged, and like clockwork, Curt relayed the message. Next, Andrew's phone did the same. Again, the message was relayed.

Both Andrew and the Admiral hung up their phones. "Let's see what happens," Andrew said. "Until we know for sure, let's reduce the amount of info we share on cell phones. Petrov is a massive prize, and we can't afford to lose him. There's been too many close calls with him already."

The Admiral nodded.

Again, at an intelligence processing center on a Russian military installation, somewhere near Moscow, an intelligence collector typed the transcript from Admiral Hershey's phone, at the top of it, he placed a small synopsis which read.

# Russian Puppeteer

*'Victor Petrov declared dead by U.S. Citizen (Nover?) to former*
*U.S. Defense Chief, Admiral Hershey*

The name Victor Petrov flagged to the highest levels of intelligence dissemination.  President Volkov and Stefan smiled, nearly in unison as the messages flashed onto their desks.  It also circulated much further, to include into the Russian Embassy of Washington, D.C.  Ambassador Tarlov would also crack a smile, and a shot of vodka.  It was worth celebrating.


*******************

Before her meeting with Ambassador Tarlov, President Crawford had one other meeting on her calendar.  Steve escorted National Political Party Chairman Thomas Agnew into the Oval Office.  He walked with confidence and a warming smile.  "Good afternoon, Madam President.  Congratulations on your appointment."

"Thanks Thomas, I appreciate it, although I am not sure what I've gotten myself into.  Hell of a first day."

"I can imagine, Ma'am."

"Please Thomas, let's sit down."  The two sat and Steve sat with the President on her sofa.  His move spoke volumes to Thomas as he'd never seen a Chief of Staff sit that close to the President.  "Thomas.  I'd normally ask what your thoughts are on a special election, but given the amount of press coverage that is splashing across televisions as well as the D.C. social media PR machines, I believe I know your answer."

It was an awkward start to their first meeting.  "Well, ma'am, I am not sure my feelings matter as much as the public.  I think you can understand their desire to have an elected official in the office.  A special election quells that concern.  Should you run in a primary and win, you'll have the full backing of the party."  Thomas had practiced that line numerous times as he'd said it to many candidates, both those that had a chance, and those that didn't. He'd gotten so good at delivering it, there was no discerning.

"Yes, Thomas. Thanks. I appreciate that. But I also believe the people expect their elected officials to uphold the constitution. At the quickest, a special election could happen in a few months. If there is a primary, then there would need to be a general election. Through all that, you'd maybe be able to finish a year or so before the actual presidential election in two years. Is that really worth it?"

"Worth, Madam President? I don't have that answer. I am not sure it's about money. It's about what the people want."

Stacy smiled at him. "Thomas, I may not have the donors other candidates have, and I may not have raked in millions for the party, but please. Let's refrain from the comedic line *'I am not sure it's about money.'* Clearly, when the party offered forty million for Petrov, it was all about the money."

Steve smiled at Thomas, who drew a blank stare. The first day and the new President was already swinging for the fences. Thomas attempted to retain his composure. "Well, Madam President, I think we both know that the deal is now dead on arrival as it was established under the previous administration."

"Thomas," Stacy smiled. "I am the previous administration. And if the deal was good enough for our former boss, I guess I am truly at a loss why it is not good enough for me?" President Crawford let the question linger, awaiting a response from Thomas. He had none.

She continued. "Unless, of course, the party desires a special election to unseat me. I never was one for playing dirty politics, but if the only cards I'm going to get dealt in this office are wild cards and aces, you can bet your ass I'm gonna play them. Now, no more bullshit. Special election or forty million. Which is it?"

Thomas cleared his throat. Part of him loved what he just witnessed in a President. But the party that was paying for his job and buying votes couldn't come to accept her. "Stacy, there's going to be a special election. I'm sorry."

"OK then, Thomas. Thanks for your honesty." She paused. "Given this is D.C., you may take that sarcastically, but I assure you. I meant it. I don't have time for games, and neither should you. And should any donors wish to meet with me, please, I'll have Steve make my calendar available. I realize I represent this party, and their voices deserve to be heard while a member of their party is in the White House."

"Madam President, that is a message I can pass to our donor list." Thomas Agnew stood up and shook Stacy's hand. Steve would walk him towards the door and whisper under his breath, "You'd be wise to give her a chance."

Thomas quizzically looked at Steve and kept walking. Mr. Agnew realized his job had just gotten much harder.

As Thomas walked through the White House halls, he passed Ambassador Tarlov, heading towards the Oval Office. The Ambassador's smile was enormous, clearly intending to enjoy his first visit.

After a few minutes, Steve walked out to greet Ambassador Tarlov and escort him into the Oval Office. Before Steve could announce the visitor, Tarlov bellowed out, "Madam President! Warmest greetings and congratulations from President Volkov."

"Thank you, Ambassador, might you please sit with us," Stacy said as both she and Steve took a seat after a brief handshake.

"Madam President, I apologize, but I must ask. Perhaps our meeting can be one on one."

Steve knew this was the standard line. It wasn't his call, but he was fine either way. Stacy looked at him and nodded. Steve stood up, then departed.

"Madam President, I must ask you, are you wearing a wire or is the office bugged?"

She was stunned. There were no such things in the Oval Office, but the mere fact the Ambassador believed there was, was telling. She laughed it off a bit, then answered. "Ambassador, it's my first day. I don't believe there are any, but I haven't had much time to look around. Would you like to come back later after I've swept? Given your President's calls, I presumed your meeting was of the utmost urgency."

Tarlov smiled. She was spicy. He liked that. It would be far more enjoyable once he dominated her and took her under his control. "Madam President. Let me ask. How do you think you arose to such a prominent position in such a short time?"

"Frankly, Ambassador, I am not sure. Please. Enlighten me."

Tarlov pulled out his phone. On it was the video of the former president and his lover.

"Yes, many have seen that video," she said. "It's disgusting and, frankly, somewhat undignified for you as an ambassador to have it."

"Perhaps, Madam President. But please note the date stamp on the email the video is attached to."

She looked. It was clear Tarlov had the video long before anyone else. "OK, Ambassador, your point?"

"Ms. Crawford. I must congratulate you. You may not realize this, but many people have gone to very great lengths to place you in the chair upon which you sit."

Stacy did not appreciate the suggestion, and her answer demonstrated that. "Ambassador Tarlov, please refer to me as Madam President, and let's drop the informalities, shall we? And for those that may or may not have helped place me in the White House. Be clear, this is not something I asked for."

"Fair enough, Madam President, but don't be surprised if those that worked so hard to get you here start asking for something in return."

Stacy smiled. "I presume they'd already have some ideas in mind?"

"Perhaps. I think a shift in the U.S. position on the Ukraine war would go a long way to make them happy."

"I see," said Stacy. "And, just for clarity, what would happen if that weren't to happen?"

Tarlov's eyes narrowed. "Well, I presume they'd be disappointed, and perhaps work just as hard to find another replacement that would curry favor in their position."

Stacy smiled and sat quietly.

"Madam President," Tarlov said. "Did I say something funny?"

"No, Ambassador Tarlov. In fact, I want to thank you. I am clearly beginning to see opportunity. And I think this may help both of us soon. May we meet again within the next week?"

"Of course, Madam President, I am at your disposal. May I tell my President that you welcomed our message?"

"By all means, tell him I enjoyed our visit and was grateful for such a helpful offer."

As Tarlov stood, he couldn't help himself take one last shot, "And Madam President. Let me be the first to offer my nations heartfelt condolences to the two Americans tragically killed in Ukraine. Such a pity they lost their life trying to capture the now deceased Victor Petrov."

The news of Beef and Jughead's death was not public. Clearly, Tarlov had excellent intelligence connections.

It was the first time Stacy was frozen... she'd almost made it through the entire first day.

"Yes. Well, I appreciate your words."

The two shook hands. Stacy escorted him to the door and politely asked Steve to escort the Ambassador out.

As Steve took him away, she leaned over to Agnus. "Get me Admiral Hershey on the phone, ASAP."

Within a minute, the call was placed by the White House Communications Office. "Mr. Hershey, you are speaking with the President of the United States."

Stacy didn't' wait to confirm he was on the line. "Squirts. When were you going to tell me?"

The Admiral was at a loss for words. "What do you mean, Madam President?"

"I just met with Russian Ambassador Tarlov. He told me Petrov is dead."

Admiral Hershey smiled. "Madam President, yes. We just got notification. I wanted to keep the entire thing quiet until we could notify the families. After that, we could release some Americans that were killed in the crash. Before I say too much, can I meet with Steve at Old Ebbits Grill in about 15 minutes to share the details of the crash and the names of the Americans who perished? I'd like to avoid open lines. Also, I think it appropriate you have all the details before it goes public. And please, let's get all the facts on the table before we talk next steps."

"OK, Squirts. I'll send him over. Truly sorry to hear you lost some folks. I look forward to learning more."

Stacy hung up, and the Admiral released a large sigh of relief.

The last thing he wanted was the President stating on a bugged line how much Petrov's head would cost.  Quickly, he packed up his office and grabbed a cab to Old Ebbits Grill.  He'd also ensure Andrew accompanied him.  There was much to discuss.

## *Chapter Forty-One*
# Miracles are in Short Supply

Buck was at the table outside the medical tent on Uman. He'd drawn a route on the map to drive, working feverishly to shorten the route as much as possible. The best he could do to the Ukraine / Polish border was ten hours.

He walked inside to talk to Smitty. "Hey buddy. How you doing?"

"I feel like shit. How are you?" Smitty smiled.

"Yea. I get ya," Buck couldn't help but believe he was talking with a dead man.

"Hey, when you landed to get us, you mentioned some Brad Swisher or something. I told you to shut up and fly. I want to know now. Who was it?"

"It doesn't matter, Smitty. Really."

"Buck. It does to me. Come on. Humor a dying man."

"OK. His name is Bernard Fisher. He was a famed Congressional Medal Honor recipient. An aviator who landed his A-1E Sky Raider on an active enemy airfield to recover his downed wingman. Not only did he land, he taxied the length of the runway, receiving 19 bullet holes in the airframe, before dragging Major Myers into his cockpit and taking off. The guy was a rockstar and I kinda thought our mission was kind like his. Stupid stuff, I know."

"Buddy. That's the best fucking story I've heard all day. Bernard must have had balls of steel... just like you. Thanks." Smitty rolled onto his back, wincing in pain, and stared at the top of the tent.

Buck could take no more. He got up and left.

Smitty's skin tone was turning yellow, and his liver was struggling to work. Curt sat with him, holding out hope. A set of traveling medical supplies and machines waited at the end of the bed. Curt was hoping they'd get a vehicle soon.

"Buddy," Smitty said with a raspy voice. "Water, please, man."

Curt picked up a small glass of water and lifted it to Smitty's mouth. "Here ya go, Buddy. Easy."

Standing behind Curt was Jackal. He was doing everything to keep a stiff upper lip but was struggling.

"Curt. Man. Can you get me a priest? It's time." Smitty said. He had no fight left in him.

Jackal ran to find one. Within a minute, he found a Ukrainian Orthodox Priest who barely spoke English. He slowly approached Smitty, placed his hand over his face and gently drew a cross over his forehead. After that, his hand lowered down Smitty's body and grabbed his hand, as if to say, *'Everything is going to be alright.'*

The priest walked away. Quietly, Curt said to Smitty. "Do you think that's gonna help?"

Smitty's cheeks flexed as his head lay back on the pillow. "At this point, what can it hurt?"

Marko's vehicle screeched to a halt outside the medical tent. He jumped out and yelled, "Buck, get Smitty ready. His ride is coming."

Marko continued into the tent and informed the other medical staff that Petrov too would be leaving. Both Smitty and Petrov would leave together in the vehicle.

Buck ran in and excitedly shared the news with Curt. "Buck," Curt responded soberly. "It's really too late. There's no way he survives a ten-hour drive. Let's let him be."

"Copy, boss." Buck said as he turned and began to walk out of the medical tent.

As Buck walked out, he heard a noise that was familiar, but one he hadn't heard for a while. A faint, Thump. Thump. Thump. The noise grew louder and louder. THUMP. THUMP. THUMP. He looked up and roughly twenty-five meters in front of him, a Ukrainian Mi-8 was rapidly lowering onto the ground in a tactical descent.

Marko stood next to Buck. "Where the fuck is Smitty! That's his ride! Let's go!"

Buck ran back into the tent. "Curt! The fucking helo is for Smitty! Let's go! Let's go!!"

Smitty's eyes opened. "I can't," he said, softly.

Curt grabbed his IV, and other gear, "The hell you can't! I'm going with you. Come on! The only easy day was yesterday, you fucker!"

A team quickly loaded Smitty onto the helo in a bed. Next to him also laying down, albeit on the helicopter floor board, was Victor Petrov. Only one medical staff other than Curt would get on the helicopter. It was still extremely dangerous to fly within the Russian S300 and S400 surface-to-air missile systems in the vicinity. The Mi-8 would do everything it could to stay low and under the lethal radar coverage.

As the door closed, the Mi-8 maintainer pulled the fuel line from the chopper's side panel. They'd take as much as they could. 650Km to Base U would be over the max operational range of a fully loaded Mi-8, but this one's load was light, and they aircrew hoped to make it the whole way. If they couldn't, the crew would have to get extra gas in Lviv, causing an even further delay.

The Mi-8 engine roared, and the crew lifted off quickly, especially given how the SBD II was downed. The nose of the helicopter spun rapidly to the west, dipped, and the helicopter lights were turned off. Rotor thumping would dissipate off into the distance. Smitty had a small chance to live.

As it lifted off, Marko pulled out his phone and placed a call. "General, the helo is airborne. Thanks."

"I'll let our team know. You're welcome."

Similarly, Buck placed a call. The Admiral's phone began to ring as he was sitting at a table in Old Ebbitt Grill with Andrew. Steve Lewis had just walked in and sat down. The Admiral said to Steve, "Excuse me, it's one of our guys," he answered the call.

"Admiral!" Buck yelled into the phone. "Smitty is on his way to Rzeszow airport via rotary wing! Now! Curt and others are with him!" Buck was careful not to say anything about Petrov after Curt had brief him.

"OK. How's he doing?"

"Admiral, he asked to have his last rites read to him. It's not good, but he left here alive."

"OK. I got it from here." The Admiral hung up. He turned his direction back to the discussion. "Again, my apologies, Steve. Turns out our wounded guy is outbound on his way to Rzeszow airport. If the President's promise was true, we hope you can help."

"Admiral, she plans to keep her word. In fact, she had a C-17 Globemaster III placed on one hour alert a few hours ago on the ramp at Warsaw. She also had State Dept work a dip clearance for flight through Poland into Germany. Text me the name of the airport and I'll send it onto DoD. Expect it airborne in about a half hour. If it's anywhere near Warsaw, the C-17 may beat your helicopter."

"Thanks, Steve. We appreciate that." The Admiral said.

"Great, now what's the deal about Petrov's death?"

Both the Admiral and Andrew turned off their phones, requesting Steve do the same. Once any chance of monitoring was secure, the Admiral began to speak. "Steve, he's not dead. On a hunch our phones were bugged, we had our guys down range send a bullshit report that Petrov was dead. It was the only mention of Petrov's death. If Tarlov told the President that he knows Tarlov is dead, it's clear Russians have tapped our phones."

"Gentlemen, Russia taps many phones." Steve responded.

"True," the Admiral said. "But the longer we can keep Russia believing he's dead, the longer we can keep moving Petrov without them trying to kill or recapture him."

"Fair. I'll inform the President. I'm sure she'll be pleased. Is there anything else?"

The Admiral shook his head no, but Andrew had another answer. "Yes. There is."

Andrew turned back on his phone and made a few swipes with his finger. "Can you explain this?"

Andrew turned his phone to Steve. It was an email to major political donors, raising money for a special election. While the email did not explicitly say the plan was to oust President Crawford, the intent was clearly there.

Steve sighed. "Yes, Thomas Agnew is pushing hard for a special election. Andrew, you've been a major donor for years. You know the game. There are other political candidates that are far deeper in major donor pockets than President Crawford is. They want a return on their investment, and with her in office, they fear that won't happen."

Andrew rubbed his chin. "You get Smitty to Landstuhl alive, and Petrov to Andrews Air Base, and I can assure you, President Crawford's concerns about a special election will ease."

Steve smiled. "I shall pass your message. I'm sure it will please the President."

\*\*\*\*\*\*\*\*\*\*\*\*\*\*\*\*\*\*\*

The two Mi-8 pilots raged over the countryside, in the dark from 15 to 50 feet above ground. On occasion, they'd received indications that radar missiles had locked on. When they did, they'd roll the helicopter to the left or right, while extending bundles of chaff and flares. The chaff was millions of tiny pieces of metal that would bloom in the air stream, temporarily blinding the missile tracking radar. The flares would blind missiles guiding on the jet engine exhaust. Each time they did, Smitty would groan as the turn and the associated G forces on his body were painful. Each groan kept Curt optimistic. Smitty was still with them. He was also pleased to see Petrov in pain as the helicopter maneuvered.

The helicopter crew member in the back with Curt pulled his headset away and yelled, "Straight thru! No gas stop!"

Curt gave him a thumbs up. That would save a little bit of time. Curt leaned down to Smitty. "Straight through, buddy. No gas stop." Smitty didn't respond.

Curt shook him and then checked Smitty's pulse. Quickly he looked up at the heart monitor screen. There was a flat line, but in the Mi-8, it was too loud to hear the associated tone.

Curt jumped up and grabbed the defibrillator paddles. Quickly rubbing them together, he placed them on Smitty's chest and yelled as loud as he could, "CLEAR!"

Smitty's body jumped, and a faint heartbeat was detected. Curt threw down the paddles and grabbed Smitty's hand, squeezing it. His other hand held back Smitty's hair while Curt leaned into him. "Almost there, you son of a bitch. Don't fucking die on me now."

The helicopter anticollision lights turned on and the aircraft began ascending quickly, climbing to a more traditional flight altitude. They'd crossed into Polish airspace and were safe. It was also an indication they'd be landing in ten minutes. They were so close.

A C-17 had taxied into parking at Rzeszow airport. The aft ramp and door opened, and the engines were kept running. Inside the C-17, a full medical pack awaited Smitty. Additionally, two armed FBI agents from U.S. Embassy Warsaw also awaited the helicopter. They would be escorting Victor Petrov.

The Mi-8 pilots had learned Smitty had received one hit of defibrillator paddles. There was little time to screw around. Rzeszow approach control attempted to put the Mi-8 on a traditional approach. The pilots turned their transponder to 'Emergency' and continued directly to the airport. As they approached, they saw the C-17 Globemaster III and flew to a portion of the ramp directly behind the aircraft, slowly setting down so that Smitty's door was closest to the C-17's aft ramp and door. The medical team raced out, grabbed Smitty, and then rushed him onto the aircraft. At the other door, the two FBI agents took Petrov onto an old metal gurney, with far less care than Smitty received. As Petrov rolled up the aircraft ramp, the C-17 crew began sealing up the aircraft.

The C-17 pilots had never seen anything like it. There was no customs delay, no checking of personal papers, nothing. It was as if two aircraft in Cuba shifted over bundles of cocaine under the cover of darkness. The only difference was this ramp had numerous police and security cars with lights blaring, as if in support of the transfer. Seconds later, the crew chief brought up a list of passengers. The copilot looked down at it and said, "Fuck me."

The aircraft commander turned to him and said, "What's up?"

"Sir, we are flying the dude who killed the Vice President." Soon, the C-17 was rolling out of parking and headed towards the runway. They'd even received an opposite direction take off to the west headed for Germany. It seemed everyone knew this mission had very little time to spare.  To Smitty, every minute was extremely precious.

## Chapter Forty-Two
# Smuggler's Delight

For the next three hours, two surgeons and three other medical staff fought to keep Smitty alive inside the C-17s cargo bay. The Globemaster III landed at Ramstein, and a full surgeon team would receive a barely alive Mark Smith. His surgery would last six hours and be performed under the dead of night and into the morning. Smitty would need to fight for just a few more hours if he wished to live.

As for Petrov, the two FBI agents walked him casually down the ramp pushing his gurney towards an awaiting C-37 VIPSAM aircraft that was bound for Andrews Air Force Base.

Standing on the ramp, the USAFE Commander, General 'Cobra' Harrigian, was overseeing the entire effort. He and a handful of others were the only ones who knew what was going on. He stood there in his flight suit and was easily identifiable by the four stars on each shoulder.

Curt found him and began approaching him from across the ramp. "General! General!" Curt yelled.

Cobra began walking towards him. "Yes, how can I help you?"

"Sir, are the two FBI agents and Petrov the only two flying on that aircraft?"

"Yes. Who are you?" The General asked.

"I'm Dr. Curt Nover. I don't have time to explain. The patient that just raced off to Landstuhl was on a mission that captured Petrov. In Petrov's hand was a tracking chip. That chip was removed and is inside this slog of lead. It cannot be turned off, and the lead is shielding the transmission. If that aircraft is going to Andrews, someone needs to escort this item and make sure it gets to the NSA."

Cobra's executive officer was already on the phone checking out who Curt Nover was. It wasn't necessary. Cobra knew the name from the stories about NISSASSA. Cobra looked at his executive officer and spoke, "Who's on the ramp with us that's in our intelligence division?"

His exec, BamBam, said, "Sir, senior guy on the ramp is Maj Tack Atteberry. He's right over there." BamBam pointed about thirty feet away.

"BamBam, bring him here," Cobra commanded. BamBam ran off and within seconds, Tack was standing in front of the Commander.

"Sir?" he said.

"Tack, take this. Don't let go of it. Go get on that plane. Orders will meet you once you land. You're going to Andrews. When you get there, you'll get a ride to NSA. Once there, you're going to give this to…" General Harrigian paused and looked back at BamBam, "Hey, who's the exec you work with at NSA?"

BamBam said, "Lieutenant Colonel Hejda."

The General turned back. "Hejda. No one else. Do you understand?"

"Too easy, boss. I don't have my passport with me, but I'll figure it out."

Cobra turned to his Exec. "BamBam, contact Hejda and tell him everything you heard. Then get me a Top Secret Video Conference ASAP with the NSA Director. I want him to know what he's getting."

"Yes, Sir. Wilco."

Tack took the lead slug in his hand and got on the aircraft once BamBam told the pilots it was directed by the USAFE Commander. Within fifteen minutes, the plane would take off. Petrov was reunited with Boris' beacon. Unfortunately, it was no longer communicating with the Rasputin Firm.

As General Cobra Harrigian watched the C-37 Gulfstream V take off, his phone vibrated. He looked down and saw there was breaking news. The headline read, *'Suspected killer of the Vice President, Victor Petrov, is dead.'*

Cobra chuckled and whispered under his breath, "Sure he is. You're just a few months ahead of his execution."

The crowd on the ramp began disbursing and Curt was able to catch a ride over to the Landstuhl hospital. As he rode, he placed a call to the Admiral.

"Sir, we made it to Landstuhl. Smitty is in surgery."

"Good news. I presume everything went well."

"Sir, it was as if the President herself was flying. Hey, I have some critical info for you. Let me know when you can copy."

"Actually," the Admiral said. "Why don't you get to Landstuhl and see if you can get on secure comms. I'll pass you a number of an old Pentagon buddy who can relay what you pass him via a written note."

"Yes, Sir. Will do. Send me the digits via text."

"Wilco. And Curt. Everyone here is praying for Smitty."

"So am I, boss. So am I." Curt hung up. He'd eventually get to the hospital and find a secure phone that called from military line to military line. He dialed the number and passed the following.

"Admiral. Two issues. First. Victor Petrov is on the flight to Andrews right now, escorted by two FBI agents. Will land in six hours. Second issue. A U.S. Air Force Officer named Major Tack Atteberry is also on the flight. He is carrying a Rasputin Firm tracking device that was embedded in a dead man's hand. Major Atteberry is under order to get it to DIRNSA's exec. Petrov also had a tracker, but it's been removed – Out."

The message was received by the Admiral's old staff officer. He departed the Pentagon and met the Admiral who was still sitting at Old Ebbitt Grill. He and Andrew hadn't left since their meeting with Steve and were on their fourth appetizer.

As the Admiral read the note, his face broke into a grin.

"What does it say," Andrew said.

"Andrew, our package is on his way to U.S. soil, and it appears there is another little gift that our team was able to secure.

Every time the news above the bar flashed the 'Breaking News' Banner stating Petrov's death, the Admiral and Andrew ching'ed their beer glasses. They'd not get drunk, merely taking small sips. But it was good to be on the right side of the fight.

## *Chapter Forty-Three*
# Turning Tables

A few hours prior to daybreak, the C-37 landed at Andrews under the cover of darkness. Victor Petrov was led off the plane with a black cloth bag over his head to hide his identity from any prying cameras along the flight line.

Major Atteberry was met by LtCol Hejda as well as two armed Security Forces personnel. The lead blob was handed over and placed in a metal box roughly the size of a jewelry box, then sealed. A van would escort Major Atteberry to a hotel. After a few days and getting his passport sent to him via DHL, he'd return to Germany.

Two SUVs pulled off the ramp, one containing Victor Petrov and the other was full of FBI agents with over one thousand rounds of ammunition. They'd drive to an undisclosed maximum-security location, for both the agents' security and Petrov's.

Eventually, the sun would rise over D.C. and as it did, it shone into the White House private residence. This morning, Stacy Crawford and Ryan Murphy would be able to sleep in for a while. There was no crisis demanding the President's attention before daybreak.

*********************

Curt woke fairly refreshed and had a large breakfast across the street from the Landstuhl hospital at The Fisher House. Many U.S. military bases had such facilities. Fisher House is a non-profit organization that provides a 'home' for family members of military personnel undergoing medical care. Since Landstuhl was a primary hub for wounded coming out of Afghanistan and Iraq, the Landstuhl Fisher House was one of the bigger ones, but they were all nice. As he walked out of the Fisher House, Curt dropped $60 in the donation jar. It was all he had in his pocket.  He made a mental note to donate more online later when he had time.

He entered the hospital to learn that Smitty was still in the ICU and under constant observation.  According to the floor nurse, he'd survived the surgery, barely.  Curt sat outside the ICU, waiting.  Eventually, one of the doctors that performed the surgery arrived and was able to talk to Curt.

"Your friend is a stubborn one," the doctor said.

"Yeah, he doesn't quit easily," Curt responded.

"Actually, I meant the other way.  We lost him twice.  Seemed like he didn't want to stick around much longer.  The good news is, we were able to save a portion of the liver.  It will be a day or so if we know if it will truly function.  It was a long delay from the packing to surgery.  I wish we'd gotten him sooner."

Curt looked at the doctor.  "The only way you'd gotten him sooner is if Star Trek beaming was viable technology.  How are his vitals?"

"He's stable now.  Blood pressure, heart rate and O2 levels are decent.  Again, it's all up to that liver.  Let me go check on him around noon.  If he's good, I'll let you see him."

"Thanks, Doctor.  I appreciate it."

Curt pulled out his phone and drafted up a quick text.

*Team,*
*Smitty out of surgery.  In ICU.  Vitals are OK.  Partial liver saved.  Next 24-48 are critical.  Hope liver functions return.*

*Curt*

The message was sent to Andrew, Admiral Hershey, Buck, Jackal and JT.  Each one responded with positive messages.  Curt then checked his watch.  It was nearly 0500Hrs in D.C. and after all this, he needed to hear a set of voices he hadn't heard for a very long time.

A groggy female voice answered.  "Hello?"

"Hey Baby. It's me," Curt said.

"Curt! Are you OK?" Allison demanded.

"Yes, yes, baby. I'm fine," tears were welling up in his eyes. "How are Noorullah and baby Bo?"

"Sweetheart! They're great. We all miss you. Where are you? Can you say?"

"Yes. I'm in Germany at Landstuhl Medical Center."

"Hospital? What happened?"

Curt began to break down. "Smitty. He got shot and we could barely get him out. His heart stopped half a dozen times. I had to literally give him blood from myself while he was in the OR. Now, he's through surgery, but we don't know if his liver is going to start functioning again."

Allison paused. "Baby. I love you. I'll pray for him. What about the rest of the team?"

"Buck is good. We lost another pilot and team member. You didn't know them," Curt answered, shifting from being somber to almost robotic.

"When are you coming home?"

"Allison, I don't know. I can't leave Smitty. Give me a few days. The doctor said it could be 24-48 hours before we know if his liver recovers."

"OK. Will you be on this phone? Can we call you? The kids would love to see you."

"Sure. I'll be here," Curt responded. "I love you."

Finally, in Curt's mind, the mission was over. He'd begin decompressing, again facing all the demons. At least he was on a military base and staying at a facility like The Fisher House that not only understood his needs, but was compassionate to them.


*********************


Stacy rolled over and looked at Ryan. "Do you think day two is gonna be worse than day one?"

"Stac, I think it will be as good or as bad as you make it.

Today's result is all about you. You're the President."

She kissed him. "You're right. I am. Now, why no breakfast today?"

Ryan laughed. "You're gonna have to talk to the White House staff. I wasn't allowed into the kitchen yesterday."

She laughed and gave him a hug. The two would get up and enjoy a nice breakfast together.

Downstairs, Steve was doing everything he could to organize the President's schedule, along with starting the prebriefs. It was what a normal day looked like in the White House, and far more manageable than the prior day.

Eventually, Stacy walked down the stairs, watching the hustle and bustle of the staff. Most would pass and say, "Good morning, Madam President." She responded in kind.

She walked towards the Oval Office, stopping at Agnus' desk. "Good morning, Agnus. How you holding up?"

"Good morning, Ma'am. I'm good. Still learning a lot of stuff unique to you. It's overwhelming and far different from your predecessor."

"Agnus, you're great. You have my utmost trust and confidence. What more do you need?" Frankly, there were far better secretaries than Agnus. She was old, with a demonstrated inability to adapt quickly to new presidents. But Agnus was also a staple at the White House. And those are treasures one does not just toss away.

The two smiled as Stacy continued her walk into the Oval Office. There, she found Steve, standing and waiting for her.

"Good morning, Madam President. Did you sleep well?"

"Good morning, Steve. Yes. Thanks for asking. How about you?"

Steve smiled. "Also good. Thanks. We have a busy day for you. I've prepared talking points for you as well as some background information on a few of your meetings. I confess though, I wanna make sure I stay away from 'mansplain-ees.'"

Stacy laughed. "Steve, do what you'd do for the previous guy. I'll deal with it."

The two sat down and began going over notes. They spoke, laughed and learned together. It was a very cordial event, and

Stacy enjoyed it greatly. Keeping Steve onboard was the right decision. As the meeting wrapped up, Steve said, "Ma'am, as you requested, Secretary Baker's resignation letter is on your desk. Just let me know when you'd like to go public with it."

Stacy walked over and looked at it. "Interesting. Steve, do you recall what I specifically told the Secretary?"

"I thought you said you wanted to talk about the letter, not that you asked for one."

"That's correct. At this time, I have no intent to accept this nor do I wish for it. Please schedule me another meeting with the Secretary." Although Stacy didn't want the letter, she carefully took it and placed it in her top drawer, not the trash can.

"Yes, ma'am, but you'll see her in an hour. You have your first Security Council meeting. Do you want to make it a sidebar?"

"Sure, Steve. Good idea. Now, let me go over some of this stack of paper you dumped on me." She smiled and he closed the door.

Stacy was able to perform about fifteen minutes of work before Attorney General Erwin Reese was standing at her door. It was the first appointment of the day, and she was hoping he had good news.

"Erwin, good to see you. Please come in." Both Erwin and Stacy were long time government employees in D.C. They had known each other for quite a while, via professional connections, and on occasion were able to collaborate and cooperate to advance their issues.

"Thanks, Madam President. How are you fitting in?"

"I'm not," she joked. "And I doubt I ever will, but perhaps that's a good thing and perhaps that's what this office needs. Someone who never feels comfortable in it."

"True. Well, I have news for you."

"Erwin, you left out the word 'good.' Was that on purpose?"

"Yes, ma'am, because it's not good, it's great. We have Victor Petrov in custody. He's healthy, minus some broken bones. We can hold him for up to 24 hours, but given the majority of the world thinks he's dead, I'm fairly certain not too many attorneys are going to rush to defend him."

"That is great news. When can you have charges prepared against him?"

"They'll be good enough to go public around noon, or anytime you'd like to after that."

"Great. I'd like you here later today, around four PM. Please do not share any of this with anyone who doesn't have a need to know."

"Will do, Madam President. Do you have anything else?"

"Yes. Actually, I do. The woman the previous President had an affair with. She was supposedly attacked by what she believes was personnel from the U.S. Government. I know there was an agent on that case. What ever happened?"

"Ma'am. Nothing. It's a cold case, and frankly, Ms. Benson, the victim has disappeared. We can contact her attorney, but she won millions in a lawsuit and is gone."

"I see," Stacy said. "And your personal thoughts?"

"I don't think it was USG, but it was clearly someone who could mimic it and wanted it to look legit. Mafia? I don't know. There never seemed to be a motive. The young lady was clean."

"Got it. Thanks Erwin. Have a good day and I'll see you later."

Erwin stood up and shook her hand, then departed.

"Agnus," Stacy called out. "Can you get Steve for me?"

"Yes, Ma'am." Agnus yelled back.

Steve was preparing the briefing room for the Security Council. He quickly scurried to the Oval Office. "Yes, ma'am?"

"Steve, today, I want another meeting with Ambassador Tarlov at 1500, then I want the Press Corps available at 1600. Can we do that?"

"Ma'am. You're the President. We can do anything. But do you want to let me know what you're planning or if you need help?"

"Steve. As soon as I put it all together, you'll be the first to figure it out."

\*\*\*\*\*\*\*\*\*\*\*\*\*\*\*\*\*\*

297

Stefan Balakin sat at his desk monitoring his operations and ensuring the transition to a new and secure 'FindMe2' was successful. Eventually, on his computer map, beacons began popping up, and on his iPhone 'FindMe' original App, they were all gone. *'Perfect,'* he thought.

As he scrolled across the globe, he saw numerous beacons reporting from D.C., just as they were assigned, however, one beacon began reporting north of D.C. and south of Baltimore. Then it stopped. Then it started again. Before he could click on it, the beacon stopped, and never restarted. Stefan dismissed this as part of the change over to the new system. Plus, there were far greater issues to solve. He had to replace the vehicles lost in the rail yard explosion, hire more operatives for the ones lost, and more.

*********************

Somewhere in an undisclosed location of D.C., the FBI's best interrogators and others took their turns questioning Victor Petrov. He wouldn't talk, especially given the techniques they were using. Operatives from the Rasputin Firm had been subjected to far worse interrogation tactics in training than they'd experience from the United States or any other nation that abided by the Geneva Conventions. While he wasn't officially a military member, enemy combatant, or even a U.S. citizen, he was afforded rights and protections under the U.S. Constitution, even if he assassinated Vice President Banks.

For hours, interrogators used sleep deprivation, played loud music, threatened him with attacks on his family. Nothing worked. There was something about Russians and the Russian culture. Suffering and struggling were commonplace, almost a comfort zone.

## *Chapter Forty-Four*
# Resetting the Chess Board

Buck, JT and Jackal remained on the base at Uman. The three had worked together to get Old Girl ready to fly. She was ready, but would likely not be taking to the skies anytime soon. The Ukrainian aviation officials confirmed SBD II was in fact shot down. Small fragments of metal were embedded in some of the wood and plastic of the left wing. The tell-tale sign, however, was a spent RPG- 7 rocket-propelled grenade motor and booster laying near the crash site in an open field. Officials would perform diagnostics on the metal fragments, but many already believed they were consistent with an RPG-7. Ironically, Buck and Admiral Hershey were correct. Modern weapons were not a threat to the glider design. To down these gliders required older technology. The Russian made RPG-7 was first used in 1958. Circulation of the system proliferated the globe. Against modern military aircraft, an RPG-7 would be a waste of a grenade. However, against a slow, lumbering glider at one to two hundred feet, chances of success were quite good.

Marko approached the three, who were bored and awaiting orders. It was a common occurrence in warfare, and is the attributor to the military adage, *'Hurry up and wait.'* "Hey, gentlemen," Marko said. "How is Old Girl?"

Buck proudly replied, "She's ready to fly. Just need an OK." That wasn't really true. Even if the Admiral authorized flights, Buck was holding personal reservations after watching Old Girl's sister, the SBD II, get knocked out of the sky.

"Good to hear," Marko shot back. "Any word from the U.S.? The news of Petrov's death is dominating the news here in Ukraine."

"Yeah, same in the U.S.," JT answered. "Not sure when the truth will come out, but man, when it does, it's gonna be a fun time to tune in and eat some popcorn."

The group chuckled, then Marko continued. "Hey, Jackal, what's your plan?"

"Same as the rest of you. Wait for some tasking, then execute." Jackal was bored, but well trained. He knew this was part of the process.

"Well, if you're willing, and if your boss agrees, the Ukrainian military may have a job for you. Ukrainian military will provide over-watch protection. My leadership was impressed with your shot on Ivan."

"I'm game if TVG is. Let me ask." Jackal tried to suppress his excitement. More chances to shoot and more money. It was a win-win.

"OK," Marko said. "I do have another bit of unsavory business to discuss with you."

Buck, the most senior of the three, answered. "Yes. What is it?"

"The bodies of Jughead and Beef. Because of the war, our morgues are full. We can cremate them if you wish, but in their current state, we can't keep them for much longer. I know it's only been a day, but local officials are pushing to get them out."

Buck was understanding, but partially frustrated. "I get it, but our team is kinda stuck here." Buck then had an idea. "Hold on," he said. Buck pulled out his phone and dialed the Admiral. "Hey, Admiral. Buck here. Colonel Marko Taran, our Ukrainian liaison, is with me. I think the two of you should talk."

The Admiral replied, "Please, put him on."

Marko took the phone and greeted the Admiral. After the pleasantries, he relayed the concerns of the local authorities.

"I understand," The Admiral said. "What options do we have?" He asked. "I don't want anyone flying our aircraft out until the assessment of the crash is final."

"Admiral, I'd say even if the assessment is done, you likely won't fly. Initial indications are it was shot down by an RPG-7."

'Damn it,' the Admiral thought. *They figured it out.* He knew old style weapons were the Achilles heel to his project. "OK. So, no aircraft. What else?"

"I'm working on that," Marko replied. "If I can get you a climate-controlled bread truck, would you consider trading it for Old Girl?"

Buck's eyebrows raised. He wasn't part of the phone conversation but butted in anyway. "Old Girl is one of a kind and cost hundreds of thousands in man hours and parts. I don't see that trade being acceptable."

The Admiral heard Buck in the background. "Marko, sorry about Buck, but he has a point. There seems to be a bit of a cost imbalance."

Marko calmly responded. "Admiral, your aircraft could be worth a million dollars, but if she can't fly, she isn't worth much. And I think it was very generous of our government to dedicate a helicopter to Smitty's extraction. It likely saved his life."

The Admiral realized Marko had a point. "Yes, I do, thank you for that."

"Admiral," Marko continued. "I see great opportunities for you and your company here in Ukraine for the foreseeable future. Let's not waste that opportunity. In fact, if you're amenable, we would like to provide Jackal with some opportunities, of course, paying for his services. We would also provide over-watch protection until you can get a team back to Ukraine. You can talk money with our Defense Attache or Ambassador in D.C., as well as the specifics."

The Admiral knew Old Girl's days of flying were likely done for a while, and the offer of new business was too much to pass up. "Sure. Deal. Get a climate-controlled truck. Buck and JT can come back. You keep Jackal. Please, put Buck back on the phone."

"Thank you, Admiral, for your agreement." Marko handed over the phone.

Before Buck could weigh in, the Admiral spoke. "Buck, stow it. There will be other opportunities. We need to get Jughead and Beef home, and I presume you'd like to be there for the funerals with the families. That Mi-8 mission is what allowed Smitty to be holding onto life. That's worth more than Old Girl. Lastly, if we wanted another aircraft like her, we know we can build one. The Ukraine war is nowhere near done. Let's get back here, regroup, and find new options."

' Buck bit his lip. "Yes, boss... you're right."

"OK. Get the truck and get to Warsaw. From there, if you don't hear from me, get to the Embassy. Things here are a bit hectic, but hopefully I'll figure out how to get them home.

"Yes, Sir. I'll do it."

"And tell Jackal to be safe. If he doesn't like the over-watch Ukraine is providing, he doesn't go. I'll make that clear to the Ukrainian Ambassador. Do you copy?"

"Yes, boss. I'll relay it. Anything else?"

"No. That's it. Buck, I know this is hard. I'm proud of you for the missions you flew. You made a difference in the war, and you'll make more in the future. Also, your efforts put the Valyrian Group on the map. We owe you a debt of gratitude. I assure you."

Buck lifted his head a bit. "Thanks, boss. I needed that. Cheers." The two hung up.

\*\*\*\*\*\*\*\*\*\*\*\*\*\*\*\*\*\*\*\*

President Crawford's first National Security Council meeting went well. It differed slightly from others, including an overarching set of guidance she wanted the entire team to hear. For years, she had formulated what she believed the U.S. National security strategy should be. Now, with guidance pushed out, she was confident the team would all be rowing together. More importantly, any member not rowing correctly could be dismissed for cause. Should there be a special election and if she were to win, Stacy would formulate her guidance into an actual National Security Strategy document. For now, with an uncertain horizon, there was no need to place such stress on the Defense, State, and other departments.

As the meeting wrapped up, the President looked at Secretary Baker. "Marleen, can you stay back for a quick sidebar?"

"Yes, Madam President," she responded.

The rest of the group departed the briefing room until the two were alone.

"Marleen, perhaps I didn't make myself clear. I wished to discuss the topic of your resignation; I did not ask for it. Do you wish to resign?"

Marleen had misunderstood. She was also angered by the comment. "Madam President, perhaps I misunderstood, but I presumed you wanted my resignation, given you held two high-level meetings with foreign leadership without my presence. We both know I should have been a party to those events. I wasn't and the logical conclusion was my services were no longer desired. You deserve to have a Secretary of State you can rely on. Clearly, that isn't me."

Stacy thought about it for a bit, then said. "Marleen, if you were me, what would you have done? If you had a direct subordinate promise unwavering loyalty and in less than five minutes, break that vow? Perhaps you did misunderstand and I understand you are angered. But, who are you really mad at?"

Marleen was stuck again. "Madam President, I don't know what I would do," she said. It wasn't true. She did. She would have fired the subordinate. But in the back of her mind, aspirations to retain power lingered. If Stacy were to go unopposed now, it could be another eight years before she had a D.C. power play job. Secretary Baker remained silent. Committed to her last words. No matter how disingenuous they were.

"Marleen, I'm going to give you a second chance. Later today, I am going to have a press conference with the Russian Ambassador, and I'd like you to be there, standing behind me. Can you do that?"

"Yes, Madam President. I'd welcome that." Marleen couldn't hide her grin. She was back on the inside and would have access to critical information, helpful to her party chairman and any future campaign.

"Great. I'll see you then."

Marleen departed and Stacy walked back to the Oval Office. She passed Agnus and offered a brief hello, then walked in. Standing there waiting for her was Andrew Denney. It was a private meeting.

"Andrew, I am happy you could come on such short notice," she offered.

"Madam President, it's an honor, but I thought we had concluded our business."

Stacy offered him to sit as she closed the door. "Yes, we did for The Valyrian Group, but this is another issue." The two sat, and she continued. "I'd like to discuss the notion of a Special Election under the guise of the 9th Amendment."

"Yes, ma'am."

"I am curious. Do you support this course of action?"

Andrew was leery of answering. "Madam President, may I inquire why you wish to know my answer?"

"I spoke to Steve today. He said from your meeting yesterday, you suggested I may not need to worry too much about this election if I were to deliver Petrov to U.S. Soil."

"That's correct. I said that," Andrew answered.

"Well, he's here. And you've succeeded. I now need to find a way to come up with $20M. But as you likely know, Thomas Agnew and the party aren't supportive of me. It appears I don't have enough gaffs in me from large donor fishermen."

Andrew smirked at her analogy. "Yes, I understand there are some who believe that."

"Therefore, I want to know what you think. Andrew, you have long been one of the largest campaign donors in D.C. I've never taken a dime from you, or anyone else for that matter. I'm a career civil servant and political novice. It seems to me you'd rather have another party member as president. One that you've long bought and paid for."

"Madam President, you'd be wrong. Frankly, I'd welcome the opportunity for you to remain President. Given our recent dealings, I'd perhaps argue I'm the only fisherman with a gaff in ya, albeit not an outright donation."

"Perhaps," Stacy answered. "But I never intend to sell my soul in this office. Ever. Not to a donor and not to another nation." Stacy was adamant.

"Madam President. If I had a dime for every time I heard a politician chirp that line. Perhaps you're different. Time will tell. What can I do for you?"

"Andrew, I'd like you to donate to my campaign, and I'd like you to help me get other donors. Additionally, I need a small favor from The Valyrian Group. Do you have men in D.C. that can perform a small task tonight? Nothing more criminal than a misdemeanor."

Andrew's eyes lit up. "Madam President. I will donate to your campaign and am honored you asked. For the record, my donation will not be anonymous. I will ensure other donors know where I stand. As for your minor task. I'm intrigued. Please, go on."

Stacy explained her task and Andrew listened. It was truly nothing that nefarious, but Andrew loved the idea. He'd make it happen, free of charge.

Stacy wished Andrew a fond farewell, as almost all the pieces were in place for her press conference today. As she walked Andrew to the Oval Office door, Agnus stood there, holding a small, gift-wrapped box.

"Madam President," Agnus said. "Ryan dropped this off for you. He said it's a 'Day one do-over gift.' Should I place it on your desk?"

"No, Agnus, I'll take it. Thanks." Stacy took the box, walked into the Oval Office and closed the door. Quickly, she unpacked the gift. It was exactly what she had asked for. *'Thanks, my love.'* She thought to herself.

## Chapter Forty-Five
# An Unforeseen & Unfortunate State of Affairs

Ambassador Tarlov arrived at the White House as scheduled. He'd brought a three-hundred-dollar bottle of the finest Russian Vodka as a gift. It was his token offering, paid for by the Russian government. The Ambassador and the bottle were both scanned and X-rayed. They were clean. Tarlov was escorted to the Oval Office where Stacy was waiting for him. She had changed into a sleeveless jumper style outfit. Her shoulders were revealed, but the outfit was professional and not too risqué.

"Mr. Ambassador, it is good to see you again," she offered as he entered the room.

"You as well, Madam President, and I brought a gift from our nation."

Stacy took the bottle and set it down on the table. Agnus closed the Oval Office door, as Stacy had asked. The two were alone.

"Ambassador Tarlov. I've thought much about our meeting yesterday and would like to discuss things further… shall we say, discretely." Stacy raised her arms as a demonstration she had no listening devices.

"I'd welcome that," Tarlov said. "But we are in this office. Perhaps a walk in the Rose Garden?" He offered.

"Certainly," Stacy responded. She opened the door. The weather outside was a bit windy. She held the door for him and as he walked out, she said, "Forgive me ambassador, it's a bit too chilly for this outfit." She ran back to her desk and grabbed a hand knitted shawl, a gift from a long-time friend. Stacy threw it over her shoulders to keep warm and stepped outside, closing the door. With her hands, she motioned for her Security Detail to remain at a distance. Out of earshot. "Perhaps not the best outfit for a stroll in the garden," she said to Tarlov.

"No, I presume not. Women always are always too cold, I've found." It was Russian humor and, like most jokes, it fell flat with an underlying sexist jab.

"Yes. You're right." Stacy appeased his comment through cut teeth.

"Ambassador. Yesterday, you suggested it was in my best interest to support the ideas you and Russia offer. Now that we are alone, I must ask. Why did you frame my predecessor with that video? Wasn't he doing what you wanted?"

Tarlov smiled. "No. He wasn't, but I'd suggest your notion that we had him framed was wrong?"

Stacy smiled. "Well, I guess we don't need to walk alone in the Rose Garden if that's going to be your response. Look, I may have been born at night, but it wasn't last night. I get the game. You want my support, fine. But help me understand. We both know it wasn't the U.S. government that targeted Rachel Benson, don't we?"

Tarlov let down his guard and smiled. "That was a fun one for my men," he replied. "She was perfect. I bet the FBI is still trying to figure out who shot up her house."

"Yes. Ironically, I asked our AG yesterday. You're right. It's a cold case and likely won't ever be solved."

"You see, Madam President. It is not difficult to lead in this nation. I'm hopeful we can work together. Things like Ms. Benson's targeting or Vice President Banks' assassination can be unpleasant memories of the past."

Stacy chuckled. "I think you mean work 'for Russia' and not necessarily together."

"As I said yesterday, Russia went to great lengths to place you in this office. We are hoping for a return on our investment. Yes, it came with risks," he said almost matter-of-factly. "If it doesn't pay off, we will invest in another."

"Well, I hate to say it, but I think your return on investment is going to be short-lived. It looks like there will be a special election soon and I have no campaign war chest. I also don't have the support of the party, at least not yet."

"Ah, Madam President," Tarlov replied. "These things are small issues. You will have all the money you need. You merely have to ask."

Stacy looked at him. "Well, I don't know how, but I appreciate the offer. Under our laws, foreign campaign contributions are illegal."

Tarlov bellowed out a laugh. "Perhaps you were born last night. There are many ways to change rubles to dollars. You let us worry about that."

The wind whipped up and Stacy grabbed her shawl tight around her neck. "The breeze out here. I wish there were trees. Nothing stops the wind." Stacy was getting cold.

Ambassador Tarlov had said all he wished to say. "Shall we head back in? Perhaps we can have a small glass of vodka. I believe you mentioned something about a press conference later today, so not too much."

"Yes, please. That would be great," the President answered. The two went back inside, and Stacy removed her shawl, laying it on the chair behind her desk. "Mr. Ambassador, in about a half hour, I plan to announce some of my ideas. It won't be anything earth shattering. As you know, it will take time to put in place all the changes I do hope for. I held my first Security Council meeting today. I want you to know, I've directed my staff to focus on our relationship with Russia. Specifically, I've reinforced the notion we should deep dive into Russian narratives. I am hopeful that is acceptable." She'd chosen her words carefully. Tarlov heard what he wanted to hear. "Might you be available to be there?"

Ambassador Tarlov was flattered but was in no shape to be on camera. "Madam President, thank you, but I have no desire to be on camera yet. Perhaps when the population is more favorable."

"Oh, I'm sorry. I didn't mean on camera. I meant in the crowd, to watch. You can sit in the audience or with the press corps, your choice."

Ambassador Tarlov could barely control his excitement. "I'd like that, Madam President. Let me pour you a glass of Vodka."

Tarlov opened the bottle and poured two small shots. The two clinked glasses and drank.

"Mr. Ambassador, if you don't mind, I need just a few minutes to have my makeup done and prepare for the event. I'll have Steve show you to the waiting area."

"Thank you."

The President called in Steve, who did as instructed. Stacy ran back to her shawl, removing a recording device from it. The gift she had received earlier from Ryan was a recording device, something only he would be able to get past White House security into the Oval Office. She rewound the tape quickly and confirmed she'd caught it all. Hastily, she threw the shawl down on the Oval Office desk. The microphone wire laid exposed on top.

After a few minutes in make-up and reviewing her notes, Stacy put on her jacket and walked out into the hall where she was met by Secretary Baker.

"Madam President, I didn't see a draft of your speech yet. That's not really the protocol."

"Yes, I know, Marleen. I am sorry. It's day two. I am hoping to get better and catch on. Please forgive me."

"I understand," Marleen responded. She made a mental note about the sloppy start of Stacy's presidency and would consider its use in a future campaign.

The two walked together up the hallway towards the podium and microphone. As expected, Stacy immediately noticed Ambassador Tarlov in the audience. So did Secretary Baker, who was puzzled by his presence.

News agencies all broke from their currently televised schedule, "Ladies and Gentlemen, the President of the United States."

Stacy began. "Fellow Americans. Today is a good day. I'd like to start my speech today by thanking our Secretary of State, Marleen Baker and Russian Ambassador Tarlov who's in the audience here today, for their exceptional support to myself and the U.S. over the past few days."

She paused and shuffled papers. "Today, I'd like to share with you how, over the past few days, U.S. and Russia have worked together. To begin, the news of Victor Petrov's death is inaccurate. Currently, he is in custody on U.S. soil, being held for the assassination of Vice President Banks."

Tarlov's eyes turned a fiery red. Camera crews in the Press Corps had turned to him and began snapping photos. As much as he tried to hide his rage, it was clearly present. President Crawford was far from done.

"As most in the media know, the initial reports of Petrov's death originated from Russian media. This false reporting greatly eased our effort to extradite him and I'd like to take this opportunity to thank the Russian media for a job well done." She paused, ensuring the appropriate level of sting could be enacted across Moscow. "Presently, Attorney General Reese is submitting the indictment papers. Based on the evidence, we are confident the judicial system will direct a no bail ruling until legal proceedings can begin." The camera flashes died down and President Crawford again shuffled some papers.

She looked up and continued. "Russia isn't the only entity that deserves credit. As I mentioned earlier, Marleen Baker was instrumental in these efforts. Under constitutional and international law, U.S. forces and federal agents were unable to secure Mr. Petrov. Marleen, with the help of the national party leadership, funded a private firm to find, capture and bring Mr. Petrov to justice. By the time I learned of the mission, Petrov had already been captured and was on his way to the U.S. While I am grateful that Petrov is in U.S. custody, please know this. I would not have supported such an effort, as I don't believe the funding to be ethical. Further, as I remain president, I will not secretly fund the use of private security firms. I will, however, support Congress, the purse branch of our government, to fund security efforts it deems worthy. Should the House and Senate choose to contract private security firms, that is their choice. That is how the people's government is supposed to work. I realize some may find private military companies distasteful. I understand and accept that. But the world has changed since World War II, and the Geneva Convention hasn't. Other nations, arguably led by Russia, have leveraged private military companies to do their bidding. I refuse to sit idly by while others continually break the rules. My position may not be popular with our allies, but I look forward to explaining it in detail. Perhaps they have some options to make it better, and if so, I welcome them. Until then, I stand by my decision."

Marleen wanted to run and hide, but there was no chance. Millions around the world were watching.

"On my last topic. People have asked if I support a special election. My answer is simple. I will support whatever the U.S. people desire. I know full well, should there be an election, I will possibly lose, as I have no long-standing political base or massive donors. To some, this is perhaps refreshing in the White House. To wealthy donors and Super PACs, that is a liability. A special election is a decision for Americans. So, what I intend to ask Congress to do is the following. Fund an effort that accurately garners the will of the people on this simple question. 'Should there be a special election?' Not via polling, and not via pundits. The question should be answered by the people. Should they vote yes, we will have the election as soon as Congress can organize it."

Stacy set down her papers. She was done with her prepared remarks. "It's been an eventful two days, and I am just getting started. May God Bless You, and Our United States of America."

Stacy stepped back from the podium and nodded at Secretary Baker. Questions were shouted out from the media gallery, but none would receive answers.

Stacy and Marleen walked back down the hall until they were out of sight. "You fucking set me up!" Marleen yelled. Losing her composure.

"Marleen. It's my bully pulpit, not yours. You have the party war chest, and I have a microphone. Let's see who wins, shall we? I'll announce your resignation later today. You can sort out with the press why you resigned. Given the funding of Petrov's capture, they may draw other conclusions."

Marleen stormed off.

Stacy strolled to the Oval Office. Standing outside, under escort, was Ambassador Tarlov, who was fit to be tied. "Ambassador, please come in."

"You hold me hostage in your White House! I want to leave, now!" He refused to move.

"Mr. Ambassador, this will only take a minute, please."

The two secret service agents nudged him, and he begrudgingly entered. The door closed and Tarlov raged. "You slut!"

"Easy, Tarlov. The recorder is still on." Stacy pointed down at the Shawl. There, the wires, microphone, and recorder were clearly visible.

Tarlov's eyes widened as if in fright. His jaw dropped, and he did not know what to say. What he'd said in the rose garden was damning, and he knew it. Eventually, he was able to speak. "You cunt. You will pay! You will pay dearly! You Americans never learn. Moscow owns you. Moscow pulls your strings. I PULL your strings. I am the Russian Puppeteer! You are nothing but a character in my play."

Stacy smiled. "Ambassador. It must be enjoyable in your fantasy world. In reality, you are no Russian Puppeteer. Perhaps a Moscow Muppet, but that's it. Threaten me, my family, or my administration at all, and this tape goes public. Do you understand?"

"Make it public! I don't care. I have diplomatic immunity!"

"Yes, you do. But should it go public, the judicial branch may not be able to judge you, but the American public will. You've lost your power."

Tarlov steamed. She was right. He'd never go to jail, but any leverage he had against Stacy, now or in the future, was lost.

"You're free to go," Stacy said, as she picked up the shawl.

Tarlov stormed out of the office, off the White House grounds, and into his awaiting embassy staff car. His phone was ringing off the hook, mostly calls from Moscow. He chose not to answer any of them.

For the Press Corps, the White House Spokespersons shared current photos of Victor Petrov. Full explanations were provided about his surviving an air accident. Media outlets splashed the photos via every medium they could, along with Secretary Baker's resignation letter. There'd be many questions, and perhaps The Valyrian Group would be exposed, but that was a small price to pay in Andrew's eyes for keeping Stacy in the White House.  Should it be necessary, he could stand up another security firm in days.

## *Chapter Forty-Six*
# The Ugliness of Rage

Tarlov directed his driver to Café Berlin. He was a regular there and would be protected from a hounding media. As angered as he was, Tarlov knew he needed to let off some steam. His driver pulled up. The rear door opened, then slammed shut. Tarlov knocked on the front passenger window. It rolled down.

"Come in. I may need protection."

His driver would do as instructed, driving only a few meters up Massachusetts Ave, finding a handicapped parking spot to parallel park in. It was the way of many D.C. diplomats. With diplomatic plates, anywhere was a possible parking spot. Rules and regulations be damned. Tarlov's driver locked the car and entered the restaurant.

Minutes later, a large black van that had been following the car from the White House, pulled alongside the Russian Ambassador's staff car. A door between the two vehicles opened, and two men jumped out. Within seconds, each had removed the front and rear diplomatic license plate. With a swift strike, the rear assailant cracked a taillight open and removed the bulb. Hastily, he collected up the debris. They departed as quickly as they arrived. Andrew's team had done well.

After the black van drove away, another man, strolling down Mass Ave on a cool evening, walked by the vehicle. On one arm, a large sleeve led down to an industrial glove. Two fingers of the glove delicately held a small slip of paper. As the man walked by the Ambassador's car, he wiped the paper along the bumpers and side of the vehicle. Once complete, he continued strolling along Mass Ave, without a care in the world.

\*\*\*\*\*\*\*\*\*\*\*\*\*\*\*\*\*\*\*\*

Back in the White House, Steve and the President were sitting in the Oval Office, swirling glasses of scotch. "So, how was my second day, Steve?"

"Madam President. I'm not sure I can handle a day three." Steve enjoyed working for Stacy. She wasn't polished, no President could be under current constructs, but she was far cleaner than the others. Steve appreciated that. President Crawford was as close to the ideals he held dear, or at least as close as one could get. He was in for the ride... wherever it went.

"OK, Steve. Day three, tomorrow. What's on the books?"

"Ma'am, I have your schedule here, but promise me, no nukes or radiation fall out? OK?"

Stacy laughed. "Who told you?" She said comically. They talked about the schedule, and she was comfortable with it. "OK, Steve. I think that's it... oh, wait. One final thing. Tomorrow morning, President Volkov will likely call, given they are eight hours ahead of us. If he does, please tell him I'll call him back as soon as I am awake and in the office."

"Will do, ma'am."

"Great. Good night, Steve." Steve retired to his residence.

Slowly, Stacy carried her microphone and recorder to the private residence. Ryan was still watching the press conference, rewinding it over and over.

"Fun day two, huh, Stacy!" He spoke.

"Killer, buddy." She hugged him and they kissed.

"Come with me. You gotta hear this shit," Stacy said, leading Ryan to the bedroom. For the next hour, they sat and listened to Tarlov's comments. They laughed, and gasped.

After a while, Ryan had stopped laughing and just stared at his wife. Stacy eventually noticed. Feeling awkward, she asked, "Hey. What's a matter?"

Ryan took a breath and spoke. "Stacy, is this really something you want?"

Her face turned serious, almost somber. "No. It's not, Ryan. I never wanted to be president." She paused and exhaled a massive breath. "But more importantly than that, I don't want our country to remain this way. If I don't fix it, who will?"

Ryan looked at her. "What are you? A Marine now?" Ryan smiled at his poorly timed joke.

"I'm serious. As a nation, we are too dysfunctional."

"I know and agree." He hugged Stacy close and held her. "Baby, I'm with ya. Wherever this ride leads us."

She squeezed him back. "And why do I need to be a Marine? I married one." She smiled, as did Ryan. Then, somewhat inappropriately, Stacy said, "Not to mention, I have about a dozen young, cute Marines running around our house."

Ryan realized it was a return zinger, marginally letting it pass. "Yes, Madam President. Easy does it."

*******************

Now completely drunk, Tarlov stumbled out of Café Berlin, under the assistance of his driver. The driver, completely sober, focused on ensuring no media or cameras were around. He poured his boss into the car. Hastily, he circled to the driver's door, angrily snatched a parking ticket from the window. As he got into the driver's seat, he tossed the ticket onto the ground. *'Diplomats don't pay tickets,'* he thought to himself.

Slowly, he pulled out onto Mass Ave, heading northwest back to the Ambassador's residence. He'd only make it a quarter mile before a D.C. metro police officer stopped the car.

The officer got out and approached. "License and registration." He requested.

The driver held up a diplomatic card to the window. The officer walked to the front of the car, then the back. There were no diplomatic license plates. In fact, there were no plates at all.

"Sir, please roll down the window. You have no license plates. I need to see that card."

The driver refused. Per international law, that car and its contents were considered territory of Russia, exempt from search.

"Sir, I cannot verify you are a diplomat. Please roll down the window, or I will be forced to break it." Another police car pulled up. The D.C. Metro officers faced a unique situation. Without a license plate number to run, there was no way to verify the driver's claims.

The senior officer returned to the driver's side door and began pounding on the window with the back of his MagLite flashlight. "Open the Window."

Tarlov had enough. He rolled down his passenger window from the back and began screaming at the police, waving his diplomat identification card wildly in the air.

As trained, once the window was open, the officer reached in and unlocked the door, then swung it open. Russian Ambassador Tarlov was seconds away from being in police custody.

Tarlov's driver hastily jumped out from his seat, planning to confront the police. The scene quickly escalated until both Tarlov and his driver were handcuffed face down on the pavement.

After a while, the two were taken for processing. While they both had diplomatic immunity from many crimes, they were not exempt from being apprehended for disobeying as well as resisting arrest. Eventually, the charges would be dropped, but for now, they were under arrest.

Once booked in, Tarlov was escorted into a room with a mirrored window. After the guards left him, electronics transitioned the mirror into a window. In the adjacent room, Ambassador Tarlov saw Victor Petrov, sitting in a wheelchair with two broken legs, but very much alive. Along with Victor were two other men interrogating him. As Victor spoke, the two feverishly scribbled down everything he said. While Tarlov couldn't hear the conversation, his emotions raged just considering what Petrov could be saying. Tarlov ran over to the glass, pounding on it. There was no use. It was multiple layers and mirrored on the other side.

The actual discussion Tarlov observed had nothing to do with criminality but was rather Petrov describing an old Russian sport of 'Bandy,' a form of hockey. The agents acted quite interested as Petrov showed moves of checking and holding. Without audio, Tarlov assumed the worst. Just as he was supposed to.

A local wrecking company began to tow Tarlov's vehicle towards the Washington D.C. impound lot. Strangely, as it passed the Capitol building on Mass Ave, alarms and sensors blared and traffic was stopped. Police stopped the tow truck under gunpoint and the driver obliged. A quick scan of the car showed positive levels of radiation. Procedures were immediately followed, just as they had been practiced in numerous exercises. The tow truck and car were rapidly removed and placed in special quarantine. A hazmat unit from the Washington D.C. National Guard would evaluate the car and find trace amounts of Polonium-210, the same agent used to assassinate Vice President Banks.

Tarlov's and his driver's rap sheet grew longer. Accomplice to murder of the United States Vice President.


\*\*\*\*\*\*\*\*\*\*\*\*\*\*\*\*\*\*\*\*


Allison couldn't believe the news. She picked up her phone and called Curt.

"Hello?" Curt answered, waking from a nap.

"Curt! Did you see the news?"

"Yeah. Petrov is alive. I know. Crazy." He'd known all along.

"Not only that! The Russian Ambassador was arrested, and they found Polonium-210 traces on his car."

Curt rubbed his eyes. That was a piece of info he didn't know. "Wow. I hadn't heard. It's late here. Sorry."

"No, I'm sorry. I shouldn't have woken you. Just wanted to tell someone. Hey, any update on Smitty?"

"Not really. He's turning yellow, which is expected. Folks with liver failure are often yellow. The hope is his liver starts to function on its own and cleans out all the crud. The positive news is that his blood pressure is stronger and his O2 levels are up. Seems he's producing his own blood now, which is good news. He fades in and out. Not much talking."

"Curt, when are you coming home? We miss you."

"I know. A few more days. Then I'll be there... but."

"But what?"

"Allison. After coming home, I'd like to go back to Poland for a bit more. I was doing what I've longed to do. Save lives. When I come home, can we work out a schedule where I can do that for a time and then be home for a time? Hell, maybe you come to Poland with me."

Allison could sense his passion. "Yes. Baby. We will figure it out. Just come home. And bring Smitty with you."

"OK. I will. Give the kids a hug and kiss from me. I love you, Allison."

"I love you too, Curt. You crazy man."

The two hung up. Curt faded back to sleep.

## *Chapter Forty-Seven*
# Iron Balls McGinty

As Steve Lewis lay in bed, a phone call rang in from the D.C. Mayor, explaining what had happened. Steve was shocked and thanked the mayor for the information.

He called the White House private residence and was put through to President Crawford. "Madam President, I am very sorry to wake you, but there is urgent news."

Stacy groggily replied, "Yes, Steve. It's fine. Please, tell me what's going on."

Steve relayed the information he had just received, focusing in on all the details surrounding the information regarding Polonium-210 traces on the Russian Ambassador's vehicle.

President Crawford acted surprised. When Steve asked what course of action she desired, Stacy asked if there was enough to ensure both the ambassador and his driver could remain imprisoned until the morning.

"Madam President, I presume anyone in possession of the rare radioactive substance that killed Vice President Banks will remain in custody."

Stacy paused. "Yes. Actually, I retract that question. This is the mayor's jurisdiction. Whatever she wants, it's her call." I do not want the White House interfering in this. Do you understand?"

"Yes, Madam President. That makes sense. I'll relay your message. Again sorry for.."

President Crawford cut him off. "Steve, don't apologize. I accepted the job. It comes with late night calls. All good. See ya in the morning." The two hung up.

Stacy rolled over in bed. "Checkmate," she said to Ryan who smiled. The two fell asleep content with the days events. The next morning, she was certain she'd have a phone call from President Volkov, on her schedule.

D.C. awoke to a gloomy sunrise. Heavy cloud cover blanketed the entire national capital region. Stacy and Ryan woke and had a lovely breakfast. They watched the news, which

320

was slathered full of pundits and analysts trying to make sense of yesterday's events. A D.C. Metro Spokesperson briefing would soon air with details of an unfortunate event the previous night, where a senior foreign diplomat refused a lawful order and was detained. Questions flew from the media regarding diplomatic immunity as well as exactly what ensued.

The spokesperson stiff armed the questions and continued with the rest of his prepared remarks. When the issue of Polonium-210 arose, the press grew silent, focused on the details.

Stacy and Ryan would watch the presser all the way to its conclusion. Overall, she was pleased with it. She arose from the table, walked over to Ryan, and kissed him on the head. "Time to go to work," she said.

"What's day three hold?" Ryan asked.

"Some final coffin nailing," Stacy replied. Then she walked to her office.

"Good morning, Steve," President Crawford called out as she approached her office. Steve stood there with the day's agenda and some staff packages he wanted to review before the day's start.

Steve responded, "Good morning, Madam President. I have…"

Stacy cut him off. "Steve, I need to talk to President Volkov. I presumed he's called several times."

Steve smiled. "Only fourteen times. I'll get him."

Stacy sat at her desk, mentally reviewing what she wanted to say.

Agnus announced the Russian President was on the line.

"President Volkov, good morning or should I say good afternoon to you."

Volkov was in no mood for formalities. "Madam President, release our ambassador. Now. Not in an hour, not tomorrow. Now."

"President Volkov. I understand your request. I truly do, but given his car demonstrated traces of polonium-210, we are holding him for his own good."

"Own good?" Volkov screamed. "What on earth do you mean?"

"Mr. President. Ambassador Tarlov declared during questioning he does not know how the polonium-210 got onto his vehicle. Until we know further, we must take him at his word. This leaves two likely possibilities. Either he or his vehicle had something to do with the murder of the Vice President, or someone is now trying to assassinate Ambassador Tarlov."

"Madam President, please stop with the games. Seriously? The license plates were stolen from the vehicle. The taillight was broken out, and an immediate traffic stop ensued. There was polonium-210 on the car, weeks after the murder? Is it even from the same source? This has all the fingerprints of a setup."

"Mr. President, I don't know if it's from the same source, but we do have forensics looking at it."

"That doesn't address all the coincidences I brought up." President Volkov responded.

Stacy took a deep breath. "Perhaps it is a setup. But it seems to me that over my many years working for the U.S. Government, the amount of strange coincidences when it comes to diplomatic relations between the U.S. and Russia are heavily slighted to your side."

"Madam President, please do not insinuate such things."

Stacy shot back. "Mr. President, I'm not insinuating. I'm stating a fact. I'd also gently suggest your ability to recognize a setup is perhaps based on professional experience."

President Volkov did not reply. He was furious, but smart enough to realize no comment was his best response.

President Crawford continued, "I would also say this. Should things between our nations continue to erode, there's a strong likelihood that the ratio will even out."

Volkov tried to butt in, but President Crawford wasn't finished. "Further, I am directing the closure of our Moscow Embassy. Until the last American is out, if one hair on any of their heads is harmed, Tarlov will not be released and if that isn't enough of a threat, I'll find more. Your nation's long standing 'eye for an eye' diplomacy is going to end, one way or another.

And lastly. The United States, under my leadership should I stay in office, will drastically increase its support of Ukraine."

Volkov paused before responding, taking a deep breath. "Madam President, I fear you are making a grave mistake."

"President Volkov, I know you haven't had the luxury to speak to your ambassador. When you do, he'll relay what he told me in private. He will also relay I captured it all on tape. Perhaps unprofessional, I know, but when wrestling with pigs, one needs to get a bit dirty. On a personal note, I want to thank you and the Russian government for having the faith and confidence in me to perform as the President. As for your efforts, you won't receive my thanks. It was criminal, and you killed a good man in Steve Banks." She paused, then continued. "I realize that tape will never be evidence in a court of law, but it is gold for public opinion as well as informing our NATO allies. Don't test me."

Volkov had regained his composure. "I will expect the announcement of your embassy closer. Americans will be free to depart Moscow on their schedule unhindered by my government. Do you assure me Ambassador Volkov will be released?"

"Yes. You have my word."

"And what about Petrov?"

"He will be tried in our court system and receive a fair trial. It is the best I can offer."

It wasn't enough for President Volkov, but he had no more diplomatic chips to offer. "Good day, Madam President." President Volkov hung up.

Stacy fell back in her chair, exhausted, as if she'd run a marathon. "Jesus, this is hard. And it's only nine in the morning," she said.

\*\*\*\*\*\*\*\*\*\*\*\*\*\*\*\*\*\*\*

The Beast idled in front of the White House. Stacy and Ryan entered, and the motorcade pulled away. They would drive out of the city towards the northwest, then onto the Dulles Toll Road. Once close to the airport, the presidential limo would transition onto the airfield from a back gate, and head over to a small hangar. She'd arrived roughly five minutes after the others had.

Inside the hangar were two caskets, each draped in an American Flag. Buck and JT were there, consoling the families of Jughead and Beef respectfully. Additionally, Admiral Hershey and Andrew stood by, quietly.

As Stacy and Ryan exited the Beast, the hangar grew quiet. Everyone inside watched as the President of the United States entered the ceremony unannounced. Stacy approached the wife of Jughead, Ms. Tamara Souza. "On behalf of a grateful nation, I want to thank you and your family for the sacrifices you've made." Stacy offered her a presidential medal and citation. It would never be public. Ms. Souza didn't care. She thanked the President, stoically.

Next, Stacy approached Beef's mother, Ms. Wormley. She was there with her husband and sobbing. Antonio was her only son. He loved the military, and she knew it, but it didn't take away the pain. Ms. Wormley began to hear the same comments from President Crawford and instead of listening, wrapped her arms around Stacy, crying. Ryan looked away. Even for a Marine, it was too much.

For Stacy, it was hard, too. She was never one to display affection. This was awkward for her, especially with a large black woman. Slowly, Stacy's arms raised, and she held Ms. Wormley back. After a while, they separated. Stacy handed over the citation, then walked up to the caskets. On each, she placed a presidential coin, then walked towards the Beast.

Near the car, Andrew and the Admiral were waiting. "Tough stuff. Thanks, Madam President, for doing this."

"Thanks, Andrew, for waving the $20M. You're helping me keep my promise of not paying a security firm directly."

Andrew smiled. "I wouldn't say I waived it. Perhaps better framed as an investment in our future. I saw your speech. It was good."

"You're the expert, Andrew. Do you think it will make a difference?"

"In a normal country? Likely." Andrew said. "In the U.S.? Who knows?"

The three chuckled. "OK, I need to get back. This wasn't on my official schedule, and I don't want to be gone too long. Let's talk soon... and Andrew, get those donors lined up."

They all shook hands. Stacy and Ryan entered the Beast and it pulled away.

\*\*\*\*\*\*\*\*\*\*\*\*\*\*\*\*\*\*\*

The sun had set over Landstuhl. Curt had gone to the base gym and then to dinner. Smitty wasn't much company over the past few days and he wanted to get some things done.

As he walked into Smitty's room, he found his friend, sitting up, with far better color, and flirting with an Army med tech who was ten years his junior.

Curt smiled. "I guess I should leave you two alone."

The med tech giggled.

"Ha. We are just talking," Smitty said.

"Talking? Man, I was about ready to tell you to get a room, but you appear to already have one."

A voice from behind Curt spoke up. "What's all the fuss in here?" It was the Landstuhl doctor making his evening rounds. "Mr. Smith. Look at your color. Far improved." He turned to the medical tech standing in the room. "Get me some blood work, now, please." He then returned his attention to Smitty. "Either your liver is healing, or you've qualified for a chance at sainthood with a miracle."

Smitty tried to sit up a bit more to address the doc, but his abdomen was still in great pain. "Ah," he winced. "Yeah, I'm gonna need far more than one miracle to make sainthood, Doc."

They all chuckled, but it was clear, Smitty was going to live.

Curt stepped out of the room and called the Admiral to spread the good news. Given he was still in the hangar, the celebration was muted, but everyone was pleased to hear about Smitty.

The doctor exited and the med tech had already gone to process the blood. Curt went back in.

"Dude, great to see you up. What do you remember?"

"Not much. I know we were all in Uman and then I kinda blacked out. Is the team still there? Are they taking on more missions?"

Curt sat on the side of Smitty's bed. "No buddy. Everyone is back home." Technically, it was the truth, other than Jackal.

"OK, but we are gonna get back out, right? We're building up, two airplanes now and soon we'll have three. Get some more guys for a few more teams..."

Curt stopped him. "Jughead and Beef didn't make it. They were killed in a plane crash. It was shot down. Admiral Hershey asked us to regroup for a while. Jackal is working in Ukraine with a local overwatch team."

Smitty sunk back down into his bed. "Fuckers," is all he said, then rolled over, a bit on his side. He wouldn't sleep, but it was clear he didn't want to talk anymore. It was how Smitty processed such news.

Curt got up and walked out to the nurse's station. He informed them that he'd retire to his room in the Fisher House for the night, but that he was, in fact, a doctor and would like to know the blood work results as soon as they came back. The nurses took his number and agreed.

Curt walked back across the Street to the Fisher House. In the common living room downstairs, a young woman and her child sat, nervous.

"Hello," Curt said.

"Hello," she answered, clearly not American.

"Where are you from?"

"Ukraine," she answered, somewhat scared. "Sorry. English not good."

"It's OK. I understand. Is your husband in the hospital?"

"Yes. Husband," she responded. She used her hands in a swiping motion as if to cut off legs. "These, gone." She began to tear up. Her husband had stepped on a land mine. While it

326

didn't make his wife feel any better, he was actually lucky. Without dedicated aerial medivac in Ukraine, it was amazing he made it to Landstuhl at all.

Curt set his hand on her shoulder, as any doctor would. "He must be a fighter if he is here. I am praying for you."

She nodded in appreciation, and her baby began to whine.

Curt walked away, up to his room. As he did, a text came in, it was Smitty's blood work. His liver had clearly begun functioning. '*Yes!*' Curt thought as he made a small fist pump.

## Chapter Forty-Eight
# You Sow What You Reap

After three days, all American diplomats had exited Moscow. Media coverage surrounding the event was heavy, and the Russian President had 'hoped' the U.S. would reconsider and release their Ambassador. That happened, just as President Crawford had predicted.

Tarlov was released and immediately slapped with a persona non grata letter, demanding he leave the U.S. within 48 hours. It was the last thing he wanted. While he despised being in prison, he enjoyed the distance it placed between him and Moscow. Not having to answer for his mistakes was now no longer a luxury. Years ago, Tarlov was the one who pitched the idea on placing an unpolished female government servant into the White House. Once Moscow approved, Tarlvo crafted the steps and executed them, continually lauding the effort to Kremlin leadership. Returning to Moscow meant a life prison sentence or worse. Staying in the U.S. was not an option. Frankly, Ambassador Tarlov was running out of options.

After walking out of the D.C. prison, Tarlov took a cab to his residence. He opened a bottle of vodka and began drinking as he wrote out a thoughtful suicide note. Much of it blamed the United States and how he truly loved Mother Russia. Once finished, he grabbed a hefty rope and tied it to a pillar on his balcony that overlooked Washington D.C.'s 16th Street. He stood up on top of the balcony and screamed something in Russian to draw attention, then jumped. The noose of the rope tightened as he fell. As the slack was eliminated, he'd reach halfway down between the first and second floor. The fall was far greater than he'd anticipated and the strain on his neck was excessive. Tarlov's head was decapitated from his body, the now bloody rope serving more as a guillotine. Both parts fell to the ground, then came to a rest on the sidewalk. Onlookers were horrified. Given Ambassador Tarlov's initial scream, some passers by had enough time to capture the event on their mobile device. D.C.'s closed circuit television security cameras also captured the event.  Tarlov's death would fill social media outlets as well as news outlets, but the CCTV would not be made public.

While it took longer than originally intended, Ambassador Tarlov would eventually return to Russia; however, it would be in a casket.

\*\*\*\*\*\*\*\*\*\*\*\*\*\*\*\*\*\*\*\*

Weeks had passed.  Petrov's trial would consume much of the news.  The talk of a special election simmered away as congressional members and supreme court justices all had informally helped scuttle much of the propaganda generated by the national political party.  Both the Speaker of the House and the Senate agreed to have an up or down vote versus a full nationwide election.  Given President Crawford's approval rating, few politicians wanted to vote against the President that stood up to Russia and won.  Those congressional members that supported her would do so on camera, gleefully.  Those that didn't would claim a 9th Amendment stance, but in private were beholden to their donors that mandated their vote.  Eventually, there was too little time left before the next scheduled presidential election... and there were better uses of taxpayer dollars.

Stacy would remain in office and settle in.  The Valyran Group would also survive, and not be collateral damage from Marleen Baker's fall from grace.  She wouldn't fall far however.  K Street always had a place for former State Secretaries.

\*\*\*\*\*\*\*\*\*\*\*\*\*\*\*\*\*\*\*\*

The Ukraine war continued.  It would for a while.  The Pentagon, State Department and other Agencies would do what they could to thwart Russia's advances.  Somewhere in a secured federal laboratory, a middle-aged man with black horn rimmed glasses was tinkering at his desk with some wires and circuit cards. He was clearly a computer tech expert as servers hummed in the background standing on a false floor which had massive wiring running underneath. He'd been given a task to decipher an object which he had been playing with it for weeks. Common for the NSA, he was not told what the item was that he kept attempting to crack. It was, in fact, the Rasputin Firm's capsule tracker brought back into the U.S. with Petrov. He'd spent countless hours attempting to back-channel into the host server and download supporting software.

Numerous efforts yielded no results, but eventually, a program opened up on his computer. Then a map display opened up on his computer. Slowly, dots and information began to populate the map, all in Cyrillic.

The man smiled, and jumped up and down! "Boss! I think I have something here!" He screamed.

His boss, another somewhat computer nerdy looking fellow, ran over, looked at the screen and said, "What is it?"

"I don't know. But I have a feeling it's important."

"OK. Let's get the NSA analysts down here. Maybe they can make something of it."

The NSA analyst came down and within seconds, knew what he was looking at. 'Mother of God,' he thought to himself.

He stepped outside the secure facility and called to NSA headquarters. "Hey, get DIRSNA (Director of the NSA) down here now. We have a game changer on our hands."

The line went dead.


The End.

Russian Puppeteer

To all who struggle with PTSD, please remember, help is never further than a phone call away.

The National Suicide Prevention Lifeline:  988

The Veteran's Crisis Help Line:  1-800-273-8255

***You are not alone.***

\*\*\*\*\*\*\*\*\*\*\*\*\*\*\*\*\*\*\*\*\*\*\*\*\*\*\*\*\*\*\*\*\*\*\*\*

Thanks for reading!  Please consider leaving a review on Amazon.  Just use your mobile device camera on the QR code below!

**DEPARTMENT OF DEFENSE**
DEFENSE OFFICE OF PREPUBLICATION AND SECURITY REVIEW
1155 DEFENSE PENTAGON
WASHINGTON, DC 20301-1155

Ref: 22-SB-0186
October 7, 2022

Colonel (Ret.) Jeffrey Fischer

███████████████████████

Dear Colonel (Ret.) Fischer:

This responds to your September 9, 2022, correspondence requesting public release clearance of the manuscript titled, "Russian Puppeteer". The manuscript submitted for prepublication security review is CLEARED for public release.

This clearance does not include any photograph, picture, exhibit, caption, or other supplemental material not specifically approved by this office, nor does this clearance imply Department of Defense (DoD) endorsement or factual accuracy of the material. The appearance of external hyperlinks does not constitute endorsement by the DoD of the linked websites, or the information, products or services contained therein. The DoD does not exercise any editorial, security, or other control over the information found at these locations.

This office notes that your manuscript may include the names and other personally identifiable information (PII) of former or active duty Service members, DoD employees, and third party individuals, the release of which could be a violation of the privacy rights of these individuals. As the author, you are solely responsible for the release of any PII and its legal implications. If you have not done so already, you may wish to consult these individuals and obtain permission to include their PII in the manuscript.

This office requires that you add the following disclaimers prior to publishing the manuscript: "The views expressed in this publication are those of the author and do not necessarily reflect the official policy or position of the Department of Defense or the U.S. government." and; "The public release clearance of this publication by the Department of Defense does not imply Department of Defense endorsement or factual accuracy of the material."

A copy of the first page of the manuscript with our clearance stamp is enclosed. Please direct any questions regarding this case to ███████████████████████

for ████████████████████████████████

Enclosure(s):
As stated

## THE AUTHOR:

Colonel (Retired) Jeffrey H. Fischer is a 30-year aviator with seven combat tours in Iraq, Afghanistan, and the Balkans. Additionally, he served at the U.S. Air Force Headquarters, Pentagon, as well as a Defense Official in both Austria and Kosovo Embassies. Jeff ended his extensive military career at NATO Special Operations Headquarters. He currently resides in Austria with his wife Barbara and son Tobias.

www.ingramcontent.com/pod-product-compliance
Lightning Source LLC
Chambersburg PA
CBHW022209010726
47493CB00002B/487